DUCK THE HALLS

"Andrews leavens the action with her trademark humor, including dueling Christmas dinners and an extravagant—and extravagantly funny—live Nativity scene."
—*Publishers Weekly*

"*Duck the Halls* offers a wealth of yuletide yuks amid the Christmas carnage, and Andrews' faithful fans will flock to greet the birth of her latest funfest."
—*Richmond Times-Dispatch*

"Meg, as well as her quirky extended family, makes this humorous cozy a holiday treat."   —*Booklist*

THE HEN OF THE BASKERVILLES

"The 15th novel in this bird-themed popular cozy mystery series offers more fine-feathered foibles to chuckle over. Andrews' ever-present humor and detailed animal lore will be familiar pleasures, and the grounded and endearing heroine offers the perfect balance to the silly shenanigans in this neatly plotted potboiler."   —*RT Book Reviews*

"Diverting . . . Enjoyable."   —*Publishers Weekly*

SOME LIKE IT HAWK

"Uproarious."   —*Criminal Element*

"[This] series gets better all the time."   —*Booklist*

THE REAL MACAW

"As always, Andrews laces this entertaining whodunit with wit, a fine storyline, and characters we've come to know and love."   —*Richmond Times-Dispatch*

STORK RAVING MAD

"Meg grows more endearing with each book, and her fans will enjoy seeing her take to motherhood."
    —*Richmond Times-Dispatch*

SWAN FOR THE MONEY

"As usual in this hilarious series . . . a good time is guaranteed for everyone except Meg."
    —*Kirkus Reviews*

"The Meg Langslow series just keeps getting better. Lots of cozy writers use punny titles, but Andrews backs them up with consistently hilarious story lines."   —*Booklist*

SIX GEESE A-SLAYING

"Fans will enjoy [this] entry in Andrews's fine-feathered series."   —*Publishers Weekly*

"Fans of comic cozies who have never read Andrews' Meg Langslow mysteries have a real treat in store. . . . Lots of silly but infectious humor and just enough mystery."
    —*Booklist*

COCKATIELS AT SEVEN

"Suspense, laughter and a whole passel of good clean fun."
    —*Publishers Weekly*

"More fun than seven cocktails—and a lot safer, too."
    —*Richmond Times-Dispatch*

"The plot, in true 'You Can't Take It With You' fashion, involves plenty of snakes, as well as the titular cockatiels and assorted exotic birds. The author has a fine sense of pacing and a droll...sense of humor. This is character-driven fiction, and Andrews maintains the action within the confines and sensibilities of her town-and-gown setting." —*The State* (Columbia, SC)

THE PENGUIN WHO KNEW TOO MUCH
"Deliciously daffy."—*Publishers Weekly* (starred review)

"Andrews always leavens the mayhem with laughs. So march yourself down to the bookstore or library and check out *The Penguin Who Knew Too Much*."
—*Richmond Times-Dispatch*

"Andrews' eighth Meg-centric mystery moves along like the best beach reads." —*Entertainment Weekly*

"The levelheaded, unflappable Meg takes it all in stride . . . This eighth cozy in the series makes the most of humorous situations, zany relatives, and lovable characters."
—*Booklist*

"A classic whodunit . . . wraps suspense, humor, and a screwball cast of characters into a mystery novel with stand-up quality." —About.com

"Andrews has mastered the art of writing farce with style and wit." —*Mystery Scene*

DON'T MISS THESE OTHER MYSTERIES BY
AWARD-WINNING AUTHOR
DONNA ANDREWS

The Good, the Bad, and the Emus

A Meg Langslow Mystery

Donna Andrews

St. Martin's Paperbacks

This is a work of fiction. All of the characters, organizations, and events portrayed in this novel are either products of the author's imagination or are used fictitiously.

THE GOOD, THE BAD, AND THE EMUS

Copyright © 2014 by Donna Andrews.
Excerpt from *Lord of the Wings* copyright © 2015 by Donna Andrews.

For information address St. Martin's Press, 175 Fifth Avenue, New York, NY 10010.

ISBN: 978-1-250-00937-1

Printed in the United States of America

Minotaur hardcover edition / July 2014
St. Martin's Paperbacks edition / May 2015

St. Martin's Paperbacks are published by St. Martin's Press, 175 Fifth Avenue, New York, NY 10010.

10 9 8 7 6 5 4 3 2 1

Acknowledgments

Thanks, as always, to everyone at St. Martin's/Minotaur, including (but not limited to) Matt Baldacci, Anne Brewer, Hector DeJean, Paul Hoch, Andrew Martin, Sarah Melnyk, Courtney Sanks, Talia Sherer, Mary Willems, and my editor, Pete Wolverton. And thanks again to David Rotstein and the art department for yet another fabulous cover. Who knew emus could look so fetching?

More thanks to my agent, Ellen Geiger, and the staff at the Frances Goldin Literary Agency for handling the boring (to me) practical stuff so I can focus on writing.

Many thanks to the friends—writers and readers alike—who brainstorm and critique with me, give me good ideas, or help keep me sane while I'm writing: Stuart, Elke, Aidan, and Liam Andrews, Renee Brown, Erin Bush, Carla Coupe, Meriah Crawford, Ellen Crosby, Kathy Deligianis, Laura Durham, John Gilstrap, Barb Goffman, Peggy Hansen, C. Ellett Logan, Alan Orloff, Valerie Patterson, Shelley Shearer, Art Taylor, Robin Templeton, Dina Willner, and Sandi Wilson. Thanks for all kinds of moral support and practical help to my blog sisters and brother at the Femmes Fatales: Dana Cameron, Charlaine Harris, Dean James, Toni L.P. Kelner, Catriona McPherson, Kris Neri, Hank Phillipi Ryan, Mary Saums, Marcia Talley, and Elaine Viets. And thanks to all the TeaBuds for years of friendship.

Thanks to Mo Heedles, who gave generously at the Bouchercon Albany charity auction to have a character named after her. I hope Chief Heedles pleases. Thanks also to my fellow Malice Domestic board members Joni Langevoort and Anne Murphy, who graciously allowed me to borrow their names when I was writing furiously and had no energy left to christen characters with suitable panache. And of course thanks, as always, to Dina Willner for allowing me to name Dr. Blake's frequent co-conspirator after her late mother.

Without David Niemi, Dr. Blake would speak even less Norwegian than he does. David also served as my technical resource on generators—any mistakes you find in my description of them must have crept in after the draft he read.

Without the brainstorming I do, online with Suzanne Frisbee and in person with Chris Cowan and Barb Goffman, I'd probably still be figuring out what to write. Chris also shared her mineralogical knowledge and samples of the kyanite that plays a part in the story.

I probably would never have even started this book if, at the 2012 Writer's Police Academy, my writer friend Ashley McConnell hadn't greeted me by saying, "Oh, I was hoping I'd see you here. I've heard something you might want to use. Did you know they have feral emus down in Blacksburg, Virginia?"

And above all, thanks to the readers who continue to read Meg's adventures.

Chapter 1

"Be careful!" I said, looking up from the boxwood hedge I was pruning. "We don't want another trip to the emergency room. We've used up our family quota for the week."

My twin four-year-old sons paid no attention, of course. Josh, who was supposed to be collecting the fallen twigs and leaves into small piles, continued to battle an invisible opponent, now using a particularly large, sharp stick I'd just pruned off the hedge. Jamie had volunteered for the task of loading the small piles into the wheelbarrow and ferrying them to the large pile by the driveway that was awaiting the eventual arrival of a borrowed chipper/shredder, but his active imagination had transformed the bright red wheelbarrow into a high-powered race car, to judge by his repeated growls of "Vroom! Vroom!" His racetrack was starting to inch near the street in front of our house, and while it was a little-traveled country road, cars did pass by often enough that I didn't want the boys getting complacent about playing there.

Neither of them heard me. But I wasn't really talking to the boys. My seventeen-year-old niece, Natalie, who would be serving as the boys' babysitter this summer, snapped to attention.

"Josh!" she called out. "Drop that stick before you put someone's eye out! Jamie! Out of the street! Inside the hedge!"

I returned to my snipping, satisfied that Natalie was on the case. And that she was beginning to get a handle on her job. She had taken care of the boys two summers ago, but apparently had forgotten how lively they could be. Then again, compared to two summers ago, their capacity for mischief and mayhem had grown exponentially. I'd gotten used to the change gradually, as they'd grown. Natalie was still catching up.

In a day or so, once she was really up to speed, I could retreat for hours each day to the barn where I had my blacksmith's workshop. In fact, I could start retreating the day after tomorrow, when Michael's spring semester ended, and he'd have several weeks off before the summer session began. I could delegate training Natalie to him while I hit the anvil. I hadn't had much time for iron work since the boys were born, and had almost given up selling at craft shows. Hard enough to get routine household chores done safely with two increasingly active munchkins underfoot. No way did I want them in the same room when I was heating steel to 2000 degrees Fahrenheit and then whacking on it with a three-pound hammer. I managed to get in a little time at the anvil during Caerphilly College's semester breaks, when Michael was not only willing but eager to spend time with the boys. But I never had enough time to stock my booth for even a modest-sized craft show. And while the higher salary Michael now earned as a tenured professor in the drama department meant we could manage without my crafting income, the money I'd earn would be helpful. Besides, I didn't want to lose my hard-won skills.

So with Natalie around all summer, I was planning a frenzy of iron work. As soon as I was sure she really understood just how carefully she had to watch "Trouble" and "Danger," as my brother, Rob, had nicknamed his nephews.

Today we were easing into what I hoped would become our routine, with her keeping an eye on the boys while I did neglected yard work and repairs and kept an eye on her. It was a beautiful mid-June day, sunny, but not hot—

perfect weather for being outdoors and enjoying the wealth of flowers in our yard. The azaleas were past, but the mountain laurels, rhododendrons, and magnolias were in bloom, and the scent of the lilacs was almost overpowering. And daylilies were everywhere—not just the common orange and yellow ones, but daylilies in every possible shade of red, white, purple, lilac, and pink. A glorious day to be outside.

I was relieved to find that Natalie didn't seem to mind being outside. I'd been a little worried when she'd showed up that first day in a Morticia Addams black dress with trailing, fluttery sleeves. Apparently, since the last time we'd seen her, she'd taken to dressing entirely in black except for the odd bit of skull- and spider-themed silver jewelry, and her skin was so pale I was afraid she'd blister if she stepped outside.

But I soon realized that her pallor was due to sunscreen and careful use of makeup, and in spite of looking like a refugee from a low-budget vampire film, she was still the same cheerful, organized, responsible kid she'd always been. And she'd put away the dress after the first night and was now wearing black jeans, a black T-shirt, black sneakers, and a black baseball cap. I anticipated that some of the more sedate citizens of Caerphilly would look askance at our choice of babysitters, but Michael and I were content. And we'd gladly complied with her request to take over a corner of the back yard for her own gardening project, which seemed to involve growing as many black plants as possible. Already, dark-flowered hellebores and nearly black pansies were blooming in her bed, surrounded by neatly raked black mulch, and she'd used black ribbons to tie her black tomato and pepper plants to their black iron stakes. I'd actually decided that it made a nice restful contrast with the multicolored profusion of the rest of the yard.

The four of us had weeded the vegetable garden right after breakfast, and now I was pruning the hedge. Our black-and-copper Welsummer hens were hovering nearby, pouncing on any insects disturbed by my pruning. It was slow going, because I was using hand tools—the power hedge clipper, like any other power tool, was too attractive to small eyes and fingers—and even the manual clippers were dangerous enough, given the constant danger that an overeager hen would trip me on her way to nab a particularly tempting insect.

I switched to the hand pruners to do some fine tuning and continued snipping away, listening carefully to Natalie's interactions with the boys and stifling the urge to offer advice every five seconds or so.

"Josh, leave the chicken alone. I don't think she wants to play tag."

"Jamie, don't jump on the brush pile."

"Take that out of your mouth."

"Stop throwing rocks at your brother."

"I don't think the doggie wants to eat holly leaves."

"Leave that alone."

"No, I said later."

She was learning. And I was making good progress. Should I try to finish the hedge before lunch? Or would it be wiser to break now, get the boys fed, and have Natalie learn how to put them down for naps? I could finish the hedge while they were asleep and—

"Eeeeeeeeeeeeeeeeeee!"

Natalie's bloodcurdling scream startled me. My right hand slipped, and I felt a searing pain as the pruners sliced into my left fingers. Just a laceration, though; the fingers themselves were still attached, I noted, as I ran to the other end of the hedge where Natalie and the boys were, wrapping my hand in my shirttail as I ran.

"I'm sorry," Jamie was saying.

"Only a grass snake," Josh was saying. "See?"

He held up the writhing green reptile that had provoked Natalie's scream. She backed away slightly.

"Josh, put the snake down," I said. "Maybe Cousin Natalie doesn't like snakes." Which would be rather ironic, since her favorite earrings were a pair of long, dangly silver serpents, but you never knew.

"I'm sorry, Meg," Natalie began. "I'm not scared of snakes; really, I'm not. I was just startled and—oh! What happened?"

I looked down at my hand. Blood was pouring out of my fingers.

"I'll get a bandage." Natalie headed for the house.

"Blast." It wasn't nearly as satisfying as the "damn" I'd have uttered if the boys were not around. "I was hoping we'd seen the last of the ER for the week."

I gave in to Natalie's insistence that she drive me to the ER. But on the way, I managed to pull out my cell phone and make arrangements for her to take the boys over to visit Mother and Dad for the afternoon.

"You know how long it always takes at the ER," I said. "And how restless the boys get."

Natalie nodded and looked more cheerful at the prospect of going to her grandparents' house instead of spending more hours at the ER. Two days ago Jamie had fallen out of the barn loft and cut his forehead. Yesterday, it had been Josh's turn to get stitches, thanks to a close encounter with a broken pickle jar. Both days, I'd accompanied the injured twin back to see the doctor while Natalie tried to keep the other entertained and protect the ER waiting room from collateral damage. She'd gone to bed early the last two nights—about ten minutes behind the boys.

"Mommy okay?" Jamie asked, as I got out in front of the ER.

"I'll be fine," I said. "I'm just going to get some stitches from Grandpa's friend in the ER, like the ones you guys got."

"Mommy get ice cream now?" Josh asked. A trip to the Caerphilly Ice Cream Parlor had become the standard reward for brave behavior at the ER.

"Not until later, when you can come with me," I said.

That idea was well received, and both boys stopped looking anxious.

"Now don't forget to show Grandpa your stitches so he can make sure they're healing properly." I shut the minivan's door.

I watched for a moment as Natalie pulled out of the parking lot. She was a careful driver. And there was a limit to how much mischief the boys could cause while strapped into their car seats. Right?

I turned and walked into the ER.

"Not you again. Which one is it this time?"

Crystal, a friend who worked at the hospital, was sitting behind the admissions desk.

"Me," I said. I held up my hand and pulled off the once-clean dish towel wrapped around it. The bleeding had mostly stopped, but since this allowed me a better view of the four deep lacerations along the inside of my fingers, it wasn't entirely an improvement.

"Yuck," she said, wincing. "Wrap it up again and keep the pressure on. Let's get you checked in. Kitchen knife?"

"Pruning shears."

I filled out the now-familiar paperwork—actually, I only had to complete a few fields on the form Crystal handed me. A couple of months ago she'd added our household to what she called her frequent filer program, which meant that she kept a set of prefilled forms for us in her computer and could just print them out when we came through the door.

Then I was ushered back to an even-more-familiar

cubicle. Another nurse inspected my hand and then dashed out, apparently satisfied that I was in no immediate danger of bleeding out. No doubt if Dad was in the hospital she'd send him in. Although he was, in theory, semiretired, he still spent rather a lot of time here and in the consulting office he'd opened in his barn. Meanwhile, the doctor's daughter in me began trying to figure out what was up with all the other patients in the ER, based on what I'd seen on my way to my cubicle and what I could overhear now. A possible heart attack in one cubicle. And a kid with a possible concussion in another. Possible appendicitis in a third. Rats. Everyone sounded more dire than me.

I sat back and resigned myself to a long wait.

My cell phone rang. I answered it quickly—always aware of the possibility Natalie was calling to report a new crisis.

But it wasn't Natalie. It was Stanley Denton, a private investigator who had set up his office in Caerphilly a few years ago.

"Could I come out to your house to ask you about something?" he asked, after we'd exchanged the usual greetings.

"Not right now," I said. "I'm actually in the ER at Caerphilly Hospital waiting to get stitches. Just some cuts," I hastened to add. "But I have no idea how long I'll be here."

"Even better," he said. "Not the cuts, of course, but I could just stop by the hospital. Only a few blocks from my office, you know. I could talk to you while you're waiting to see the doctor. Help you while away the long delay."

"Talk to me about what?"

"I'll explain when I get there. Shouldn't be more than a few minutes."

It took Stanley about five minutes, and by the time he arrived, Dr. Gridwell, the duty ER doctor, had arrived to examine my hand.

"We don't give group discounts, you know," the doctor was saying. "Not even if you come in together, and certainly not if you straggle in one by one all week. Your father coming down to supervise again?"

Beneath his nonchalant, bantering tone I detected a note of tension. Gridwell had been the one to stitch up both boys. Not every doctor likes having his patients' regular doctor supervising every move he makes. Especially when the doctor was also the patients' very opinionated grandfather. Of course, I understood what Dad was up to. Gridwell had only recently joined the staff at Caerphilly Hospital, and Dad was still assessing this new colleague's skills.

"Dad didn't come with me," I said. "He might still show up if he hears I'm here. But maybe if you kick me out pretty soon he won't bother."

"Hmph." From the alacrity with which Gridwell bounced out of the room and began throwing around orders to the rest of the staff, I deduced that yes, he would rather get me stitched up and discharged before Dad arrived to second-guess him. And the fact that he was willing to try was good news for the other patients, who presumably were stable, under observation, and in no need of anything urgent.

"Well played," Denton said. "I wonder if I should drop your father's name next time I show up here."

"Can't hurt," I said. "What can I do for you?"

"If you have time to talk," he said, glancing around.

"Dr. Gridwell can't do anything until someone gets here with the Mayo tray," I said.

"Mayo tray? He's sent out for sandwiches?"

"That's what the medical people call that metal rolling cart that you or I would probably call the suture tray. That thing," I added, as the med tech rolled it in.

"I'd probably call it the thing they use to bring in the

scissors and the sutures and the bandages and all the other stuff the doc needs to put you back together again." Stanley shuddered slightly as the tech began arranging the contents of the tray. "Anyway, I want to ask you something about a case."

"Ask away," I said.

"I was wondering if you could come down to Riverton to help me out."

I closed my eyes and sighed slightly.

"It's only about forty miles from here, and—"

"Look," I said. "I know my dad seems to think I'm Caerphilly County's answer to Nancy Drew or Miss Marple, but he exaggerates my sleuthing skills. And I'm pretty busy—now that we have a reliable babysitter, I plan to get a lot of blacksmithing done for the fall craft-fair season."

"Not with that hand." Gridwell was back. "Trust me, you won't want to be doing much blacksmithing for a few days."

"That's perfect," Stanley said. "This won't take long. And I really don't need for you to do anything. I just need to borrow your face."

Chapter 2

"Borrow my face?"

Gridwell didn't say anything, but he was clearly following our conversation with interest. He stepped to the doorway of the cubicle and looked out, tapping his foot impatiently, but he didn't roar out orders to the staff, which I knew from my earlier visits was his usual style.

"Yup." Stanley looked as if he was enjoying himself. "I just want to show it to someone."

A nurse bustled in and handed Gridwell a syringe.

"Hold your hand still while I numb you up," Gridwell said. "You want him to stay?"

"Yes, if it's okay with you." I gritted my teeth as he began poking needles into my fingers. "He'll distract me from whatever you're about to do to me. Who do you want to show my face to?" I went on, turning back to Denton.

"Someone who may have known your grandmother," Stanley said. "Your grandfather hired me to find her."

"After all this time?"

Stanley shrugged.

"How long's she been missing?" Gridwell asked. He had finished with the needles and a welcome numbness was spreading through my fingers.

"All my life," I said. "And all Dad's life, for that matter."

Gridwell paused in the middle of rummaging through the Mayo tray and gave us a puzzled frown. Stanley had pulled out his pocket notebook and was looking over his glasses at it.

"Dr. Langslow was found as an infant in a basket in a

library in Charlottesville, Virginia," he explained to Gridwell.

"In the mystery section, according to Dad," I added. "Although I think he made that part up."

"And adopted by one of the librarians there," Stanley went on. "He never knew who his blood parents were until a few years ago, when Dr. Montgomery Blake showed up."

"The zoologist?" Gridwell asked. "The one who keeps appearing on Animal Planet and National Geographic?"

"That's him," Stanley said. "He was in Caerphilly for an environmental conference at the college, and happened to see Meg's picture in the local rag. Turns out she's a dead ringer for Dr. Blake's college girlfriend."

"Cordelia," I said. Not that Gridwell would care what my grandmother's name was, but I liked the sound of it.

"Back when Dr. Blake and Cordelia knew each other, some seventy-odd years ago, he had received a fellowship to study for a couple of years on the Galápagos Islands," Stanley went on. "They had parted on good terms, but she never answered any of his letters."

"Dad's had a grudge against the Ecuadorian postal service ever since he found out," I said. "That's who delivers mail to the Galápagos. Or fails to deliver it."

"And when Dr. Blake came back to the States, he couldn't find her," Stanley continued. "So he moved on with his life. But when he saw Meg's picture, he got curious. And when he found out Meg's dad had been found in the same library where Cordelia had been employed, he obtained DNA samples and confirmed that he was, in fact, Dr. Langslow's father."

"And my grandfather," I said. "And presumably Cordelia was the mother, but since when has Grandfather been trying to find her?"

"Apparently he brooded about it for a year and then decided he had to know what happened to her," Stanley said. "But his investigative methods weren't yielding any fruit."

"Don't tell me—I bet he stormed into the library where Dad was found and demanded that they tell him where Cordelia had gone."

"Something like that," Stanley said. "And he kicked up a fuss with the Charlottesville police, too, with no success. Luckily, he had no idea where her hometown was, or he'd have poisoned the well there, too. Last week he hired me."

"And you've found something already?"

"Someone who may have known Cordelia."

"Known," I said. "Past tense. She's dead?"

"Apparently."

I felt a curiously strong surge of grief. I'd never known Grandmother Cordelia—hadn't even known her name until Grandfather showed up in my life. Even then I had told myself, sensibly, that I would almost certainly never meet her. Presumably, she had been the one to leave Dad in the library. The Charlottesville papers had carried the story of the library foundling and his adoption by the childless, forty-something head librarian and her much older physician husband—the adoptive grandparents who hadn't lived long enough for me to meet them. Cordelia could have found Dad—and the rest of us—at any time. I didn't blame her for not doing so. I tried to imagine how she must have felt—seventy-some years ago, the stigma of being an unwed mother could ruin a young woman's life. And I'd always known there was a possibility she was no longer alive. Grandfather was in his nineties, and Cordelia couldn't have been that much younger.

But somehow knowing her name made it harder, not easier, to accept her absence from my life. And I'd hoped one day I'd meet her. Was it silly to grieve for someone I'd never known? Or maybe I was grieving because now I never would.

"Hold your thumb still," Gridwell said. "Unless you want me to suture that, too."

I started slightly. While Stanley and I had been talking—and while I'd been lost in thought—Gridwell had already stitched two of my lacerations.

I looked up to see Stanley's face frowning slightly in concern.

"How long ago did she die?" I asked.

"That's the strange part," he said. "Less than a year ago. And she didn't just die. She may have been murdered."

"Murdered? How?"

Gridwell paused in his stitching and looked up to hear the answer.

"She was killed when her garden shed burned down," Stanley said. "Arson, according to some people in town. Accidental, according to others. Or maybe her own fault— there was a power outage and she'd gone out there with a kerosene lantern to tend the generator."

"Killed in a fire—are they sure it was her?"

"The police got a positive ID from her dental records," Stanley said. "And there's an invalid cousin who lived with her. She reported seeing Cordelia go into the shed. Of course, she also testified that she saw someone sneaking away from the shed with a gas can just before the fire blazed up, but the police don't seem to buy that part."

"We could talk to the cousin," I said. "She could tell us more about Cordelia."

"That's my plan," Stanley said. "That's why I want to borrow your face. The cousin won't talk to me. She's gotten it into her head that I'm from the insurance company and trying to prove her cousin was at fault so they won't have to pay her claim."

"Couldn't you tell her who really hired you?"

"I tried," he said. "She's stubborn. And the town recluse. Won't even open the door to me."

"You could show her my picture?"

"I tried that already. She pays no attention. And why should she? I could have found the picture anywhere. Could have Photoshopped one of her cousin, for all she knows. But I figure if you show up in person, a dead ringer for the cousin she grew up with—"

"You're on," I said. "When do we leave?"

"Not until I finish suturing your cuts," Gridwell said. "And let's check when you last had a tetanus shot."

"How's early tomorrow morning sound?" Stanley suggested.

"My face and I will be ready," I said.

Chapter 3

The next morning, a Tuesday, Stanley Denton and I set off for Riverton, the town where Cordelia lived. Not as early as he had hoped. I'd arranged for Natalie to spend the day over at my parents' house again, where she'd get plenty of help from Dad and supervision from Mother. But it still took forever to get Natalie and the boys packed up and on their way.

Stanley, to his credit, watched the whole thing with obvious amusement, but refrained from making any annoying comments about how in his day kids got along just fine without car seats and sunscreen.

On our way to Riverton, I interrogated him about what he'd found, but either he didn't yet know much or he wanted me to approach the cousin without being biased by what he did know. So eventually I gave up, and we chatted about other things while the countryside gradually grew more and more hilly. Evidently Riverton was in the foothills of the Blue Ridge mountains. As we approached the town limits, the horizon was filled with mountains—the green slopes of the smaller ones that surrounded the town on three sides, and beyond those the blue shadows of larger, more distant peaks.

By that time, I knew what Stanley thought of the Caerphilly College baseball team's season and how much he was looking forward to the town's big annual fall fair, but I hadn't learned much about our mission.

"Riverton, two miles," I read on the road sign. "So isn't

there anything I need to know before we get to town? Like maybe the name of this newfound distant cousin of mine?"

"Annabel Lee. Like the Edgar Allan Poe poem," Stanley said, with a chuckle. "She's Cordelia's first cousin— their fathers were brothers—which makes her your first cousin twice removed, I suppose."

"Cordelia Lee." I liked the sound of it. "Grandfather never mentioned her last name."

"That's because he didn't remember it," Stanley said. "All he remembered was that it was something short and common, like Smith or Jones. Well, Lee is common—the twenty-fourth most common name in the country."

"But Cordelia's not that common."

"No," he said. "So I started by looking through the social columns of the Charlottesville papers for the year before your father was born. Looking for Cordelias. When I found a note about a tea welcoming newcomers to town, including Miss Cordelia Lee of Riverton, Virginia, I knew I'd found the trail."

"And she just went back to her hometown?" It didn't seem possible that the answer could be so simple.

"Went home, then moved to Richmond when she married a man named Mason," Stanley said. "No children, or at least none surviving. Widowed relatively young, and sold her house in Richmond to move in with Annabel, who never married and by now was living in the ancestral home. Which we'll be seeing in a few minutes."

He pointed to a sign by the side of the road that said, simply, WELCOME TO RIVERTON. You could see that they'd painted over smaller letters that had once proclaimed the town's population. They'd probably grown tired of revising the number downward. It looked like the sort of town that inspired the occasional tourist to gush about how unspoiled it was and drove most of the high school graduates to leave in search of gainful employment.

Between the outskirts of town and the central business district, all but one or two buildings were over a hundred years old. A few solid brick houses or gingerbread-trimmed Victorians with rolling lawns and well-established banks of azaleas. A lot more plain frame houses with overgrown yards behind fading picket or wrought-iron fences.

Most of the storefronts in the main business district were occupied, but it was only a block long and the buildings, like the houses, were at least a hundred years old and looked as if they'd been kept going rather than well maintained.

"Makes Caerphilly look like a metropolis," Stanley said.

Once we passed the business district, we were back to old, mostly run-down houses. And we were climbing steadily uphill. We'd climbed at least five hundred feet and nearly run out of town. For a quarter of a mile, I could see nothing but woods along both sides of the road.

"I thought Cordelia and Annabel lived in town," I said.

"Within the town limits," Stanley said. "But just barely. That's their house up on the right."

We had come to a cluster of four large houses—mansions, really, to my eyes—set far back on generous lots. Stanley was pointing to the largest, a sprawling white Victorian house in better shape than most in town. In fact, all four of these houses were larger and better maintained than anything back in the center of town, and I had the feeling we had arrived at what passed in Riverton for an upscale neighborhood.

I studied Cordelia's and Annabel's house. The requisite banks of azaleas nestled around the foundations—the place must have been spectacular in full bloom. Hundreds of orange daylilies lined the high black iron fence that surrounded the yard as far as we could see, and a few bright blooms peeped through the railings to the street side. The fence defined a large yard, and I could see several out-buildings—an old-fashioned detached garage, a gazebo, a white frame toolshed. Big, well-grown trees—oaks, tulip poplars, and mulberries. And several bird feeders of various types hanging from the trees or standing on poles guarded by metal squirrel baffles.

Beyond the iron fence on the left side of the yard the landscape became wooded again. The return to trees probably marked the edge of town—I could see the back of what looked to be another welcome sign. On the right side of the house, the fence was lined by a tall boxwood hedge. About halfway back along the fence's length, a short, stout man in a straw hat was pruning the hedge. The fingers on my left hand began throbbing in time to the steady *snick-snick-snick* of his manual hedge clippers.

"There's a 'no soliciting' sign on the gate," I pointed out, as Stanley parked the car along the street.

"We're not soliciting," he said. "And it doesn't say 'no trespassing.'"

"Tell that to the man with the hedge clippers," I murmured.

The stout man had climbed carefully down from the ladder and was trotting over to meet us at the gate.

"This is private property," he called out as he approached. "You can't—oh, my!"

He seemed to be staring at me.

"We're here to see Miss Annabel Lee," Stanley said.

Not for the first time since I heard her name, scraps of Poe's lyric flitted through my brain, and I only just stopped myself from reciting "It was many and many a year ago/ In a kingdom by the sea . . ."

The man stared a few more moments, holding the hedge clippers in front of him, blades spread wide, as if preparing to defend himself. He looked to be in his sixties, perhaps even his seventies. If he was a longtime resident, then he was old enough to know what Cordelia had looked like when she was my age. No wonder he was staring.

Stanley reached into his pocket, took out a business card, and offered it through the gate.

After staring at the card for a bit, the man closed the clippers with a sharp snick and reached out to take it.

"I will see if she's at home," he said. He turned and trotted rapidly toward the front door.

"Of course she's home," Stanley muttered. "She's a recluse. Doesn't leave the house from one month to the next."

"Yes, but she may not be *at* home, at least not to us," I said.

"Still, this is more than I got last time I was here," he said. "I rang the doorbell a dozen times with no response, unless you count seeing the front curtains flutter once or twice, as if someone was peeking out at me."

An unseen hand opened the door for the man, and he disappeared inside without looking back at us.

We stood in front of the gate. Birds trilled, insects buzzed, and in the distance I could hear the steady drone of a lawnmower. I wondered if Stanley had a contingency plan in case the hedgeclipper/gatekeeper simply stayed inside and waited for us to leave. Before I got around to asking, the man reappeared. He walked out to the gate at a much slower, steadier pace, and when he got closer I could see that he was frowning.

"Miss Lee will see you," he said. "Briefly."

He opened the gate—not very wide, as if he still hoped to discourage us from entering.

Stanley stood aside and graciously beckoned for me to go first. Or maybe he wasn't being gracious, just hoping I'd succeed in shoving the gate open a little wider, to accommodate his somewhat bulkier form. I obliged. When he was inside, he offered his hand to the man.

"Thank you," he said. "Mr.—?"

"Doctor," the man said. "Dr. Dwight Ffollett. Two f's, two l's, two t's." He turned back toward the house, and we fell into step on either side of him.

A doctor. Odds were he was a volunteer gardener, then, unless the medical business here in Riverton had fallen off precipitously.

"Nice of you to help Miss Lee," I said. "Such a beautiful yard."

"Yes," he said. "A lot of work, though, and she can't do it herself."

"Did you plant all this?" Stanley asked.

Dr. Ffollett frowned as if this were a trick question.

"No," he said, finally. "Mrs. Mason did it all."

So my grandmother had been a gardener. Like Dad.

"Mrs. Cordelia Mason?" Stanley asked. "Miss Lee's late cousin?" Dr. Ffollett flinched at the name, then nodded.

"Yes," he said, his voice shaky.

He fell back to let us climb the steps without him. Stanley rang the doorbell. I glanced down to see Dr. Ffollett clutching his pruning shears the way Josh and Jamie clutched their favorite stuffed animals in a thunderstorm.

Stanley and I stood there for a few moments, both of us studying our surroundings. We were on a broad old-fashioned porch that ran along the whole front of the house and wrapped around both sides. To our left were a couple of comfortable-looking white Adirondack chairs with blue cushions on the seats and a wrought-iron table between them. To our right, a pair of white wicker chairs with a matching table. An empty white china cup and saucer suggested that someone had been having tea this morning on the wicker. There were bamboo roll-down shades you could use to block out the sun if the afternoon was too hot, and ceiling fans on either side to stir up a little breeze. An assortment of Boston ferns, spider plants, begonias, and geraniums hung from the porch ceiling in brown macramé holders or on chains from wrought-iron plant brackets attached to the walls or posts. Very nice wrought-iron brackets. Just the sort of things I'd be making now if I hadn't injured my hand. And would get back to making as soon as my hand healed.

"Don't look now, but someone's watching us," Stanley murmured.

I had noticed it, too—the slight twitching of the curtains in the glass panel to the left of the door.

And why were we pretending not to notice that the woman whose doorbell we'd rung was peeking out at us instead of opening the door?

I smiled and waved cheerfully at the glass panel.

The curtain fell shut.

Stanley smothered a chuckle.

Then the door slowly opened, and we found ourselves face-to-face with a tallish, angular, elderly woman. Her gray hair was pulled back in a bun, and her brown eyes studied us intently over a pair of gold reading glasses.

"I don't need to ask who you are and why you're here," she said to me. "Not sure I like the look of him, but come on in, both of you."

She stepped back and opened the door wider so we could enter. She wasn't that much shorter than me. Maybe five six or seven. If, like most people, she'd lost height as she grew older, she must once have been eye to eye with my five foot ten. Or maybe taller.

And she was wearing a green T-shirt emblazoned with the words COMPOST HAPPENS.

I made a provisional decision that I liked Annabel, in spite of the tepid welcome.

"Have a seat," she said, gesturing to an archway that led to the living room. "You come in, too, Dwight," she called out the doorway.

She left the door open to follow us into the living room.

Dr. Ffollett scurried up the front steps and inside, closing the door carefully behind him.

I liked the house. At least the parts I'd seen, the foyer and now the living room. Both were high-ceilinged and airy, with both walls and woodwork painted white. And although the house and some of the furniture were Victorian in style, I appreciated the most un-Victorian lack of clutter and fussy details.

"Miss Annabel Lee?" Stanley held out out his hand. "I'm—"

"Stanley Denton, private investigator," Annabel said. "I read the card." She ignored his outstretched hand and turned to me. "And you are?"

"Meg Langslow." I held out my hand and, after a beat, she took it and gave me a firm handshake.

"James's daughter," she said, nodding. "Go on, sit."

I tried not to show how surprised I was that she knew Dad's name. Stanley and I sat down in two wing-back chairs while Annabel took the matching love seat and Dr. Ffollett perched on the edge of a Windsor chair just inside the archway from the hall.

"So you know about us," I said. "That we exist, I mean."

"Oh, Cordelia kept an eye on all of you," she said. "She was proud of you."

"But she never got in touch," I said. "Why?"

Annabel shrugged.

"Maybe she thought you were doing just fine without her," she said. "Maybe she didn't want to shake things up after so long. Rake up the old scandal. Who knows? Well, she would have, but it's not as if we can ask her now. She's dead."

Dr. Ffollett made a choking noise.

"Sorry, Dwight," Annabel said. "He thinks I'm very indelicate. Thinks I should say she 'passed away,' or 'went beyond.' I like plain speaking. And so did Cordelia."

"Tell me more about her," I said.

Annabel frowned and studied me.

"You were her cousin," I went on. "I understand you grew up together."

"Only six months apart," she said with a nod.

"You must know a lot about her."

"I do," Annabel said. "And I'll tell you whatever I can. Show you all the photo albums. I can probably even round up a few home movies. But there's one condition."

She paused. I wasn't sure if she was just pausing for effect or if I was supposed to ask what condition. Stanley beat me to it.

"What's the condition?" he asked.

"You need to solve her murder," Annabel said.

Chapter 4

"Her murder?" Although it wasn't really a question. Stanley had already told me that Annabel thought Cordelia had been murdered. But sitting here comfortably in the cousins' brightly lit old-fashioned room—the room where Cordelia had probably sat hundreds of times—the idea seemed both more horrible and a lot less plausible. "You really think she was murdered, then?"

"She was." Annabel looked grim. "Find out who killed her and prove it, and I'll tell you everything you could possibly want to know about Cordelia. In fact, it's easier than that, because I can tell you who did it—Theo Weaver, that no good son-of-a—"

"Now, now," Dr. Ffollett murmured.

"Theo Weaver," she repeated. "I know it, you know it, half the town knows it, and if our numbskull of a police chief had any gumption—"

She clamped her mouth shut and shook her head.

"What did the police do?" Stanley asked. I noticed he'd taken out his notebook.

"Nothing," Annabel said. "Oh, they poked around the remains of the shed a little. And then they apparently decided her death was merely an unfortunate accident."

"They haven't even—" Dr. Ffollett began.

"As I said," Annabel said, frowning at the interruption. "They did nothing."

"What do you think happened?" Stanley asked.

"Here's what I know happened." Annabel sat back with

a rather satisfied look on her face. And why not? It looked as if she was getting her way.

"It was December," she said. "The day we had that early snow. And of course the power went out. Three drops of rain or more than a single snowflake and the power goes out around here, regular as clockwork, as far back as I can remember. And I don't care what the power company says, it's not getting any better. So we installed a generator about twenty years back. Smartest thing we ever did."

I nodded in agreement. Living as far out of town as Michael and I did, we also lost power much too often. A generator was on my home improvement list. As soon as we dealt with the need for a new furnace and possibly new air conditioning.

"But we don't like to run the thing all night," Annabel went on. "No need, really. In the summer it usually cools off enough after dark to get by, and in the winter we can bundle up."

"There's also the fact that Mr. Weaver keeps complaining about the noise," Dr. Ffollett said.

"Theo Weaver?" Stanley asked. "The one you think . . ."

"Theo Weaver, yes," Annabel said. "He lives next door."

"Beyond the hedge," Dr. Ffollett added.

"He's the reason for the hedge, actually," Annabel said. "To cut down on his snooping. And we didn't turn the generator off to please him. He could have bought himself some earplugs. Or installed his own generator. But having it on while we slept fretted us. Cordelia, mainly. She kept worrying it would catch on fire or poison us both with carbon monoxide. That's why we installed it way at the far corner of the yard, behind the garden shed. For safety. Cost an arm and a leg, running the line so far, but it kept her happy. And even way out there the noise bothered me at night. So one of us would go out and turn it off at bedtime. Usually her."

"So she went out that night to turn off the generator?" Stanley asked.

"And I kept an eye on her, because I was afraid the path might be icy. She disappeared around the back of the shed and a few moments later, the generator stopped. But she didn't reappear, and just when I was getting worried and starting to get my coat to go out and check on her, I heard a loud *whomp!* and the shed went up in a ball of flames. And there was enough light from that fire that I could get a glimpse of the killer sneaking away. It was Theo Weaver."

"What do the police say?" Stanley asked.

"That it must have been an accident. That she was carrying a kerosene lantern and the open flame must have ignited the gasoline vapors."

"Sounds plausible," Stanley said.

It didn't sound plausible to me, and I was trying to find a polite way to say so. Annabel beat me to it, possibly because she wasn't worrying about being polite.

"Plausible, my eye," she said. "Don't you know the first thing about how a generator works? It was behind the shed, not in it—for safety. You want a well-ventilated site for a generator. And it was a cold, windy night. No way for vapor to build up even if there had been gasoline there in the first place—which there wasn't. And besides, she wasn't carrying a kerosene lantern. Those things are a fire hazard. She had a perfectly nice LED headlight that she kept on her bedside table in case she needed to get up in the night. One of these."

Annabel reached over to her left and opened a small drawer in the end table that flanked her love seat. She took out something and pulled it onto her head. A small headlight, similar to what a miner would wear, but attached to a light elastic strap instead of a helmet.

"We try to keep one handy in every room, for the outages. Better than a flashlight, because you have both hands free." She reached up and pressed a button on the side of the headlight. A light shone out, bright enough to make me blink even though the room, while shaded, was far from dark. "And with something like this, why in the world would she haul out a stinky old kerosene lantern?"

"A good point." Stanley had raised his hand over his eyes to protect them from the LED beam. "Surely, then, if the police didn't find a kerosene lantern . . ."

"They found one, all right," she said. "I expect we had one out in the shed, along with a lot of other old junk that we should have thrown out years ago. They might have found a butter churn and an old wooden washboard in the debris, too, but that doesn't mean we were using them that night. Or maybe the killer planted the lantern. The point is, she wasn't using a kerosene lantern or any other kind of open flame, so the police explanation of how it happened is nonsense."

Stanley was scribbling rapidly. I was just listening, and trying to decide if Annabel's version of events sounded plausible. Was she a keen-eyed witness being ignored by the police—and if so, why? Or was she a lonely old woman who was taking the death of her cousin hard and looking for someone to blame?

"Cordelia and I have been running that generator for twenty years now," Annabel said. "I know how the thing works. What I saw wasn't consistent with any kind of accident with a kerosene lamp. But it's exactly what would happen if you poured gasoline around the shed and then threw in a match just as Cordelia showed up."

"And you think it was your neighbor, Theo Weaver, who did this?" Stanley asked.

"Damn right I do," Cordelia said. "I told you, I saw him slinking away from the shed and hopping over the fence."

Hopping over the fence? It was eight feet tall if it was

an inch. Was their neighbor a recreational pole vaulter? I could see Stanley frown at this, too.

"You recognized him?" he said aloud. "Wasn't it dark?"

"It wasn't that dark. There was a full moon, so with all the snow around, you could see pretty well when there was a break in the clouds. And not that bad even when the clouds were there. Wasn't so much the darkness as the glare from the flames that made it hard to see. Hard, but not impossible. And I know Weaver well enough to recognize him. He was carrying something that could easily have been one of those red plastic gas cans, slipping along the hedge and then jumping the fence into his own yard."

Stanley glanced over at me. If he was waiting for a signal, or the answer to some unspoken question, he was doomed to disappointment. I shrugged. Whatever question he was asking, that answer seemed to satisfy him.

"It does sound as if there may be some scope for investigation," Stanley said.

"Good," Annabel said. "You can start today. No time like the present."

"There are a couple of things I need to do before I agree to go forward with this," Stanley said. "First, I need to consult my client."

"Consult away," she said. "If you two want some privacy, use the study."

"My client is actually Meg's grandfather, Dr. Blake," Stanley said.

"Wait—Blake hired you to find Cordelia?" Annabel asked.

Stanley nodded.

Annabel looked puzzled, and not entirely pleased.

"A little late in the day, don't you think?" she asked.

"Better late than never," I said.

Annabel's face wore a thunderous look. Clearly she was not a fan of her late cousin's lover.

"Dr. Blake was unaware, until a few years ago, that his relationship with Cordelia had produced a son," Stanley said.

"He should have known it was a possibility," Annabel retorted. "Some biologist he is."

Stanley nodded, conceding the point.

"Technically, I've completed the task Dr. Blake hired me for," he said. "Find Cordelia. If she was alive, see if she wanted any contact with her son and his family. If she was dead, tell him what I'd learned about her life since their parting. We never anticipated this—finding she'd been murdered and being asked to investigate it. I need to clear it with him before I can continue."

"And if Blake says forget about it, case closed?" Annabel snapped. "What then?"

"Then Stanley will talk to my dad," I said. "Who obviously has an even stronger reason for wanting to find out what happened to his mother. For that matter, so do I, and I bet my brother and sister will, too."

"I feel reasonably sure Dr. Blake will authorize the expanded investigation," Stanley said. "And if he doesn't, I can terminate my contract with him and work with others in the family. But I do have to talk to him first."

"That works," Annabel said, with a brisk nod. "And you know, the more I think about it, the more I like the idea of old Monty footing the bill for this. From what I hear, he can certainly afford it. So one way or another, you can move ahead, then, once you clear up the question of who's the client."

"Correct," Stanley said. "I'll also need to talk to the local police." His pen was poised over his notebook. "Can you give me the name of the police detective who worked the case?"

"Detective!" Annabel snorted. "We don't have police detectives here in Riverton. We have Chief Heedles and four patrol officers. The chief did the investigation, if you can call it that."

"Chief Heedles," Stanley repeated. "No involvement from the county sheriff's office, or the state police?"

"Riverton's an incorporated town," Annabel said. "County doesn't have jurisdiction. I hear they offered, but Chief Heedles didn't seem to want any interference."

"I'll need to talk to Chief Heedles, then—could you spell it?"

"H-e-e-d-l-e-s," Annabel said. "First name, Mo."

I could tell from her tone that she probably wasn't crazy about Stanley wanting to consult the chief. Evidently, Stanley picked up on that as well.

"It's a touchy business," he said. "Coming onto a law enforcement officer's turf and conducting an investigation of what's probably considered a closed case. It'll go better if I contact the chief up front, try to smooth any ruffled feathers beforehand."

"Suit yourself," Annabel said. "Just don't let her snow you."

"Her?" Stanley was the one who made the mistake of saying this aloud.

"Surprised?" Annabel's tone was sharp, and just a little triumphant. "The Mo is short for Maureen. So you think a police chief has to be a man?"

"No," he said. "But I know quite a few very competent women law enforcement officers who are still banging their heads against the glass ceiling. I'm pleasantly surprised that Riverton is so progressive."

"Nice save," she said. "And we're not that progressive— her daddy was the chief of police before her, and she didn't have any brothers. Anyway, don't let her snow you. There was nothing accidental about Cordelia's death. Wait a minute. I've got something for you."

She stood up and strode briskly across the room to

where some papers were lying on a side table. My heart beat faster suddenly. I had the feeling she was about to show us something of Cordelia's. A photo, perhaps. Or a letter she'd left in case her son or any of her grandchildren ever showed up after her death. Romantic nonsense, I knew, but still—

"Here's a copy of my file on the case," she said, holding out a slender manila folder. "I put it together so I'd have something to show the state police if I ever got them interested."

Stanley took the folder and tucked it under his arm. Annabel must have seen my disappointment.

"Not what you were hoping for?" She patted my arm. "Don't worry. Give me her killer and I'll give you her life story, all of it. Dwight, see them safely on their way."

She turned and left through a door at the back of the room. I suspected it led to the kitchen. She wasn't quite fleeing, but still—I was reminded that she was a recluse. Maybe she had used up her tolerance for other human beings for the day.

Dr. Ffollett escorted us out of the house. He was hustling us down the front walk when Stanley stopped.

"Before we go," he said. "May we inspect the shed?"

Ffollett blinked.

"The shed?" he said finally. "It burned down."

"Sorry," Stanley said. "Imprecise of me. The remains of the shed. The scene of the crime."

Dr. Ffollett looked anxious and hunched his shoulders slightly as if bracing himself to repel an assault. Then he sighed, and stepped to the side, as if getting out of our way.

"It's back there," he said, pointing. "At the back of the lot, on the right side of the yard. The right side as you're facing the house."

"The side with the hedge," I said.

He nodded.

"We won't take too long," Stanley said.

He strode ahead, and Dr. Ffollett followed him toward the shed.

The remains of the shed.

Chapter 5

As I followed Stanley and Dr. Ffollett into the backyard, I studied the gardens. I suspected that Dad would be beaming with pride if he were with us. Even my less expert eye could tell that Cordelia had been quite a gardener. I spotted more azaleas and daylilies—though I noted with satisfaction that she didn't have the wide variety of daylilies we did. I could smell a lilac somewhere nearby, though I couldn't spot it. Perhaps it was hidden behind the enormous pink and purple rhododendrons. I spotted beds of pink, white, red, and yellow peonies and roses, and an extensive herb garden, neatly labeled.

But the herbs gave me the first clue that not everything was rosy in the garden. The perennials, including multiple varieties of rosemary, sage, thyme, mint, oregano, and lavender, were thriving, but annuals like basil and marjoram were represented by bare spots. Nearby a large space clearly once devoted to vegetables held only a few rows of beans and some tomato plants. In fact, throughout the garden, the perennials were going strong, and the annuals were either few in number or missing entirely. Clearly Cordelia had been the one who loved and slaved over the garden. Annabel and Dr. Ffollett were carrying on as best they could, but their hearts weren't really in it, and it showed.

They were keeping up with the bird feeders, though. Another half-dozen were scattered throughout the backyard. Their perches were getting lively traffic from cardinals, chickadees, titmice, goldfinches, bluebirds, and a lot of birds that Dad would probably have identified in an instant as either familiar friends or rare and welcome visitors, but which I just lumped together as "small, nondescript brown birds."

"Not much left, is there?" Stanley said.

I was about to protest that unless your gardening focus was completely on edibles, there was quite a lot left. Then I realized he wasn't sharing my focus on the landscape.

He was looking at what remained of the shed.

My stomach tightened suddenly, and I wondered if this was really such a good idea. I stared at the debris. The shed had probably been about six by eight feet. The charred front wall was partly standing, and the rest of the building had collapsed into a jumbled pile of half-blackened boards and timbers, with bits of glass and shingles mixed in. The charred and now rusting hulk of the generator was clearly visible behind what had been the back wall of the shed. In life, its useful but pedestrian, boxy shape would probably have been hidden entirely by the shed.

And the whole scene was fenced in with a double row of crime-scene tape.

"Chief Heedles hasn't yet taken the crime-scene tape down," Stanley said. "Maybe we should check with her first."

"She hasn't taken it down because she never put any up," Dr. Ffollett said. "That was her idea." He nodded slightly toward the house. "Did you know you can buy that stuff on the Internet now?"

"Ah," Stanley said. "Well, then."

He lifted up one section of the tape and ducked under.

I tried to think of a good reason to be somewhere else. Surely there must be more clues to be found in the herb garden. Or a need for someone to walk nonchalantly up and down in front of the house next door, where Annabel's chief suspect lived, and jot down any suspicious activity. I was almost hoping for a call from Natalie—as long as it wasn't about something that would kick off another round of stitches.

Why was I so reluctant to follow Stanley into the ruins of the shed? Cordelia's body would be long gone. I could easily see Annabel wanting to preserve any gruesome details of the scene, like a tape outline or other visible signs of where the body had been found. On the other hand, the ruins of the shed were uncovered, so time and the elements would have had a chance to soften everything.

But my grandmother died there. Never mind that I hadn't known her, and that she, apparently, had been content to keep it that way. She was still my grandmother.

I glanced up at the house. I spotted Annabel peering out from one of the windows.

Get over it, I told myself. Cordelia's body wasn't here, and I would be damned if I was going to let Annabel think I was squeamish. I stepped forward, lifted up the tape, and followed Stanley—

Who wasn't wading into the thick of the rubble, thank goodness. He was circling the ruins at a careful distance, peering closely at everything and snapping photos every few seconds with his digital camera.

"Where was Mrs. Mason found?" he asked.

"By the generator." Dr. Ffollett pointed.

Stanley began to pick his way around the perimeter toward the remains of the generator. I stayed where I was for now and tried to picture the scene as it must have been six months ago. I remembered that big storm Annabel had mentioned. A foot of heavy, wet snow fell, knocking out all the power, and then temperatures in the twenties set in for the long haul. Not fun for our household, even with plenty of able-bodied family members to shovel and haul firewood. And Cordelia and Annabel were two ladies in their late eighties or thereabouts, living in a house that looked at least as old as ours and was probably just as badly insulated. I half closed my eyes and tried to imagine the scene. Night instead of day—though it would have been bright; I remember how useful it was having a full moon in mid-power-outage. Moonlight over the unbroken snow of the yard—wait.

"Someone had shoveled a path to the shed, I assume?" I opened my eyes again and turned to Dr. Ffollett.

"They hired a high school kid to do chores like that," Dr. Ffollett said. "And to drive the ladies around to their events. Church, garden club, bird-watching society."

"Both of them?" I asked.

"Cordelia, mostly," he said. "Miss Annabel never went out much, even before the fire. Thor—Thor Larsen, the kid who was working for them for the last year or two—came over and shoveled the paths for them. And the whole area around the generator. He and Cordelia probably had the usual argument over starting the generator."

"Usual argument?" Stanley, who had been squatting and examining the generator, stood up and took out his notebook.

"Thor thought he should be allowed to start it," Dr. Ffollett said. "He's quite mechanically minded. Works part time down at his uncle's car repair shop. Cordelia didn't want anyone but herself touching it. Lucky, as it turned out; if he'd been the one to start the generator, I think Chief Heedles might have tried to lay the blame on him. Claimed he'd done something wrong. It would have made his life a misery. He's fond of both of the ladies. Well, is fond of her"—he gestured toward the house—"and was fond of her cousin."

Stanley nodded and scribbled.

I went back to my efforts to imagine that night. Cordelia following Thor's shoveled path out to the shed, any sound she made drowned out by the steady mechanical throbbing of the generator. She reaches the shed—and then what? Does she disappear from view?

"How high was the shed?" I asked.

"The top of the roof was level with the top of the hedge," Dr. Ffollett said.

"And set catty-cornered to the property lines." Stanley traced a rough rectangle in the air to mark the shed's position. "So the front of the shed faced Cordelia and Annabel's house, and the generator was in this back corner of the lot, completely concealed from the house and the street."

Dr. Ffollett nodded.

"Cost a pretty penny, I imagine," Stanley said. "Running the line that far from there to the house."

Dr. Ffollett didn't respond.

I walked over to where Stanley was. Yes, with an eight-foot shed where the ruins now lay, no one in the house could see the generator. I turned toward the front of the lot. My view of the road was almost completely blocked by several big camellia bushes planted between it and the shed—though fortunately far enough from the shed that they hadn't been consumed by the fire. They were evergreen, so they'd have done the same in December. Definitely the place to ambush someone, if you were so inclined.

And close up, the sound of the generator would have concealed any noise the killer made. Or any screams from his victim—presumably he'd knocked her down, or maybe even out, to ensure that she'd stay put for the explosion he was about to set off. But I knew from experience that a generator would be ample cover. My parents had installed a generator at their farmhouse, and now Mother was campaigning to have it moved farther from the house. The ladies had been wiser when they'd installed theirs. The generator probably hadn't really sounded all that loud to them, since it was at the far corner of their very large lot, with the shed between it and the house. I made a mental note that if we installed a generator, we should try to put it behind the barn, at the far edge of our property, and screen it with evergreen shrubs.

And we had no close neighbors to complain no matter where we put our generator. On one side of us were sheep fields belonging to our nearest neighbor, Seth Early. On the other three, more fields belonging to my parents' farm. But both Seth's house and my parents' were at least a mile away.

Here, I could understand Theo Weaver's annoyance. His yard, though not miniscule, was much smaller than Cordelia and Annabel's, and the generator was a lot closer to his house than theirs. I'd have tried to placate him by inviting him in to share the benefits that came with the noise. If they didn't want to offer him a spare bedroom, would it have been possible to run a line to his house as well? Possible, but no doubt expensive. And presumably the enmity between the two households predated the generator.

Still, something about the scene bothered me.

"I see now what Miss Annabel meant by hopping over the fence," Stanley said, pointing. The eight-foot iron fence ended at either side at what I assumed was the rear boundary line of the property. That rear boundary was delineated with a low wire fence. There was a gate approximately in the middle of the fence, leading into a field beyond.

"Easy enough for any reasonably agile person to hop over the fence," Stanley remarked as we gazed at the wire.

"Yes," Dr. Ffollett said. "That's just what she thinks happened. He hopped over the fence, ran through the field, and then hopped over his own fence to get back into his yard. You didn't really think she meant the iron fence, did you?"

"What's the field used for?" I asked.

"Nothing, at the moment," Dr. Ffollett said. "Used to be the Lee family's pasture back when you needed horses for transportation and a cow or two for fresh milk. Cordelia had gotten fired up about the idea of keeping some sheep, and she had the fence fixed up last fall. She was going to start her flock this spring. Guess that won't be happening now."

"What's beyond the field?" I asked.

"Woods," Dr. Ffollett said. "And mountains, eventually, unless you're heading toward town. Pretty isolated out here."

"I know the ladies didn't get along with Mr. Weaver next door," Stanley said. "How about the neighbors across the street?"

"They get along with them fine when they're here," Dr. Ffollett said. "But they're not home now, and wouldn't have been the night of the explosion. The house on the left belongs to a colonel from the army. Plans to retire here, but right now he's only here when he's home on leave. Other house belongs to a retired couple who only spend spring and fall here. Winters they have a condo in Florida, and summers they're up in Maine. No, Theo Weaver's the only real neighbor the ladies have, and they wish they could be rid of him. Cordelia always says—said—that having Theo Weaver around was worse than being all alone."

"Very isolated," Stanley said. "Must have been hard on the ladies."

"Wasn't hard on Cordelia, because she was always gadding about," Dr. Ffollett said. "And Annabel preferred the peace and quiet."

"Preferred?" I said. "She doesn't now?"

Dr. Ffollett looked startled for a few moments. Then his face fell.

"I can't exactly speak for her," he said. "But I think she's lonely."

Lonely? Maybe. But if Annabel was right about Theo Weaver, now she was practically alone in the woods with her cousin's killer. Maybe lonely wasn't the problem. Maybe she was scared.

I finally put my finger on what had been bothering me.

"Were there tracks in the snow that night?" I asked. "Showing where someone had gone over the fence?"

"No way of telling, after all the firemen had finished trampling around," Dr. Ffollett said.

Stanley reached inside his jacket and pulled out a pair of gloves and a folded brown paper bag. He put the gloves on, reached into the charred debris, and pulled out something. A bit of metal, blackened and twisted, but still recognizable.

"The kerosene lantern?" I asked.

"*A* kerosene lantern," Stanley said. "No way of telling if it's the one Chief Heedles thinks set off the explosion. But even if she's sure this was a tragic accident, it does seem a little careless, leaving this lying around."

We studied the charred lantern for a few moments. Then he tucked it into the brown paper bag, reached into his pocket, and sealed the bag with a large sticker.

"Just in case there are any questions about this thing," he said. He fished a pen out of his pocket and scrawled his signature, half on the bag and half on the sticker. "Meg, if you don't mind?"

I followed suit, and Dr. Ffollett, after a moment's hesitation, stepped forward and did the same.

"I think we've done as much as we can reasonably do before talking to Dr. Blake," Stanley said. "Dr. Ffollett, thank you for your help. Tell Miss Annabel we'll be in touch."

Dr. Ffollett nodded. He escorted us to the gate and stood watching as we drove off. I couldn't tell if Annabel was watching, too, but I could swear I felt her eyes on us.

Chapter 6

"Well, overall I think that went well," Stanley said. "We got a lot farther than I expected."

"So you think there's something worth investigating?" I certainly did, but I knew I could be biased. "About Cordelia's death, I mean. You think it's murder?"

"I didn't at first," he said. "But if Chief Heedles really went in with her mind made up that this was a tragic accident . . ."

"And if she really thinks my grandmother was such a doddering old fool that she'd traipse around with a kerosene lantern when she had a perfectly good LED headlight at her bedside." I realized I sounded cross. "Sorry," I added. "Not mad at you—just venting."

"I think it's definitely worth investigating," he said. "Although, even if there was evidence to be found in December, there's no guarantee it will still be around in June. Still—worth a try. Could you come with me to see your grandfather? I think it will go better."

"You think he's going to be upset to find that Cordelia's dead?" I asked. "Because, frankly, I doubt it. More likely he'll be peeved that she inconsiderately managed to get herself knocked off before he got around to hiring you to find her."

"I'm not going to argue with that prediction," he said, with a chuckle. "I wasn't so much worried about his feelings as strategizing the best way to enlist his support for expanding my investigation. If he's alone when I tell him, I have a feeling his answer will be thanks, but now he knows what happened to her, and would I like to see his latest litter of some endangered animal he's breeding in captivity."

"You're right," I said. "Even down to the animals—which will be either black-footed ferrets or red wolves; he has new litters of both this week."

"But if I ask him in front of you, maybe he'll stop and realize that even if he no longer cares what happened to Cordelia, you do."

"Good point." I took out my cell phone and called Dad.

"How are the fingers?" he asked, by way of a greeting.

"They're fine." Actually, they were throbbing like crazy, but if I told him that, Dad would explain that it was perfectly normal, which I already knew, so I thought I'd save us both the trouble. "Gridwell did a nice job. How are the boys?"

"Fine," he said. "Your grandfather and Natalie are taking them on a nature walk. Is your terrarium large enough for a few more toads?"

"It's not large enough for the toads we already have," I said. "Please enforce a catch-and-release policy on all reptiles and amphibians. Do you think you can keep Grandfather there till I get back?"

"I doubt if I could chase him away if I wanted to," Dad said. "Rose Noire and Natalie are making homemade ice cream, and I'm going to start up the grill before too long. Ribs and corn on the cob for dinner."

"May I bring a guest?" I said.

"You and Michael aren't guests," Dad said. "You're expected. I want to inspect Gridwell's work. He seems to be shaping up, but I still want to keep an eye on him till I'm sure."

"I was thinking of bringing Stanley Denton," I said. "I've been helping him with a case."

"A case? Here in Caerphilly? Does he need any more

help?" Dad devoured at least half-a-dozen mystery books in a slow week and was always fascinated by the idea of getting involved in real-life investigations. Curious that Grandfather hadn't told Dad he'd hired Stanley. Or maybe not so curious; maybe Grandfather was trying to ensure that his hired PI wasn't saddled with too much volunteer help.

"The case is out of town, but we might need your help." I could almost hear him beaming. "As long as you have enough ribs and corn for one more, I'll bring Stanley to supper and you can hear all about it. Just make sure Grandfather's there."

"There's plenty," Dad said. "I may have overbought the ribs and corn. See you soon!"

With that we hung up.

"So there's plenty for me?" Stanley asked.

"If even Dad realizes he overbought, there's plenty for a small army," I said. "And this should work even better, Rob will be there, so you can tell Grandfather in front of his son and two out of his three grandchildren. Not to mention three out of eight great-grandchildren. Plenty of family pressure to shame him into continuing the investigation even if he's not so inclined for his own sake."

"That should work very nicely," he said. "Thank you."

"So is there anything else you want to do while we're here?" I asked. "Visit the police station, perhaps?"

"I'd rather save that until we have your grandfather officially on board with the expansion," Stanley said. "I have a feeling Dr. Blake has connections that will make it a lot harder for the Riverton police to stonewall me."

"Checking back files of the local paper, if they still have one?"

"The *Riverton Record,* and I already did," he said. "Hang on a sec and I'll show you."

When he stopped at the next stop sign, he reached into the backseat and retrieved a manila folder.

"Here," he said, handing it to me. "You can check it out. If it's okay with you, I'm going to take the long way home. Scope out the countryside a little. And I can think better when I'm driving on a sane road instead of an interstate."

"Fine by me," I said. I was already delving into the file.

It was mainly printouts from microfilm. They were fuzzy and hard to read, so I merely leafed through, saving the close study for later, when it was less apt to make me carsick. The articles were in chronological order, and most were merely passing mentions of Annabel, Cordelia, and other members of their family. I found the obituaries of Cordelia's and Annabel's parents. Apparently Cordelia's mother—my great-grandmother—was a member of the National Genealogical Society. Might there be family trees going back even farther? Another thing we could hope to get from Annabel eventually. A notice of the widowed Cordelia's return from Richmond to Riverton to live with her cousin. By this time, she seemed to have been using her married name, and Delia rather than her full name, I noticed with a frown. I liked Cordelia better.

After that the file contained mostly passing mentions of their attendance at parties or Cordelia's participation in the Garden Club. In the last few years, she'd been active in the campaign to set up some kind of bird refuge somewhere in the mountains outside town. I wasn't quite sure I understood the need for a refuge. From what I could see, the whole area was a bird refuge. Apart from the songbirds that swarmed Annabel's feeders, I'd spotted quail, pheasants, and even a wild turkey. But there was probably some good ornithological reason for the refuge. Perhaps the local hunters were a little too zealous, and Cordelia felt the need to provide some protection for the local ducks, geese, partridge, grouse, quail, wild turkey, and—

"Whoa!" Stanley slammed on the brakes and the papers went flying onto the floor. "Did you see that?"

"See what?" I glanced up but all I saw was the two-lane road, stretching downhill in front of us, and the trees pressing close to it on either side.

Stanley was staring at the woods to the right of the road.

"Something ran across the road," he said. "You didn't see it?"

"Sorry," I said. "I was studying the file you gave me. Could it have been a deer?"

"No." He was shaking his head slowly. "Actually, it looked like a small ostrich. I didn't realize we had ostriches in Virginia."

"I'm pretty sure we don't," I said. "Not in the wild, anyway. Not in any part of the U.S."

"It looked smaller than I'd imagine an ostrich to be," he said. "Do we have anything that lives in Virginia that looks like an ostrich, only slightly smaller?"

"Not that I know of," I said. "But you can ask Grandfather over dinner."

Chapter 7

"No," Grandfather said. "You couldn't possibly have seen a wild ostrich here in Virginia. There are no living species of ratites native to North America."

"Ratites, I assume, is the scientific name for ostriches?" I put in from my end of my parents' picnic table.

"For the taxonomic order that includes ostriches." Grandfather licked the butter from his fingers and went on, using the corn cob he'd just finished gnawing as a pointer. "None native to North America, and there's only scant, unreliable evidence to indicate we ever had any. You have the ostrich in Africa. At nine feet or so, the largest extant ratite."

"I don't think what I saw was quite that tall," Stanley said, helping himself to more green beans.

"Then in Australia you have the emus, about six feet, and the cassowaries, a little smaller, but not to be trifled with, because of their razor-sharp talons."

"Either one sounds more the size of what I saw," Stanley said. "Although I can't speak to the presence or absence of talons."

"South America has several species of rhea, four or five feet tall." Grandfather was drowning a buttermilk biscuit in butter. "Though before you ask, no, I doubt if they ever stray this far north. And then in New Zealand there are the kiwis, which are pretty much the size of a chicken. Well, bigger than those," he added, waving a bit dismissively at one of the sleek bantam whatzits that had wandered away from Mother's elegantly decorated chicken coop. "The size of a normal chicken. But none of them would be running around wild here in Virginia."

"Are you missing any ratites from your zoo?" Rob asked, his words slightly garbled by the rib bone he was gnawing.

"No." Grandfather shook his head. "I was showing them to the boys about an hour ago. Was there a zoo in the town where you saw it? They could have escaped from some other zoo."

"There's barely even a town," Stanley said. "Definitely no zoo."

"Where was it you thought you saw this ostrich?" Grandfather asked.

"Or emu," Stanley said. "Out near Riverton."

"Riverton?" Grandfather frowned as if the name rang a bell.

"That's in the foothills of the Blue Ridge, isn't it?" Dad asked. "Were you out there on your case?"

"Actually, I was," Stanley said. "On Dr. Blake's case."

"My case?" Grandfather sat up, looking alert. "You were out there on my case? Why didn't you say so earlier?"

"Because it was dinnertime when we got here," I said. "And Mother always disapproves of talking business over dinner."

"Thank you, dear," Mother said.

There was also the fact that Grandfather had been a little testy when we first arrived, probably because he'd just spent several hours patiently answering questions from the boys, and we'd decided to wait until the meal had mellowed him. He was incredibly spry for a man in his nineties, but neither his legs nor his patience could take too much of the boys all at once.

"What's the case?" Dad asked.

"I hired him to see if he could find any trace of your mother," Grandfather said. "What were you doing up in Riverton?"

"That's where Cordelia lived for the last twenty or so years of her life."

"Lived?" Grandfather said. "Past tense? She's dead?"

Stanley nodded.

That news cast a predictable pall on the gathering, and we all fell silent. No doubt the rest of the family were thinking the same gloomy thoughts that had come to me when I'd first learned that I'd lost my grandmother before ever having the chance to meet her. Stanley glanced around and evidently decided to give everyone some time to digest the news. He applied himself to the last bits of his meal.

Either everyone had finished eating or no one quite felt comfortable asking for seconds on potato salad quite so soon after hearing such bad news. The silence might have dragged on quite a bit longer if we hadn't been startled out of it by sudden shrieks of alarm from the boys. They had been over by the chicken coop, throwing small handfuls of grain at the bantams, while Natalie hovered over them like a protective mother crow. One of the bantams had begun chasing the boys and pecking at their ankles. Natalie rescued them handily enough but Spike, our eight-and-a-half-pound furball, who had appointed himself the boys' canine guardian angel, had counterattacked, and we all dashed over to save the chickens from Spike or possibly Spike from the chickens. By the time we'd separated all the combatants and soothed everyone's ruffled feathers and feelings, the mood at the table had lightened a bit.

"Well, it's sad," Grandfather said. "But not surprising when you come to think of it. Slip of a girl like that—you can't expect her to last as long as a tough old goat like me."

"She lasted just fine until this past December," Stanley said. "And she didn't just fade away or anything of the sort—she was killed by a fire, and it may have been murder."

"Murder!" Dad looked stricken. I felt guilty. He'd been so excited at the idea of helping Stanley with a case. And few things excited him more than the notion of getting involved in a real-life murder investigation. But if the victim was his own mother . . .

"According to her cousin," Stanley said. He quickly sketched in what we'd learned about Cordelia's death from Annabel and the *Riverton Record*.

"What did the local police have to say?" Grandfather asked.

"I haven't talked to them yet," Stanley said. "It seemed to go a little beyond the original scope of the case, and I wanted to make sure you were comfortable with my taking it in this direction."

Grandfather was frowning, but before he could open his mouth, Dad spoke up.

"Comfortable with it! We insist on it!" Dad pounded his fist on the table.

"Yeah," my brother, Rob, said, through a mouthful of watermelon. "You think we want someone to get away with knocking off my grandmother?"

"I agree," I said. "And Stanley can probably also find out a lot of information about Cordelia. Her cousin Annabel is reclusive, but she knows a lot about Cordelia's life, and she's very interested in helping us solve the case."

Stanley and I had agreed that it was better not to come right out and say that she was holding her information hostage to our solving the murder. That was the sort of thing that would set Grandfather off.

"Just think," I went on. "Photos. Journals. Home movies. Genealogy files—apparently Cordelia's mother was interested in that."

"Fabulous!" Dad looked a little less lugubrious.

"Well," Grandfather said. "It's not exactly what I would have hoped you'd be finding. But it does sound like the reasonable thing to do."

"Awesome," Rob said.

"And you know, the more I think of it, the madder I get," Grandfather went on. "She survives all this time, and just as I was about to reunite her with her family, some miscreant kills her? Unacceptable."

Even better. A riled-up Grandfather would be more than a match for any opposition the local police tried to put in Stanley's way.

"So I should accept Annabel's request that we investigate Cordelia's death as a possible homicide?" Stanley asked.

"Absolutely!" Grandfather pounded the picnic table by way of emphasis.

"I'll head back down in the morning."

"It might take me a day or two to get things organized to join you," Grandfather said.

"Join me?" Stanley looked taken aback. As well he might. The investigation was clearly going to be a delicate mission. Grandfather had many sterling qualities, but subtlety, tact, and diplomacy were not among them.

"I think maybe Stanley can probably handle this better alone," I said. "He already knows it's going to be difficult dealing with the local police. I'm not even sure he would have needed me at all, except that my face seems to reassure people who knew Cordelia."

"And you think I'm going to barge in like a bull in a china shop," Grandfather said. "Don't worry. I have the perfect cover story for being there."

"Do tell," Stanley said, his voice sounding faint with dismay.

"I knew there was something familiar about the name

Riverton," Grandfather went on. "It's near Biscuit Mountain, isn't it?"

"I'm afraid I'm not yet that familiar with the local geography," Stanley said. "What's the significance of Biscuit Mountain?"

"They've got a feral emu problem down there," Grandfather said. "And possibly feral ostriches as well, though most of the sightings have been of emus."

"I thought you said there couldn't be any ostriches or emus down there." Stanley sounded cross, and I didn't blame him.

"I said there couldn't be any wild ones," Grandfather said. "Feral is a different matter."

"A wild animal is one that has never been domesticated," I explained. "Feral means it was domesticated, but has gone back to the wild."

"There used to be a place up in the mountains near Riverton called the Biscuit Mountain Ostrich and Emu Ranch," Grandfather said. "Some aging hippie decided it would be an easy way to earn a living, so he bought a lot of pasture land and turned the birds out on it. Only emus, apparently, in spite of the name. I suppose he never got around to the ostriches."

"It was a big thing in the nineties," Dad said. "Ostrich and emu ranches were springing up all over."

"What do they raise them for?" Stanley asked.

"Meat, leather, feathers, and with emus, the emu oil," Dad said.

"The Australian aborigines used emu oil along with eucalyptus oil in all their traditional remedies," Rose Noire put in. "It's supposed to have healing properties for wounds and arthritic joints."

"You use the stuff in all those herbal balms you sell?" Grandfather often pretended to make fun of Rose Noire's passion for all things New Age, but I'd noticed that he'd started experimenting with some of her essential oils to enhance the well-being of some of his zoo animals. And he did suffer from arthritis.

"Oh, no!" Rose Noire said. "I think you have to kill the emu to get it. Everything I use is natural, organic, and *vegetarian*."

"I have yet to see any really reliable studies that prove the benefits," Dad said. "And—"

"Whether or not it works miracles for arthritis and wounds, the emu oil didn't do much for the owner of the ranch." Grandfather was definitely getting better at herding family conversations back on track, or at least in the direction he wanted them to go. "He went bust, and couldn't get anyone to buy his stock, so he just turned them loose."

"And they survived?" Dad asked. "Astonishing."

"Well, we have no idea how well they're surviving," Grandfather said. "It's possible that they're hanging on, but not thriving, in which case we need to rescue them and re-home them in a place that can give them proper care."

"And if they're doing just fine on their own?" Stanley asked.

"Then they're probably having a detrimental effect on the native ecosystem, in which case we need to capture them and confine them in a place that can care for them without damaging the environment."

"Like the Willner Wildlife Sanctuary?" Dad suggested.

"Precisely my idea," Grandfather said.

"Are you just going to show up at the sanctuary with an as-yet-undetermined number of ostriches and emus?" I asked. "Or are you going to give Caroline Willner a heads up on what you're up to?"

"I plan to invite her to join the expedition," Grandfather said. "She'll love it."

He and Dad immediately began making elaborate plans, as if Riverton were half a continent away instead of forty minutes' drive. For some unfathomable reason they decided it would be more effective to camp out there for however long the ratite roundup would take, rather than sensibly coming home to sleep in their beds every night.

I borrowed Stanley's folder again and began reading some of the articles in it while he picked at his homemade organic strawberry ice cream.

"Well, at least I know I'm not going crazy," he said. "I did see an ostrich cross the road. Or possibly an emu."

"Let me just call the SPOOR members," Dad was saying. "They'll all want to get in on this."

"What is SPOOR?" Stanley asked me.

"The Society to Preserve Our Owls and Raptors," I said. "A local bird conservation and appreciation group."

"Ah," he said, nodding. "That makes sense. Are there many of them?"

"Several dozen," I said.

"Oh, dear. I wasn't hoping for quite this much enthusiasm."

"Well, it will probably please Annabel," I said. "Because the whole feral emu thing explains why she and Cordelia were trying to start a bird sanctuary there. Have you read this?" I held up one of the articles from the folder.

"I confess, as yet I've only skimmed all those articles," he said. "It's always been one of my least favorite parts of the job, wading through page after page of fuzzy fine print. I was planning to study them this evening. What did you find?"

"Cordelia was heading up a campaign," I said. "She and some other locals were trying to raise enough money to buy the former ostrich and emu ranch and set it up as a sanctuary for the abandoned birds."

I passed over the article. Stanley studied it for a few

moments. Then he lifted his head, gazed at my Grandfather, and spoke up.

"Dr. Blake," he said. "Just how did you happen to find out about the feral emus in Riverton?" he asked.

"Someone from down there contacted me," he said. "Asked for my help dealing with the problem."

"Recently?" I asked.

"A few months back," Grandfather said.

"Was it a Mrs. Mason who contacted you?" I asked. The article listed Delia Mason as the leader of the project.

"No," Grandfather said. "It was a Miss somebody. With a Civil War name."

"Civil War name?" Stanley looked at me for a translation.

"You mean something like Grant or Lincoln or Jackson?" I asked Grandfather.

"That's right," he said. "Can't remember which one."

"Could it have been Lee?" Stanley asked.

"That's it," he said. "A Miss Lee."

Stanley and I looked at each other.

"Well, it makes sense Cordelia wouldn't want to contact him directly," I said.

"Yes," he said. "If Annabel's attitude is anything to go by, Dr. Blake would have been the last person Cordelia wanted to see."

I applied myself to the last bits of my meal. Eventually everyone—even the boys—gravitated to the end of the table where Dad and Grandfather were plotting their expedition. Rose Noire slipped a bowl of organic chocolate walnut ice cream in front of me, and I closed my eyes, the better to enjoy it.

"Meg?" I opened my eyes to see that my husband, Michael, had sat down at the picnic table opposite me. The boys climbed up and sat, one on either side of him. Natalie was hovering behind them, her black-clad shoulders slightly hunched, making her look more like a buzzard than a crow. Mother was right—we would need to work on her confidence and posture this summer. Like so many tall girls, she tended to slouch. Nothing a summer of intense exposure to Mother's tall-is-beautiful philosophy couldn't cure.

"What's wrong?" I asked aloud.

"Nothing's wrong," he said. "But the boys want to know if they can go on the camping trip with Grandfather."

"I don't mind," Natalie said. "And I think the emu roundup sounds pretty cool."

"We were talking about a camping trip later this summer," Michael said. "Why not just go now, with the rest of the family? Tomorrow's the first day of my break—let's do it!"

They all stared at me, eagerly. The boys seemed to be holding their breath.

"Why not?" I said.

"We're going camping! We're going camping!" The boys began running around yelling at the top of their lungs. Natalie was following in their wake, and looked as if only the grave responsibility of her position as babysitter was keeping her from shouting "We're going camping!" along with them.

"Of course, that's assuming we find a campground," Dad said, joining us at the table. "The closest one seems to be almost as far away from Riverton as Caerphilly is."

"I have an idea." I pulled out my phone. "Stanley, do you have Annabel's phone number?"

"I do." He took out his phone and began tapping on it. "She tends not to answer it, though."

"She can't answer at all if I don't call," I said.

He read me the number and I dialed. After four rings, Annabel's brisk, no-nonsense message told me the number I reached and ordered me to leave a message.

"Miss Lee," I said. "This is Meg Langslow. I was—"

"What's the verdict?" Annabel's live voice interrupted me in mid-message.

"It's a go," I said. "Mr. Denton will be back tomorrow to start working on the case."

"Good," she said. "See you tomorrow."

"I have more news," I said. "Good news, I think. Stanley saw what he thought was an emu while we were leaving town."

"Yes, we have feral emus running amok around here," she said. "Cordelia had me write your grandfather, suggesting that he do a rescue on them instead of running off to Africa or Australia or some such place. Never heard back."

"You will soon," I said. "When we mentioned seeing the emu, it reminded him that he'd been intending to do something about your problem. He's organizing a roundup now."

"Hmph," Annabel said. "Probably feels guilty that he ignored our problem while your grandmother was alive."

"Very likely," I said. "But at least it will get done."

"And where are you planning to put them when you get them rounded up?" she asked. "We haven't got the sanctuary set up. The bank that repossessed the land's being difficult, and so's the town council."

"He has a friend who runs a sanctuary," I said. "She can probably take them, at least in the short term. Though I have no idea if she wants a whole herd of ratites for the long haul, so if you like, I'll see if I can get Grandfather fired up about your proposed sanctuary. Nothing he likes more than browbeating governments and financial institutions that are standing in the way of environmental progress and animal welfare."

"Ha!" she snorted. "He just likes browbeating people, period. Cordelia had his number, all right."

I was opening my mouth to defend Grandfather and thought better of it. After all, we needed her cooperation. Besides, she wasn't saying anything about Grandfather that I hadn't said to myself in moments of exasperation. And if anyone had grounds for ongoing exasperation with him, surely Cordelia and Annabel did. I decided to change the subject slightly.

"Speaking of the roundup," I said. "He's having trouble finding a campground nearby."

"Campground?"

"He wants to get the roundup done with maximum efficiency, so he and his team are planning to camp nearby until they finish. Do you know anyone who would rent them a field for however many days it will take?"

Silence. At least thirty seconds of silence. I was just about to ask if Annabel was still there when she spoke up.

"We own the field in back of the house," she said. "Well, now I own it. I suppose I could let you camp there. How many people are we talking about?"

I looked up from the phone. Grandfather and Dad were sitting at the other picnic table, and already three people I recognized as avid local SPOOR members were sitting with them. Maps and notepads were starting to cover the table. Grandfather was shouting into his cell phone.

"Yes, a full camera crew," he was saying. "And how soon can you get the editing trailer down there?"

I shut my eyes for a moment. Apparently Grandfather was also going to film the emu roundup for another of his popular *Animals in Peril* documentaries.

"Meg?" Annabel sounded impatient.

"I have no idea how many people," I said. "Dozens."

"Dozens?"

I had a feeling she was about to rescind the invitation.

"Dozens," I said. "And you might not want them in your backyard. Grandfather's crews tend to get a little rowdy around the campfire after a hard day of rescuing. Your neighbors will hate it."

"The only neighbor close enough to that field to be bothered is Theo Weaver, and I damn well hope they make his life a misery," she said. "Blake can bring a whole damned army if he likes. But they can't use my toilet. Got to draw the line somewhere."

"I'll tell him he'll need port-a-potties," I said.

"There's a side road leading to the field," she said. "About a quarter of a mile beyond my gate. Have them use that. I don't want a whole mob tromping through the yard."

"I'll pass that along," I said. "Oh, and Michael and the boys and I are probably going to come down, too. And their summer babysitter, Natalie—my sister Pam's next-to-youngest. The kids are all excited about going camping with Great-Grandpa. I'd love for them to meet you while we're there. If that's okay with you."

Another silence. Not quite so long this time. Still, I wondered if Annabel's curiosity about her cousin's grandchildren would outweigh her reclusiveness. And her already clearly expressed distaste for her cousin's seducer.

"I'll think about it. As long as it's just a few of you. And I don't want to meet Blake."

"I can understand that," I said. "We should be down sometime in the next day or so. I'll let you know."

"Fine," she said. "Good-bye."

I looked back at the table where Dad and Grandfather and the rest of the troops were studying their maps.

"Good news," I said. "I've found you a place to camp."

Chapter 8

Michael and I headed down to Riverton first thing the next morning. Luckily, we'd been considering a camping trip, and I had already gathered most of the equipment and supplies we'd need. With the camping checklist in my notebook-that-tells-me-when-to-breathe, it only took an hour or so after dinner to gather the remaining items and pack them in the Twinmobile, our sturdy minivan.

If anyone had asked Why the rush? I'd have told them that we only had two weeks before Michael's summer session began. But that wasn't my real reason for haste. I wanted to be there as a buffer between the rest of the rescuers and Annabel. Particularly between Grandfather and Annabel. Even those of us who loved him dearly often found Grandfather exasperating. And Annabel had already shown clear signs of animosity toward him—obviously resenting what he had done to her cousin. Even if Grandfather was savvy enough to steer clear of her, I couldn't be sure that the rest of the campers would, and I suspected Annabel did not suffer fools gladly.

And this gathering could get rather large. In addition to the film crew—Grandfather never passed up the chance to document his exploits for the television audience—there would be the usual motley assortment of volunteers who always showed up when he put out the call, drawn both by their eagerness to serve the environment and their desire to be seen doing so on one of Grandfather's specials.

As we pulled into Riverton at a little past eleven o'clock

Wednesday morning, I was already planning how I'd handle it. I was driving—partly to prove that my hand didn't hurt that badly and partly so I could feel no guilt at abandoning Michael to set up camp and tend the boys while I headed over to charm—or at least distract—Cousin Annabel. Probably a good idea not to spring the boys on her just yet. Not until we'd found something very active for them to do, to drain off all the extra energy they'd built up on the ride. And I'd be there to ease any anxiety she felt as the other campers trickled in, swelling our small beach-head into the full camp.

So I wasn't thrilled when I turned the Twinmobile onto the dirt road that led to our borrowed campground and realized—

"Blast!" I exclaimed. "We're not the first."

"How can you tell?" Michael was sitting back in the third row, with Josh, and probably hadn't spotted the tell-tale clues.

"Because there's already a sign over the road up ahead," I called back. "Saying Welcome to Camp Emu."

Someone had hung the sign between the last two trees before the lane left the woods for the open field. So when I drove under it, I found myself in the midst of an already thriving camp. Cars, vans, pickups, trailers, and RVs were everywhere, and I could see at least half-a-dozen tents already set up, with more in progress.

"Meg!" A man I recognized as a longtime SPOOR member raced up to my window. He was wearing an orange safety vest, a hard hat, and an armband with the word STAFF printed on it. I rolled my window down.

"I see we're not quite the first," I said.

"Oh, no!" he said. "Some of us have been here since dawn! Your grandfather is saving a spot for your tent near his."

Since I wasn't sure how restful it would be, camping

near Grandfather, I was about to protest that we didn't want any special treatment, but—

"See the mess tent? The big tent just to the left of that first port-a-pottie? Your spot's right behind it."

After a moment of consideration, I decided that proximity to the food and bathrooms was worth being near the noise and drama that always accompanied Grandfather, so I thanked the volunteer and drove on toward where Grandfather's familiar battered Airstream was parked in a nice shady spot, midway between the mess tent and the area where a truck was delivering more port-a-potties, along with a shower trailer and a huge water tank.

The tents and trailers belonging to Grandfather's staff, including the film crew, were clustered together to the left of the Airstream. I headed for the area at the right, where I recognized Dad's tent, with Tinkerbell, Rob's Irish Wolfhound, lying in front as if on guard. Inside I could see that Dad had begun setting up his equipment so the tent could double as a field medical station. Nearby was a space with a hand-lettered sign in the middle of it proclaiming THIS SPOT RESERVED FOR THE WATERSTON FAMILY.

"We're here," I said.

"Give your hand a rest," Michael said. "The boys and Natalie can help me set up our tent."

"Good idea." I could imagine how much help the boys would be but managed to keep a straight face. "Then I'll go over to see how Annabel's taking the invasion."

I hopped out and came around to the passenger side to haul out the dog crate containing Spike. I'd have preferred leaving him at home, but the boys insisted, and it turned out everyone who'd be willing to feed and walk him was coming on the expedition anyway.

"Meg! Michael! Welcome!"

Dad and several of his fellow SPOOR members bounced up to greet us and quickly began helping to unload the van.

"Mommy! Playhouse!"

Jamie was tugging at the hem of my shirt. I looked up and saw that Josh was trying to drag Natalie over to a nearby vehicle that looked like an old-fashioned gypsy caravan, straight out of a movie.

It was set on tall wheels and towered over the drab tents and cars nearby. Every inch of its surface was painted or decorated with gilded carvings. Painted lions and tigers stalked along the sides, while cranes and flamingos flanked the windows and a peacock with tail outspread graced the door.

"Mommy! Go see!" Jamie whined.

"Let's make sure whoever owns the caravan wants company," I said. I turned Jamie over to Natalie and walked up to the caravan. I noticed that while it had the shafts you'd use to hitch a horse up to it, it also had a contraption to allow the caravan to be towed behind a car if needed.

The two shutters that formed the top half of the door flew open, narrowly missing me, and my old friend Caroline Willner peered out.

"Meg! Welcome! How do you like my new toy?" she crowed. "Isn't it splendid?"

"I love it," I said. "And the boys are dying to come inside."

"Bring them in!"

I beckoned to Natalie and the boys, who raced over. Within minutes, the boys were bouncing on the built-in divan at the back of the wagon. It probably served as Caroline's bed at night, but now it was piled high with brightly covered scarves and pillows and had a small table in front of it that held a plate of fruit and cheese.

"Do you mind if I leave Natalie and the boys with you for a bit?" I said. "I want to check in with our hostess."

"I thought this was Monty's shindig," Caroline said.

"The lady who's letting us camp in her field," I elaborated. "I'm not sure she realized quite what an army Grandfather would be bringing."

"Never does anything quietly, your grandfather," she said. "They're fine here, and if I get tired I can tell your niece to drag them away. Come back later, and I'll give you the tour. You'd be amazed how much hidden storage my carpenter managed to fit into this thing," she added, as she followed me to the door. "Don't worry. Along with the storage, my carpenter was under orders to make everything nearly impossible to break or hurt yourself on."

"Good," I said. "The boys will be the acid test of how well he succeeded. How in the world did you all get here so fast?"

"Well, we were already planning an expedition," she said. "Not quite such a big one, of course. Just a follow-up on the Toad Wars."

"The what?"

"The Toad Wars. That's what the brigade calls that expedition to southwest Virginia two years ago, where we managed to stop a strip mine and save that new species of toads."

"The poisonous ones that they're going to name after Grandfather?" I asked.

"Turns out they're not poisonous after all," she said. "Only foul-tasting, so he's not interested. He's going to arrange to have them named after me. *Anaxyrus willneri* instead of *Anaxyrus blakei*."

"Congratulations," I said.

"Thanks," She beamed—clearly she had no prejudice against the nonlethal toads. "So we were planning to go down and shoot the final segment: your grandfather standing and gloating over having saved all those verdant hills, and some more footage of the toads. We were gearing up for that when you came along with the emu rescue, which sounded much more interesting to him, so the camera crew just headed here instead of Abingdon."

"That explains you and the camera crew," I said. "But where is he going to get provisions for this crowd?"

"One of our stalwart volunteers runs a catering company." She pointed toward the mess tent, where a twenty-five-foot truck was carefully maneuvering into position, with another truck just beyond, waiting its turn. "He doesn't do it for free, of course, but he's willing to drop everything and get a crew out to wherever we're filming."

"In return for a few well-placed shots of his trucks on the show, I assume."

"Exactly. Well, I'd better go keep the boys from tearing my caravan apart."

She began climbing up into the caravan. I was turning to leave when a blond Valkyrie in a white shirt and khaki shorts bustled up to me, wielding a clipboard.

"Have you signed your releases yet?" she asked.

"Releases? Oh, right—"

"Dr. Blake plans to develop a documentary about the emu roundup," she said, and she began to recite a spiel warning me that anyone who refused to sign their photo release would be escorted to the gate and—

"I get it, I get it," I said, as soon as I could interrupt her. "Give me four of the forms and I'll turn them in later today. Dr. Blake's my grandfather and I know the drill." In fact, I'd done her job a time or two, and hoped I'd managed to be less annoying.

"I see." She was studying me with a slight frown, as if not quite sure I measured up to the exalted position of Dr. Blake's granddaughter. I got the feeling that she was trying to look down her nose at me. She was nearly six feet tall, with an elegant if slightly aquiline nose, and I suspected she got a lot of practice looking down it at most women and quite a few men. But since I was five foot ten in bare feet and had chosen to wear thick-soled clogs today, she had to look me eye to eye. It seemed to throw her off her game.

I noticed she was wearing a name tag with a big smiley face on it that read HI! MY NAME IS SHERRY S. SMITH! If she tried to enforce the wearing of cute name tags with superfluous exclamation points, she was going to have a rebellion on her hands.

"You can turn your forms in at the information desk," she said. "Center of the camp, right in front of Dr. Blake's trailer."

After saying that, she strode off. I noticed, enviously, that her hair was arranged in a perfect French braid, something I had never in my life achieved without professional help. I resolved to make an effort not to hold that against her. I stowed the forms on the passenger seat of the Twinmobile for safekeeping and began to pick my way through the camp toward the gate that led into Annabel's backyard.

The camp wasn't really as huge as I'd first thought. Not yet, anyway—only fifteen or twenty tents, trailers, or RVs apart from Grandfather's little headquarters cluster. But every time I looked, someone else was arriving.

Luckily, the campers were settling in precisely where I would have tried to put them—mostly in the part of the field that backed up to Theo Weaver's house. The part immediately in back of Annabel's yard was vacant, and several volunteers were setting up fence posts in a line that would divide it off from the other half of the field.

"Setting up a holding pen for the birds," one explained, when I stopped to watch for a few moments.

"Good idea," I said, and moved on.

A rather substantial holding pen. I found myself suddenly wondering if anyone had recently confirmed the continued existence of the emus and ostriches. What if the emu Stanley had seen was the last of his kind, the rest having succumbed to the rigors of the recent unusually harsh winter?

Not my problem. My job was to charm Annabel.

In addition to the wire fence that outlined the pasture, a weathered split-rail fence ran along the back of Theo Weaver's lot. And inside his fence were a lot of overgrown bushes. Mostly prickly hollies and thorny pyracanthas, in an almost unbroken line, as if twenty years ago Mr. Weaver had anticipated the need for a substantial barrier between his yard and Camp Emu.

Someone was watching us over the two fences: a tall, though slightly stooped figure in a battered fishing hat. Presumably the infamous neighbor himself.

I smiled and waved at him, and he started slightly, as if surprised that he could be seen. I paused, and wondered if now would be a good time to go over and introduce myself to him. As good a time as any. I headed his way.

But when I was about ten feet from Weaver, he turned and stumped away toward his house.

"Mr. Weaver!" I called over the back of his fence. "May I speak to you for a moment?"

He ignored me, at least until he reached his back stoop, when he turned around to glare venomously at me before going inside and slamming the door behind him.

"So much for our welcome to the neighborhood," I muttered.

I changed direction again, heading back toward the gate that led to Annabel's yard. I was lost in thought, and almost fell flat on my face when my foot hit something more solid than the tall grass and weeds I'd been walking through. I glanced down to see something black and silver in the grass.

I bent down to look at it.

It was an LED headlight. Even if I hadn't recognized the black and silver metal shape of the lamp itself, the elastic head strap had LED HEADLIGHT woven into its design in white letters on a black background.

I reached down to pick it up and then stopped myself. Was I disturbing evidence at a crime scene? Should I leave the headlight in place?

I looked around to see if I could spot anything to mark where it was. Nothing in sight, just tall grass. And I almost couldn't find the headlight again when I looked back down, even though I hadn't moved. Probably not a good idea to leave it. I'd never find it again. And after all, this wasn't a fresh crime scene.

I pulled out my phone and took some pictures of the headlight in place. And I found some small sticks and made a triangle in the place where I'd found it. I didn't have gloves, but I did manage to find a couple of large yellowed tulip poplar leaves. I picked the headlight up, careful not to touch it except with the leaves, and continued toward the house.

I was planning to go around to the front door and ring the doorbell, in case Annabel was a stickler for formalities, but I was only ten feet into the yard when the back door opened and Annabel stuck her head out.

"Over here," she stage whispered. "Hurry."

I veered toward the back door and soon found myself in a comfortable, if old-fashioned, kitchen. It was a big, airy room with white cabinets and countertops and a huge, well-worn oak table in the middle. Along one wall was a display of art pottery in tones of blue and turquoise, and on the table was a matching vase containing a huge bouquet of white hydrangea blossoms.

Although blacksmithing was my craft, I knew a lot of potters, and liked to think I'd developed a pretty good eye for a nicely made pot. These were very nice indeed. They had an Arts and Crafts feel to them—the sort of thing you'd find in a Frank Lloyd Wright house. But were they

antiques or a modern reinterpretation? My fingers itched
to pick up one of the pieces to see who'd made it, but I
mentally swatted my hand away. Probably not the best way
to ingratiate myself with my new cousin, mauling her
crockery collection.

"Hope it's okay that I came through the backyard," I
said.

"What's that you're carrying?" she asked.

"Good question," I said. "You tell me."

I set the LED headlight down on her kitchen table and
tucked my makeshift leaf pot holders into my pocket. Annabel bent down and looked over her reading glasses at it.
She made a move to pick it up and then stopped herself.

"Ah," she said. "I see why you were being careful not
to touch it. It's her headlight."

"A headlight," I said.

"It's just like the one she'd have been wearing that
night," Annabel said. She yanked open a drawer beside the
sink, pulled out another little LED headlight, and set it
down on the table beside the one I'd found. Mine had mud
caked on it and showed signs of rust and corrosion. But
apart from that, they were identical.

We both stared down at the two headlights for a few
moments. I had no idea what Annabel was thinking. For
my part, I was pondering an apology. Maybe there was
more than I thought to her theory about Cordelia's murder.

"We should call that detective of yours," she said finally.

"And the police, surely."

"What good would that do? I told them to look for her
headlight. They claimed they did a good search, but they
didn't find this. You're here half an hour and you find it.
Hmph."

"I stumbled over it," I said. "Quite literally and very
much by accident."

"In the field, near the fence? Precisely where Weaver would have dropped it on his way back to his house?"

"No, it was a good fifteen or twenty feet back from the fence," I said.

"Even better." Annabel nodded. "He was running back to his house and he chucked it out into the field, as far as it would go."

"But why would he have taken away Cordelia's headlight and then chucked it away?" I asked.

"For the same reason he left that old kerosene lantern there," she said. "To make it look as if Cordelia herself had started the fire by being careless with an open flame. It's obvious."

Not that obvious to me, but I didn't want to argue with her.

I pulled out my phone and dialed Stanley's number. He didn't answer, so I left a voice mail.

"It's Meg," I said. "I found what Miss Annabel thinks could be Cordelia's discarded headlight. Want to take a look at it before I turn it over to the local cops?"

"Of course he does," Annabel muttered as I was hanging up.

"May I use your phone book?" I asked.

Annabel pointed to the counter where it lay, and I looked up the nonemergency number for the Riverton police and scribbled it down in my notebook-that-tells-me-when-to-breathe. I could call them later, when Annabel wasn't around to be annoyed.

"Do you have a paper bag we can put the headlight in?" I asked. "Preferably one that's never been used."

"What about a plastic sandwich bag?" Annabel asked.

"No, it's damp. Dew, most likely. Wet evidence should go in paper, to keep it from deteriorating."

"I thought you were a blacksmith, not a cop." She

stepped into the pantry and I could hear little scuffling noises as she rummaged through the shelves. "Would a lunch bag work?"

"A lunch bag would be perfect. My cousin Horace is a forensic crime-scene expert," I explained. "You pick up a few things. Oh, and may I keep this, too, for the time being?" I held up the newer headlight. "So we have another one for comparison?"

"Fine with me," she said. "We buy them by the dozen. Well, I do, now. Keep them all over the house. I have a horror of stumbling during a blackout and breaking my neck. I assume you'll need two bags."

"Please," I said.

She emerged from the pantry carrying a package of brown paper lunch bags, a tape dispenser, and a box containing a pair of brand-new, lime-green kitchen gloves. I put a glove on my uninjured hand and I tucked the rusty headlight into a brown paper bag. Then we taped it shut and scribbled our initials over the tape and the bag, as Stanley had done the day before with the bag in which he'd stowed the kerosene lamp. I dumped the other headlight into its own bag without all the formalities.

"Thanks." I took off the glove and its mate and held them out.

"No, keep them," she said. "You might come across more evidence. And take the bags, too. I've got more. I buy them in bulk for when I pack bag lunches for the shelter."

"Good idea." I tucked the gloves into my pocket. "I'd better get back to Camp Emu and help Michael set up our tent."

"You're camping out with the rest of Blake's Brigade?" she asked.

"We are," I said. Blake's Brigade was the nickname used on and off camera for the paid and volunteer crew Grandfather brought to his projects. I was a little surprised

Annabel knew it. Perhaps the cousins were keeping a closer eye on Grandfather than I'd imagined. "I confess, I'm not sure I see the necessity for camping here when an hour's drive would see us safely in our own beds. But the boys love the idea of camping."

"Makes for better television," Annabel said. "If he let you all go home to your own beds, you wouldn't have all that footage of the volunteers crawling out of their sleeping bags before dawn and singing 'Kumbayah' around the campfire after a hard day's work. Yes, I've watched some of the shows. I expect Cordelia snuck a peek occasionally, too. And thanked her lucky stars nobody expected her to tag along. Probably a good thing if you stay here with the brigade," she added. "From what I've seen, Blake's expeditions are long on book learning and theatrics and short on common sense."

"That settles it," I said, with a laugh. "You must have met Grandfather at some time in his life."

Her face stiffened.

"Only through Cordelia's memories," she said. "Which you can understand were not entirely cordial."

"I was kidding," I said. "Sorry. I just meant that you had his style pegged."

"Male foolishness can be much of a muchness," she said. "And I have no patience for it. Which, in case you're wondering, is probably why I stayed single all these years. Let me know what the PI says about the headlight."

I could recognize a dismissal when I heard it, so I wished her a good morning and headed for the back door. I had to smile when I noticed a pair of binoculars lying on the counter beside the sink. Was Miss Annabel bird-watching this morning? Or was she, perhaps, keeping an eye on what was happening in camp?

"One thing before you go."

I turned to find Miss Annabel holding out a sheet of

paper. I took it and glanced down. It was a formal letter granting permission to use the field to me and anyone else I cared to invite.

"No idea if it has any legal worth, of course," she said. "But it'll give you something to wave in the air if Chief Heedles comes and tries to claim you're trespassing."

"Good thinking," I said. "Thanks."

I reached into my pocket for my notebook, tucked the paper between its pages, and headed back for Camp Emu.

Chapter 9

The construction crew had made progress. They'd outlined an area of about half an acre with tall fence posts and were starting to enclose it with six-foot-tall chain-link.

"I gather a few strands of wire won't stop a charging emu," I said, as I stopped to watch.

"This might not even stop a really determined emu," said a man who appeared to be the foreman. "But we don't intend to keep them here too long. The truck from the wildlife sanctuary's already here. We'll haul them down in batches as soon as we catch them. By the way, I'm Jim Williams. Relatively new recruit."

He held out his hand. He was tall and lean, with a tanned, craggy face.

"Meg Langslow," I said, as I shook the proffered hand. A good handshake, I thought, firm and no-nonsense. Nothing like Grandfather's bone-crushing style. "Haven't we met at one or two previous events?"

"Yes, and I hope you'll be seeing a little more of me now that I'm retired. Let me know if there's anything I can do for you."

"Well, since you offered," I said. "If you have any leftover fencing, can we borrow some? The boys insisted on bringing our dogs camping, but I don't think taking them to the woods with us is a good idea. If we had some fencing we could put up a temporary dog run."

"We can do that for you," Williams said. "No, it's no bother," he added, before I could even open my mouth to protest. "We'll just enclose that corner of the pen for them. Right there in the shade. They can help guard the emus."

Actually, the two of them together probably could. Tinkerbell wouldn't hurt the proverbial fly, but a hundred-pound Irish wolfhound is every burglar's nightmare. Spike, in spite of his purse-dog appearance, had more than once repelled intruders from our house, although unfortunately, most of them were repairmen and other people we actually wanted to keep.

"That would be perfect," I said. "Thanks."

I set out again toward the main body of the camp. Which had grown, even in my brief absence. Amazing how many people were showing up on less than a day's notice, and most of them were probably veterans of more than one of Grandfather's projects. I overheard two people swapping tales of past expeditions. Bird and animal cleanups in the wake of various oil spills. Roundups of abandoned animals after hurricanes. Raids on dogfighting rings and puppy mills. Interventions with animal hoarders. Quests to save endangered species from extinction. Battles to stop greedy companies from building strip mines and golf courses in irreplaceable green spaces.

And getting lots of volunteers was probably easier now that Grandfather was doing more of his events close to home, in Virginia or the neighboring states. If anyone pointed this out, he'd claim he wanted to spend more time with his newly discovered family. And I'm sure he did. But I suspected he was also relieved to have a plausible reason for slowing down just a little now that he'd reached his nineties. Trips to Riverton and the Dismal Swamp were a lot less taxing than safaris to Africa and China.

I dropped by the family tent and grabbed a canvas tote bag to carry the two headlights, the lime-green gloves, and the unused lunch bags. I figured I'd show them to Stanley and then—

"Is this thing on?" Grandfather's voice, amplified and distorted by feedback. I followed the squawking sounds and found myself in the mess tent, which also doubled as the general gathering space.

"That's better." Grandfather nodded his thanks to the techies who had fixed the portable sound system. I found a place at the very back of the tent where I could slip out if the meeting went on too long.

"Let's go over what we're up against here," Grandfather said.

Clearly the expedition's work had begun. Or at least the filming. A camera was pointed at Grandfather, who stood on a small raised platform at the front end of the tent, while another was panning the audience for reactions. Grandfather was wearing his expedition outfit. Olive-green cargo pants already stained with mud—or perhaps unwashed since their last outing. Muddy hiking boots. His tan shirt appeared to be clean, but it was hard to tell, since it was almost precisely the same color as the mud on his pants and boots. Over it, he wore a khaki fishing vest whose dozen or so pockets, like those of the cargo pants, bulged with unidentified objects. At least he wasn't yet wearing his pith helmet—though it was sitting nearby on a table—so he hadn't yet acquired his usual dramatic case of hat hair.

I noticed Sherry, the blond Valkyrie, standing by clutching her clipboard to her chest, obviously intent on Grandfather's every word. And she'd added a khaki fishing vest to her white shirt and khaki shorts. Was it entirely an accident that her outfit looked like the feminine version of his standard expedition garb?

"Now here's the location of the defunct ostrich and emu ranch," he was saying. He was tapping the map with his well-worn hickory hiking stick. "And this is the approximate location where my operatives spotted an emu yesterday."

His operatives. The phrase conjured up visions of an army of professional emu trackers beating the bushes, instead of one startled PI and his unobservant passenger.

I heard a brief, quickly smothered chuckle and traced it to Stanley Denton, who was sitting in the audience with his hand covering his mouth and his shoulders shaking with suppressed laughter.

"Our scouts will start at the ranch and spread out from there," Grandfather said.

"Will the emus be in a herd?" someone asked. "Or scattered around?"

"Unknown," Grandfather boomed. "In their native habitat, they tend to travel in mated pairs. But here? We have no idea what to expect. Solo birds, pairs, flocks—who knows?"

As Grandfather continued to dispense emu lore, I sat back and studied the crowd. I recognized half-a-dozen people from Mother's side of my family. Not surprising; many of my relatives had been involved in environmental and animal welfare projects long before Grandfather had come into our lives, and they'd thrown themselves into his expeditions with enthusiasm. I was a little surprised to see Seth Early, the sheep farmer who lived across the road from us, sitting at a table with Lad, his rescued border collie, at his feet. I wouldn't have thought Seth cared for any animals apart from Lad and his prize Lincoln sheep. But perhaps it wasn't the emus that had enticed him but the presence of Rose Noire—he was among the legions of men apparently smitten with her.

My friend Crystal, from the hospital—also a longtime SPOOR member—timidly raised her hand.

"Is this roundup going to be dangerous, Dr. Blake?"

Grandfather beamed. Clearly she had just asked his favorite question. Was she a plant or had she come up with it on her own?

"Dangerous? Of course!" he boomed. "Emus are as tall as we are, with a kick like a mule—and unlike mules, they also have sharp claws. I've seen them gut a man in seconds. Moreover—"

Just then a middle-aged man seated a few rows in front of me shrieked and keeled over, splashing several nearby spectators with the contents of his coffee mug. I could see Dad running from the front of the tent, pushing his way through the people clustered around the fallen man. Maybe the man was only panicking at the thought of encountering a rogue emu, but I hadn't liked the sound of that shriek, so I pulled out my cell phone and dialed 9-1-1.

"It's Fred," someone said. "He's having convulsions!"

Dad and Crystal and several other volunteers who presumably also had medical training had reached the patient, though their efforts were slightly hampered by the onlookers. Someone should make them move back. When I finished calling the ambulance—

"Move back, everyone! Move back, now!" Sherry apparently had the same thought.

The Riverton emergency dispatcher answered.

"We need an ambulance out in the field behind Miss Annabel Lee's house," I said.

"Where the bird people are camping?" the dispatcher asked.

"Yes," I said. "One of our volunteers has collapsed and is having convulsions."

"I think Fred's been poisoned," Dad said over his shoulder.

"The doctor on hand thinks he might have been poisoned," I relayed.

"Let me talk to them." Crystal rushed up to me and took the phone.

I let her have my phone and hovered nearby to reclaim it when she was finished. And wondered if maybe someone should mention to the dispatcher that poison was a hobby of Dad's, and that he had been known to be just a little too eager to diágnose it.

"Nothing to see here! Let's clear out!" Sherry was still trying to shoo people away, not entirely successfully. Did the rest of the brigade find her as annoying as I did? But I decided to cut her some slack. She kept turning to stare at Fred and then jerking her head away. She was obviously quite shaken by what was happening.

"Let's give him air, folks!" Grandfather shouted. "The food trucks will be serving in a few minutes. Clear the mess tent! Today's lunch will be a picnic."

At Grandfather's urging, the crowds left. I hoped not too many of them had heard Dad's comment about the possibility of poison, or lunch could be something of a bust, even though the coffee hadn't come from the newly arrived food trucks.

One of the volunteers scurried in with an armload of medical equipment—from Dad's tent, I assumed.

I heard a siren in the distance. I glanced back at the patient in time to see him vomiting copiously.

"Excellent!" Dad exclaimed. He was hooking up an IV. From his triumphant expression, I deduced that vomiting was something he'd been trying to bring about, not a sign that his patient was deteriorating.

Crystal handed me my phone and rushed back to her patient. I decided to make sure someone was clearing a path for the medics. I headed toward the sound of the ambulances.

Just outside the tent, I ran into a woman who was scrubbing at her blouse with a paper towel. Scrubbing what looked like coffee stains.

"Well, at least I wasn't scalded," she muttered when she saw me looking at her stains.

"Were you sitting next to Fred?" I asked.

"Just in front of him," she said. "He's not usually this bad."

"What do you mean, not usually this bad?" I asked. "You mean he's had convulsions at brigade outings before?"

"No, that's new," she said. "I mean he usually gets a little tiddly around the campfire in the evening, but not this early, and not like this. Do you think it's DTs?"

"You think he's drunk?"

"I think he's been drinking," she said. "More Scotch than coffee in that cup of his. Smell this." She held out the paper towel. I took a hesitant sniff and detected a faint odor of coffee overlaid with a much stronger smell of Scotch.

"I should go and change," she said. "And find a plastic bag to stow this blouse in, or my tent will smell like a distillery for the rest of the week."

"How about if I take it off your hands for the time being?" I asked. "If Dad is right and Fred was poisoned, your blouse could be evidence. We should turn it over to the police."

"Poisoned?" She pulled the blouse away from her body as if afraid the poison would seep into her skin. Which some poisons could do, of course. "In the coffee?"

"No idea," I said. "Dad can't necessarily be sure it's poison at this point. But since your blouse is saturated with the coffee Fred was drinking just before his collapse—"

"My tent's this way. Let me find something else to put on and you can keep the blouse." She set off at a fast pace.

I followed her to her tent and stored her blouse in another of Annabel's paper bags. And then I went back to the mess tent and spotted a coffee mug that had fallen on the ground near where Dad and his crew were working on Fred. I was pretty sure it was Fred's mug, because it, too, gave off a strong odor of Scotch. I hesitated for a moment. Should I leave it where it had fallen? No, all too likely that the cleanup crew would whisk it away. And if Dad was right about Fred being poisoned—and if it turned out to be intentional rather than accidental—the cup would be evidence. Not a good idea to leave it where the poisoner could find and dispose of it. I bagged it and stowed it and the blouse in my tote. It was getting bulky. But surely the police would arrive soon to investigate the suspected poisoning, and I could turn everything over to them. Should I hunt down Stanley first and show him the contents of the tote? Or—

"Ms. Langslow?"

I turned to find Dr. Ffollett standing behind me. He seemed tense and kept darting glances around him, making him look rather like a mouse making his way through an encampment of cats.

"Welcome to Camp Emu," I said. "I'm afraid you've caught us in the middle of a medical emergency."

Dad would have perked up at that news but Dr. Ffollett didn't.

"She's having a fit," he said. Annabel, of course. "People keep showing up at the gate and trying to get in. She sent me out to give directions to the first few, but she's not happy."

"Tell her we'll take care of it," I said.

"Right." He turned and fled, looking more mouselike than ever.

We'll take care of it. More likely me. Although perhaps it would be nice to have something I could take care of, since there was nothing I could do for poor Fred. I could hear Natalie and the boys still chattering happily in Caroline's caravan. Good. I strolled through camp, passing clumps of picnickers at every turn. I made my way to Grandfather's Airstream. In front of it was a tarp that sheltered a small folding table and chairs that served as the command center. Grandfather wasn't there—no doubt he'd taken his place at the head of the chow line, and by now was having his first spoonful of the chili whose odor was wafting through camp. But a woman I recognized as one of his assistants was on duty—a harried-looking thirtyish woman in jeans and a BLAKE'S BRIGADE T-shirt. She was typing on a laptop. She looked up when I approached, and braced herself, as if afraid I was bringing her another problem.

"Any news about Fred?" she asked.

"Not yet," I said. "Look, we need to keep people from bothering the woman who owns this field. People keep going up and knocking on her gates instead of going round. She's a recluse, remember?"

"We said that in our directions," she said. "Which nobody reads, apparently. We could put up a sign."

"A sign would be nice," I said. "And do you have someone you could spare to sit out there and snarl at anyone who doesn't read the sign? Just for today. I assume most of the brigade will be here by the end of the day."

She frowned, and then a sudden look of delight crossed her face. She pulled out her cell phone and dialed a number.

"Evan," she said. "Come see me ASAP. I have an important job for you."

She hung up and began to rummage through a stack of supplies under the table.

"This Evan," I said. "Someone who'll be a good watchdog?"

"If the job involves loitering for hours on end and bossing people around, Evan can do it," she said. "And he'll love putting some distance between him and Sherry. What do you want your sign to say?"

We started our sign with DO NOT BOTHER HOMEOWNER! and followed that with both written instructions and a small map. Evan had not appeared by the time we'd finished, so I set out to post the sign and guard the gate until his arrival.

"I'm going to take a shortcut through Miss Annabel's yard," I said. "But only in the interest of getting the sign up as soon as possible. Tell Evan to come the long way round."

The woman nodded, and I set off with my sign and a roll of duct tape.

The ambulance had arrived and was parked near the mess tent. But no police vehicles, so I took my tote bag full of evidence with me.

I could see curtains flutter along the side of the house as I passed, and then in the front as I taped the sign to the tall iron gate, where Dr. Ffollett was standing on guard.

"You think they'll bother to read this?" he asked, watching me tape up the sign.

"We'll have a guard out here to reinforce it, at least for today," I said. "The first shift is already en route."

"Good." He nodded and headed back to the house.

I resigned myself to waiting for the elusive Evan. Who had better not show up reeking of chili.

I loitered by the gate for a while. Then, growing restless, I began strolling up and down the length of the iron fence. In fact, when I reached the end that bordered Theo Weaver's lot I decided to stretch my legs a little more. So I kept going past the borderline and sauntered along the road, studying the Weaver house in sidelong glances.

It was a white Victorian, much like Annabel's, though slightly smaller. Neatly maintained, though not as homey looking—no bird feeders, no porch furniture, nothing to indicate the occupant made any use of his yard or porch. And while the lawn was neatly mowed, it was more weed than lawn. He had a few bushes around the foundations of the house, but they were the sort of low-maintenance kind you'd have put in if you didn't want to bother much with gardening. Nothing that would shed fruit or blossoms on the tidy if unimpressive lawn.

And then, just as I drew level with the closer end of Mr.

Weaver's house, I realized, in one of those sidelong glances, that someone was in the yard. Doing something in the border next to Miss Annabel's fence.

I made a show of peering down the road to see if anything was coming, then turned, and pretended to notice Mr. Weaver for the first time.

"Good afternoon," I called out, in my most cheerful tone.

Weaver froze, then glanced up and stared at me for a few moments before replying.

Was it Cordelia's face working its magic again? Not necessarily. He'd frozen—almost flinched, actually—as soon as he heard my voice.

"Afternoon," he said. His facial expression suggested that, whatever I might think, his afternoon wasn't good. Though it might improve slightly if I left.

He had the pallor of someone who doesn't go outdoors all that much. I guessed he was in his sixties, and surmised, from the pattern of the wrinkles on his long, rather horsy face, that over those sixty-odd years he'd spent a great deal more time frowning than smiling.

He continued to stare up at me for a few moments. Then he turned his attention back to the flower bed. Actually, flower bed probably wasn't the right word. I'd have called it a weed bed. If he plucked out every sprig of dandelion, pigweed, plantain, crabgrass, curly dock, chickweed, knotweed, and ragweed, he'd have nothing left but bare dirt.

Probably not an observation that would charm him. I found myself wishing I'd spent more time preparing a conversational gambit. "Hello, I was wondering if you murdered my grandmother?" wasn't exactly a question I could ask. I decided to go with the other, less sensitive reason I was in town.

"By the way, I was just wondering if you had any information about the emus," I said.

"Emus?" He had frozen again and was frowning up at me as if this were a trick question.

"They're large, flightless, gray-brown birds—a lot like ostriches, but a little smaller. They—"

"I know what an emu is," he snapped. "Seen enough of them these last few years. Don't belong here. Someone should deal with them before it's too late. But why are you so interested in the emus?"

"My grandfather's here to deal with them," I said. "He's going to round them up and take them away to a wildlife sanctuary."

"Take them away?" Weaver was all attention now. "Out of Riverton?"

He wasn't suddenly getting possessive about the town emus, was he?

"To the Willner Wildlife Sanctuary," I said. "It's only about an hour from here."

"Good riddance," he said. "There's some people in town who want to turn the farm those damned emus escaped from into a sanctuary for them."

From his tone, I deduced that he wasn't a supporter of the proposed ratite sanctuary.

"That's an interesting idea," I said. "But it hasn't happened yet, and Grandfather doesn't think we can afford to wait any longer to do something about the emus. Especially since there's an established sanctuary so close."

That seemed to please him.

"So that's what the commotion behind my house is all about?" He seemed to find this amusing. "Bunch of bird nuts come to rescue the emus?"

"Pretty much."

"How long are they going to be there? They're not sleeping over there, are they?" Suddenly his face changed, as he realized the commotion might be going on into the night. "Not even noon and the police have already been out there. Don't deny it—I heard the siren."

"It was an ambulance," I said. "One of the volunteers was taken ill."

"This is a quiet, respectable neighborhood," he said.

"I know it will be annoying," I said. "Miss Annabel's already pretty steamed about the commotion, too, but she knows if she makes a fuss, Grandfather could very well lose his temper and storm off without rescuing the emus."

"And what's more—steamed about it, is she?" A slow smile was spreading across his face.

"Livid," I said. "I certainly hope she doesn't have a heart problem, or high blood pressure, because this could set it off. You'll probably see me running in and out a dozen times a day, trying to placate her and keep her from kicking us out."

"She's too fussy by half," he said. "What's the big deal about a little noise? How long's this thing gonna take, anyway?"

"I have no idea," I said. "I wish I did; it would calm Miss Annabel down a bit. First we have to find the emus. As I said before, I was wondering if, living out here at the edge of town, you ever saw any of them nearby."

"Not for a year or more," he said. "Not since Chief Heedles gave her men orders to shoot the damned things on sight. But if I see any I'll let you know."

"Thanks," I said.

He returned to his weeding—or perhaps returned to contemplating his weeds and keeping an eye on the comings and goings next door. And no doubt gloating at the annoyance our presence was causing to his unloved neighbor.

Or maybe he was just waiting for me to leave.

Chapter 10

Just then my phone rang. I was relieved to find that it was Michael calling.

"Are you coming back soon?" he asked.

"As soon as someone named Evan turns up to guard Miss Annabel's gate," I said. "What's up?"

"He's on his way," Michael said. "And should be there soon if he isn't already. Any chance you can come back to play diplomat? A police car just showed up. They're searching one of the tents—the one that belongs to the guy who collapsed during the meeting. And the chief of police is supposedly en route. You know how your grandfather is with authority figures."

"Yes, he likes to be the only one around," I said. "On my way."

I hoped no callers arrived before Evan, but greeting the police chief seemed more important than waiting for him. I jogged back through Miss Annabel's yard and vaulted over the wire back fence, since detouring to the gate would slow me down. Easy enough for me, though I found myself wondering if the sedentary-looking Weaver could ever have managed it. I could see a police car stopped by the side of the road at the edge of camp, so I headed that way.

A woman in a khaki uniform was standing beside it, talking on her cell phone. As I approached her car, she nodded to me, held up a finger as if asking me for a moment.

I stayed far enough away that I could pretend I wasn't eavesdropping, and her end of the conversation wasn't very interesting anyway, just "Yes, I see," and "Right," and "I agree."

She was rather nondescript. She was a few inches shorter than me, which made her of average height. I'd have had a hard time guessing her age—she could have been anywhere from midthirties to midfifties. Her uniform was sharply pressed, but it and everything about her seemed beige and faded. She had light brown hair pulled tightly back, pale brown eyes, and features so regular and ordinary that if she showed up out of uniform I'd probably have trouble recognizing her again. She'd have been good at undercover work in a larger town. And either she wore no makeup or she went in for a really subtle natural look.

"Talk to you later, then." She pressed a button, stuck the phone in her pocket, and turned back to me.

"Can I help you, Ms . . . ?"

"Meg Langslow." I offered my hand.

"You in charge of this bird rescue thing?" she asked. Her handshake was as brisk and no nonsense as the rest of her.

"My grandfather is," I said. "I'm mostly in charge of seeing that Grandfather and the rest of the bird nuts don't wear out our welcome with Miss Annabel, our hostess, or annoy the rest of the town too much."

"I'm assuming you have permission from Miss Annabel to camp here," she said.

I held out the letter Miss Annabel had given me earlier. She read it, nodded again, and handed it back.

"Seems in order," she said. "I understand you're taking the birds someplace out of town."

"To a licensed wildlife sanctuary and rehabilitation center," I said. "Where they'll be well treated and—"

"Out of my town," she said. "Frankly, that's all that matters to me. Those birds have been nothing but trouble to this town. Not just the birds, but all the fighting over the birds. Whole town's been taking sides. If Dr. Blake's willing to round them up and haul them off, fine by me, just as long as it doesn't cost the town anything."

"It shouldn't." I wanted to ask if it was true that she'd given orders to shoot the emus on sight, and decided not to.

"But that's not why I'm here," she said. "You know anything about this alleged poisoning?"

I told her what I'd seen, and handed over my collection of paper bags.

"Only two of them are related to the poisoning," I said. "The coffee-stained blouse and the coffee mug. The other two are a rusted LED headlight I found in the field behind Miss Annabel's house, and a brand new one from her supply, for comparison. Miss Annabel thinks they could be related to her cousin's death."

Chief Heedles looked a lot more thrilled with the Scotch-scented blouse and cup than the headlights, but she stowed all of the bags in her trunk.

"Can you show me where this happened?" she asked.

"Of course." I turned to lead the way back into camp, and she fell into step beside me.

She wasn't what I expected. From Miss Annabel's account, I'd expected more bluster and bombast. A stereotypical backwoods bungler. A rare female beneficiary of the old boy network. But the first impression Chief Heedles made on me was one of calm and quiet competence. She said nothing as we walked, only looked and nodded as I pointed out the emu pen and a few other salient features of the camp.

"Seems like a nice setup," she said, when we had reached the mess tent. "Any reason why that PI feller's staying out here with you? He a bird lover, too?"

Her tone was perfectly neutral, but just the fact that she

asked the question made me suspect she wasn't thrilled by Stanley's presence.

"Stanley Denton? Grandfather hired him," I said. "He's a local PI—local to where we live, that is, in Caerphilly County. Frankly, hiring him's all part of the price of placating Miss Annabel."

"Hiring him to prove I'm covering up a murder?" Her voice didn't seem to hold any rancor, but I'd already figured out she didn't show much emotion.

"To investigate her cousin's death," I said. "And give her an honest report on the investigation."

"I've known Theo Weaver all my life," the chief said. "Friend of my late father. Cranky old geezer, but I can't see him as a killer. Still—if your PI finds anything suspicious, I'd appreciate it if he'd share with me."

"How odd," I said. "That's exactly the polite way our police chief at home phrases it when he wants to warn people about not withholding evidence from the proper authorities."

That earned a brief smile from Heedles. For all I knew, it might have been her version of a broad grin. She didn't seem like the kind of person who would be a lot of fun at parties.

Then again, she was on duty. And she seemed pretty calm about the idea of having Stanley working on a case in her jurisdiction.

She turned and went into the mess tent. A good third of it—the area where Fred had collapsed, and a broad buffer zone around it—was fenced in with yellow crime-scene tape and guarded by a Riverton police officer. The rest of the tent was filled with volunteers, pretending to be still eating, but quite obviously just gawking.

I snagged a cup of chili. Then I spotted Stanley and went over to have a word with him while I ate.

"So the guy really was poisoned?" he asked.

"Dad thinks so," I said. "And evidently the local police are taking it seriously." I brought him up to speed on what I'd learned, and the bits of evidence I'd turned over to Chief Heedles.

The chief had finished talking to her officer. She looked around, spotted me, and strode over.

"I understand your grandfather is in charge here?"

"Let me introduce you," I said. "By the way, this is Stanley Denton, the PI."

They shook hands and exchanged a few pleasantries. I knew Stanley's promise to share any important evidence he found was sincere, though I noticed he didn't promise to do so immediately. Time would tell whether the chief's offer to provide any assistance Stanley needed was genuine or just for show.

Then I led the chief over to Grandfather, who was sitting at the other end of the mess tent, doing a better job than most of pretending he was just finishing up his meal.

"Pleased to meet you," he boomed. I'd been hoping against hope that he'd refrain from his usual bone-crushing handshake. No such luck. Though Chief Heedles looked as if she could give him a taste of his own medicine if she wanted to. "What a charming area this is!" he went on. "Such beautiful countryside!"

"Glad you like it," she said. "Do you have any idea who might have wanted to poison one of your volunteers?"

I had to suppress a chuckle at that. She didn't waste time. Of course Grandfather liked that, and beamed at her.

"Not a regular feature of our expeditions," he said. "Are we sure he was poisoned?"

"Dad thinks so," I put in.

"Well, he should know," Grandfather said. "Quite a specialty of his, poisons."

"Detecting and treating them," I added for the chief's benefit.

"Precisely," Grandfather said. "If he thinks it might be poison, you should definitely look into it. Any clues yet?"

"Fortunately, Ms. Langslow had the forethought to secure the victim's mug and a garment on which he spilled some of his coffee," Chief Heedles said. "I'll be sending those down to the crime lab in Richmond as soon as possible, along with any other evidence my officers gather here."

"Unfortunately," I said, "if they're as backed up as usual, it could be days before the crime lab tells the chief whether Fred's mug contained anything other than coffee and Scotch. I have a cousin who's a crime-scene technician," I added to the chief. "And he's always complaining about that."

Chief Heedles frowned and nodded.

"Well, I'm sure you'll manage," Grandfather said. "In fact—Scotch?"

"Scotch," the chief said. "Whatever else was in the mug, it was self-evident that it contained both coffee and a healthy dash of Scotch."

Grandfather frowned as if this both puzzled and troubled him. Then he got up and strode off.

"Come with me," he called over his shoulder. "Show you something odd."

The chief looked at me. I shrugged to show I had no idea what was up. She took off after Grandfather. I tagged along.

We found Grandfather in his Airstream, pulling bits of trash out of a brown paper shopping bag and strewing them on the floor.

"You wanted to show me something?" the chief asked.

"Here it is." He held out a crumpled wad of green wrapping paper and a length of purple ribbon with a gift tag attached.

The chief put on a pair of gloves before taking the

ribbon and paper from him. Then she turned the card so she could read it. There, in a block print that seemed deliberately chosen to be as anonymous as possible, were the words WELCOME TO RIVERTON.

"This has something to do with the suspected poisoning?" the chief asked.

"I came in here sometime this morning and found this purple and green package," Grandfather said. "Thought it was a present from the local Chamber of Commerce or something of the sort. So I opened it to find a peculiar decanter shaped like a stag being savaged by a couple of wolves."

"Someone must know how much you love wolves," I said.

"A pity they don't also know how much I detest cheap booze," Grandfather snapped. "It was full of some off-brand of Scotch."

"Grandfather only drinks designer Scotch," I said.

"I only drink good brands. Laphroaig, Lagavulin, Macallan—"

"What did you do with the decanter?" Chief Heedles asked.

"Gave it to the first person who stuck his head in the trailer," Grandfather said. "Told him to find someone who could use it."

"And was that person—"

"Fred," Grandfather said. "The one who keeled over during my orientation speech."

Chief Heedles bagged the wrappings as evidence. And then she thanked Grandfather and headed over to Fred's tent where, shortly afterward, a flurry of excitement announced the discovery of the mysterious decanter. I managed to be nearby when she showed it to Grandfather for identification.

"That's it," he said. "A singularly unprepossessing object."

I had to agree. I'd never have guessed it was a decanter—it looked more like a ceramic statue. It was about a foot high, painted with great detail, and featured a wild-eyed stag being attacked by two wolves, one on either side. At least the artist had depicted the three animals a few moments before the wolves drew blood. I thought it was ghastly, but I suspected that if it had come filled with better Scotch, Grandfather would have found it charming.

"I'll be keeping this for the time being," Chief Heedles said.

The chief and her officers departed, leaving behind them an unsettled camp. To my surprise, no one left, although I did overhear a couple of people discussing the advisability of driving to the next town to buy their own supply of coffee, in case the poisoner tried to strike again.

Grandfather strode around looking as if he'd cheated death through strength, courage, and intellect, instead of by having persnickety taste in Scotch. Caroline quickly organized round-the-clock teams of volunteers to keep an eye on him, in case the poisoner made another, more direct attempt on his life, and quite a few volunteers independently decided he needed watching over and joined in the vigil, so that he couldn't go anywhere without a flock of five or six anxious people hovering over him and starting at their own shadows.

I hunted down Caroline, who was evidently conferring with Sherry on additional security measures.

"We'll make sure he's never left unguarded," Sherry was saying. "We could even assign a couple of men to sleep outside his door."

"That would drive him crazy," Caroline said. "Let's

think about it. Come up with something a little more subtle."

"Has this happened before on any of Grandfather's missions?" I asked. "People getting attacked?"

"Not usually by other people," Caroline said. "Usually only by the animals we were rescuing."

"We've had death threats before," Sherry put in. "But never anything like this."

"We don't usually get death threats unless we're taking on some scummy company," Caroline said. "We've had to hire security guards a couple of times over the last few years when we were going up against rogue mining companies, for example. Some of them play rough. But it's hard to imagine anyone would make death threats over a bunch of emus."

"If this keeps on, he'll have to give up this kind of thing," Sherry said. "It's not safe." She shook her head and strode away.

"Fat chance of that," Caroline muttered. "Look, Meg— I'm going to take your boys for a ride in the caravan. Get them away from all the stress here at camp."

"Thanks," I said. "I'd appreciate that."

"I'd appreciate it if you could keep an eye on things," Caroline said in an undertone. "Pour oil on the troubled waters if Sherry gets too bossy."

"I was planning to go to town for a while," I said.

"Don't change your plans," she said. "But while you're in camp, just keep your eyes open and be ready to intervene if she goes too far."

"Can do."

"Yes," she said "You can. And I can. But unless she learns to stop troubling the waters . . ." She shook her head.

"Is she new to the brigade?" I asked. "I don't remember meeting her before."

"Relatively new," Caroline said. "She comes from a

small West Virginia town that was devastated by the mining industry, economically and environmentally. Can't remember if she was part of the Toad Wars expedition or if she joined up right afterward, but she's definitely passionate about evil mining companies. A little obsessive, really, but that's understandable, given how much her family has suffered. But don't get her started on it. And don't let her run people ragged. She has a tendency to forget we're all volunteers."

"I'll do what I can," I said.

I waited until Caroline had hitched her caravan up behind her horse—an enormous, placid Percheron who seemed to make light of pulling the caravan—and waved good-bye as Michael, Natalie, and the boys set out on a horse-drawn tour of town. Then I went in search of Stanley.

"What do you think?" I asked.

"I think someone doesn't like us," he said. "And I think maybe I'm glad I'm planning to get away from here for the afternoon. Going down to Richmond."

"For anything exciting?" I asked.

"I thought I'd do a little more checking on Mr. Weaver's business interests," he said. "And also find out a little about your grandmother's life when she was there. It needs doing, and it will keep me out of Chief Heedles's hair for a while. And you?"

"I thought I'd go into town and check out the library," I said.

"Good idea," he said. "The more we know about the town and the cast of characters the better."

"Any chance you could do some research on what people and companies Grandfather has ticked off recently, and whether any of them have any connection to Riverton?" I asked. "I could try from the library, but in a small town like this—"

"They might learn we're looking for them before we actually find them. Can do. You concentrate on the family angle."

I started up the Twinmobile and headed into town myself, passing the caravan almost as soon as I hit the main road.

Considering the small size of the town, I was favorably impressed with the Riverton Public Library. It occupied what had obviously once been a large Victorian-era house—in fact almost a mansion. And not the only mansion in town, though most now seemed to be broken up into apartments or offices. Clearly at some point Riverton had been a lot more prosperous than it was now—sometime between the Civil War and World War I, to judge by the vintage of the mansions. I wondered how the owners had made their fortunes and where it had all gone. Finding out wasn't going to solve Cordelia's murder—if it was murder—but it might help me understand her life. And Stanley had said that the more we knew about the town, the better able we'd be to solve this. I scribbled "research town history—affluence?" in my notebook-that-tells-me-when-to-breathe and focused on the task at hand.

I strolled into the library and over to the information desk. A smiling, sixtyish woman looked up when she heard my footsteps. And then her mouth fell open in surprise.

"Oh, my goodness!" she exclaimed, and then put both hands over her mouth for a moment. "You absolutely have to be a Lee!"

Chapter 11

Stanley was right—my face was a pretty good passport here in Riverton.

"A distant cousin of Miss Annabel Lee." I offered my hand. "Meg Langslow."

"Anne Murphy," she said, shaking my hand with enthusiasm. "Call me Anne. I knew it as soon as I saw you. You do favor her a bit. And you're a dead ringer for her late cousin, poor Ms. Delia, when she was younger."

"So I gathered," I said. "I'll have to take your word for it. I never met Delia."

"What a pity," she said. "If you and Miss Annabel are related on her father's side, then Ms. Delia would also have been a cousin. Her father and Judge Lee, Annabel's father, were brothers, and the judge raised Ms. Delia after her father died when she was still in grade school."

Strange and rather frustrating that almost any citizen of Riverton knew more about my grandmother's life than I did. Then again, Anne was a librarian, and thus possessed of almost mysterious powers of information gathering, so she didn't count as just any citizen.

"I'm hoping to find out all about that," I said. "So far I've only just got my foot in the front door."

Anne was frowning in puzzlement.

"Long story," I said. "Our branches of the family lost touch decades ago, and I'm trying to reestablish cordial relations. Which isn't easy with someone I'm told is the town recluse."

"Oh, my, yes." Anne was shaking her head sympatheti-cally. "Your project would have been so much easier when Ms. Delia was alive."

"Exactly," I said. "I'm very worried that I'll offend Miss Annabel and have the door permanently slammed on my genealogy research. Frankly, I'm looking for someone who can tell me a little more about my cousins. Help me avoid putting my foot in my mouth again."

"Again?" Anne raised one eyebrow in interrogation.

"I almost sank the whole project from the start by wish-ing her neighbor a good morning as I passed him," I said. "I was just trying to be mannerly, but I gather they don't get on."

"Mr. Weaver?" Anne's eyes grew wide. "Oh, my good-ness, no. Not at all. They've been bitter enemies for years. It all started not quite twenty years ago when Mr. Weaver chopped down Miss Annabel's mulberry tree."

Clearly I'd come to the right place.

"Chopped it down?" I asked. "Why?"

"It was a big old red mulberry tree, thirty feet high and almost as wide," she said. "Shaded the south side of the yard so well that they got along fine without air condition-ing until well into the sixties. It was on the Lee family side of the property line, but at least half of the fruit fell in Mr. Weaver's yard."

"Ah," I said. "Very messy fruit, mulberries. Not the sort of thing he'd want on that super-tidy lawn of his."

"Exactly," she said. "Mr. Weaver had just moved in, and he didn't like the mess. Asked old Judge Lee to chop the tree down. Which the judge ignored. They sniped back and forth for some months, and then the judge died, and be-fore he was cold in the grave, Mr. Weaver up and hired a tree company to chop down the mulberry."

"I'm surprised any local company would do it," I said. "Wouldn't everyone around here know they were stepping in the middle of a feud? Not to mention the fact that he had no legal right to do it?"

"He hired an out-of-town firm." She pronounced "out of town" as if it were something rather worse than "bloodsucking insectoids from outer space" and almost as bad as "damned Yankee."

"What did Miss Annabel do?"

"Miss Annabel wouldn't have done anything," she said. "Wouldn't say boo to a goose, poor thing. But Miss Delia was in town for the funeral and stayed over to help. You should have seen how she went after Mr. Weaver!"

"Good!"

"She sued him and the tree-cutting firm, and tried to get them both arrested for trespassing and destruction of property and I don't know what else," Anne said. "And in Judge Lee's time, Mr. Weaver would never have gotten away with it."

"But he did?"

"The chief of police was a friend of his," Anne said. "Chief Heedles—father of the present chief. Mr. Weaver swore up and down that before he died, Judge Lee gave him verbal permission to cut down the tree. He couldn't prove it, but then no one could disprove it, either. And he offered to pay for planting a new tree to replace the one he'd cut down, and the chief wouldn't do anything. Told the ladies to have a new tree planted and send Mr. Weaver the bill and be done with it."

"Hardly fair," I said. "They're left with a sapling instead of a full-grown shade tree."

"Oh, but Ms. Delia took care of that," Anne said. "She found a company that would dig up a full-grown mulberry from somewhere and plant it in the yard, right where the old one had been. Not quite as big as the old one, but big enough to drop a whole heck of a lot of mulberries across the property line."

"That must have cost a pretty penny."

"You know it!" She shook her head as if in awe of Cordelia's gall. "And she sent that great big bill to Mr. Weaver. Took her forever to get him to pay it, but he did, finally."

"Good for her!"

"And the ladies put everyone in town on notice," Anne said. "That anyone who wanted to take down the new tree had better have written permission from both of them, and that if anything happened to the new tree, they'd raise holy hell. Pardon my French, but that's what Ms. Delia said. And ever since then, they've been at each other's throats. I think maybe Ms. Delia would have gone back to Richmond, where she'd been living, if not for Mr. Weaver. She was so mad at him. I think she moved back here to make sure he didn't run roughshod over Miss Annabel."

Somehow the Annabel I'd met didn't seem like someone who'd be easy to run roughshod over. But maybe several decades of living with Cordelia had toughened her up.

Then again, Annabel hadn't had much success in getting the local police to investigate her suspicions of Weaver.

"This is exactly the sort of thing I want to hear about," I said. "Family history. Town history."

"I'd love to talk to you," she said. "Except that I've got a busy afternoon today. How long are you staying?"

"I don't know yet," I said. "That rather depends on the emus."

"The emus?"

"My grandfather's come to town to rescue them," I said.

"Your grandfather?" she said. "Is he part of Dr. Montgomery Blake's rescue team?"

"News travels fast here," I said. "Actually, Dr. Blake *is* my grandfather."

"Oh, my goodness!" She was standing with her mouth open, staring at me as if I had suddenly achieved celebrity status. In a way I had. Any second now she probably would tell me she watched all of Grandfather's TV shows.

"Dr. Montgomery Blake is your grandfather!" she exclaimed. "I am *such* a fan! I have all his books. My own copies, I mean, not just in the library."

Shame on me. I should have realized a librarian would focus on Grandfather's printed oeuvre. I wondered if it would be discreet to tell her that he actually did write them, for the most part, although he did keep a tame English major on staff to clean up his syntax.

"If you like, I'll ask him to drop by and sign them while he's in town," I said instead.

"I would be so honored!" she said. "Do you suppose there's any way we could prevail on him to speak here at the library? On any topic he chooses."

Would Grandfather object to her handing him an audience to perform for? Clearly she didn't know him as I did.

"I'll ask," I said. "And frankly, if you want to make him immensely grateful, you could help me out with a personal project of his."

"If I can," she said.

"I think Grandfather intended to get down here to rescue the emus before now," I said. "But it took a while to arrange, and—well, he's disappointed that Ms. Delia won't get to see the rescue."

"They were friends?"

"Not that I know of." Not anymore, anyway. I was trying not to lie too much, in case the whole story eventually came out. "But she and Miss Annabel were the ones who brought the plight of the emus to his attention. And he knows about Miss Annabel's belief that her cousin was murdered."

"I'm not sure she's wrong," the librarian said. "But there's not a whole lot any of us can do if the police won't take any action."

"I think maybe Grandfather feels a little guilty that he waited too long for Ms. Delia to have the satisfaction of seeing the rescue," I said. "Or maybe he actually agrees with Miss Annabel. Whatever the reason, he's hired a private investigator to look back over the evidence. To see if there's anything that would convince Chief Heedles to re-open the case. Or get the state police involved. Or maybe just leak it to the press."

"Oh, my!"

"And I've decided that helping the PI might be cooler, cleaner, less tiring work than chasing after emus."

"Lord, yes," she said. "So what would you like to research?"

"The Lee family. Riverton itself, past and present. Mr. Weaver. Cordelia's demise. Any and all local history you've got."

"You have a seat in there, where it's comfortable," Anne said, pointing to a smaller side room containing several stout oak tables with comfortable chairs around them. "I'll start bringing you local history material. Goodness knows, we've got enough of it."

She wasn't kidding. After delivering a second armload of books to my table, she giggled at my startled expression.

"Just let me know when you need more," she said, and returned to her work.

I studied the volumes she'd selected. I was puzzled by the first book in the stack—a cookbook published by St. Sebastian Episcopal Church in the 1970s. But when I checked the index, I found three different Lees had recipes in it—Ginevra, Morgana, and Annabel. Annabel had six recipes in it, which was two more than anyone else in the book. Cordelia wasn't represented, under either Lee or Mason. Was she not Episcopal like the rest of her family? Not a cook like her cousin? Or simply not living in town when the book was published? I opened up my notebook-that-tells-me-when-to-breathe and made a note to find out. And was either Ginevra or Morgana my great-grandmother? Another note. I also jotted down a reminder to copy out a few of the family recipes and reached up to grab the next book on the stack, a thick coffee-table-sized book.

To my astonishment, its cover featured a beautiful color photo of a piece of the same white-and-aqua pottery that decorated Annabel's kitchen. The title of the book was *Biscuit Mountain Art Pottery*.

And the author's name was Jeremiah Lee. Another ancestor, or at least cousin? Was this pottery factory merely a piece of town history, and did it have some connection to my family?

I opened the book and eagerly began scanning the photos. In addition to the white-and-turquoise pots Annabel collected, there were other striking color schemes—gray and rose, salmon and teal, and a surprisingly modern purple and green.

I tore myself away from the pictures and began racing through the text. Apparently my ancestors had settled on Biscuit Mountain in colonial times, intending to farm, and found they'd landed in the middle of a morass of clay. They'd had a lean time of it until they stopped trying to grow crops on their land and began digging it up and baking it into pots. After that, the family's star began to rise. The book mentioned that they made both stoneware and porcelain, and were among the first to make porcelain on this side of the Atlantic.

They really hit their stride in the 1880s when they jumped onto the bandwagon of the Art Pottery Movement, and for a while Biscuit Mountain's wares had rivaled those of more famous Art Pottery manufacturers, like Roseville, Rookwood, Van Briggle, and Weller. They'd had a commercial advantage, since they were able to dig several kinds of useful clay out of their mountain. Riverton grew from a sleepy village to a prosperous town. The Lee family grew rich, and many of their employees had also made small fortunes.

But the company's prosperity began to decline after World War I. Apparently, my ancestors were savvy enough to have invested most of their money in something other than pottery, so when the pottery business went belly up during the Depression, they managed to hang onto their position as the town's wealthiest and most influential family. But only because everybody else had lost so much more. Riverton had never recovered, and its population had been in a long, slow decline for the last eighty years.

I looked around to see if the library offered Internet access to patrons. Yes, and one of the two slightly outdated computers was unoccupied. I went to eBay to see if any Biscuit Mountain pottery was on sale. I found two pieces, each going for several hundred dollars. If people really paid that much for the stuff, Annabel had several thousand dollars' worth of the family crockery in her kitchen. And I'd bet that wasn't her only stash.

But still, Biscuit Mountain was small potatoes compared to its rivals. There were over 800 listings for Van Briggle pottery, for prices up to $5,000. Over a thousand Rookwood, over two thousand Weller, and nearly eight thousand Rosevilles, all at even steeper prices than Biscuit Mountain pots.

I went back to my stack of books, loyally telling myself that I'd rather have my family's pots than any of that other stuff. Well, than most of it. And at least, since the Biscuit Mountain crockery was selling in the low three figures, maybe I could splurge and buy a bit of the family history.

Next on the stack was a slim pamphlet about the Biscuit Mountain Ostrich and Emu Ranch. Which, according to the text, had been founded in 1992 by Mr. Hosmer Eaton on property that had formerly been part of the Biscuit Mountain Art Pottery Works. I wondered if that meant Mr. Eaton had bought the land directly from some of my family, or if they'd lost the land when the pottery factory went out of business. And was the ranch—

Just then my stomach growled, and I realized it had been a long time since my chili lunch.

I pushed back my chair and stood up. Anne came bustling over.

"You're probably going to kick me out before too long," I said.

"Not for another hour," she said. "Nine-to-six weekdays, ten-to-five on weekends."

"Would it be okay if I left these books here?" I asked. "I didn't even get to look at more than the first few."

"No problem," she said. "This is now officially your carrel, for as long as you need it. And if Dr. Blake would like a peaceful place to think and write, he's more than welcome to a table."

"I'll let him know," I said.

Leaving the library was like stepping into a sauna. Were the boys out in this? I stopped on the steps, pulled out my cell phone, and called Michael.

"How's the research going?" he asked.

"Well enough for today," I said. "I decided to quit before I go cross-eyed. Where are you guys?"

"At the lake. Don't ask me what lake, because it has an unpronounceable six-syllable Native American name, and don't ask me where it is, because Caroline brought us here in the caravan. It can't be too far from Riverton; the horse only goes so far. It's got a swimming area with a lifeguard, and a snack stand that serves pizza by the slice, and I plan to bring the boys home cooled off, well fed, and so tired that they will sleep like angels tonight."

"Good plan," I said. "I'll see you back at Camp Emu."

"Could be a few hours," he said. "And if we're late, don't worry. We can bed the boys down in the caravan on the trip home."

"Sounds good," I said. "Give them my love."

A car had pulled into the parking lot while I was talking to Michael—a familiar and very distinctive car, painted lavender with a few purple and green vines twining around it. My cousin Rose Noire hopped out. She was wearing an odd outfit—loose-fitting white pants tucked into knee-high brown faux-suede boots, a flowing white tunic belted with a lavender sash, and a broad-brimmed straw hat decorated with dried flowers and lavender ribbons. Presumably, this was her equivalent of my grandfather's multipocketed expedition outfit.

She seemed taken aback when she saw me.

"It's not closed is it?" she asked.

"The library? No, it's open for another hour."

"Good! I need to look up a few things. I had such a fascinating time up at the emu ranch!"

"I didn't realize anyone was going up there today."

"They weren't," she said. "But I was worried about what we might find, so I went up there to see if I needed to do a cleansing to make it safe for the rest of the brigade. And Meg! It's really lovely up there! A beautiful aura! I smudged the area with some sage and herbs, just to be sure, but you can tell it's a happy place that's only recently been through hard times. And it's looking forward to having nice people back. You can just feel it."

"That's nice." I didn't entirely believe in Rose Noire's self-proclaimed ability to read the auras of people, pets, and now geographical areas. But I did believe she had sound instincts. If she thought the emu ranch was a good place, maybe I wouldn't worry quite so much about taking the boys up there tomorrow.

"Did you see any emus?" I asked aloud.

"No, but I found a couple of their feathers. And such a lot of interesting other stuff. I'll show you later—I need to look something up before the library closes. See you back at camp!"

She was running up the steps by this time, with her lavender sash and lavender hat ribbons trailing behind her.

I hoped Anne was ready for such an energetic new patron this close to closing.

My stomach growled again, and I hopped into my car and headed back toward camp.

Although when I reached the stretch of road in front of Miss Annabel's house, I decided to stop in and check on her. Make sure the denizens of Camp Emu hadn't done anything to annoy her during my absence.

And maybe enjoy a bit of her air conditioning while the day still remained hot. If I was correctly remembering the schedule they'd posted on the bulletin board, I still had half an hour to go before dinner was served.

A twenty-something man was seated in a folding lawn chair to the left of the gate, doing something on his smartphone. He came to attention when I stopped my car in front of the house, but then recognized me, waved genially in my direction, and focused his attention back on his phone.

Dr. Ffollett wasn't in the yard, so after calling out "hello!" from the gate a few times, I tried it. Unlocked. I let myself in and strolled up to the porch.

She opened the door before I had a chance to knock.

Chapter 12

"Noisy crew, your bird lovers," Annabel said as I stepped inside. "Want some lemonade?"

"I'd love some. Dr. Ffollett not around?"

"He doesn't live here," she said. "Just comes over to be helpful."

She ushered me into the living room and then disappeared into the kitchen. Before sitting down, I strolled around the room, looking at things. I spotted a couple of purple-and-green pots that looked to be from the Biscuit Mountain Pottery Works. And a framed picture facedown on a table. When I picked it up to set it right, I found myself looking at my own face.

Well, not actually my own face, but very close. Cordelia, clearly, and probably Annabel beside her. They were both wearing light blouses and dark, square-shouldered jackets. From the 1940s, I guessed, although I was no expert on fashion history. But they looked as if they could step into a movie beside Joan Crawford or Bette Davis and fit in just fine. They were standing in front of a white frame house with a picket fence, and looked tall and happy. Their heads were almost level—in fact, Cordelia was perhaps an inch or so taller. Clearly I'd gotten my height from her.

"That's us up at the Biscuit Mountain Farm." Annabel had returned with the lemonade. "Cordelia and me."

"Your family owned the farm."

"Not by then." She shook her head. "After the factory went out of business, my grandfather didn't see any use in keeping it. Some sheep farmer bought it. Name of Virgil

Eaton. Cordelia and I never lived there. We just went up to see it one day and my father had his camera with him. Always liked that picture."

"So you grew up here?" I took a seat in one of the wing-back chairs and sipped my lemonade.

"Me here, and Cordelia next door, until her father died," she said. "Wish we'd held on to the other house, too."

"The one where Theo Weaver lives?"

She nodded.

"We kept it for years," she said. "Uncle Moss and Aunt Morgana lived there. But they both died and their kids had left town, and twenty years ago Weaver offered Papa a fortune for it. We should have known better."

She shook her head as if blaming herself for not spotting her neighbor's homicidal tendencies from the start:

"How did the sheep farm become an emu ranch?" I asked, to distract her from what appeared to be a recurring source of bitterness.

"When Mr. Eaton decided to retire, he turned the farm over to his son," she said. "Hosmer had grown up with sheep, and wasn't keen on them. He decided to raise emus. It was all the rage back in the nineties."

"And he couldn't make a go of it," I said, nodding. "I hear it's a lot of work."

"He made a go of it just fine for seventeen years," she said. "Up until two years ago. Hosmer had nothing against hard work. Just sheep. It was the recession that did him in—that and the fact that the bank wouldn't work with him. Just about every business in downtown Riverton got a loan or had their loan terms renegotiated, but not the emu farm. It's as if the damned bank wanted it to go under."

"What puzzles me is why this Mr. Eaton just turned the emus loose," I said. "What a jerk!"

"He wasn't a bad man." She sounded a little puzzled at my vehemence. "Just caught in an impossible situation."

"Why didn't he try to sell them?" I asked. "And for that matter, why didn't the bank sell them after they repossessed the property?"

"He tried, and the bank tried," Annabel said. "It doesn't work the same as cattle or sheep. With them, you only have to raise the animals and sell them to a wholesaler or a meat packer. You might not get the price you want, but there's a whole support system for selling them. With emus, according to what I heard, there are no packers buying them. You have to slaughter them yourself, pluck the feathers, render the oil, tan the hide—it's messy and labor intensive. Not something I'd like to take on."

"Me neither," I said. "But weren't there any other emu farmers out there?"

"Yes, but apparently they had all the emus they could handle. Or at least all they could afford to keep—a lot of farmers were hit hard by the recession. Eaton couldn't even find anyone who would take them off his hands for free. And once the bank figured out they'd taken ownership of a bunch of hungry livestock with no ready market, they hired a couple of guys to kill the flock and dispose of the carcasses. When Eaton heard that, he snuck back up to the farm and turned the birds loose. Said at least that way they'd have a fighting chance. A pity he didn't think of offering them to a wildlife sanctuary, but he had a lot going on in his life back then."

A clanging sound rang out from outside. My stomach growled as if to answer it.

"That must be the dinner bell," she said. "I won't keep you from it."

She stood up and held out her hand for my glass.

"Thanks for the lemonade," I said.

"You're welcome," she said. "By the way, you have any idea who I should thank for the candy?"

"Candy?"

"Not you, then? Must be someone from the camp, though." Seeing my puzzled face, she walked over to a small side table and picked up a box. "This was on my doorstep this morning. With a note that said 'Thanks for your hospitality.' No signature."

She was holding a small rectangular box wrapped in green paper with a purple ribbon trailing from it. It looked like the same paper and ribbon I'd seen Grandfather pull out of his trash. I bent over so I could read the attached note without touching it. The block-printed letters were also a match. The wrapping paper had been opened on one end, and I could see beneath it the corner of a box of a familiar, inexpensive brand of chocolates.

"You didn't eat any of this?" I asked. Although I was pretty sure she hadn't. The cellophane wrapping seemed slightly loose, but that could have happened when she was tearing the package open. She hadn't even fully removed the purple paper.

"Didn't even open it all the way," she said. "I have to watch my sugar. I cheat sometimes, but frankly a box of cheap, drugstore candy like this isn't much temptation."

"Thank goodness."

"I'd thought of asking you to take it back to camp and pass it around," she said. "But then I realized that whoever sent it would realize I hadn't liked the gift. So maybe you could take it into town and give it to Anne at the library. She likes to have treats to give the children when they drop by."

"I will not be taking this to Anne to give out to the town children," I said. "And thank goodness I was the one you asked to take it."

I explained about the attempt to poison Grandfather and what had happened to the unfortunate to whom he'd given his anonymous gift. Annabel fell silent for a few moments after I'd finished my explanation. She was frowning and staring at the chocolate box.

"Not sure which I like least," she said finally. "The fact that someone tried to poison me or the company they tried to poison me in."

"Fortunately, the would-be poisoner didn't know either you or Grandfather very well," I said. "We need to get this to Chief Heedles."

"Fine. You take it. It's nothing to do with me." She picked up the box and shoved it toward me. "No, wait." She jerked the box back. "No need to add your fingerprints to mine. You still have those gloves I gave you?"

I pulled a lime-green kitchen glove out of my tote and pulled it on before accepting the box.

"I'll turn it over to the chief." I said. "But she'll probably want to talk to you."

"Not sure I'll feel up to it," Annabel said. "Gives me a funny feeling, having someone try to poison me. I may have to take to my bed. Call Dwight—Dr. Ffollett, will you? Ask him to come out to see me."

She rattled off a number. I pulled out my notebook and scribbled it down.

"It might be nice to warn him if you're in need of medical assistance or if you merely want him here to help fend off the chief," I suggested.

"Just tell him to come," she said.

"Want me to stay and look after you until he does?" I asked.

"I can manage," she said. "Go get your dinner."

"Call me if you need anything," I said. I flipped to a blank page in my notebook, wrote down my name and cell phone number, tore it out, and handed it to her. "Or if the campers keep getting on your nerves."

She studied it for a second, then nodded.

"I will," she said. "Thank you."

"And don't eat or drink anything unless you know where it came from!"

I tucked the candy box in my tote and left. I could feel her eyes on my back as I walked to my car. She didn't look so overcome with shock that she needed to take to her bed. More like someone who wanted some peace and quiet in which to figure out who was after her and plot revenge. Or was I projecting how I'd be feeling onto my distant cousin?

I waited until I was almost back at camp to call Chief Heedles and tell her about the suspicious candy.

"Keep the thing safe and out of sight," she said. "And don't mention it to anyone. I'll be out to collect it as soon as I can."

Back in camp, the food truck was turning out steaming pans of lasagna, with or without meat, and huge vats of tossed salad. Michael, Natalie, and the boys were still on their way back, and Dad was still off attending to his poisoned patient. I filled my plate and managed to find a seat at Grandfather's table—along with the eight or ten volunteers who were currently watching over him. Several were hovering behind him, standing to attention like meerkats on guard, swiveling in unison at every nearby sound or motion. Others were perched on either side of him, sniffing his food and drink and combing through both salad and lasagna attempting to spot foreign objects. Grandfather was having an uphill battle getting enough to eat. So far he was only reacting with mild annoyance, swatting at their hands or snarling orders at them—a clear sign that his brush with death had rattled him. But I could tell he was rapidly approaching the point at which he'd explode and insist that they all get the devil away from him. We needed Grandfather cooperating with his bodyguards, not defying and evading them. Clearly someone was going to need to crack down on the bodyguards. Caroline was still out with the boys. And Sherry the Valkyrie was sitting at the other end of the table, looking on approvingly. She probably didn't know Grandfather well enough to realize the danger.

"Damn it all!" Grandfather exploded. "Are you trying to save my life or starve me out!"

"Makes you understand why all those Renaissance kings and potentates were so quick to shout 'off with his head,' doesn't it?" I asked. "Of course they had food tasters. Anyone want to volunteer for that?"

Everyone fell silent. But a couple of them were frowning as if they might be actually considering the idea.

They probably were. Grandfather might be one of the most difficult, exasperating people on the planet, but he managed to inspire an almost fanatical loyalty in the members of Blake's Brigade. Probably because they knew that beneath his sometimes bombastic exterior was a man who genuinely loved animals and had spent his life trying to protect them.

"Look, I know everyone in camp wants to protect Grandfather—" I began.

"Almost everybody," someone put in. "Don't forget the poisoner."

"But the more the merrier doesn't apply in this case," I went on. "Grandfather, how many guards do you think would be reasonable?"

"Am I allowed to suggest none?" he growled.

After a few minutes of debate, we settled on two. I took down the names of the volunteers on hand, chose two of them to continue the current shift, and got the rest signed up for four-hour shifts that would last throughout the night. And put out the word that anyone who wanted to take a shift tomorrow should see me in the morning.

Almost all of the off-duty guards either settled down to eat their own dinners or went back to their tents to nap before coming on duty. One or two kept up the meerkat imitation, but they did so less annoyingly, from a distance. Grandfather seemed to be in a much better mood. Sherry did not. I suspected from her surly glances at me that she felt I'd usurped one of her responsibilities. Well, tough luck.

I was hoping to get some clue about how Grandfather planned to locate the emus in the morning, but all he said was that he had scouts out working on it. So instead I ended up listening to him and some of his stalwarts swapping stories about past expeditions. Sherry the Valkyrie drank in every word, but didn't contribute anything to the conversation. I felt a little sorry for her. However essential it was to achieve total compliance on the photo release front, it didn't give you any bragging rights afterward. Then again, I suspected from what Caroline had said that Sherry's motive for joining the brigade wasn't so much a love of wildlife as a desire for revenge on rapacious mining corporations. Maybe she was just as happy in camp organizing things as the rest of the volunteers were out in the woods communing with nature.

In the middle of dinner, Dad arrived with the good news that Fred was expected to survive, and the less cheerful news that he was expecting the toxicology results to show that Fred had ingested aconite.

"A good thing he was sipping that Scotch in his coffee rather than drinking it neat," he said. "Or it could have turned out much worse."

After dinner, Grandfather announced that he was going to work on writing up his report on the expedition, and retired into his trailer. I suspected he was actually tired out and in need of an early night. About the time the catering trucks had finished packing up and were driving away, promising to return in time for breakfast, Chief Heedles arrived.

"Mind coming with me over to Miss Annabel's?" she said.

"Sure," I said. "But it's late, you know. Past ten. I'm not sure she'll let us in, even if she's still up."

"Not sure she'll let me in, you mean." We got into her car and she started the engine. "Especially considering that on my way here I spotted Dr. Ffollett's car in front of her house. I know if I ask to see her he'll tell me she's taken a sedative and gone to bed. And I can imagine how she'd react if I flashed my badge and forced my way in. Hang on a sec."

She had just turned from the dirt road onto the highway. She pulled her car over onto the shoulder and stopped. We were out of sight of anyone in camp and not yet visible from Miss Annabel's house.

"Want to give me that candy box now?"

I pulled my trusty lime-green glove out of my pocket, put it on, then fished the box out of my tote. The chief pulled out gloves of her own—much more official-looking ones—and studied the box with interest.

"Dare I hope you were wearing those gloves when she handed it to you?" she asked.

I nodded.

"But I assume Miss Annabel handled it," she said. "No reason for her not to. We probably still have her prints on file from when her cousin was killed. At least I hope so. Lord knows how much of a fuss she'll make if we have to send over someone to fingerprint her again. Let's go on to the house. Maybe I can interview her through the front door."

She started up the car and we drove the rest of the way to Miss Annabel's house. Dr. Ffollett opened the door as she was parking the car and came dashing down to the gate.

"She was very upset," he said. "She's—"

"Asleep and under sedation?" the chief finished for him. Dr. Ffollett nodded. "I expected as much. Any chance she told you what happened before she dropped off? Like when she found this box of candy?"

"Actually, I found it," Dr. Ffollett said. "People looking for the campground kept knocking on her door, so sometime around ten I came over to fend them off. The candy was lying on her doormat when I got here. She didn't even know it was there until I brought it in."

Was he telling the truth? Or was he pretending to have found the candy so Annabel wouldn't have to talk to the police? The chief questioned him sharply but he didn't seem to have any more useful information.

"Call me if you think of anything else useful," she said finally. "That goes for Miss Annabel, too. And don't tell anyone about this. We're going to keep it quiet for now."

Dr. Ffollett nodded solemnly and watched through the gate as the chief and I got back into her car. Chief Heedles seemed to be brooding over something as she started the car and headed back to camp.

"So I should keep quiet about the candy, too?" I asked after a few moments.

"Please."

"So are you planning to get an identical box of chocolates, pass them around, and see who turns pale and refuses to eat any?"

"It's a thought," she said.

"I could do it, you know," I said. "I could say she ate a few and gave me the rest for my sons. And I could do it sometime when you're out at camp so you could watch."

"I'll think about it," she said.

"So do you think Dr. Ffollett's telling the truth?" I asked after a few moments.

"Did anything he said contradict what she told you?" the chief asked.

I thought it over and then shook my head.

"We may never know," she said. "Any idea why some-one would want to kill both Miss Annabel and your grand-father? Any connection between the two of them?"

"Apart from the fact that they both want to rescue the emus?" I felt a little guilty about concealing the one other connection I knew about, but I couldn't see how it could possibly be relevant.

"If you think of anything," she said as she dropped me off at the edge of camp. "Or hear anything."

I nodded, and watched as she slowly drove off.

Camp had grown quiet. Grandfather's Airstream was dark. Two men in lawn chairs sat just outside its door. One appeared to be playing a game on his phone and the other was sipping from a mug and contemplating the increas-ingly cloudy sky.

I had to smile when I reached Rose Noire's tent, which was just across from ours. It had originally been white can-vas, but she'd dyed it lavender and invited the whole family to help paint or stencil decorations on it in purple and green paint along with several pounds of gold glitter. Even the boys had contributed, and the tent rivaled the multi-colored glory of Caroline's caravan.

She was sitting cross-legged in front of her tent, using a flashlight to read a thick book. A stack of other books rested on the ground beside her.

"What's up?" I asked.

"You can't believe how exciting this is!" she said. "I be-lieve one of the rocks I found up at the emu ranch today is actually a blue kyanite! Look!"

She held out a book—property, I noticed, of the River-ton Public Library—had she really managed to wangle a library card from Anne in the scant hour she'd spent in the library? Or was she on another of her "information wants to be free" kicks? At least she always returned the books she borrowed without permission.

I focused back on the book page she was pointing to, which showed a photo of several squarish shards of translucent crystal in sort of a faded blue color, like old denim. Making allowances for the fact that her crystal was slightly damp from washing and that one end of it was stuck into a chunk of white quartz, they did look much the same.

"Pretty," I said. I was about to leave her to her mineralogical studies when suddenly a whole scenario flashed into my mind—what if Cordelia had been murdered because of that pretty little stone in Rose Noire's hands, that stone and all its brothers and sisters up on Biscuit Mountain? What if someone had discovered that you could mine kyanite stones on the former emu ranch, and had murdered Cordelia to thwart her plan to turn the ranch into a sanctuary? And what if that same someone was afraid Grandfather's expedition would discover the kyanite and block their plans, and had tried to poison him and Annabel in an attempt to frighten us all away?

Of course, this was only a plausible motive for murder if the stuff was valuable. I'd never heard of kyanite, but then I'd never heard of musgravite and grandidierite until a few months ago when I'd seen an article someplace about precious stones more rare and expensive than diamonds. So if this kyanite was another little known treasure—

"Is it valuable?" I asked aloud.

"It's almost unique!" she said. "It's so hard that unlike most other crystals it doesn't absorb negative energy, so it never needs cleansing. And it's a very peaceful, calming, healthy stone. It would be a great thing to keep in your room, or even better, in the boys' rooms. And blue like this is very good for the throat chakra. It doesn't just heal throat ailments, it also helps communication and self-expression."

I knew better than to say that I'd been asking about commercial value rather than spiritual—I was in no mood for another lecture on crass materialism. So I tried another tack.

"I'll keep my eyes out for more bits of it, then," I said. "Or maybe if it's so beneficial, we could just buy some for the boys' rooms from some ethical, fair-trade crystal seller. Would it cost much?"

"I don't think the world has recognized its value," Rose Noire said. "I'm sure you could buy them for a few dollars."

So much for my grandiose murder scenario. Actually, I decided I liked kyanite all the better for not being fabulously expensive.

"I'll keep my eye open for it when I go up to the ranch," I said.

"Do," she said. "And I might go up there and hunt for some more, if your grandfather can spare me from helping locate the emus."

Since she had already suggested using a dowsing rod to locate the emus—a suggestion Grandfather, with unusual politeness, had ignored rather than ridiculing—I suspected he'd be glad to see her otherwise occupied.

"I'm sure he won't mind," I said. "In fact, he might approve of your mineralogical quest."

"Do you think he's asleep?" Rose Noire asked. "I wanted to smudge a protective circle around his Airstream before I go to bed. But I didn't want to alarm him."

Actually, having her circling his trailer, chanting and waving burning herbs, was more apt to annoy than alarm him. But what he didn't know wouldn't hurt him.

"There are two volunteers guarding his door," I said. "Why don't you ask them to let you know when they can hear him snoring? And you can do it then."

"Good idea," she murmured. "If you see any crystals

that look like this, only moss green, be sure to get them, too. They could be green kyanite. Very useful for balancing us with nature."

I left her to her studies.

The boys were fast asleep when Caroline's caravan finally pulled into its space. I was pleased to see that one of her staffers had stayed up to tend the horse, since I had no doubt that spending the day in the company of Josh and Jamie would have exhausted Caroline.

The boys never woke up as Michael and I carried them to our tent. I was afraid we'd have to carry Natalie as well, but she managed to mumble goodnight and stumble the few feet into her own small tent—which I noted, with amusement, was now draped with a black tarp, the better to fit into her chosen color scheme.

"So, tomorrow we get up at dawn to watch them round up emus?" Michael asked through yawns.

"Tomorrow we get up at dawn to watch them look for emus," I said. "Which might not be nearly as much fun for the boys as a roundup. Do we have a backup plan?"

"I'm working on one," he said.

He fell asleep a few minutes later. Ah, well. Rose Noire was fond of suggesting that if we needed a solution to a knotty problem, we should think about it just before going to sleep and let our subconscious minds solve it. I would leave Michael's subconscious mind to its work.

If only I could follow his example. But with every passing minute I grew more restless.

After what seemed like several centuries, I gave up. No sense tossing and turning and waking up the rest of the family. I slipped my shoes back on and crept quietly out of the tent to see what was happening.

Not much at the moment. It was only midnight, but no doubt everyone else, like Michael and the boys, was full of enthusiasm for tomorrow's first day of real work and had gone to bed early. Maybe some of them were even planning to join the early morning owl-watching expedition, which meant they'd have to be up in about four hours. I could still see lights on in some trailers and tents, but no one sitting around the group campfires strumming guitars and singing. No one having a late night snack in the mess tent. No campers lounging in lawn chairs outside their RVs. And several of the lights winked out as I passed them.

Apart from Grandfather's guards, I was probably the only person in camp still awake. I was glad the soft grass and weeds underfoot muffled my footsteps.

Still, I felt relieved when I finally passed the last few tents and trailers and stepped out into the open pasture. I stopped when I came to the tall chain-link fence defining the emu holding pen and turned to face Miss Annabel's house. It was slightly uphill from the pasture—only slightly, but with its tall lines and gleaming white Victorian fretwork it looked even farther above me, like an ornate wedding cake sitting on top of the hill.

There were lights on in two rooms on the ground floor. I couldn't see anything, because all the shades were drawn. Was Dr. Ffollett still there, watching over Miss Annabel? Or had he lied about her being sedated and asleep? Should I have arranged for guards for her, too? I made a mental note to broach the subject tomorrow.

A couple of times I saw a shadow flicker across the blinds, but it was a useless and rather uneventful vigil I was keeping.

Or a very peaceful one, depending on how you looked at it. The noises from the camp had pretty much died down, so I heard only the bugs and frogs and the occasional distant peal of thunder. I glanced back and forth between the house on the hill and the camp down here in the pasture, with an occasional side glance at Theo Weaver's house, which had been and remained completely dark. Eventually one of the lights in Annabel's house blinked out. A light upstairs came on—then another. I heard the sound of a car starting and then driving away. Presumably Dr. Ffollett leaving. The remaining downstairs room went dark. The reclusive Miss Annabel, secure in her lair, was moving upstairs to retire for the night.

I had a sudden, unexpected vision of a dragon settling down for a nap on its treasure hoard, folding its wings and coiling its scaly tail, knocking a jeweled goblet off the pile of gleaming objects and sending a small avalanche of glittering gold coins falling down.

"Curious what the subconscious sends up when you're overtired," I murmured.

But yes, the image of Annabel as a dragon wasn't off base. There she was, sitting on who knows how rich a hoard of family history. Pictures, letters, journals, and her own memories of my grandmother. The house was less a wedding cake than a castle hiding a treasure chest inside, with dragon Annabel guarding the gate. And it wasn't our job to slay the dragon but to charm it. To win it over by completing the quest it had set. To—

I suddenly realized that for the last several minutes—maybe longer—I had been feeling the uneasy prickling that we humans feel—or think we feel—when we are being watched.

Chapter 13

I had to fight the urge to whirl around, darting glances in all directions, trying to spot whoever was watching me. Instead, I took a slow survey, moving only my eyes.

Who could possibly have any reason for watching me? I suspected Annabel had been keeping an eye on the camp earlier, with those binoculars I'd seen on her kitchen counter. But even if she was still peering out of those now-darkened windows, I was in shadow. She couldn't see much from this distance. The idea of her watching didn't creep me out. And I was definitely feeling creeped out.

But if not Annabel, who? Was it only my imagination? Had I spooked myself with the image of the now-slumbering dragon? Or was it the thought of someone sneaking around with more potentially lethal purple-and-green packages that was making me nervous?

Then I spotted him. Him or her, I couldn't tell which, only that someone was watching from the bushes behind Theo Weaver's house, right on the border with Annabel's lot, at the foot of the eight-foot iron fence. Was it Weaver himself?

I stood there for a while, pretending to be watching Annabel's house, but keeping my eye on Weaver or whoever was lurking in Weaver's yard. Was he watching me or the camp?

Standing here by the emu pen wasn't going to get me any answers. I took one long, last, obvious look at Miss Annabel's house, heaved my shoulders in a sigh, and ambled off in the general direction of the tents. But I took care to veer a little to my right, so I could pass as close as possible to Weaver's yard. I stared up at the sky while I walked, as if fascinated by the stars—or, more likely, assessing whether the predicted thunderstorm was about to break—and let myself drift even farther to the right.

Suddenly I saw a flurry of motion in the distance. I heard a faint rustling of leaves as a shadowy figure extracted itself from the shrubbery along Weaver's fence. Then I saw the figure, half running, half tiptoeing, across the lawn to the back door of Weaver's house. The door opened and closed slowly, as if someone was trying to minimize the noise it made.

I drifted over to the fence and loitered there for several long minutes. No lights came on in the house.

Then I heard a slight rustling farther down the fence. Had I only imagined him going inside?

I set out again, paralleling the fence, pretending to be merely strolling along, enjoying the evening. And meanwhile I fished in my pocket with my healthy hand until I found the tiny flashlight I was keeping there for midnight bathroom trips. When I got level with the place where I'd heard the latest rustling, I whipped out the flashlight and turned it on.

"Shut that thing off!" Stanley Denton snapped.

I obeyed. Probably not as quickly as Stanley would have liked, but the bandages prevented me from helping with my other hand.

"Sorry," I said, while fumbling over it. "I thought you were Weaver."

"He went inside."

Stanley extracted himself from the shrubbery in which he'd been hiding and came over to join me.

"So I saw," I said. "But what's to keep him from sneaking back out again? He could have gone in the back door, out the front, and snuck around the back of the house again."

"I wouldn't put it past him," Stanley said. "But I'm not going to spend another hour and a half watching him crouch furtively in the shrubbery staring at the camp."

"Sorry I scared him off," I said.

"Don't be." He stretched and then rolled his shoulders, and I gathered he'd been crouching there motionless for an uncomfortable length of time. "I was looking for an excuse to stop watching him."

"Happy to oblige, then."

"Look," he said. "I'm pretty sure you and I and Theo Weaver are the only ones skulking about here tonight, but just in case I'm wrong, let's go someplace where we can talk in peace."

"I think Riverton rolled up the sidewalks hours ago," I said. "And Camp Emu isn't exactly awash with privacy."

"My trailer's over there," he said, pointing to a shape a little apart from the main encampment.

"Then let's—what's that?"

Stanley whirled to see where I was pointing, but the slight shadow I'd seen was already gone.

"What was it?"

"I don't know," I said. "Someone in the bushes? Someone else, I mean."

We spent a few minutes searching up and down the edge of the field, peering into all the bushes in both Miss Annabel's backyard and Weaver's, but found nothing. Unless you counted the place where the shrubbery had been slightly broken or trampled, but it could easily have been done by one of the three deer we'd startled during our search.

We hopped the fence into Miss Annabel's yard and circled the house, making sure nothing looked amiss. No signs that anyone was awake.

"No sinister packages outside any of the doors," I muttered.

"Were you expecting any?"

"Someone left a box of chocolates for Annabel," I said. "Wrapped in the same paper and ribbon as Grandfather's decanter. In case it comes up, pretend I told you earlier today, before Chief Heedles asked me to keep it quiet. But I thought you should know."

"Right," he said. "I think we've done all we can here."

We headed for Stanley's trailer. I stood by while he unlocked his door. It was an old Shasta trailer—I guessed 1960s vintage—and small, but well maintained and neatly organized. Just inside the door was a built-in table with banquette seating on either side. The sink and stove were on the wall across from the door, the refrigerator and a closet opposite, and built-in drawers and cabinets ran from floor to ceiling on either side. A curtain at the far end probably concealed the built-in bed. Not an inch was wasted, and hardly a single unnecessary item was visible.

"Used to belong to my parents," he said, noting my appraising look. "We took family vacations in it when I was a kid, and the first ten years after Dad retired they dragged this thing all over the country. Useful sometimes, when I'm on a case someplace remote."

I sat at the banquette on one side of the dinette table while Stanley opened the small refrigerator.

"I'd offer you coffee," he said over his shoulder. "But I don't think either of us needs the caffeine at this time of night. Decaf iced tea or lemonade?"

"Whatever's easiest," I said.

We heard another distant rumble of thunder.

"That's getting closer," I said.

"Big front coming through," Stanley said. "Thunderstorms sometime between now and dawn, according to the local weather."

He brought a large pitcher of iced tea and two glasses to the table, poured us each a glass, and sat down on the banquette opposite me. In fact, he almost collapsed.

"Long day?" I asked.

He nodded and sipped.

"So why were you capping off a long day by skulking behind Theo Weaver's house?" I asked. "Do you actually think there might be something to Miss Annabel's theory about Weaver?"

He was silent for a few moments.

"Could be," he said finally. "When she told us, I thought no. At least ten to one against. I figured it was the grief talking. Grief does peculiar things to people sometimes."

"Not just grief," I said. "Add in the fact that she believes her cousin died in a stupid accident that might have been her own fault. Cordelia's own fault, I mean, although maybe Annabel also blames herself for letting Cordelia do all the generator-tending. Even if Cordelia didn't have a kerosene lantern with her, maybe she unwisely tinkered with the generator. And maybe Annabel finds it a lot more satisfactory to think Weaver could be responsible."

"Precisely," Stanley said. "But dismissing her notion out of hand wasn't going to get us anywhere—to say nothing of the possibility, however small, that she was right. So I decided to start my investigation by checking out Mr. Weaver."

"Any interesting findings?"

"Not really." He reached onto the seat beside him, picked up a manila folder with perhaps half an inch of paper in it, and handed it to me.

"I can summarize it if you like. He's retired from some kind of investment banking firm. He was an assistant vice president, which sounds impressive, unless you do a little poking around their annual report and figure out that AVP was actually pretty low on the totem pole there. The place currently has about a hundred employees, and at least half of them are assistant vice presidents, associate vice presidents, senior vice presidents, executive vice presidents, or just plain vice presidents."

"Impresses the client, no doubt," I suggested.

"I suppose. He retired from that five years ago. Still serves on the boards of a couple of small companies."

I nodded. I was looking at the list of Mr. Weaver's directorships. A Richmond real estate firm. First Undermountain Bank, a tiny Riverton-based institution that had somehow managed to escape being gobbled up by one of the big fish. A mutual fund I'd never heard of. A mining company.

"Smedlock Mining," I said. "What is smedlock, and where do you mine it?"

"Smedlock's the founder," Stanley said, with a chuckle. "A hundred years ago he was quite the robber baron, but while his children inherited his fondness for high living they didn't get his business acumen. They lost their West Virginia coal fields and these days the company only has a couple of small mines producing quartz and amazonite and a few other decorative minerals. Rumor has it that the current generation of Smedlocks would be delirious if some big company mounted a takeover bid, but no one has, because they don't really have anything worth taking over. Rather the same with the bank whose board Weaver serves on. So small that it would have been gobbled up by now if it weren't one step above worthless. I'm told they dabbled too deeply in real estate derivatives, whatever that is."

"So these directorships are small potatoes," I said. "Meaning he's not a major mover and shaker in the Virginia business community."

"I expect his former employer arranged the directorships," Stanley said. "It's the sort of small perk that probably would get handed out to a loyal if minor retiree. The directors usually get paid for attending meetings, so it's a little extra something on top of your pension."

"Is that all he does?" I asked. "He sits on boards?"

"And meddles in town affairs," Stanley said. "He's on

the town council. And squabbles with the ladies—at least he did when Cordelia was alive. Haven't been many fireworks between him and Miss Annabel over the last six months, if you don't count her repeated letters to the editor calling for him to be arrested for Cordelia's murder. And to everyone's surprise, he's taking her campaign quite philosophically. Seems out of character."

"Maybe not if it was Cordelia, rather than both ladies, leading the charge against him," I said. "Maybe he knows that no matter how much Miss Annabel hates and suspects him, she can't cause him much trouble if she won't poke her nose outside her own front door. So if that's all you've found, why do you seem to be coming around to Miss Annabel's point of view?"

He frowned and leaned back in his seat as if the question required some thought.

"Not sure yet," he said, after a few moments.

"Hunch?" I suggested. "Or gut feeling, if you prefer that term."

"Try taking that into court," he said, with a grimace.

"My cousin, Rose Noire, says that a hunch is a deduction your subconscious has made from evidence you don't yet know you have," I said. "And all you need to do is bring the evidence up into your conscious mind."

"I agree with her, but that's easier said than done," he said. "So far the only thing my conscious mind has found is that there is bad blood between the two households, going way back. I've been reading the letters to the editor in the local rag. Can't do too much at a time without coming down with a killer eyestrain headache, so I'm only five years into it, but some of Weaver's letters are downright scary. And these are the letters the paper printed."

"His letters," I repeated. "What about Cordelia's side of the quarrel?"

"She comes off well, if you ask me," he said. "She

doesn't mince words, but she's logical, articulate, credible. Rational, even when angry. She's wielding a rapier. Weaver's just spewing bile and lava. The venom pulses off the page. I'm thinking of running the texts by a shrink I know. Because the man who wrote those letters—I can see him committing murder."

"He seemed pretty normal when I talked to him this afternoon," I said. "Grouchy but rational."

"The same with his letters to the editor in the last six months," Stanley said. "A changed man. Clearly her death removed a major stressor from his life."

"So is he merely feeling mellow because he outlived his worst enemy," I asked. "Or is he also smug because he's gotten away with murder?"

"Gotten away with it so far." Stanley frowned and shook his head. "But what if he's starting to worry?"

"Because of our arrival, you mean?" I asked. "You're worried that having us here—and more particularly you—might make him decide he needs to get rid of Annabel, too."

"The thought had crossed my mind," he said. "That's the reason I was lurking there behind the houses. Well, that and the mysterious, possibly lethal present someone left for your grandfather. I thought it might be a good idea to keep an eye on things. But I can't do that full time, even if I didn't have the murder case to pursue. Maybe Weaver is just worried that some of the campers will trespass on his lawn, and maybe it was only a deer you spotted after he went inside—but you never know. Can you talk to Miss Annabel? I'd feel a lot better if I knew she had a good security system installed in the house."

He rummaged for a few moments in the tall but tidy stack of papers that sat beside him on the banquette and held out a business card.

"Friend of mine who does stuff like that," he said.

"Mention my name and he'll give her fast service and a rock-bottom rate."

I nodded as I took out my notebook and tucked the card safely in the front pocket.

"Weaver's behavior is another reason I'm taking Annabel's theory a little more seriously," Stanley said.

"The way he was lurking around tonight, you mean?" I was scribbling a note on my task list to remind me to talk to Annabel about the security issue.

"It's not just the lurking tonight," Stanley said. "He's behaving furtively. Like a man with something to hide. Spent a lot of time weeding his flower beds today, all on the side closest to Miss Annabel's house, and if he pulled more than a dozen weeds I'd be astonished. Then he didn't answer the doorbell when I went over to interview him this afternoon."

"Are you sure he was home?"

"I did an hour or so of surveillance before ringing the doorbell. That's how I know he was pretending to weed. He was there all right. And ignored fifteen minutes of doorbell ringing. Then, about half an hour after I disappeared from his doorstep, he dashed out his front door and drove away as if en route to a fire. Of course, there's no law against behaving furtively. And no law requiring anyone to talk to a private eye who shows up on your doorstep. But still . ..."

"And no law against keeping an eye on our camp, but I think it's creepy of him to turn out the lights, sneak to the back of his property, and gawk at us from the shrubbery."

"With binoculars," Stanley added, nodding.

"Binoculars? You're sure?"

"I was using night-vision goggles," he said, pulling them out of his pocket and placing them on the table. "And a camera designed for taking pictures in darkness. I got some nice shots of his Peeping Tom act."

"You private eyes have all the fun," I said. "And all the cool toys."

He smiled and sipped his tea. I pulled out my notebook and added a few tasks. Including finding out where to get night-vision goggles. The boys would adore them.

"Did you see Weaver over at camp at any time today?" he asked.

"No," I said. "But I wasn't really there a whole lot. You're thinking maybe he snuck out the back door while you were watching the front and left the present for Grandfather?"

"Crossed my mind," he said. "Seems unlikely. The candy might have been a last-minute improvisation, but someone went to a bit of trouble beforehand to pick out that wolf decanter for your grandfather. I'm betting someone had that thing all ready to go a while ago and took advantage of the chaotic first day of camp to sneak it into his trailer."

I nodded.

"What are you planning for tomorrow?" he asked, after watching me scribble for a few moments.

"Grandfather and the troops are going up to the defunct emu ranch first thing in the morning," I said. "All the zoologists and volunteers will be looking for traces of the birds, and the film crew will be tagging along, capturing everything that might be useful for the eventual television special. I think their working title is something like *In Search of the Feral Emu*.

"That's what Dr. Blake is up to," he said. "What about you?"

"I'm going to tag along long enough to satisfy my curiosity about the emu ranch," I said. "And then I plan to leave Michael and the boys to enjoy the roundup and come back here. Talk Miss Annabel into hiring your friend for home security. Probably take a nap while the tent is quiet."

"Any chance you could spend some more time at the library?" he said.

"Sure," I said. "What do you want me to look up?"

"If I knew that, I'd go down and do it myself," he said with a sigh. "Follow your nose. We know about Weaver's feud with the ladies, but what if Cordelia had other enemies that Annabel didn't think were important? The more we know about this town, the better our chances of solving this. And see what you can do to befriend some of the townspeople. Use that familiar face of yours and see if you can get some of them to open up. And while you're at it—if you get a chance to talk to Chief Heedles, see what you can find out."

"You want me to tackle her instead of you?" I asked. "Play the fellow-woman-in-a-male-dominated-profession card?"

"Only if you see a chance to do it naturally," he said. "But yes, I have a feeling she'd talk more readily to you than to me. Funny—not the first time I've felt a little resentment from a law enforcement officer, but I always attributed it to testosterone, not turf."

I nodded and scribbled a few more lines in my notebook. And then I glanced down the page and sighed.

"What's wrong?" Stanley asked.

"My to-do list is growing like a kudzu vine and I don't see an end in sight," I said. "And half the new items have something to do with Cordelia, and I'm starting to wonder why I'm spending so much time trying to find out about her."

"She's your grandmother."

"A grandmother who never bothered to get in touch with us while she was alive," I said.

"Think what it must have been like for her," Stanley replied. "She was barely eighteen, and pregnant, and remember what a stigma that would have been seventy-some years ago."

"Yes, but times have changed."

"Times have, but maybe she never did," he said. "You never know. Maybe if she'd met you she would have."

"Or maybe not," I said. "Maybe it's a good thing Grandfather didn't start looking for her while she was still alive. I'm having a hard time dealing with the rejection as it is. Can you imagine how bad it would have been if we'd shown up and she had slammed the door in our faces? And however bad I feel about it, I know it's much, much worse for Dad."

We fell silent. Not for the first time, I tried to imagine how Dad must be feeling about all this. At times in my life—especially in my teens—I'd been very critical of Mother. She hadn't always lived up to my vision of an ideal mother, which wasn't surprising, considering that my idea had been shaped by *Little Women*, *Little House on the Prairie*, and *The Waltons*.

But she'd always been there. Giving me dangly earrings for Christmas instead of the welding set I'd asked for. Critiquing my posture instead of praising my grades. But there, always.

Dad had grown up knowing only his own history, knowing his adopted mother loved him dearly, but with nothing but a big question mark in place of his biological mother. And now to learn that she'd been so close and never bothered to contact us?

A sudden not-so-distant rumble of thunder interrupted my thoughts and made us both glance over at the windows.

"I should head back to my tent," I said. "Before that breaks. May I borrow this?"

I held up the file on Weaver.

"Be my guest," he said. "And if you can add to it tomorrow, all the better."

When I arrived back at the tent, Michael and the boys were still sound asleep. They didn't even wake up when the big storm hit, a few minutes later, which was lucky, because both boys were a little afraid of thunder and lightning.

Chapter 14

"Mommy! Pancakes!" Josh.

"Ssshhh! Mommy's sleeping." Jamie. I'd have called him the considerate one, except that his rebuke was at least twice as loud as his twin's original remark. I glanced up to see the two of them peeking through the tent flap.

"Mommy will be out in a few minutes," I said. Both tousled little heads vanished, and I lay back for a moment, trying to remember if I'd packed a comb, and wondering what was it about being a parent that made people start talking about themselves in the third person.

I pulled on the first clothes I could find and stumbled out of the tent.

Dawn. Not ever my favorite time of day, and even less welcome today, given how late I'd been up keeping watch over Annabel, worrying about Grandfather, strategizing with Stanley, and riding out the thunderstorm. I was glad Michael seemed well rested. I planned to let him take the wheel for the drive up to the abandoned emu ranch. My lacerations were throbbing. I'd probably overdone it yesterday, in my efforts to prove I was too tough to let a minor injury slow me down.

Thanks to the high winds that had accompanied the previous night's thunderstorms, our departure couldn't take place until a volunteer crew with chain saws removed the several large trees that were blocking the dirt road out of camp.

As I strolled round the camp, checking to see if the storm had caused any other damage, I noticed with dismay that Rose Noire's beautiful hand-painted tent had collapsed overnight. I hoped she'd find a way to get the mud out without washing out all the decoration. She had festooned it with so many banners, flags, amulets, crystals, and tokens that you'd think even a thunderstorm would take notice and tiptoe around it, instead of flattening it in the wee small hours, forcing her to take refuge in Caroline's nearby caravan.

Seth Early and two other volunteers were trying to get the tent back in working order, a little hampered by the fact that one of the tent poles had broken and some other part of the tent that they considered essential had never been installed in the first place.

"We need to find a sporting goods store," Seth was saying. The other two occasionally stopped what they were doing to wave their cell phones in the air.

"Still no signal," one of them said, after one such break.

"You think anyone's got a good, old-fashioned paper copy of the Yellow Pages so we could look up the address of the nearest one?" the other man asked.

Undaunted by her ailing tent, Rose Noire was spending the interval before our departure reorganizing the camp along proper feng shui lines, and getting a surprising degree of cooperation. I'd have expected people to balk at taking camping advice from someone whose first night's efforts had left her homeless and looking like a drowned rat, but I soon realized that the people who signed on for Blake's Brigade were remarkably tolerant and kindhearted, and thus willing to re-stake their tents two or three times and arrange their campfires and folding chairs into the sometimes odd and inconvenient configurations Rose Noire felt they needed to be in to cure the camp's chi.

Or maybe they were all glad to have something to do while the chain saws were at work.

A pity we weren't getting the early start we'd planned.

I couldn't call up a weather report on my cell phone—in fact, I couldn't get a signal at all, which probably meant that the cell towers were out because of the storm. And the air was already warm and muggy.

The boys were busy making mud pies, mud cookies, and mud pancakes with rainwater for syrup. I decided to while away the time until the convoy left with a visit to Miss Annabel. Make sure she was all right. Maybe bask in her air conditioning a while if she had any. And if she wasn't up, I could leave her a note with the security company's business card.

But I had barely tapped on her front door before it flew open.

"I see you all survived the storm," she said. "Come in."

She waved me into the living room. She was dressed for the heat, in a loose caftanlike garment and sandals. And she was wearing a little headlight on her head—turned off, but ready whenever she needed it. Clearly she didn't in the high-ceilinged living room. The Venetian blinds were down, but slanted to let in maximum sunlight while keeping out prying eyes.

"Want some lemonade?" she asked. "Lukewarm, but we should drink it up before it spoils completely."

"That would be nice," I said. "I gather the power's out?"

"You gather right."

She made a beckoning gesture and I followed her into the kitchen.

"Cooler back here," she said, as she took two vintage glasses from an overhead cabinet and poured out the lemonade. "Times like these, I really miss the generator. Good thing I don't keep much in the refrigerator and freezer these days. I'm not much for cooking. Not anymore," she added after a moment. "Hard to see the point, cooking for one."

"Have you considered getting another generator?" I

asked. "Or has losing your cousin to the generator explosion made you not want one around anymore?"

"Oh, I want one all right," she said. "I just didn't want to get it installed until Chief Heedles had finished with the crime scene. And here it is, six months later, and if you ask me, she hasn't even started with the crime scene."

"Maybe you could install the new generator in the other back corner of the yard," I suggested. "Then you could preserve the crime scene as long as you liked. Of course, the down side is that the new generator wouldn't be quite as close to Mr. Weaver's yard, so it wouldn't annoy him quite as much. But right now, you're hardly annoying him at all, so anything would be an improvement, right?"

She looked at me in surprise for a moment, then burst out laughing.

"I like the way you think!" she exclaimed. "I'm calling the generator company as soon as I get my phone back."

"Think about calling this guy, too." I pulled out the business card Stanley had given me. "Friend of Stanley's. Installs security systems."

"You think I need a security system?" She cocked her head, birdlike.

"If I were living this far from town with only three houses for miles and one of those occupied by someone I believed to be a cold-blooded killer, with both power and cell phone service this prone to interruption, and someone leaving possibly poisoned gifts on my front step, I'd want a security system."

"You forgot 'at your age,'" Annabel said, with a chuckle. "Everyone always has an idea what I should do at my age."

"And at my age, too," I said. "I'd get one. I'd get the generator first, and then I'd make sure my security system was hooked up to it."

She nodded.

"In fact, odds are I'll find a working phone before you

do," I added. "Want me to call both contractors and have them come to give you an estimate? I copied down the security company's number in case I needed one."

She appeared to be studying me for a few moments. Then she nodded briskly.

"Yes," she said. "I'd like that. Hang on a minute."

She stood up and walked out of the room. I sipped my lemonade and enjoyed my view of the Biscuit Mountain pottery display. And then I noticed that her back door was open, with just a screen door between her and any possible intruders. Was she being careless or was I being paranoid?

"Here's the place where we got the first generator." Annabel returned and handed me a business card. "Cordelia checked out several vendors and picked this company. And if they don't sell the same generator anymore, we want one very similar. If she were here, I bet she'd agree that there was nothing wrong with the generator until her killer meddled with it. Our requirements haven't changed."

"How about one change?" I suggested. "I bet you could have a switch installed so you could turn it off from the house. And if this company can't do it, I know one that can."

"I wanted that in the first place," she said. "But for some reason she objected. No idea why. A switch right here in the utility room. You tell them that."

Just then another chain saw started up, not far away. Miss Annabel started slightly.

"You'd think I'd be used to that by now," she said.

She drifted over toward the back window and stared out.

"Must be costing your grandfather a fortune to hire all these people," she said.

"Except for the film crew, I think they're all volunteers," I said. "Bird lovers, animal lovers, environmental activists."

"He just waves his hand and they show up to work for him for nothing?" She shook her head in disbelief.

"I'm not sure it's entirely due to his magnetic personality," I said. "There's also the fact that they're all dying to be on television."

She laughed softly at that.

"Well, I wanted to stir things up and make things happen," she said. "They always say be careful what you wish for."

But she continued to watch the camp with a worried look on her face.

"I'll make sure Grandfather gives everyone strict orders to stay on the other side of your fence," I said.

"It's not the ones who follow orders that I'm thinking about," she said.

Clearly she was worried. And as I walked back to my car, I realized it was contagious. Now I was worried about the horde of people we'd invited into her back yard. All those people camped so close to that flimsy screen door.

When I got back to camp, the chain saws were still going. I hunted down Caroline. She was scribbling away on a legal pad and looked busy.

"Mind if I interrupt you for just a minute or two?" I asked.

"Of course not." She looked up with a smile on her face, but I could tell her mind was still on whatever she'd been working on and that this wasn't the most convenient moment.

"This may sound like a stupid question," I said. "But how do the Blake's Brigade people find out about Grandfather's projects?"

"Same way you do, I suppose." She glanced down at her legal pad and then forced her eyes up again with a bright smile.

"I doubt it," I said. "I usually hear about them at the

dinner table when he's staying with us or with Mother and Dad. 'By the way, I'm going to Australia tomorrow to rescue some endangered kangaroos. Want to come along?' "

"It wasn't kangaroos," she said. "Wombats, wallabies, and fruit bats. And that wasn't an official Blake's Brigade effort. Just him and me and the film crew. Couldn't expect the whole brigade to traipse off to Australia on short notice and at their own expense."

"But a whole bunch of people showed up here less than twenty-four hours after he decided to come," I said. "How did they all find out?"

"We have a group e-mail list," she said. "Didn't we add you to it? Your dad sent out word five minutes after Monty decided to come, and people started signing on and volunteering for crews within the hour."

"But who are these people?" I said. "Do you really know them all?"

"Some better than others," she said. "Some I've known for twenty years, even before they started working with Monty. Others I meet when they first show up for a project. Everyone's new once. Why are you asking so many questions about the brigade members all of a sudden? You think one of them tried to poison Monty?"

"I think it's quite possible," I said. "Don't you?"

"Maybe," she said. "More likely it's someone who took advantage of all the chaos of the setup to slip into camp. It's not as if every one of the volunteers knows every other volunteer."

"But does anyone know all of them?"

"Not sure if anyone knows all of them, but I probably come pretty close." She pointed at a woman standing nearby. "Retired teacher. Here with her husband, a retired insurance executive. We get a lot of retirees, especially for the expeditions with short notice, like this one. Right beside her: college student, studying environmental science.

We get a lot of students, too. The woman manning the information desk—now she might be a little suspicious. Made out so well in her latest divorce that she has no need to work, so she volunteers for every cause she sees. Then again, this might be her first and last expedition. I'm not sure how she likes roughing it in her half-million-dollar RV. The bright pink one that's only slightly smaller than the *Queen Mary*," she added, pointing to the vehicle in question. "I pretty much know them all. But I was tied up much of yesterday and didn't get around camp as much as I usually do."

Tied up amusing Josh and Jamie, I remembered. Should I feel guilty and apologize for distracting Caroline from her commitment to the brigade?

"Does anyone even have a list of everyone who's here?" I asked aloud.

"Sherry would," she said. "You've seen her—tall, blond, thirtyish, with the big faux tortoiseshell glasses."

"Runs around with a clipboard collecting photo releases?" I asked.

"That's her," Caroline said, with a nod.

The Valkyrie.

"She's been doing a lot of volunteer administrative work for some of our projects in the last year or so," Caroline went on. "And one of the things Monty dumped on—er, delegated to her was making sure we had a photo release from everyone in camp. Last thing we want to do is have some great footage of volunteers herding an emu into the pen and realize we have no idea who the gawkers in the background are and whether we have releases from them. So—you show up in camp, and Sherry doesn't know who you are, she finds out, and if you refuse to sign a photo release, she makes sure you hit the road. You'd like her. She's very organized and efficient."

"I've met her, remember," I said. And the word I'd have

used was officious, and I hadn't liked her all that much. But then again, Grandfather had rounded up more than his usual number of cats and made her one of the chief cat herders. Having been in a similar position myself more than once, I resolved to give her a reasonable amount of slack.

"I'll ask her to give you a list," Caroline said. "Better yet—I'll ask her to give me a copy. I need it anyway. And you never know—she might have overheard Monty going on about how organized you are. She's a little touchy— heaven knows, we don't want her thinking you're invading her turf."

"I have no desire to offend the Valkyrie with the clipboard," I said. "Just give me a copy of the list when you get it. And while you're at it, give Stanley a copy, too."

"You're not going to have him investigating our volunteers are you?" Caroline sounded shocked. Investigating them actually sounded like a pretty good idea to me if we had unlimited time and money and a dozen or so Stanleys to do it.

"Not practical even if we wanted to," I said. "But Stanley's investigating my grandmother's murder. I just want him to know who's here, in case he runs across any of the names in some other context."

"You think Cordelia's killer is here in our camp?"

"I doubt it," I said. "Grandfather only decided to come down here this week, right? Before that there was no connection between him and Riverton."

"No publicly known connection," Caroline corrected. "Stanley has been poking around for a few weeks."

"Discreetly," I said.

"He could have talked to the killer," she said. "And if I'd killed someone, and a private investigator turned up looking for her, that would get my attention."

"Yes, but I think the odds are pretty low that the killer was a member of your e-mail list," I said.

"True. We only have a few thousand people. No one from Riverton. I won't swear we don't have a few bad eggs in the basket, but I doubt any of them killed your grandmother. So what good will it do to give you and Stanley the list?"

"I don't know," I said. "Maybe I just need to be able to tell Annabel that we know who everyone in camp is. Someone did kill her cousin, you know, right there in her backyard. And now here she is with that same backyard filled with dozens of strangers. That has to be tough for anyone, and she's a recluse who's recently had a front row seat for a homicide."

"But she's totally convinced her next door neighbor did it," Caroline pointed out. "Why should she be worried about a bunch of strangers? In fact, why doesn't having us here make her less anxious—it's like having several dozen witnesses and potential bodyguards in her backyard."

"Maybe she's not as convinced anymore," I said. "Maybe the police chief's skepticism and ours is rubbing off. Anyway, if Stanley does run across any of the Blake's Brigade people in the course of his investigation, it will be a major red flag, won't it?"

She nodded.

Another thought struck me.

"You said something about the brigade going up against rogue mining companies that played rough," I said. "Does Smedlock Mining ring a bell?" I asked.

"No." She shook her head. "But my memory for names isn't what it used to be. Your grandfather's administrative assistant could put together a full list. Companies your grandfather has done battle with, or testified against, or has on his radar to tackle. I'll get that to Stanley along with the list of people here in camp."

"Thanks," I said.

"And when I get a chance, I'll go online and check to

see if any of our volunteers joined fairly recently. I assume you'd find them more suspicious. But I hope you're worrying for nothing."

I probably was. But as I strolled through the chaotic camp, I felt better knowing that someone knew who each and every one of these volunteers were. In fact, though I couldn't imagine myself singing songs around the campfire with Sherry, I rather liked knowing it was the blond Valkyrie with the clipboard who had everybody on her radar.

I heard a cheer go up.

"The road is clear!" someone called as he ran past me. "We're taking off."

Chapter 15

Of course, even after the road was clear, the camera crew had to film our departure from several angles. We didn't get underway until nearly nine, and our progress up the mountain was slower than it could have been. Every time the director spotted a new, picturesque bit of scenery, the whole caravan would grind to a halt so the crew could scamper ahead to lie in wait and film us passing through it. Meadows, mountain streams, rustic bridges, wooded hillsides—it was all new and exciting to the camera crew. A good thing we were traveling mostly on small back roads where we hardly ever ran into other vehicles.

To my surprise, Grandfather tolerated these interruptions with remarkable patience. Or perhaps not so surprising, since the camera crew put him front and center in most of their sequences. I could see what he was up to because Michael had snagged a choice spot as second vehicle in line, right behind Grandfather's open Jeep. During the occasional moments when the deep woods on either side gave way to meadows, we could glance over our shoulders and see the long, sinuous line of trucks, SUVs, Jeeps, and motorcycles snaking up the steep road in our wake. And then the woods would close in around us again.

The woods made me anxious. I kept thinking how easy it would be for someone to ambush us. Someone who knew our destination, and knew the woods well enough to take a shortcut. Someone who knew the best places to lie in wait with a rifle. One quick shot from the woods would be all it would take. I cringed every time the caravan stopped and Grandfather stood up in the back of the jeep to pose for the camera. Didn't he realize that he was also making himself a target?

Or was it that plausible that someone could switch so quickly from poison to firearms? Was I worrying unnecessarily?

I didn't seem to be the only one. Michael was eyeing the woods with a frown, and in the Jeep ahead of us, so were Dad, Caroline, and Jim Williams, who was one of the bodyguards assigned to Grandfather this morning.

"Evidently, Biscuit Mountain really is a mountain," Michael said, during one particularly long, dark wooded stretch. "But I think we're finally getting close to the emu ranch."

"How can you tell?" I asked, peering through the windshield.

"Sign up ahead."

He slowed and pointed. I didn't spot the sign at first. This part of the woods was particularly dark because all the trees were festooned with vines. Vines with thick, hairy stems. Vines that sometimes met overhead, threatening to turn the narrow road into a tunnel. Up ahead, Grandfather was gesticulating. Pointing up at the vines. I had the sinking feeling that the vines would turn out to be an alien invasive species—kudzu or its ilk—and we'd call yet another halt to the caravan while Grandfather filmed a ringing denunciation of the sinister vegetation. But then I realized that between one particularly thick swathe of vines was a faded sign. Half the letters were obscured by leaves, but I could still decipher the words BISCUIT MOUNTAIN OSTRICH AND EMU RANCH.

Then I noticed something else.

"Those vines," I said. "The ones with the hairy stems. They're poison ivy." Just the thought of being that close to such a huge stand of poison ivy made my skin itch all over. "I don't want the boys within ten feet of those vines."

"Roger," Natalie said from her post in the third seat. I noticed this morning that she was wearing a pith helmet, like her great-grandfather, only hers had been dyed black, and around it she'd tied a filmy black scarf accented with silver glitter.

Michael drove on, following my grandfather beneath the sign. We came into an open and relatively flat area, rather like an oversized ledge on the side of the mountain. The road ended up ahead at a ramshackle picket fence around a faded old farmhouse. There were pastures on either side of the road and a barn to our left. I also spotted the remains of a tall chain-link fence that had presumably once enclosed the pastures. In some places it had merely fallen down, but in others it appeared to have been bulldozed.

Grandfather parked just outside the picket fence, and Michael pulled in beside him. All the other vehicles followed suit, and the volunteers poured out. Grandfather's bodyguards hurried to his side. I noticed that they were equipped with binoculars, communications radios, and stout walking sticks that could double as weapons in a pinch. Caroline began organizing the rest of the volunteers into parties. Grandfather headed toward the barn, trailed by his bodyguards and the film crew, who were capturing his philosophical pronouncements about the rapidity with which nature claimed its own after humans had abandoned formerly cultivated land. The twins scurried in Grandfather's wake, which suited me, since the barn looked free of poison ivy and Michael and Natalie were following them.

I headed for the house. Original site of the Biscuit Mountain Art Pottery workshop. Ancestral home of Cordelia's family. An important bit of the history of the one branch of my family I'd never known anything about until this week. It was a weather-beaten gray farmhouse with a rusty tin roof. The front door was closed, but when I tried the doorknob I found it was unlocked.

I stepped inside, looked around, and immediately realized that Miss Annabel's father had made a wise decision, building the enormous gingerbread-trimmed Victorian mansion where she still lived.

The Biscuit Mountain house wasn't a hovel, but it looked exactly like what it was: a very old farmhouse that had been added onto or modernized haphazardly over the years, with an eye more attuned to function than beauty. The ceilings were low—maybe seven and a half feet. The rooms were small and pokey, and full of awkward angles where they had been retrofitted with small closets. The one bathroom was large and antiquated—although rusty water still ran from the vintage taps in the sink and the toilet flushed when I tried it.

The rooms were empty except for a few broken pieces of furniture and enough trash to suggest that the house had occasionally given shelter to passing hikers or teenagers in search of a hangout.

Everything seemed structurally sound, but still— Mother would have called it a fixer-upper, and then sniffed and added, "though why anyone would bother is beyond me."

I wandered back into the living room, feeling vaguely disappointed. I was hoping for something magical. I felt a sudden surge of sympathy for Rob, who had taken it badly when one of Mother's cousins had disproved the old family legend that one of our ancestors had been a noted Yorkshire highwayman.

Sometimes getting to the bottom of something wasn't what it was cracked up to be. Couldn't the cousin have kept his mouth shut and let Rob go on reveling in his notorious

ancestor? And should I keep my mouth shut about this being an ancestral home? Annabel's Victorian mansion was
also a family home, and would make a much nicer memory.

I felt a sudden random twinge of resentment at Grandfather for starting all this in the first place. Which was
unfair. Because if I'd heard he was planning to look for
Cordelia, I'd have been all for it.

Of course, I'd been hoping we'd find a Cordelia who had
always wanted to track down her son and grandchildren
but for some reason had been unable. It might even have
been somewhat comforting to learn that she'd died shortly
after Dad's birth, longing to be reunited with him but prevented by cruel fate. I wasn't at all happy with what we'd
found so far—a grandmother who seemed to have led a
full and perfectly contented life less than an hour from us,
well aware of our existence and yet happy to keep her own
a secret. And if the current state of affairs bothered me,
how much harder was it for poor Dad?

Still brooding on the unfairness of life, I drifted to the
back of the living room, where the back wall was entirely
made up of several sets of large, rough plywood doors—
retrofitted closets perhaps? No, apparently they led out into
the backyard.

Correction: out onto the back terrace, a wide flagstone
area surrounded with a low stone wall, offering one of the
most spectacular views I'd ever seen. The plywood doors
had clearly replaced what was once a wall of floor-to-
ceiling windows.

"We really are on a mountain," I murmured. The terrace
had a hundred-and-eighty-degree view of the surrounding countryside, all the hills and valleys sloping away beneath me, mostly dense woods interrupted with occasional
pastures, all the way to the town of Riverton, nestled at
the bottom of the valley like a toy village beneath a
Christmas tree.

"Okay," I said aloud. "All is forgiven. This is magical enough."

A pity the previous occupant hadn't left behind a few chairs or benches. I sat down on the wall that surrounded the terrace and drank in the scenery.

Below and to my right, I could see the first of the emu hunters fanning out through the meadow. A little farther to the left, Rose Noire was picking her way across a sort of rocky scree, bent almost double so she could scan the rocks beneath her. As I watched she pounced on something and held it up—something that glittered white and silver in the sunlight. Probably a quartz crystal. I couldn't quite share her excitement at finding yet another pretty bit of quartz—she must have a ton of the stuff back home—but it made her happy. Or maybe she was finding more of the blue stuff she'd showed me back at camp.

"Mommy, look!" Josh came running out, waving an emu feather.

"Look what I found!" Jamie, also carrying a feather.

"Have they found the emus, then?" I asked.

"Not yet," Michael said. "But evidently they left some feathers behind in the barn."

"Mine is longer," Josh said.

"Mine is more prettier," Jamie countered.

"Just prettier," I said. "Not more prettier. And they're both very nice. Come look at the view."

The boys marveled at the view, and we got them settled in with their small but powerful binoculars—a gift from my father, who was hoping to inspire the boys to share his love of birding. They alternated between watching the emu trackers and scanning the hillsides, hoping to spot emus themselves.

The binoculars kept the boys busy for a whole half hour. Rock hunting with Rose Noire proved more absorbing, especially since the shallow, pebble-covered slope where she was working also offered a rich variety of insects and lizards.

"This should keep them busy till lunchtime," I said. "Mind if I take off and get a few things done back in town?"

"Fine with me," Michael said. "We'll call if we can't hitch a ride back to town with someone."

When I climbed back up to the house, I found that Grandfather had taken up a post on the terrace, though he didn't seem to be enjoying the view as much as I had. He was studying the landscape beneath him through binoculars and growling sporadically. His bodyguards stood at either end of the terrace, starting and scowling whenever anyone came near.

"We're not seeing any signs of the emus," Caroline murmured.

"I'm sure it's only a matter of time," I said.

"It's only a matter of time before I heave his cantankerous carcass over the side of the terrace," she said.

I decided it was a good thing I was leaving.

Driving back solo was a lot faster than the trip up. As I cruised slowly toward the center of town, I tried to think where I could accomplish my first mission—making those phone calls for Annabel.

Downtown Riverton was remarkably quiet, and none of the businesses looked open. Of course, they hadn't looked all that lively yesterday, but today you could have used the whole area around the town square to film one of those post-apocalyptic science fiction B-movies where most of the human race has been wiped out and the few survivors would spend the next hour and a half battling invaders from outer space or giant mutant cockroaches.

I spotted Chief Heedles's blue sedan pulling into a parking space in front of a tree-shaded brick building. Perfect. She'd probably know where there was a pay phone, if such a thing still existed. I had the feeling they still might in Riverton. And maybe I could get her into conversation about Cordelia's murder, as Stanley had suggested. I pulled into the slot next to her. She spotted me and waited on the steps of the building—which, as I now noticed, was the police station.

"Afternoon," she said, as I got out of my car. "Were you looking for me?"

"Not specifically," I said. "But when I saw you I realized you could probably tell me where I can find a working pay phone. Or a kind soul willing to let me make a couple of calls. My cell phone's still out."

"Everyone's cell phones are still out," she said. "Last night's storm took out power all over town and the cell towers aren't back up yet. But we have some land lines at the station that were still working when I left. Are these local calls?"

"Not sure." I pulled out my notebook and glanced at the numbers Stanley and Annabel had given me. "Both toll-free numbers actually."

"That's fine, then."

She led the way up the steps. The station's front door was propped open. Just inside, at the desk, was a trim, middle-aged black woman whose tan uniform still looked surprisingly well-pressed in spite of the heat and humidity. She was fanning herself with an old-fashioned cardboard church fan.

"You doing okay?" the chief asked.

"Hanging in there." She handed the chief a small stack of pink WHILE YOU WERE OUT slips.

"Thanks," Heedles said, patting the woman on the shoulder. Then she led the way back to her office and pointed to the phone on her desk.

"I don't want to tie up your line," I said. "I want to make those calls, but neither is urgent."

"It'll give me a chance to triage these," she said, waving the message slips as she sat down in her battered leather desk chair.

And a chance to eavesdrop on my conversations, I thought, as I sat down in one of her guest chairs and reached for the phone. But it wasn't as if either call was private.

The generator installation company was, understandably, swamped with both requests for new generators and service calls on existing ones, but promised to come out as soon as they could. Stanley's security expert promised to be out the next day, but wasn't sure how much he could get done if Miss Annabel didn't have power.

The chief looked up from her stack of message slips when I'd finished my second call.

"Miss Annabel feeling nervous all of a sudden?" she asked.

"Wouldn't you if someone tried to poison you?" I asked. "Not to mention the fact that she's got dozens of strange people in her backyard, any one of whom could have done the poisoning as far as she knows. I wanted to get the contractors out there before she changed her mind."

"Sensible," she said. "She's pretty far out of town, and there's only so often my officers can cruise by. Anything else I can do for you?"

"No," I said. "Unless you have any inside scoop on when the power's coming back."

She shook her head. Then she just sat there, waiting for me to speak, holding the message slips in her hand.

"Then I should let you get back to your work." I took my time stowing my notebook back in my purse. I was trying to think of a way to start a conversation about Cordelia's murder, but she didn't make it easy. "And thanks again for letting me use your phone," I said, as I stood up. "As I said, it wasn't an emergency, but I did want to be able to tell Miss Annabel that I'd made those calls."

"And you have to keep Miss Annabel happy if you don't want to lose your campground," the chief said. "I understand that. At least you have her to deal with, not Ms. Delia."

"You didn't like Ms. Delia?" I asked.

"I liked her fine," she said. "Even if she was a bit bossy. Miss Annabel is just much easier to deal with. At least she was before her agoraphobia or anthrophopobia or whatever it is got so bad. She was always the mellow one."

"Good grief," I said. "If Annabel's the mellow one, Cordelia must really have been something."

"She was a pistol all right," the chief said, with a chuckle. "But she always did a lot for the town, so people would overlook it if she was a bit high-handed."

"High-handed?" I echoed.

"There was a time when the Lees and a couple of other families pretty much ran this town." The chief leaned back, clasped her hands behind her head, and stretched out her legs so that I could see the toe of one sturdy work shoe beneath the bottom of her desk. "And sometimes it did seem as if she and Miss Annabel thought they still should be running it."

"For example?" I asked.

"For example—the old emu ranch. The land used to belong to their family—eighty years ago. Some of the locals used to work up there, making bits of pottery for the Lee family."

Bits of pottery? I nodded, but it seemed to me that she was trying to downplay the importance of the pottery works. Or had the book, written by a Lee, exaggerated when it said that half the town had once been employed there?

"That's an interesting fact," the chief went on. "An interesting bit of town history. But it doesn't give them any more rights than anyone else to the property now."

"Do they seem to think it does?" I asked.

"Ms. Delia was in a high dudgeon about the bank's refusal to sell her the property," she said. "Not sure the bank agreed with her about the importance of having a museum to her family history."

"I thought she wanted it for a sanctuary for the emus," I said.

"That, too," she said. "An emu sanctuary on the land, and a pottery museum in the old house. I'm not saying those are bad ideas. If they're willing to pay what the bank wants for the land, they can do what they like with it. But if they can't pay the freight, they don't get to boss the rest of the town around."

"According to what Miss Annabel said, it wasn't a question of not paying what the bank asked," I said. "The bank wouldn't even talk to them about selling."

"No law says they have to," she said, with a shrug. "Maybe the bank's got other plans for the land. Not sure what, though. I remember when they first repossessed the land, they sent a geologist up there to see if there were any minerals worth mining, but nothing ever came of it."

"Maybe they hope to sell it to a developer for a resort or something," I suggested.

"You think that's a possibility?" She sounded surprised, and not displeased at the idea.

"The place has a million-dollar view," I said. "But still—doesn't seem likely to me. Maybe the bank thinks differently."

"Doesn't seem likely to me, either," she said. "More's the pity. The town could use the jobs. And it's not as if a Lee Family Museum would do much for the tourist trade."

"You never know," I said. "The Biscuit Mountain Pottery Works was famous. Still is to pottery collectors. People pay hundreds of dollars for some of those little bits of pottery."

"Seriously?" The idea seemed to unsettle her.

"Seriously. Check it out on eBay."

"I just may do that," she said. "My mama's got an attic full of the stuff. A lot of her family used to work there, back in the day. Maybe she could earn a little mad money by selling it."

"If she has an attic full, she might be able to put her grandkids through college by selling it," I said. "And did you know the Lees were among the first potters in America to make porcelain in addition to stoneware? Maybe the museum wasn't such a crazy idea after all. You could turn the place into a tourist site. Get some potters working up there in Colonial era costumes. You know how big historical tourism is in Virginia."

"Good point," she said. "Maybe Ms. Delia had something there after all. But with her gone, I don't think any of that's likely to happen. Not unless Miss Annabel finds someone else to help her with it. A very nice lady, Miss Annabel, but Ms. Delia was the mover and shaker. With her gone . . ."

Her voice trailed off and she shook her head.

"Speaking of Ms. Delia's death," I said.

"Death," she said. "Not murder? I thought you shared Miss Annabel's belief that I'm a lazy, incompetent investigator who is ignoring irrefutable evidence that her cousin was murdered by one Theophilus Herodotus Weaver."

She didn't sound angry. Maybe a little sarcastic. I wondered if she'd have reacted more strongly if Stanley had been here.

"I share her concern that we find out exactly what happened to Cordelia," I said. "I don't have any preconceived notion that it was murder, or who's responsible if it was."

"But Miss Annabel does," she said. "On both counts."

"Miss Annabel doesn't think what she saw could have

been caused by a kerosene lamp igniting gasoline vapor," I said.

"Neither do I," she said. "As I've tried to tell her more than once. It's a little hard to get the point across shouting through a heavy wooden door."

"Then what do you think happened?" I asked.

"I think someone whacked Ms. Delia over the head, poured gasoline over her dead or unconscious body, and set her on fire," she said.

I was speechless for a few moments.

"So you think it was murder?" I asked.

"I know it was murder."

"No chance of an accident?" I persisted. "Like if she spilled gasoline while filling the generator and it caught on fire?"

"No chance of an accident," Chief Heedles said. "Because there was no reason at all for Ms. Delia to be pouring gasoline out there. It was a propane generator."

She let that settle in for a while. She seemed to be enjoying my astonishment.

"But if you knew it was murder—"

"Why didn't I arrest anyone?" She shook her head. "No evidence. I know what happened, more or less. Someone hit her over the head. The medical examiner found traces of the blow on her skull. And then someone poured gasoline on her and set her on fire. Samples we took at the scene can prove that. But there's no evidence at all to indicate who did it."

"You never explained this to Miss Annabel?"

"She's never given me the chance," she said. "And I doubt she'd have listened if I did, because she's convinced Theo Weaver is the killer. And even if I agreed with her on that, what good would that do me? I have no evidence. No sane DA would take the case to court. No jury would convict."

"So there's nothing you can do?" I asked.

"Nothing except what I'm already doing," she said. "Keeping my ears and eyes open. If it was murder, the killer will brag about it sooner or later, when he thinks he's gotten away with it. Or his suddenly ex-girlfriend will waltz in here and tell me about the night he came home, reeking of gasoline, with his eyebrows scorched off. Or something that belonged to Ms. Delia will turn up in a pawn shop. It's a small town. Something like that happens, I'll hear about it."

"And if it happens, you'll reopen the case?"

"I haven't actually closed the case," she said. "And I won't. You can tell Miss Annabel that. But I'm not going to arrest Mr. Weaver on her say-so. Knowing he and Ms. Delia hated each other's guts makes me want to keep an eye on him, but it doesn't give me grounds to arrest him. If anything untoward ever happened to Mr. Weaver, Miss Annabel might appreciate that."

"There is the fact that she reports seeing him flee the scene."

"Do you have any idea how unreliable eyewitness testimony is?" the chief asked. "No sane prosecutor goes into court with nothing but a single eyewitness. Especially if your eyewitness is an elderly lady with bad eyesight who saw a fleeing figure from half a football field away. Saw it by firelight and moonlight, and was probably in a state of panic already. And on top of it all, she had a known grudge against the person she claims to have seen. The defense attorney would tear her apart."

I nodded, conceding her point.

"Look," she said. "The case isn't closed. But it's not going anywhere right now, because I've already done what little I can do, and found nothing. Maybe you'll get lucky—you, or that PI you hired. Either of you comes up with even a shred of evidence I can use, I'd appreciate seeing it."

"Speaking of evidence, what happened with the LED headlight I found out in the field behind Miss Annabel's house?"

"We sent it down to Richmond to see if they could get any evidence off of it. Which I hate to say is probably a waste of money. Those things are a dime a dozen around here."

She opened one of her desk drawers and pulled out two little headlights that looked identical to Miss Annabel's.

"Ms. Delia was the one who introduced these things," she said. "But these days, everyone in town uses them. Hardware store stocks them by the case. But we'll see what the crime lab can do with the one you found."

"I understand," I said. "Thanks for your time."

"Thank you for yours," she said.

I had the distinct and not unpleasant feeling that having this conversation had been on her to-do list as well as mine.

A thought occurred to me.

"Just one more thing," I said. "Is it true you've given your officers orders to shoot the emus on sight?"

"I see you've been talking to Mr. Weaver," she said. "No, it most definitely is not true. It *is* true that he has asked me to do so on more than one occasion. And that I told him I'd take his request under advisement. If he's clueless enough to think that means I agree with him . . ." She shrugged.

"I figured it would be something like that," I said. "Thanks."

On my way out, the dispatcher looked up from a phone call long enough to shove a bottle of cold water into my hands.

"You drink that down," she ordered. "Don't want to see you hauled off to the hospital over in the county. They're full up with heatstroke cases already."

I didn't need to be told twice.

Chapter 16

Sipping my cold water, I made my way back to the car. What next? I cruised down the street, checking out the businesses on either side. A few, like the police station, had their doors propped open. One or two seemed to have generators running. Most were closed.

I had a table full of books waiting for me at the library, so I headed there. But there was only one car in its parking lot, and a sign in the front door: CLOSED.

I was turning to go when the door popped open.

"Sorry!" Anne, the librarian, had opened the door and stepped out. "We're closed because of the power outage." She was wearing an LED headlight, similar to the ones Miss Annabel and the chief had, and thoughtfully flicked it off rather than shining it in my face.

"I know," I said. I'd already figured out that the power outage explained why downtown was so moribund. Even more moribund than usual. Though I should probably still keep an eye out for those mutant cockroaches. "Just figuring out what to do with myself instead of the research I was planning."

"Sorry," she said. "I'd let you in to work by a window, but I'm only staying a few minutes myself, to make sure everything's secure. We're in for a heat wave starting today. Temperatures predicted to be in the high nineties, heat index of a hundred and ten, so in an hour or so this place will be an oven."

"I knew Miss Annabel had lost power," I said. "But I

didn't know till I came into town that it was so widespread. Is the whole town affected?"

"Half the state is affected!" She sounded remarkably cheerful about it. Or perhaps she was one of those people who found some consolation in being the first to know and share the latest bad news. Of course, she was an improvement over the chief, who probably knew all of this and hadn't said a word about it. Or maybe the chief didn't care about the power situation beyond the borders of Riverton.

"Any prediction on when we'll get power back?" I asked.

"Not a word." Her expression turned grim. "That was one huge storm system last night—there's hundreds of thousands of people in the dark, all the way from Northern Virginia down to the Outer Banks of North Carolina. They say they're still assessing the damage and calling in crews from other regions. I've heard that before. Usually means we're in for a long wait. We were out for three weeks with Hurricane Isabel and again with Irene."

"Damn," I said.

"Look, if there's anything you particularly need looked up, let me know," she said. "I can't do anything online or with microfiche until the power comes back, but I can haul a few books home and do research where it's a few degrees cooler. And if my sister down in Richmond gets power back before we do, I might go down and stay with her, and I'll just be twiddling my thumbs."

I thought about it for a few moments and decided to trust her. She was a fan of Grandfather's. And a librarian.

"Any chance you could do some research on whether anyone here in Riverton has a particular reason to hate my grandfather?" I asked.

"You mean like antienvironmental nutcases?" she said.

"Or people whose business or political plans he's

thwarted," I said. "Or people he's embarrassed. Or fired. Or whatever. He makes a lot of enemies."

"Yes, but he does a lot of good along with it," she said. "I'll see what I can turn up."

"Thanks," I said. "And don't tell anyone."

"Right," she said. "Because I don't want to get the next bottle of poisoned alcohol. Although according to our local EMTs, the poor man who drank the Scotch is going to pull through, largely due to your father's figuring out so quickly what was wrong with him."

I nodded.

"And look on the bright side," she said. "Now you're free to join in the emu roundup! How's it going, anyway? Have they got many birds?"

"I was up there this morning for a while," I said. "And when I left, they hadn't started any actual rounding up. Nothing much can happen until they locate the birds."

"They're not still hanging around Pudding Mountain?"

"Pudding Mountain?" I echoed. "Is that different from Biscuit Mountain?"

"Completely different," she said. "It's where the ladies used to feed the emus."

"You mean Miss Annabel and Ms. Delia?"

"Yes," she said. "Only in the winter, when they thought the birds might have trouble foraging. A couple of times a week Ms. Delia would have Thor Larsen borrow his uncle's truck, load up with grain at the feed store, and haul it up to where the emus hung out."

"Did Miss Annabel keep it up after Ms. Delia's death?"

"Yes," she said. "Though poor Thor had to do it all by himself, since Miss Annabel doesn't go out."

I wondered, briefly, if Miss Annabel had forgotten to mention this or if she'd deliberately withheld the information to make things harder for Grandfather.

"Where can I find Thor?" I asked aloud.

"He's working for the summer down at his uncle's car repair shop," she said. "Larsen's Auto Shop. It's on the north side, about two blocks out."

I'd already figured out that was how Rivertonians gave directions. The only two roads in town that were more than a block long met up and circumscribed what locals rather inaccurately called the town square, a small circular grassy space large enough for four benches at the base of the statue of an obscure Civil War general. Locals could say "two blocks north" or "about half a mile out to the east" and everyone knew they meant from the town square along the one road that went in that direction.

I thanked Anne, left the library—itself "a block south" in local parlance—and paused at the door of my car. The shop was only three blocks away. I felt guilty not walking such a short distance. But if I could arrange for Thor to take a break from his work to show me the location of the emus, it would help to have my car ready and waiting.

And besides, at least my car had air conditioning.

Larsen's was busy, with mechanics working in all three indoor bays and quite a few vehicles parked on the grounds, presumably awaiting either a mechanic's attention or their owners' return. Mostly pickups, which seemed to be the local norm. But the place was a lot quieter than most repair shops I'd ever visited. It took me a few moments to realize that none of the mechanics were using power tools.

"That's it," one of them snapped, tossing a wrench on the floor with a loud clatter. "Nothing more I can do without juice. Is anyone working on the damned generator?"

I walked into the small office, and found a man I assumed to be Mr. Larsen himself talking on the phone. He was burly and his face almost completely covered with a wiry red beard. He held up a finger to acknowledge my arrival and indicate that he'd be a minute. I nodded and parked myself on the available customer seating—a couch that appeared to have been constructed by chopping off the rear end of a vintage car and inserting the matching rear car seat in the space once occupied by the trunk. The car seat was black leather, the car body fire-engine red, and the effect was oddly elegant, making the utilitarian clutter of the paper- and part-filled office seem shabbier by contrast. And it was surprisingly comfortable.

I deduced from Mr. Larsen's side of the conversation that he was negotiating to get a part for his silent generator from a junkyard some half an hour's drive away.

"I'll send Thor down to get it," he said. "Thanks."

With that he hung up and looked up at me.

"Oh, dear," I said. "I couldn't help but overhear that you're sending Thor on an errand, and I was hoping to hire him."

"Hire him?" Larsen looked puzzled. "You need something repaired?"

"I wanted to hire him to take me out to find the emus," I said. "I understand he might know where they hang out."

Larsen smiled, and leaned back in his chair.

"You must be with that bunch camping in back of Miss Lee's," he said. "With that TV zoologist. He can't find them himself?"

"He can, and will eventually if there are any left to be found," I said. "But it would save a lot of time if we knew where to start. And Thor used to take Ms. Delia Mason up to feed them. I figured maybe it would work better if we started where they were fed a few months ago rather than where they lived several years back. But if you're sending him to fetch a part—"

"I can send someone else." Larsen turned around to a window in the back of his office, where a view of the busy interior of the garage was visible. He lifted the window sash with one hand and leaned slightly toward it.

"Thor!" he shouted. "In here!"

A tall, gangling teenager with a protuberant Adam's apple and a scruffy mop of rusty red hair hustled into the room. Larsen jerked his thumb at me.

"Lady wants your game tracking skills," he said, with a chuckle.

Thor turned to me with a polite but puzzled frown.

"It's a pretty long time till hunting season, you know," he said. "Or are you a photographer or something?"

His expression clearly said that I didn't look like a hunter.

"I'm looking for emus," I said.

A pained look crossed his face.

"Finding them could be pretty impossible," he said. "And I'm not sure why you'd want to. Couple of people around town have tried eating them, and they say the meat's kind of tough and stringy."

"We don't want to eat them," I said. "We want to rescue them. I'm with Dr. Blake's expedition."

"Oh, well, that's different," he said. "If my uncle doesn't need me for a while . . ."

"Go on." The elder Larsen waved his hand genially, granting permission. "I'll send Virgil down to Winchester for the part for the generator. Until he gets back, there's not much you can do around here."

"My car's outside," I said.

"No offense," Thor said. "But there isn't a paved road up there, so unless your car has four-wheel drive . . ."

"Take the truck." Mr. Larsen tossed over a set of keys as he opened the window into the garage again. "Virgil! Get in here!"

Within a few minutes Thor and I were on our way. At his suggestion, we stopped by the feed store for a few bags of the grain mix the ladies were in the habit of hauling out to the emus in wintertime. Then we headed back into town, rounded the statue in the center, and took the road that went by the library.

"So where are we going?" I asked. "Unless my mental map of the town is completely backward, we're heading south, rather than north, where the emu ranch used to be."

"You're right," he said. "When Mr. Eaton first turned the emus loose, they pretty much hung around the ranch. But then this guy who had the nearest farm started taking potshots at them 'cause they were scaring his cows and eating his crops."

"Was that true?" I asked. "Or was it just an excuse for taking potshots at the emus?"

"It was pretty much true," he said. "But it wasn't their fault! No one was feeding them anymore, and—"

"Hey, I'm on the emus' side, remember?" I said.

"Okay," he said. "Anyway, Ms. Delia said we needed to lure them away to a safer place. We started leaving feed out for them near the farm, then we gradually moved it farther and farther away till we had them trained to get fed over on Pudding Mountain. Which is completely on the opposite side of town from the ranch, so we figured they'd be a lot safer there."

Biscuit Mountain and now Pudding Mountain. I wondered if perhaps whatever early explorer had named the geological features surrounding Riverton had been low on provisions at the time.

"No trigger-happy farmers near Pudding Mountain?" I asked.

"Not many," he said. "Most of it's inside the national park, so there's no hunting allowed. And the Park Service is pretty keen on enforcing that."

"And how does the Park Service feel about their land becoming an unofficial emu refuge?"

"Probably not too happy." Thor chuckled and shook his head. "But the idea wasn't for them to live there forever.

Just to keep them from getting shot till we could get the wildlife sanctuary set up where the ranch used to be."

"You stopped feeding them at the end of the winter?" I asked.

He nodded.

"So would they be down in the national park now or would they tend to drift back toward town where they could nibble on vegetable gardens?"

He shrugged.

"Ms. Delia says they'll travel a long way for food," he said. "Which explains why even when we were feeding them, we'd hear about sightings miles away. But not many sightings over on Biscuit Mountain."

Which could mean the emus weren't returning to Biscuit Mountain, or perhaps those with an inclination to return to Biscuit Mountain fell victim to the trigger-happy farmer and were never sighted again.

"So south it is," I said. "Lead on, Macduff."

"It's Larsen, actually," he said. Evidently *Macbeth* wasn't on the syllabus at Riverton High School.

Thor was fairly taciturn on the first part of our drive. After he responded to my first couple of remarks with monosyllables, I decided to give up. Let the generation gap stand. I tried to enjoy the scenery as rolling fields gave way to steeper and steeper hills.

But as we were winding along a narrow road up the side of something that had definitely begun to earn the word "mountain" instead of "hill," Thor suddenly spoke up.

"Look," he said. "Do you think you could talk to Miss Annabel for me?"

"About what?"

"Tell her I didn't do anything to the generator."

"I think she knows that, Thor," I said.

"I don't think she believes it," he said. "I did ask her and Ms. Delia to let me work on it a few times. Okay, lots of times. I guess I bugged them a lot about it, but I was pretty sure I could make it work better."

"How?"

"Well, the problem was—wait." He looked me and frowned. "Do you want the technical explanation? Because my dad says I have an annoying tendency to lecture people on stuff like that. Mechanical and engineering stuff. I'd be happy to tell you exactly, but maybe you'd rather have the nontechnical explanation."

"Let's start with the nontechnical stuff," I said. "What did you tell the ladies was wrong with it?"

"It was too noisy, and using too much fuel," he said. "I'm pretty sure I could have fixed it—my dad's generator at home had the same problem, and I fixed it. It's running fine now. And I could have installed an on/off switch in the house, so they didn't have to go out in the cold. But the ladies never wanted me to do it—I think they were a little worried that I'd mess it up or hurt myself."

"Or maybe they didn't mind it being a little noisy, since Mr. Weaver bore the main brunt of that."

"Yeah." He grinned and chuckled softly. "That idea occurred to me, too. But the point is, I knew I could fix it—but I knew better than to do it without their permission. Can you tell Miss Annabel that?"

"You can't tell her yourself?"

"I would if I could, but she won't see me." He looked hurt. "I can understand that she doesn't need me so much anymore—it's not like she ever goes anywhere that she'd need me to drive her, like I did Ms. Delia. But I'd just like to talk to her. Give her my condolences. Tell her in person that I didn't do anything to the generator."

"She's hired my PI friend to try to prove that Theo Weaver killed her cousin," I said. "Do you really think she'd do that if she thought Ms. Delia's death was caused by something you did to the generator?"

He looked surprised, and almost cheerful.

"That's good," he said. "It'd be nice to know she doesn't blame me." His face fell again. "Still, I wish she'd talk to me. I used to like driving Ms. Delia around, and then coming back and listening to her tell Miss Annabel everything we'd seen and done. And they'd serve me cookies, and we'd talk. It was like they were actually interested in hearing what I thought about stuff, instead of telling me to shut up like most grownups. I liked them. They were nice ladies. Well, Miss Annabel is and Ms. Delia was."

"I'll see if I can bring the subject up," I said.

"Thanks," he said.

We fell silent again. I wasn't sure what Thor was thinking, but I was struggling with a sudden feeling of resentment against him. He'd known my grandmother. They'd been friends. And I'd never get to meet her.

And it wasn't his fault. Instead of resenting him, I should work on getting to know him. He was another source of information about Cordelia.

Although not, I suspected, the information I most wanted to know.

A little while later, Thor slowed down in front of a faded sign announcing that we were entering the Pudding Mountain National Park. A weathered split-rail fence ran along the road, no doubt to mark the boundaries of the park. A narrow, badly rutted dirt road led through the opening in the fence.

"Hang onto your hat," Thor said, as he pulled onto the road.

We jounced and bounced along through the woods—and rather steeply uphill—for about three miles. Neither of us spoke. Thor seemed to be concentrating on avoiding the worst of the ruts, and I was afraid if I opened my mouth, a sudden jolt might cause me to bite my tongue off.

Thor finally pulled to a stop when we reached a small clearing on the bank of a stream. The road forded the stream and continued, still uphill.

"This is where we feed them," he said. "It's about as far as you want to go—the road gets worse across the stream."

Worse? That was hard to imagine.

Thor began turning the truck around in the relatively narrow space of the clearing.

"I don't want to leave immediately," I said. "Let's look for the emus."

"I figured you'd probably say that," he said. "I just like to have the truck ready to roll in case a bear or something comes along."

If he was trying to scare me—well, no sense letting him know he'd succeeded.

"Is that likely?" I tried to sound calm and interested.

"I've only seen one once," he said. "Actually, I got in the habit of turning the truck around because when we'd bring the feed up, the emus would swarm us, and I didn't want to run over any of them while turning around."

He parked the truck, and we both got out and peered around.

"If this was February, when they'd gotten used to being fed here, they'd be lined up waiting for us," he said. "Let's put the grain out."

He hopped out of the truck, lowered its tailgate, and hefted one of the fifty-pound sacks of feed. I followed his example, a little awkwardly thanks to the bandages on my left hand.

"I can get them both if you like," he said.

"I'm fine," I replied.

I might have let him handle both sacks if I'd known he was going to carry them across the ford in the stream and over to the other side of the clearing. We couldn't have hauled them over in the truck and then turned around? Or for that matter, spread out the grain on the near side of the stream?

But I concentrated on not dropping the sack, and we came to a stop beside what I assumed was an emu feeding station. It was an eight-foot-long trough set high off the ground. Its eight legs were protected with baffles, similar to those birders used to keep the squirrels off their feeders. There was a roof to protect the grain from precipitation. I couldn't quite understand why it had bars running from the trough to the roof all the way around, so I asked Thor.

"The emus can fit their heads through the space between the bars," he said, "but it's too small for deer. Ms. Delia's idea, and it worked pretty well."

"Not a fan of deer, Ms. Delia?"

"They ate her garden," he said with a grin. "She used to say there were enough fat, lazy deer in the world without our helping them."

Thor climbed up a couple of rough steps built at one end of the trough, and I handed up the bags to him. When he was finished spreading the feed with a battered old rake that had been left lying in the trough, he picked up something that was hanging by a rope. It looked like a crudely made tomtom with a padded drumstick.

"My emu lure," he said.

He began pounding the tomtom in a two-beat rhythm: *Thump thump! Thump thump! Thump thump!*

After a while he stopped and cocked his head to listen.

"Nothing yet," he said. "Let's go across the stream and wait a while."

"So emus like percussion instruments?" I asked, as we walked.

"Emus *are* percussion instruments," he said. "They make a booming, thumping noise a lot like that drum. And also a growling noise, but I can't do that, and anyway it wouldn't carry very far."

"So when they hear that, they'll think another emu is here and come running?"

"Or maybe they just think, 'hey, that crazy human who brings the goodies is playing his drum again,'" he said, with a chuckle. "They seem to come when I do it. But they could be at the other side of the park right now. We might have to bring grain up for a few days to get them used to showing up here."

"Or maybe not," I said. "Look!"

Thor whirled and then froze, staring at the head that had suddenly appeared out of the thicket.

"Awesome," he murmured. Without taking his eyes off the emu, he reached into his pocket, took out his cell phone, and began snapping pictures of it.

I slowly lifted my binoculars to my eyes and trained them on the emu.

A knobby head that wouldn't have been out of place on a dinosaur topped a long, slender neck. Both head and neck were feathered, but sparsely, so the emu's blue skin showed through. And its eyes were a bright coppery orange. The head swiveled left and then right. Not the prettiest bird I'd ever seen, but as Thor had said, awesome.

Then it stepped out of the shrubbery and began picking its way delicately across the clearing toward the trough.

"That could be Liz," he said.

"The emu?"

"Short for Elizabeth Cady Stanton," he said. "Ms. Delia had names for all of them. She could recognize them from pretty far away."

As we watched, Liz picked her way across the clearing to the emu feeder. For something so large she moved with curious grace. Her head and body bobbed with each step in a kind of swaying rhythm like a camel.

Thump thump! Thump thump!

I glanced over at Thor, but he wasn't playing his drum. He was staring openmouthed at the emu.

I looked back at Liz and saw her throat swelling out with each thump.

Liz stopped at the trough and stared down her bill at us for a few long moments. Then she arched her long, slender neck and slipped her head through the bars to the feeder.

"They're coming," Thor murmured.

Two more emus were stepping out into the clearing. They thumped and growled a bit and then they headed for the feeding trough. Liz pulled her head out of the trough, raised it up as high as she could reach, and took a few running steps toward the approaching emus, hissing all the while. They fled, and circled around to approach the other end of the trough, giving Liz a wide berth.

"Now I'm sure it's Liz," Thor said. "Ms. Delia always said she was the boss emu. She beat Louisa May Alcott in a knock-down, drag-out fight a year and a half ago, and poor Lou was still limping months later."

"So you could probably recognize her, too, if she showed up," I said. "Are there any other emus you would recognize?"

I didn't really care if he could, actually, but I was fascinated by Cordelia's system for naming the emus.

"Ella," he said, after a few moments of thought. "She's almost a white emu—not albino, but really, really pale."

"Ella Fitzgerald?" I asked.

"No, Ella Wheeler Wilcox," he said. "I think she was a poet."

"Opinions on that differ," I said. "Look, I could watch the emus all day, but maybe we should go back and tell my grandfather where they are."

"Good idea." Still staring at the emus, he fumbled in his pocket for the keys.

"Wait." I pulled out my phone and clicked the button to start the camera app. "Before we go, let's take a few pictures of me with the emus in the background. As proof that we've found them."

Thor took my phone and took several pictures. About halfway through our photo session, one of the emus noticed us and began walking our way.

"Should we maybe get back into the truck?" I asked.

"They're usually pretty friendly once they get used to us feeding them," Thor said. "It's when they raise their heads really high that you have to keep your eye on them."

The emu raised its head really high.

"But they're not used to you feeding them at this time of year," I said, as I backed toward the truck. "And they've never seen me before."

"Well, yeah." He turned and headed for the truck as well.

We made it into the cab before the emu arrived. Emus. One of them came to my side of the truck, stuck its head right next to the window, and peered at me, cross-eyed, over its beak. Thor handed me back my phone and I snapped a photo of the emu. As if puzzled by the shutter noise the phone made when I took the picture, the emu cocked its head in curiosity. I snapped another shot of that.

The other two were peering in Thor's side. He didn't seem rattled by that, I realized with envy.

"Why are they staring at us?" I asked. I was trying to remember some of the emu lore Grandfather had been spouting so blithely for the past day or two. I didn't recall any stories of trucks being savaged by flocks of emus, so we were probably safe enough. Then again, Grandfather seemed to like emus. He was taking all this trouble to rescue them. I should have remembered that his favorite birds and animals were invariably the ones that were fierce, dangerous, and highly photogenic.

"No idea," Thor said. "They seem to like watching humans. If you like, I can start the truck moving. They'll get out of the way if I move very slowly."

"We probably should report back to Grandfather," I said. "In fact, even better idea—let's send him a couple of the photos. Oh, wait—the cell towers are probably still out. Back to camp, then."

The trip back seemed even longer than the trip out, in part because I was worried that the emus would disappear while we were gone. Although Thor assured me that another sack or two of grain and a little work with his emu caller would lure them back again.

Just as we were turning onto the dirt road into Camp Emu, I spotted Dad, driving along in his SUV. I almost fell out the window of Thor's uncle's truck waving him to a stop.

"What's wrong?" he asked.

As I ran over to his SUV, I could see he was reaching into the back for his medical bag.

"Nothing's wrong," I said. "Look!"

I held up my phone with the picture of the emu staring through the truck window on its screen.

"You found them!"

Chapter 17

Dad immediately pulled out his radio and shared the news with Grandfather, who showed up half an hour later. Although I knew Grandfather was eager to start rounding up the emus, I'd assumed that he would congratulate me on my detective work and then we'd huddle over the map so Thor and I could show him precisely where the emus were, and he and Caroline and the Valkyrie would start planning for tomorrow's expedition.

But he practically didn't wait for Caroline to bring the Jeep to a stop before leaping out of it.

"About time someone showed some initiative!" He scrambled into the passenger side of Thor's truck, taking the place I'd just vacated. "Let's go!"

"We're not waiting for the camera crew?" I asked. "And where did you ditch your bodyguards?"

"Hell with them if they can't keep up," he growled. "Take me to the emus!"

"Move over." I climbed back into the cab of the truck. "This is my grandfather, Dr. Montgomery Blake," I said to the understandably startled Thor. "Grandfather, this is Thor Larsen, who has been helping Miss Annabel and Ms. Delia feed the emus."

"A Norseman, eh!" Grandfather exclaimed. "*God efter-middag*, Thor! Drive on!"

Thor looked pained, and I suspected he was trying to find a polite way of pointing out that he didn't speak anything but English.

"If Thor's going to drive us somewhere, I should remind you that we're paying for Thor's time, right?" I asked. "And his expenses."

"*Ja!*" Grandfather said. "Certainly. *Kjapp deg!*"

"That's a yes," I said. "Even I can figure out that much."

"Wait for us!" came a shout from nearby.

Dad had parked his car and was scrambling into the Jeep beside Caroline. Two other volunteers—presumably the bodyguards—jumped in the Jeep's backseat. Thor put the truck in gear and drove off, still looking a little shell-shocked. Caroline followed.

It didn't help that Grandfather spent the first ten minutes of our drive declaiming something in whatever Scandinavian language he'd decided Thor spoke. Some sort of warlike epic poem, by the sound of it, though considering that I didn't speak a word of Swedish, Norwegian, Danish, or Icelandic, he could have been reciting a grocery list and it would have sounded the same to me. Thor just drove, seeing Grandfather out of the corner of his eye from time to time, and dodging when his grandiose gestures got a little out of hand.

Thor was probably as relieved as I was when we pulled into the little clearing by the river.

And to my delight, there were now four emus eating at the trough.

The emus looked up as we drove into the clearing, and the smallest one ran to the edge of the woods and stood there looking at us. The others just stared at us for a little while and returned to their eating.

"Fascinating." Grandfather pulled out his binoculars and studied the emus. Dad and Caroline pulled up behind us in Grandfather's Jeep. Dad hopped out, ran over to us, pulled out his binoculars, and took up the same pose as Grandfather.

I could hear Caroline back in the car shouting into her

radio, apparently giving directions to someone over a bad connection.

The bodyguards took up their posts on either side of Grandfather, and to their credit, they spent almost as much time alertly scanning their surroundings as watching the emus.

I watched Dad and Grandfather for a few moments. A pity the camera crew wasn't here yet. Grandfather would either have to keep gazing at the emus until they arrived, or reenact this first encounter with the birds.

Grandfather took a few careful steps toward the emus. I'd seen him do exactly the same thing dozens of times in his documentaries, and it seemed strange not to have the usual voice-over telling what he was up to. An irresistible urge overcame me.

"Dr. Blake approaches the emus cautiously, to avoid startling his quarry," I intoned, trying to imitate the hushed, dramatic tone that his favorite narrator would have used. "After inspecting the new arrivals, the emus return to their feeding."

Caroline, who was joining us, binoculars in hand, smothered laughter at that. Dad and Grandfather ignored me.

"What the devil's that thing they're eating from?" Grandfather asked.

"An emu feeding station," Thor said.

"Brilliant!" Grandfather said. "Whose idea was that?"

"Ms. Delia had the idea," Thor said. "And I built it."

"Ingenious." Grandfather appeared to be studying the feeding station rather than the emus, if the angle of his binoculars was anything to go by. "Excellent job! You have a real talent for this work!"

"Thanks." Thor looked shyly pleased.

"You're a college student." Grandfather lowered his binoculars and fixed Thor with what I called his interrogation look.

"This fall," Thor said. "Virginia Tech."

"Perfect!" Grandfather said. "They have an excellent wildlife sciences program."

"I'm doing engineering," Thor said.

"Hmph!" Clearly Grandfather didn't approve. "We need to talk about that."

He frowned at Thor for a few moments, then put the binoculars back to his eyes. Thor let out a deep breath when Grandfather's eyes left him.

"Of course, they don't have a department of Scandinavian languages," he said over his shoulder. "Only a handful of U.S. colleges do. What a shame."

Poor Thor tensed up again.

"I think the emus are running out of food," Dad said. "No telling if they'll stay around with no food."

"Where is that blasted camera crew?" Grandfather growled. "They're going to miss it all."

"How about if Thor and I fetch more grain for the emus?" I suggested.

"Hurry back." Grandfather returned to his binoculars. "And light a fire under that camera crew."

So Thor and I stopped by the camp to give directions to the camera crew. By the time we got back with another four bags of grain, the whole expedition had relocated to the park. Several dozen cars were parked on the shoulder of the main road, on either side of the park entrance, and there almost wasn't room for Thor's uncle's truck in the little clearing.

Apparently Michael had managed the difficult road in the Twinmobile—he, Natalie, and the boys were there, all gazing through their binoculars at the emus. And at Grandfather, who was standing in front of the empty emu feeding pen, pointing out how ingenious it was to the attending camera crew. He beamed when Thor and I appeared.

"*Velkomen!*" he called out. "*Kom hit!*"

I deduced from his gestures that he was trying to lure Thor to his side, so I gave the boy a little shove in the right direction. Grandfather insisted on filming Thor as he re-filled the emu feeder.

Now that we'd located at least a token contingent of emus, Grandfather's good humor had returned. In fact, everyone was in the best of spirits. Someone had arrived with an additional consignment of radios, which unlike our cell phones worked just fine in spite of the blackout. I snagged one for myself on general principles. Most of the volunteers headed off into the woods, armed with com-passes and GPS receivers and radios, to see if they could locate any more emus. A few stayed behind to make sure that any emu who left the feeding trough was trailed by a party of volunteers, with orders to follow them for an hour or two, get an idea of where the emus tended to hang out, and then capture their assigned birds and escort them back to the clearing. Meanwhile, Grandfather and the camera crew were having a glorious time filming the emus who were clustered around the feeding trough, pigging out on the latest supply of grain. Occasionally Thor would pipe up and identify one of the emus, or pretend to. Actually, I doubted he was pretending, partly because I'd figured out he was surprisingly literal-minded and partly because I didn't really think a kid his age would have heard of Edna St. Vincent Millay or William Jennings Bryan, much less named emus after them.

Eventually the new grain supply ran out, but the five emus who had stayed to the last seemed to have grown ac-customed to the presence of humans and continued to hang around in the part of the clearing across the river. One of them sat in the river as if to cool off and stared as if it found us vastly entertaining. Another plopped down in the dust and began preening its feathers with its beak, completely ignoring us. As for the other three—

"What are they doing, anyway?" Thor asked. "I've seen them do it a lot, but I have no idea why."

The three emus were standing in a rough triangle. One was just standing there, looking back and forth between the other two, who were strutting about, puffing out their chests, bobbing their necks up and down, and running rapidly from side to side. Every once in a while one of the active two would actually make a little dash at the other. Occasionally, the quiet emu would wave its neck around a little, but it seemed mostly content to watch the others preen and threaten. And one or more of them seemed to be making a low booming noise that carried to where we were.

"Aha! You're looking at a classic display of emu courtship behavior," Grandfather said.

"So those would be two guy emus fighting over the chick, then." Thor nodded sagely.

"Actually, those would be two hens fighting over the male," Grandfather said. "The female is dominant in emu mating behavior."

"So that one's the guy?" Thor asked, pointing to the least active of the three emus. "How can you tell?"

"They're very difficult to sex visually, at least at a distance, so I'm going by their behavior," Grandfather said.

"That explains a lot," Thor said. "Because I was pretty sure the one they're fighting over was John Stuart Mill. But I didn't want to say so in case Ms. Delia had gotten it wrong."

"I think Ms. Delia was probably quite a savvy ornithologist," I said.

Grandfather frowned and looked annoyed, as I'd intended.

We all hung around for quite a while watching the emus. Eventually the boys began showing signs that they ought to have taken an afternoon nap, so Michael whisked them away to rest before dinner.

"Which reminds me," Caroline said. "It's only two hours till sunset. Shouldn't we start rounding up some birds?"

"Good idea," Grandfather said.

That's when everything fell apart.

At Grandfather's command, the volunteers all donned heavy leather gloves and some of them crossed the stream and began trying to encircle the emus.

According to Grandfather's instructions, the approved method of capturing an emu was to corner the bird and grab it by its vestigial wings. Then you maneuvered until you were behind it, threw your arms around its body, hugged it to your chest, and frog-marched it into the door of the nearby trailer.

Cornering the birds proved easier said than done. There wasn't a fence or a wall or anything solid to corner them against—only the advancing line of volunteers, who tended to break and run when the emus charged them. Sir Arthur Conan Doyle and Zora Neale Hurston escaped from the encircling volunteers this way, by sheer intimidation. Hans Christian Andersen waited until the volunteer was about to grab him, then kicked him down and ran away. Frances Hodgson Burnett actually let a volunteer march her into one of the trailers, but as he was trying to shut the door she charged it, knocked him down, and ran off along the stream bed.

Only Edward Everett Horton, the smallest of the emus present, failed to escape, and I more than half suspected he allowed us to capture him because the other emus had been bullying him and keeping him away from the grain, and he was probably hoping he'd get first crack at the next delivery if he came with us.

Worse, about that time, teams began straggling back, reporting that their assigned emus had given them the slip, usually after leading them into thickets of brambles or down slopes so steep they couldn't climb up again.

"The damn thing kicked me down and then took off like a bat out of hell," one volunteer reported as Dad was bandaging some of his cuts. "Never seen a bird run that fast."

"Not your fault," I said. "They can sprint at thirty miles an hour." At least that's what Grandfather had been saying, with increasing irritation, as party after party returned emu-less.

Grandfather left Sherry the Valkyrie behind to wait for the stragglers and drive the truck with the empty horse trailer back to camp. The rest of us headed back to camp with the trailer carrying Edward Everett Horton. I hitched a ride in the Jeep with Dad, Grandfather, and Caroline, and for once I had no competition for my seat. The bodyguards seemed content to follow behind in a truck. Grandfather sat in the back, glaring out at the passing scenery and growling slightly whenever Caroline, who was driving, hit a bump. Dad tried to make conversation, but the only topic he could come up with was the long list of bumps, bruises, sprains, and lacerations he'd treated during the day, which didn't exactly cheer anyone up.

To my surprise, Thor arranged to drop his uncle's truck off at the repair shop and hitch a ride out to camp with some of the volunteers. Was he starting to like being part of the expedition? Or was he merely worried about Edward Everett Horton?

Grandfather's mood lifted a little as we watched the trailer unload our solitary emu into the pen.

"Well, it's a start," he said, in what I suspected was a deliberately bluff, confident tone.

"And we didn't do badly considering that we were initially given a bum steer on where the birds would be," I said.

"That's right!" The idea seemed to cheer him up. "And we'll do better tomorrow with our native guide. Isn't that so, Thor?"

He clapped Thor on the back with such hearty good humor that the kid staggered a bit.

"We'll let the emu settle in tonight, and get Clarence out here tomorrow to take a look at him."

"Clarence?" Thor repeated.

"Our regular zoo vet," Grandfather explained.

"Do you think there's something wrong with him?" Thor was frowning as if he suspected Grandfather of some evil intent toward the emu, like declaring him contagious and euthanizing him. I could have told him that Edward Everett Horton was perfectly safe, especially since, despite being the smallest of the emus, he'd managed to draw blood from two of his captors. Grandfather was a big fan of anything fierce, noisy, and dangerous.

"No, he seems to be in perfect health," Grandfather said. "But I like to make sure."

"Only a well emu visit, then," I said.

Thor seemed mollified. But still a little wary of Grandfather. I could tell Thor wasn't that keen on sitting at Grandfather's table in the mess tent, perhaps because Grandfather continued to give him unsolicited advice on his college plans and pelt him at intervals with odd bits of whatever Norse language he'd been speaking.

"Why does your grandfather keep talking to me in German?" Thor asked me in an undertone at one point when Grandfather had gone to get another helping of beef stew.

"It's not German," I said. "I'm pretty sure it's either Swedish or Norwegian. Possibly bits of both."

"Can you maybe tell him I'm not from Sweden?" Thor looked anxious. "I'd hate for him to ask me something important that I didn't understand because I don't speak the language."

"It would serve him right," I said. "But yes, I'll tell him. And I don't think you have to worry about him saying anything important in Swedish. He only knows a few words that he picked up when he was over there rescuing something."

Grandfather returned and beamed at us.

"*Korleis har du det?*" he said.

Thor flinched.

"Just what was it you were over in Sweden rescuing?" I asked. "Or was it Norway?"

"Norway, most recently," he said. "We were filming the *klappmyss*, the *brunbjørn*, the *fjellrev*, and of course the *trollflaggermus*."

"In English," I said. "Thor may have the blood of the Vikings in his veins, but Norwegian isn't my language."

"The hooded seal, the brown bear, the arctic fox, and Nathusius's pipistrelle," he said. "That last one's a bat. Not really endangered, but its habitat is threatened."

"No wolves?" I asked.

"And wolves, of course!" Grandfather exclaimed. "Astonishing animals, wolves."

As I hoped, he began talking about wolves, one of his favorite subjects, and one on which even I had to admit he could talk entertainingly for hours. Thor was probably safe from further harassment, as long as he refrained from arguing when Grandfather contended that most of the country's ills could be solved by the reintroduction of a proper number of wolves and other large predators.

I left him at it and went to check on the boys, who were fast asleep, their pajamas slightly askew, as if they'd been stuffed into them while already unconscious. Natalie hadn't even bothered with her own pajamas but lay sprawled in her tent like a discarded Halloween decoration.

And Michael, who had borne the brunt of the child care all day, had fallen asleep on his sleeping bag, with a textbook he had to read before classes began lying on his chest.

I knew I should follow their example. But I wasn't sleepy yet. And I wanted to find out if Stanley had learned anything. And check on Miss Annabel. And make sure Thor got home safely. And find out what Grandfather had planned for tomorrow. And make sure we had scheduled bodyguards for tonight and tomorrow. And—

"Meg?"

I had been standing halfway between our tent and the mess tent, undecided which way to go. I looked up to see Jim Williams standing nearby.

"I was wondering if I could talk to you about something," he said. "Just something I noticed today that worried me. I wanted someone else to know about it."

"Something you can't just tell Grandfather about?" I asked.

"It would distract him," Williams said. "You know how he gets when he's focused on a project. His passion and his laserlike focus are the biggest weapons in our arsenal."

I'd have been tempted to say his mulish stubbornness and tunnel vision, but maybe Williams was trying to be tactful.

"He might not want to listen to something unrelated to the emu project," Williams went on. "Or worse, he might listen and get so riled up that he'd switch gears in the middle of the roundup."

Clearly Williams was not only a veteran Brigade member but a close observer of Grandfather.

"No argument there," I said. "But why speak to me instead?"

"You have his ear," he said. "And you've got common sense, which is sometimes in short supply on these expeditions. Don't get me wrong," he added hastily. "You could go a long way before you'd find a group with as much heart and brain as Blake's Brigade. But good old practical common sense isn't our forte."

"Again, no argument," I said. "So what do you want me to use my common sense on?"

"This." He held out a small object.

I took the object, which appeared to be a small cylinder of rock, about an inch and a half in diameter and maybe four inches long. The ends were ragged, but the circumference oddly smooth, so much so that I suspected it was man-made. And it was actually two different kinds of rock, stuck together—one end was a pale blue-gray, the other white and crystalline, possibly quartz. If Rose Noire were here, she'd know. In fact, she'd probably whip out the mineral book she'd borrowed from the Riverton Library and tell me what both kinds of rock were and what they were good for, metaphysically speaking, but I could make nothing of it.

"My common sense is stumped," I said. "What is it, and why should it worry you?"

"It appears to be a small piece of the core you'd get from exploratory drilling," he said. "They use a round drill toughened up with diamonds so it cuts through pretty much anything it finds. Produces a round cylinder of rock just like this. I found this up near the emu ranch while I was looking for the birds. Someone's been taking core samples up there."

"Core samples?" I frowned down at the cylinder. "Is that bad? And why would someone be doing that up at Biscuit Mountain?"

"Sometimes they do it for environmental reasons," Williams said. "To test a site for contaminants. The most common reason is that someone's exploring for minerals. I've seen the process a couple of times when Dr. Blake got involved in protesting mining companies' plans to open mines in vulnerable natural areas. And neither reason's necessarily a terrible thing. They could have explored for minerals and found nothing. They might be doing environmental testing to compare Riverton with some other, less unspoiled area."

"Or someone could be planning to start an open-pit mine of some noxious carcinogenic substance," I said. "Or testing to see how far some ghastly chemical pollution has already spread. We need to figure out which."

"Precisely," he said.

"Without starting a noisy public fuss," I added. "Because that could derail the emu roundup."

"Not to mention letting the environmental bad guys know we're onto them." He was beaming at me. "You've got it."

"This core drilling—it's not brand-new technology, right?" I asked. "So we have no idea if this sample was taken last week or thirty years ago. Any possibility that this is last century's crisis?"

"It wasn't taken last week, for sure," he said. "There weren't any signs that someone had been up there recently—no tractor marks or serious trampling of the vegetation. But if you looked closely, you could see the signs where something had been going on. And I found this, too, nearby."

He held out a large monkey wrench.

"Maybe they're unrelated," he said. "But what are the odds someone would lose a nice, new monkey wrench out in the middle of the woods just two feet from where someone else was doing core drilling?"

"Slim." I turned the wrench over. Some rust was starting to form on it in a few spots, but for the most part it still looked new.

"No way that's been out there thirty years," he said. "Based on that, and the condition of the area around where

I found the rock sample, I'd say the drilling was done more than a month ago, but no more than seven or eight months."

"And we need to find out who did it," I said. "In a subtle, tactful, discreet way, which means we need to keep Grandfather out of it for the time being."

"See? I knew you were the right person to handle this. I'll leave it in your hands. I should head over to the mess tent. I'm on KP duty tonight."

He saluted—literally—and strode off.

I fingered the little rock cylinder. Such a small and apparently innocent little object. Could it have anything to do with my grandmother's murder?

I'd liked the little rock cylinder better before it was freighted with such possibly sinister meanings.

I tucked it into my pocket, stuck the monkey wrench just inside the tent, and went in search of Rose Noire and Stanley.

Chapter 18

Rose Noire's tent was still in a state of semi-collapse, so I checked to see if she was staying with Caroline. I found Caroline sitting in a chair by the steps to her caravan in a pool of light produced by a large LED camping lantern. Rose Noire was nowhere to be seen.

"Is Rose Noire inside studying her rock books?" I asked.

"She went off on an herb-gathering expedition," Caroline said.

"In the dark?"

"It's something that has to be picked by moonlight. Oh, by the way—here's that list of volunteers you wanted." She handed me a sheaf of papers. Then she kicked off her shoes and put her feet up on a battered green footlocker that was sitting a few feet in front of her chair. "Oof," she said, as she leaned back and closed her eyes.

"Has Grandfather been keeping you hopping?" I perched on the caravan steps beside her.

"No, but I've spent the last I don't know how long roaming through the camp cheering up the discouraged, calming down the overexcited, placating the quarrelsome—you know the drill."

"I do indeed." While Grandfather was brilliant at setting expeditions in motion, the job of keeping up the participants' morale fell to someone else. Usually Caroline, and occasionally me.

Caroline reached into the cooler at her elbow, took out two cold waters, handed me one, and opened the other for herself.

Sherry the Valkyrie strode up. Her French braid was still perfect, her shorts and blouse were free of wrinkles and sweat stains, and her long, tanned legs bore no scratches or bug bites. I allowed myself a few moments of profound resentment before tossing my negative feelings aside. If she could spend a day hunting for emus and still look that good, my hat was off to her. More likely, she'd spent most of the day here at camp, dealing with the kind of boring, practical tasks that made it possible for the rest of the brigade to frolic in the woods.

"New marching orders," she said, handing each of us a small sheaf of papers. "Including information on tick removal and dealing with possible poison ivy exposure."

I could have written such instructions in my sleep, and odds were Caroline had originally written these. But we both dutifully accepted our packets so Sherry could mark us off on her checklist.

"How's it going?" Caroline asked. "Nearly finished passing out the sheets, I see."

"Let me check," Sherry said.

She began counting something on her checklist.

Caroline closed her eyes briefly and sighed. Clearly she had been making conversation, not asking for a detailed progress report. Then she opened her eyes again, took a sip from her water bottle, and turned to me.

"Anything you want me to tell Rose Noire when she gets back?" she asked. "Assuming I'm even awake."

"Just tell her I found another interesting mineral for her to identify," I said.

Sherry looked up with a frown at that. Clearly she disapproved of anyone not giving full attention to the expedition's main mission. She pursed her lips and then focused back on her clipboard.

It was disconcerting having her hovering like that. I glanced at Caroline, who rolled her eyes.

"I'll tell Rose Noire about your mineral," Caroline said. "Tell me, what do you think of this?" She picked up something that had been in her lap and held it up for my inspection—a shapeless knitted wool object in a particularly vile shade of purplish brown. "Millicent made it. One of our volunteers."

"I think it looks like a giant mutant tea cozy," I said.

"Strange," she said. "Rose Noire had the same reaction, down to the little nose wrinkle of disgust at the words 'tea cozy.' Does your whole family have an unreasoning hatred of tea cozies?"

"Actually, yes," I said. "It goes back to when our cousin Sylvia was just learning how to knit. She made tea cozies for everyone in the family."

"What's wrong with that?"

"It meant for the next few years, whenever Sylvia came to tea, we all had to cover up our pretty teapots with her ghastly tea cozies. Sylvia's taste in color combinations is legendarily bad, and back then her knitting was even worse."

I glanced up to see that Sherry had pulled out her phone and was punching buttons on it. I caught a glimpse of what she was doing—using a calculator program.

"It's not a giant mutant tea cozy but an emu sweater." Caroline turned the knitted blob to a slightly different angle and held out a long knitted tube that emerged from one side of it. "That, apparently, is the neck."

"Isn't it at least twice as long as a normal emu's neck?" I asked

"It's supposed to be a turtleneck," she said. "This part folds down."

"Do the emus actually need sweaters," I asked. "They seem to be rather well insulated with feathers."

"I doubt it," she said. "And I wouldn't care to be the person trying to stuff one of the birds into this thing. Did you see some of the lacerations your father patched up? I told her to hold off on knitting any more until we see how this one fits. With any luck she'll see reason now that we've actually met the emus and got one in the pen and she can see how lively they are."

"I hope she listens," I said. "Though when I passed the campfire just a little while ago, there was someone sitting there, knitting up a storm."

"Probably Millicent," Caroline said with a sigh. "She told me she was working on the matching leggings."

"Eighty-nine percent compliance," Sherry announced.

Caroline and I both started, having forgotten that Sherry was still there, communing with her clipboard.

"That's eighty-nine so far," Sherry added. From the gleam in her eye I suspected one hundred percent compliance was not far off. She tucked her phone back into her pocket. Then her eyes fell on the emu sweater.

"That's even uglier than I expected," she said. "We're not really putting those on all the emus, are we?"

"I doubt we'll manage to get any of the emus to wear them," Caroline said. "But let's not hurt Millicent's feelings."

"Maybe someone should hurt her feelings," Sherry said. "Instead of letting her waste all that time—not to mention perfectly good yarn—on something that makes us all look ridiculous."

"The yarn won't go to waste," Caroline said. "Assuming the emus don't want the sweaters, I can donate them to a church group that knits for the homeless. They can unravel them and reuse the yarn."

Sherry didn't seem to find this thought calming.

"We've got people over there hooting like owls," she said, pointing vaguely to her left. "And some people over there who want us to declare the camp a clothing-optional zone."

"I think not," Caroline said. "We don't want to make the film crew's job any harder than it already is."

"You never know," I said. "Could do wonders for the ratings."

"That strange woman who looks like a refugee from Haight-Ashbury running around ordering people to move their tents and waving herbs at people."

"That would be my cousin, Rose Noire," I said. "And if you're not fond of the herbs, you might want to avoid drinking any tea she tries to serve you."

"And that creepy little Goth girl trailing after those destructive little brats like the wicked witch chasing Hansel and Gretel!"

"That's our babysitter," I said. "And if the brats are trying to destroy anything and she doesn't intervene, let Michael or me know and we'll deal with it."

Sherry seemed unembarrassed at having called my children brats.

"We're here on an important mission!" she exclaimed. "But how can you expect people to take us seriously when so many of us are complete flakes!"

She threw up her hands in dismay.

"Now, now," Caroline began.

But Sherry clearly wasn't in the mood to be now-nowed. She took a deep breath, smoothed down the sheets of paper on her clipboard, which might have been knocked ever so slightly askew when she threw up her hands, and strode off.

"They also serve who only stand and keep accurate records," I murmured.

"But they don't exactly endear themselves to the rest of the crew," Caroline said. "And that is why Sherry, in spite of her admirable efficiency, will never get the job she aspires to as Monty's right hand. No tolerance for the glorious diversity that is Blake's Brigade. You should have seen her face when I pulled up in the caravan."

I nodded, and kept to myself the fact that I could partly understand Sherry's point of view. After all, I'd done her job before, including the photo release drill. I didn't mind the group's colorful appearance and behavior. I only got annoyed when they did things that seemed deliberately aimed at making my job harder. Like the people who thought it was amusing to sign their photo releases under pseudonyms.

I reached into my tote and pulled out the list of camp residents Caroline had given me.

"You must not have warned Sherry to ask for a photo ID when she has people sign the photo release," I said. "What are the odds we really have both a James T. Kirk and a Leonard McCoy in the brigade?"

Caroline sighed.

"I'll have a word with her," she said. "She's only been with us for a year or so. A fast learner, but she's not onto all the tricks yet."

I found myself wondering if Sherry had merely been letting off steam, or if her brief rant was a clue that she was about to storm out of camp and swear off Grandfather's expeditions forever. On the one hand, I had been hoping someone would come along to take some of the organizational burden off of Caroline. Someone other than me. On the other, I wasn't sure I'd enjoy Camp Emu nearly as much if it was organized in the regimented fashion that would probably keep Sherry happy.

"If we all showed up in khaki uniforms with matching khaki tents and set them up in precise rows, and lined up in alphabetical order five minutes before every meal, Sherry still wouldn't be happy," Caroline said, echoing my thoughts.

"I'm not overfond of khaki," I said. "Just another name for beige."

Clearly Caroline wasn't a big Sherry fan, either. Well,

their next conversation could be the deciding moment. If Sherry didn't lose it upon discovering that two members of the brigade were impersonating officers from the starship *Enterprise,* she could probably handle anything. And if she went away in a huff, maybe it was a good thing.

Stanley wasn't in his trailer. Thor had left the mess tent and was nowhere to be found. I hoped he'd found a ride home. Grandfather and some of the film crew were gathered around a laptop watching some of the day's footage. Nearly all of the volunteers had been drooping over dinner and had disappeared soon after. The catering trucks had departed for the night. All was once more quiet in Camp Emu.

I strolled over to the emu holding pen and scanned it to see what Edward Everett Horton was up to. I finally spotted him just as I was about to send up an alarm that he'd escaped. He was lying on the ground with his legs tucked under his body, his long neck stretched out straight in front of him, and his head lying flat on the ground. I couldn't help thinking of some of the odd, uncomfortable-looking poses in which Jamie and Josh sometimes fell asleep, and made a mental note to ask Grandfather if Edward Everett Horton was the smallest of the emus because he wasn't full grown. And—

A slight flicker of light in the corner of my eye caught my attention. It appeared to be coming from the bushes between the emu pen and Miss Annabel's yard.

There it was again, a faint glowing light. A familiar, rather ghostly rectangular glow.

It was the glow from the screen of a cell phone.

I began to work my way around the perimeter of the pen, staying turned toward the emu, as if my attention was on him. When I was within ten feet of where I'd seen the cell phone light, I fished into my pocket for the tiny flashlight I kept there and aimed it at where I'd seen the glow.

"Thor," I said. "I thought you'd gone home. If you're actually getting a signal on that thing, can you let me use it for a few minutes?"

"Don't let anyone know I'm here!" he said. He was crouched in the middle of a thicket of thorny shrubs. His face was cross-hatched with scratches and dotted with fresh mosquito bites. "And I wasn't making a call. Just checking the time."

I turned the flashlight off and walked closer.

"And just why are you here?" I asked. "Lurking around the emu pen. Are you worried about Edward Everett Horton?"

"I'm not really lurking around the emu pen," he said. "I mean I am, but only because it's right behind Miss Annabel's house. I'm worried about her."

"Worried? Why?"

I sat down on the ground just outside his thicket and pretended to be gazing at the emus.

"Last fall everyone was stirred up about the emus and then Ms. Delia was killed," he said. "And now everyone's stirred up again and there was that poisoning—" He shrugged. "You probably think it's stupid."

"Not stupid at all," I said. "If it makes you feel any better, the private investigator who came with us is worried, too. He suggested that Miss Annabel get a security system installed, and I talked her into doing it."

"Good," he said. "And I can keep watch until she gets it."

"It could be days."

He hunched slightly as if to demonstrate his determination to stay put.

"Do your parents know where you are?" I asked.

"They know I'm out here at the camp," he said. "I told them that I wanted to be here to help out first thing tomorrow morning, and sort of implied that someone would lend me a cot."

The parent in me wanted to shoo him home. Better yet, to grab him by the scruff of the neck and frog-march him over to my car, like one of the emus, and drive him home.

But he wasn't a preschooler, like Josh and Jamie. He had to be seventeen or eighteen. He was going to college in a few months. And maybe if his instincts were correct—

"If you see something suspicious, do not rush in like an idiot," I said. "You make a lot of noise and run over to get help from the camp."

He nodded.

"And for heaven's sake, bring some mosquito repellant next time. Use some of this for now." I reached into my pocket and tossed him a little tin of Rose Noire's home-made organic bug repellent, chock full of citronella, lemon eucalyptus, cinnamon, cedar oil, and half a dozen other ingredients. "Drop by the first aid tent tomorrow and Dad can give you something for the itching."

"Thanks," he said.

"At the first hint of trouble," I intoned, shaking my finger at him.

He nodded and began slathering himself with Rose Noire's ointment.

I strolled back to the main part of camp.

Grandfather was sitting in the mess tent by himself, sipping from a Blake Foundation mug.

"Coffee, at this hour?" I didn't sit down, but I leaned against the table.

"Single malt Scotch," he said. "Macallan, to be precise. If I drink it in a glass, I get lectures about alcoholism and setting a bad example for youth. If I drink it in a mug, I get lectures about caffeine. I can't win."

"Drink it in a teacup," I said. "Everyone will assume you're having an herbal tisane to help you sleep."

"Good idea," he said. "Sipping tea at bedtime—is that something normal people do?"

"How would I know?" I said. "So what's on tap for tomorrow? Any strategies for rounding up the emus more efficiently."

"Tomorrow should go better," he said. "I've put out a call for my wranglers."

"Wranglers?" I echoed. "What do you mean, wranglers?"

He didn't explain—he never did—just tossed back the last swallow of his Scotch and stumped off to his trailer. He nodded goodnight to the guards occupying the lawn chairs on either side of the door—I recognized Jim Williams as one of them—and disappeared, presumably to sleep. I probably wasn't the only person in camp who went to bed wondering if the emu roundup was doomed to failure.

Or the only person less than thrilled when the wranglers arrived shortly before dawn.

Chapter 19

"Mommy, horsies!"

Josh was following the letter of the rule that he wasn't supposed to leave the tent before daylight without a grownup, but only just barely. At least half of him was hanging out the back flap of the tent.

"Mo-sickles!" Jamie exclaimed. Like his brother, he was leaning out of the tent so far that any second I expected him to topple over.

From the loud vrooming noise I could hear outside the tent, I assumed that Jamie had a better understanding of what was happening outside. Then I heard a definite whinny, and decided perhaps I needed to stick my head outside as well.

The field between our tent and the emu holding pen now held half-a-dozen horse trailers and at least a dozen motorcycles. The motorcycles weren't the large, heavily chromed kind you usually saw tooling down the highway—they were leaner, lighter, simpler looking. Dirt bikes rather than motorcycles. They were all parked in a row on the left side of the field, near the road, and the riders were gathered in little clusters, taking their helmets off and chatting. They were dressed not in scruffy leather and denim but in brightly colored racing outfits with lots of reflective silver on them, so that they looked a lot like the drivers I'd seen when we took the boys to see a car race several months ago.

At the other side of the field, several people were leading

horses out of their trailers, feeding and watering them, and saddling them. The horses didn't look thrilled at the occasional sound of motor revving from one of the motorcycles, but they weren't panicking either. I also saw Thor standing near one of the horse trailers, blinking sleepily. Good. Maybe if the equestrian part of our crew settled down that near to Miss Annabel's house tonight, Thor would trust their presence to keep her safe.

"So that's what your Grandfather meant when he said he was calling in the wranglers." Michael was at my side, peering out at the new arrivals, and holding onto Jamie's pajama top to keep him from falling into a nearby puddle.

Michael and I hurriedly dressed ourselves and the twins. He collected Natalie from her neighboring tent and they took the boys off to enjoy the twin attractions of horsies and mo-sickles. I heard Grandfather's booming voice from over in the dining tent, so I headed that way to see what I could learn.

"Excellent!" He was beaming with delight as he waved around a mug of coffee—this time I could see that it actually was coffee, and unlikely to contain any dangerous additives because Grandfather wasn't a big fan of diluting alcohol with anything. "I wasn't expecting to get both the horses and the bikes on such short notice."

"Well, we knew you might be needing us," said the leader of the bikers—who, to my surprise, was Clarence Rutledge, Caerphilly's holistic biker vet. I wasn't surprised to see him at the rescue, of course—Clarence was a sucker for any animal in trouble, and had been known to foster litters of abandoned puppies or kittens so young that they needed hourly feeding with an eyedropper. But I was surprised that he wore the same sporty racing outfit as all the other bikers. His had to be at least a size XXXL. At six five, he was an inch taller than Michael, and considerably wider, and I'd never before seen him out of his faded leather and denim biker gear—in the office he merely topped them off with a lab coat the size of a small tent.

These days, Clarence was the only vet we trusted with Spike, the Small Evil One. Of course, it helped that he was the only vet we knew who didn't pretend to be completely booked for six weeks when Spike needed tending.

He and Grandfather quickly fell into a discussion of the optimum dosage for the tranquilizer darts they planned to use, if necessary, to capture the emus. I could see Sherry lurking nearby, waiting for a lull in the conversation to thrust a photo release into Clarence's hands.

When they moved on to the enthralling topic of whether the emus were likely to need deworming, I decided to leave them to it. I headed for the chow line to fortify myself for the day. I suspected that the quality and quantity of food served in the mess tent on Grandfather's expeditions was one of the main reasons he never seemed to have trouble recruiting volunteers. I dithered between the fresh-squeezed orange juice and the organic cranapple juice before settling for small glasses of each, and then I filled my plate with scrambled eggs, bacon, sausage, hash browns, and whole wheat toast. After all, we might not have much time for lunch once the roundup began.

Even apart from the wranglers, our numbers had grown this morning, and I recognized some of the newcomers as people I'd seen in town. Evidently, interest in our work was rising among the inhabitants of Riverton. Or maybe the emu roundup sounded like more fun than anything else they could do with the power still out all over town. Or maybe they were just eager for the hot breakfasts the catering trucks were serving up to all comers. Whatever the locals' reasons, Sherry was busily circulating among them with her clipboard.

Since the only other important task I had in my notebook was to do more research at the library, which wasn't happening until the power came back, I decided to tag along and see how well the wranglers worked out. The boys were too excited about the horses and bikes to eat, so I raided the breakfast line for a large to-go package. Odds were they'd realize how hungry they were about halfway out to Pudding Mountain.

No emus were visible when we arrived at Thor's emu feeding station—if any had been breakfasting there, I'm sure the roar of the choppers would have sent them fleeing. We filled the little clearing and spilled over into the nearby woods.

Caroline got someone to give her a boost up onto the hood of her truck and began shouting out orders with a battery-powered megaphone. Dad had opened up the back of Grandfather's Jeep and was setting up his small field medical station in the cargo area.

Grandfather was standing in the middle of the clearing, staring up into the sky with binoculars. I strolled over to stand beside him.

"I'd have assumed up was the one direction we didn't need to be scoping out," I said. "Unless you think these emus have evolved here in the wild and regained the power of flight."

"Not very likely," he said. "Their wings are less than a foot long—no way they could fly. The Andean condor weighs only half of what an emu does, and they need a wingspan of eight to ten feet to fly with. So extrapolating from that, unless the emus developed a wingspan of—"

"I was kidding about the flying emus, you know," I said. "But I did wonder why you're staring up at the sky with your binoculars?"

"Looking for our air support," he said. "Aha! Here they come."

A large, rainbow-striped hot air balloon drifted into

view. Grandfather waved vigorously at it. I could see tiny hands waving back from the balloon's gondola.

"So they're going to drift around, hoping to spot the emus through the trees?" I asked.

"They're going to drift around using thermal imaging cameras to pinpoint the locations of the emus," he said. "And when they do, they can radio the birds' positions back to us. Caroline will be liaising with the horses, and your Dad with the bikers. They're all carrying radios."

I wanted to ask how the balloonists were going to tell the emus from other thermal images on their scopes, such as deer, wild turkeys, and random human hikers. Probably best not to sound a discouraging note.

For a while, the bikers and riders milled about while the balloon drifted around and radioed back reports to Grandfather. After forty-five minutes or so, Grandfather let out a whoop.

"Emu sighting! Emu sighting!"

The bikers and riders flipped a coin and the bikers won. They donned their helmets, and a couple of them pulled out GPS machines and entered the reported coordinates of the emus. Then they all sped off into the woods.

Ten minutes later the balloon reported another sighting, and the equestrians galloped off in a slightly different direction.

Doubtless everything was very lively for bike and horse riders, and even more for the film crews that were scrambling to keep up with them. But back here in the clearing with nothing to watch but Grandfather, Dad, and Caroline talking on their radios—and the ever-present volunteer guards hovering—the level of excitement dropped considerably. More of the locals began drifting away. The boys were getting restless, and after three games of Uno, they began to ask if they could go for another ride in Caroline's caravan.

"I have an idea," Michael said. "Everybody into the van!"

I didn't ask what his idea was. I wasn't even sure he had one. Maybe he was just getting us into motion and planning to think of an idea on the fly. I'd been known to do that when dealing with cranky, bored toddlers.

But he definitely had a plan today. We took off down one of the faint dirt tracks that led out of the clearing and, after several minutes of rough uphill driving, we pulled into another small clearing.

"Our official emu observation tower!" he exclaimed.

It was actually a fire lookout tower. Either it had been abandoned or the danger of fire wasn't high enough today to be worth staffing it. It looked sturdy enough, its metal was unrusted, and it was at least forty feet high and at the top of a sizable hill. We were at the foot of a steep gravel track leading up to it.

"Castle!" Jamie exclaimed.

"Space ship!" Josh countered.

"I talked to one of the forest rangers yesterday," Michael said as he downshifted and steered the Twinmobile toward the gravel road. "He said hikers are welcome to use it as long as it's unmanned. And this particular tower has an excellent view of today's search area."

"I'm glad someone has talked to the rangers," I said. "I've been worried that Grandfather might be barging in with the bikes and horses and balloons without clearing any of it with them."

"He would have," Michael said. "But Caroline had the same worry and contacted the local ranger station."

"Caroline is a wonder."

"And found that the park rangers were already aware of our mission and enthusiastic about getting rid of their unwanted ratite guests," he went on. "Miss Annabel had already called to arrange everything."

"Miss Annabel is also growing on me," I said. "If she'd just break down and talk about Cordelia—"

"Give it time," he said.

I nodded. I realized I felt guilty about Annabel. More than once since learning about my grandmother's death, I found myself wondering how different things would be if Annabel had been the one killed in the generator explosion. If I'd actually gotten to meet my grandmother. As I got to know Miss Annabel, and even to like her, in spite of her difficult and prickly personality, I was thinking that less. But still, I felt guilty that I'd thought it at all. Did it mean that subconsciously I was blaming Annabel for being alive? And wouldn't it make more sense to blame my grandfather for waiting so long before hiring Stanley? Or even blame Cordelia herself for not getting in touch for more than half a century?

Water under the bridge. Annabel might be a little eccentric, but she was intelligent, sensible, and admirably efficient. Maybe instead of regretting my lost chance of meeting Cordelia, I should focus on appreciating the cousin I had left. Not just as a doorway to Cordelia, but for her own sake.

In fact, at the moment I liked Annabel a lot better than the elusive Cordelia.

I was startled out of my reveries. The van had stopped. The boys erupted out of their car seats and dashed toward the tower.

"Hey!" Michael called as he ran after them. "Last one to the top of the tower is a rotten egg!"

Michael supervised the boys' scramble up the stairway to the tower while Natalie and I, resigned to rotten egg status, followed more slowly with the picnic provisions and mats for the boys to nap on later.

At the top of what felt like several hundred flights of stairs we entered the cabin atop the tower through a trapdoor in the floor. The cabin was only about ten feet square, but that was plenty of room for the five of us. And the windows were low enough for the boys to see through, but not so low that I'd worry about them falling out.

"Look!" Michael pointed. "You can see the balloon!"

He handed the boys their binoculars. Josh and Jamie alternated between waving at the balloon and watching it for a few minutes, while Natalie and I passed out fruit and juice boxes. Michael appeared to be scanning the hillsides below us, and I was pleased to see that there were stretches of meadow as well as woods, so we might actually see something after all. I even saw some of the horseback wranglers trotting through a clearing on the side of the next hill over, and closer at hand, we could not only see but hear a posse of bikers buzzing along a meadow. And what was that ahead of the bikers?

"Look!" Michael called. "The bikers have found some emus!"

We watched for the next several hours as both the crews of wranglers chased emus, cornered emus, and very occasionally captured them. The balloon drifted to and fro overhead, usually able to find a contrary breeze, but never quite managing to get into a useful position when there was actual spotting to be done. Eventually our tower became the expedition's main emu-spotting post, to the boys' great delight.

Toward the late afternoon, when it became obvious from the boys' steadily increasing crankiness that they were in dire need of naps that weren't going to happen here in the tower, Michael and I packed them into the Twinmobile.

"You stay here and keep spotting," Michael said, over the shrieks of agony and outrage from the boys. "I'll help Natalie put them down for their naps, and then she can watch them while I do a little more prep for my summer classes."

"Sounds good to me."

Still, I was relieved—though not surprised—when Caroline radioed to tell me that by the time they had passed her, the boys had already been asleep in their car seats.

It was a long day, but a more successful one. The horse wranglers captured three emus, while the bike wranglers managed four. Around six o'clock, Grandfather called a halt so we could transport the emus we'd already captured back well before dark. And while sunset wasn't for another two and a half hours, it had started getting dark in the long valleys on the eastern side of Pudding Mountain.

When we arrived at camp, the wranglers managed a smooth transfer of the emus into the holding pen. Grandfather and Clarence banded the birds for identification purposes and Thor provisionally identified them by name.

"Of course, Ms. Delia would have known for sure," he said, with a sigh. "She was amazing."

Grandfather harrumphed at that.

"But I'm pretty sure we have Edwin Way Teale, Claire Boothe Luce, Lucy Maud Montgomery, John Quincy Adams, John Wilkes Booth, Howard Phillips Lovecraft, and Agnes de Mille." He pointed out the emus in question, and Caroline noted the names next to their banding numbers.

"This is helpful," Caroline said. "Of course, I'm not sure how we'll ever tell when we've got them all."

"She had an inventory of all the birds," Thor said.

"Who?" Grandfather snapped to attention.

"Ms. Delia," Thor said. "I suppose it's possible that Miss Annabel still has her inventory. You'd only be missing the data on chicks born since her death, and they'd probably still be hanging with their parents a lot."

Grandfather frowned. He looked at the holding pen, with its pitiful flock of emus. Then he stared at me.

"Meg," he said. "You get on with the old lady. Get me that inventory."

"Do I hear a magic word?" I asked.

"Hmph!" he said, and stalked off.

"Just for that you're going to have to wait till after dinner," I called after him.

I only said it to be contrary, but as soon as the words were out of my mouth I realized how tired I was. Badgering Miss Annabel could wait. I headed back to the tent. Michael was outside in a folding canvas chair reading his textbook and making notes.

"They're asleep," he stage whispered.

I peeked in to see Josh and Jamie sprawled on the air mattresses in our tent, dead to the world.

I claimed the other folding canvas chair and plopped in it. I intended to take out my notebook and find something useful I could do, but apparently I dozed off, because the next thing I knew, Michael was shaking my shoulder.

"Someone here to see you," he said. And then he ducked into the tent.

It was Anne Murphy, the librarian.

"I went up to D.C. today," she said. "Did some research on that question you asked me about."

"Please don't tell me you went all that way just to do research for me," I said.

"I didn't," she said. "I went all that way to spend the day in air conditioning. I just used your research as an excuse."

"Then I'm delighted to have given you an excuse," I said.

"And I may have found something interesting," she said.

I sat up straighter in my lawn chair. Anne sat down in the chair Michael had vacated, donned a pair of reading glasses, and took a sheaf of papers from her tote bag.

"Are you familiar with an expedition your grandfather

undertook about two years ago to the southwest tip of Virginia?" she asked. "When he stopped a company from building a mine that would have destroyed the habitat of a very rare and newly discovered toad?"

"The Toad Wars," I said. "That's what the brigade members call it. I didn't go along on that one, but I've heard about it."

"The company that was trying to build the mine was called Amazonite Unlimited." She glanced down at the papers in her hand. "A name that would lead you to believe that they were planning to dig up amazonite—a green-colored form of feldspar whose main commercial use is in making inexpensive jewelry."

She looked over the top of her reading glasses at me as if this was a cue.

"But since they put up a hell of a fight to keep Grandfather from derailing their plans, I assume they were planning to mine something a lot more lucrative than amazonite," I said.

"Exactly," she said. "They were planning on extracting natural gas using hydraulic fracturing—better known as fracking, of course."

"Aha," I said. "Grandfather's not very keen on fracking."

"Many people aren't," she said. "It's controversial, but potentially quite lucrative for the company that's doing it. And while your grandfather wasn't alone in his opposition to what Amazonite Unlimited was going to do, he was their most visible opponent. Instrumental in uncovering and publicizing their plans and organizing the opposition that helped stop them."

"So Amazonite Unlimited wouldn't be terribly fond of Grandfather," I said.

"Amazonite Unlimited no longer exists," Anne said. "And its owners lost a pretty penny on the project."

"So they blame Grandfather for going broke," I said.

"They're not just broke," Anne said. "They're so deep in debt they may never dig their way out, and on top of that they're getting sued right and left by people they promised the moon to when they were trying to get their fracking operation set up. So no, I don't think they're very fond of your Grandfather right now. Caroline Willner told me that Dr. Blake has been getting death threats lately."

"He always gets death threats," I said. "He has a knack for rubbing people the wrong way."

"More death threats than usual, according to Caroline," Anne said. "And I wouldn't be surprised to find out that the owners of Amazonite Unlimited were responsible for the uptick."

"And do any of those owners live here?" I asked.

"Amazonite Unlimited was a wholly owned subsidiary of a company called Smedlock Mining," she said. "And—"

"Theo Weaver is on their board of directors," I finished for her.

"Yes." She nodded.

"Which means Theo Weaver would have a reason to hate Grandfather," I said. "And I can understand why. To listen to Grandfather, you'd think mining was up there with the seven deadly sins. But we need minerals. Even Rose Noire's healing crystals have to be mined somewhere. As long as mine owners do everything they can to protect the environment—"

"You're talking about responsible mine owners," Anne said. "Not the Smedlocks. I've done the research. This is a company that would be solvent and maybe even thriving if they'd made a reasonable investment in pollution controls and worker safety. I found an article that quotes one of them as saying that the EPA fines and court judgments are about to bankrupt them, and he's probably right, but they earned each and every one of those fines and judgments. Not that they've paid most of the fines and judgments. They'd rather spend the money on fast cars and such."

"And one of their allies lives right here in Riverton."

We both fell silent as I pondered the implications.

"Of course, it might be just a coincidence," she said.

"I'm not a big believer in coincidences," I said. "We should tell Chief Heedles about this."

"I agree," she said. "I'm going to drop by the station and try to see her. If you run into her first, fill her in, will you?"

"Roger."

"I should be going," she said. "I need to feed the dogs."

We both pried ourselves out of our lawn chairs and shook hands.

"Thank you," I said.

"Just look after that grandfather of yours."

She trotted off. I pondered her information. And then I stuck my head inside the tent. Michael was curled up with the boys, reading his textbook.

"I'm going to go over to see Miss Annabel for a few minutes," I whispered. "I'll be back in time for dinner."

He nodded and blew me a kiss.

I hurried through the camp. It was a lot more crowded than it had been earlier, and there was a big crowd around the fence. By this time I recognized most of the volunteers, even if I didn't know their names, and these were not familiar faces.

I spotted Jim Williams by the fence and went over to ask him what was going on.

"Your grandfather invited the whole town to dinner," Williams said.

"Oh, great," I said. "If whoever tried to poison him wasn't already in camp, I'm sure they'll show up for this."

Williams shook his head as if he understood my sense of frustration.

I thought Miss Annabel and I were probably on good

enough terms that I could have knocked on her kitchen door, but given the presence of so many possible onlookers from town, I decided to keep things formal and go around to the front door.

She opened it before I had finished climbing the porch steps.

"What's he up to now?" she asked. "Your grandfather, that is. I assume that mob is his doing."

"Cookout for the locals," I said.

"So he can show off the fact that he caught a few emus?"

I nodded.

"Hmph!" She sounded remarkably like Grandfather when she snorted like that. I suspected she wouldn't appreciate it if I told her that. "Well, what can I do for you?"

"Anne Murphy from the library came up with an interesting bit of information about Theo Weaver," I said. "Interesting and potentially useful, and I thought I'd share it."

I brought her up to speed on the Toad Wars expedition and Weaver's connection with Grandfather's vanquished opponents.

"Interesting," she said. "But I'm not sure I see how useful it is. There's no connection between Cordelia and this Toad War thing."

"No, it's not useful for solving Cordelia's murder," I said. "And incidentally, the police chief agrees with you that it was murder."

"Excellent!" she said. "I was hoping you'd win her over."

"I didn't have to—oh, never mind." I could relate my conversation with Chief Heedles some other time, when I was less tired. "As I said, it's not useful for solving Cordelia's murder. But it does give Weaver a very plausible motive for wanting to poison my grandfather—and that gives the chief a valid reason to investigate him."

"You think once she starts investigating she'll figure out he killed Cordelia?" Annabel said.

"It's possible," I said. "Also possible that he could end up serving time for the poisoning."

"True," she said. "Although not necessarily very much time. Attempted murder's a class three felony. Carries a penalty of five to twenty years under the Virginia penal code. Daddy and Granddaddy were both judges," she added, seeing my surprised look. "So Cordelia and I grew up knowing things like that."

"You sound like Dad," I said. "Although he gets his information mainly from reading mysteries."

"The recreation of intelligent minds," Annabel said, nodding with approval. "Daddy and Granddaddy were also big readers of mysteries, and Cordelia and I grew up on Nancy Drew and the Hardy Boys."

"You really must meet Dad," I said. "You have so much in common."

"In good time." She stiffened slightly as she said it, as if the idea still unnerved her. "Meanwhile, what are we going to do with this information about Weaver?"

"You mean, apart from giving it to Chief Heedles?" I asked.

"Hmph!" She snorted again, sounding so much like Grandfather that I had to smile.

"Look, I realize if he's convicted of the attempted murder, he won't serve as much time as you think he deserves," I said. "But at least he'd do some time," I went on. "And wouldn't even five years without a man you believe to be a killer living next door be a good thing?"

"It would," she said. "And maybe it would make the chief understand that he's not some harmless old friend of her daddy's. Who knows what might come out if she felt she had grounds to do a really thorough investigation of him?"

"That's the spirit," I said. "And maybe we can help her

out. Can you think of any connection between Cordelia and Smedlock Mining?"

She frowned and appeared to be concentrating. I waited in silence. Well, at least until my stomach growled, which appeared to break her concentration.

"I'm keeping you from your dinner," she said. "And no, I can't think of any connection. But I'll keep thinking. And I'll look through her papers."

"Good," I said. "Oh, Thor told Grandfather that Cordelia had a list of all the emus. Any chance you might still have it?"

She frowned, and I realized that mentioning Grandfather might have been a tactical error.

"Thor's worried that Grandfather will get bored and go home before we find all the emus," I added. "He figures if we have a list, Grandfather will have a harder time getting away with that."

That worked as I hoped.

"The old rascal," she said. "Yes, Cordelia had a list. I'm sure I have it somewhere. I'll look for it tonight."

As I headed back to camp, I realized that I'd enjoyed talking to Annabel and was looking forward to coming back to see what thoughts she'd had. Our relationship was becoming less weighed down by all the baggage I knew I carried about Cordelia. It wasn't Annabel's fault her cousin had kept us at a distance. I found myself imagining that perhaps Annabel had tried to talk Cordelia into contacting us. "They're your family, for heaven's sake!" she might have said. "At least go and talk to them."

Maybe I'd never know. Or maybe I was getting closer to finding out.

When I got back to the camp, the boys greeted me with delight.

"Mommy, the horses are going to fight the mo sickles!" Jamie exclaimed.

"No, they're going to race the mo sickles," Josh corrected.

Neither sounded very plausible, so I looked up at Michael, Caroline, and Natalie for enlightenment.

"Apparently the rivalry's running high between the horseback wranglers and the motorcycle wranglers," Caroline said. "One side has challenged the other to a friendly jousting match."

"A friendly jousting match?" Natalie echoed. "Just how are they going to pull that off? Isn't the whole point of jousting that the knights line up on the opposite sides of a field and then run at each other at top speed carrying long sharp pointy objects?"

"They're probably doing it the same way they do at Renaissance Faires," I said. "They aim the long sharp pointy objects at targets instead of each other. It's a test of hand/eye coordination and horsemanship."

"Or in this case, bikemanship," Caroline added.

"Sounds like fun," Michael said. "But you do realize that if we let the boys watch this, they will be jousting on their tricycles all summer, right?"

Natalie moaned slightly.

"We can make them padded armor," I said. "And lances with a lot of padding on the end. And Dad says he's very pleased with Gridwell."

"Gridwell?" Michael looked puzzled. "What's that?"

"The new ER doc," I said.

"Ah," Michael said. "Haven't met him yet."

"The summer is still young," I replied. "Let's go eat before the carnage starts."

Chapter 20

The cookout was a big hit. Those parts of the field not already filled with our campground and the emu pen were now packed with the cars and trucks of the townspeople, and volunteers were circulating with platters of hot dogs, hamburgers, and mushroom burgers. I wasn't sure whether to be relieved that so few people were worried about being poisoned or terrified at how many more potential poisoners Grandfather had invited into camp.

Then I heard Caroline's voice over the portable megaphone, ordering people to clear the roadway for the jousting. Michael and I grabbed the boys and climbed on to the roof of the Twinmobile, which was parked in a strategic location, right by the road and just outside camp—perfect for watching the joust. Caroline and Grandfather and the bodyguards were sitting in lawn chairs on the bed of a truck next door to us, and the entire length of the dirt road was lined with cars, trucks, vans, SUVs, and people, standing, sitting in lawn chairs, or reclining on blankets.

In the middle of the road were three gallowslike contraptions, each holding a ring at the end of a long string. The rings were about two inches in diameter and looked even tinier when suspended from the tall stands. Tiny and very hard to see—there was a reason that jousting was usually a daytime sport.

But tonight was an exception, because while the jousting crew were rigging the targets, the film crew had set up giant banks of lights to illuminate the course. Soon each of the rings swayed gently in its own pool of light, rendering them improbable rather than downright impossible targets.

Caroline, who had been watching the efforts of both crews, pulled out the portable battery-powered megaphone.

"Welcome, lords and ladies, to this contest. Sir Clarence of Rutledge, leader of the Knights of the Iron Horse, has challenged the Knights of the Silver Spear, led by Lady Joni of Langevoort, to a jousting competition."

The half-dozen horse wranglers who were representing their team in the joust had dressed up themselves and their horses in medieval garb, with pennants on their lances. The six motorcycle wranglers would have looked rather bland in their modern gear if they hadn't stolen the show by having their more utilitarian helmets decked with emu feathers. Presumably feathers they'd picked up while tracking the birds, since I couldn't imagine Sir Clarence of Rutledge allowing the ones in his charge to be plucked naked for a mere joust.

I was glad no one had drafted me to keep score—it was all I could do to keep Jamie from falling off the roof of the Twinmobile, so excited was he by the joust. Nearby, Michael was holding onto Josh. In keeping with their long-standing policy of always doing everything by opposites, Jamie was cheering for horse riders while Josh backed the motorcyclists. After several rounds, the competition was down to Sir Clarence and Lady Joni, the two team captains, and Michael and I rearranged our seating so we had poor Natalie between us, to help serve as a buffer in case the conclusion of the joust provoked hostilities between the two boys.

Lady Joni launched her spirited gray horse into motion and scored one ring . . . two rings . . .

"No!" Jamie wailed. Lady Joni had missed the final ring.

Clarence pulled into position at the starting line. It was

all up to him. If he made a perfect run, the bikers would win. If he missed two rings, the horse riders would win. If he missed one, the two teams would be tied. What would happen then? A runoff—or did one call it a joust off?

No time to ask anyone. Clarence fiddled briefly with his helmet and the crowd fell silent as he prepared to make his run.

In the sudden hush, I heard a burst of barking from the dog pen. Spike, barking at the emus again. Or perhaps *still* was more accurate—maybe he'd been barking all the time and we just hadn't heard it for the crowd.

Wait—it wasn't just Spike barking. I heard Tinkerbell's deep bass woofs as well.

I saw Clarence take off out of the corner of my eye. I was peering toward the emu pen.

Whose gate was hanging open. Spike and Tinkerbell were barking furiously and throwing themselves against the fence in their pen while the emus jostled each other in their haste to leave the main enclosure.

As Clarence snagged the first ring I jumped up and leaped down from the roof of our van into the truck bed next door.

"That's two!" Caroline shouted through the megaphone, as Clarence speared the second ring. "And—"

I grabbed the megaphone.

"The emus are escaping!" I shouted. "The emus are loose!"

Chapter 21

Maybe I should have waited a second or two, instead of startling Clarence and making him miss the third ring. But he didn't falter—he just threw his lance aside, braked his bike, pulled it around until he was heading in the opposite direction, and gunned it toward the emu pen.

By now all the emus were out of the pen and heading off in several directions.

Two of them headed left, toward the main part of the camp. Another two turned right, as if aiming for the road that led out of the field and back toward town. The remaining three emus were running straight ahead, toward Miss Annabel's backyard.

Wait—that only made seven emus. We'd caught eight.

The horse and bike wranglers had all scrambled onto their mounts and were racing in various directions after whichever emus they thought they could catch. Some of the townspeople were sheltering in place, in or under their vehicles, but more than a few were starting up their engines and giving chase in their trucks and SUVs.

Caroline had grabbed back her megaphone and was trying to issue orders, but between the people shouting and shrieking in terror and those who were shouting and shrieking with the excitement of the chase, she wasn't making much progress in organizing things.

"Go emus!" Josh was shouting from the roof of our van. Jamie had buried his head in Michael's chest and was sobbing uncontrollably. Michael looked calm, so Jamie wasn't hurt. Probably only upset that the emus were leaving.

"It's okay," I heard Michael say in a break in the noise. "Great-grandpa will bring them back."

I glanced over to see that Grandfather was actually still in the bed of the truck, cursing his bodyguards, who were blocking the tailgate to keep him from getting down. At least he had enough sense not to jump unaided over the side of the truck bed, although I hoped they were keeping an eye out in case the excitement overcame him.

I finally figured out what had happened to the eighth emu. He—I was pretty sure it was Edward Everett Horton—was crouching in the corner of the pen near the dogs, as if for protection. I reached up and pointed that out to Michael, so he could show Jamie that one emu, at least, wasn't deserting us.

As I watched, one of the emus who had run toward camp became tangled up in a loose rope and brought the whole mess tent down on itself. The other one flailed around on top of its fallen comrade for a while, then turned around and headed back toward the pen, pursued by the entire KP crew, waving dish towels and dirty platters.

The horses and motorcycles were concentrating on the two emus who had headed in the other direction. They had left the main road now and were running around, between and sometimes over the vehicles parked at the far end of the field.

The emus who had fled into Miss Annabel's yard had apparently been stymied by her tall iron fence. One of them was hurling himself against it repeatedly, with no success, while the other two were running up and down on either side of him, looking for an opening and trampling all the orange day lilies underfoot.

"Look!" I tugged on Caroline's sleeve. "Miss Annabel's fence is holding. They can corner them there."

I wasn't sure she heard me but she followed my pointing finger, nodded, and began bellowing instructions to the troops. Eventually they all caught on. The KP crew were the first to chase their emu in the right direction, so now there were four emus trampling Miss Annabel's flower beds. Another crew of at least a dozen volunteers was trying to pick up the mess tent with the emu still wrapped inside it so they could carry it to the holding pen.

The remaining two emus had been thwarted in their attempt to reach the woods beyond the parking lot and were milling about on or near the roadway, surrounded by a large circle of horses, motorcycles, trucks, and eager volunteers on foot. I hoped the volunteers didn't get complacent. Just because the emus were surrounded at the moment didn't mean they were caught. Getting them back into the pen was going to be a tricky job. And—

Just then a small black-and-white form trotted out into the open area around the emus. It was Lad, Seth Early's border collie.

The townspeople and some of the volunteers laughed, but a few of them had met Lad and seen him work his magic on sheep, goats, cows, pigs, llamas, and even small children. They shouted to the others to keep the circle going and see what Lad could do.

Lad trotted until he was a few yards from the emus, then he flopped down on his belly and began creeping toward them, giving them what border collie trainers called *the Eye*. It was supposed to hypnotize sheep. I'm not sure the emus were hypnotized, but clearly they had never seen anything like it and they seemed to be watching him curiously.

"Go, Lad!" Jamie shouted. He was wiping away tears with his fists and snuffling into the handkerchief Michael was holding to his nose.

"Go, emus," Josh countered, looking as if he might take his turn at crying any second.

A silence fell over the crowd as Lad alternately crept

and ran, barked and stared. He eventually worked his way behind the emus and set them in motion toward the pen, running back and forth and nipping at the heels of any would-be escapee. Occasionally one of the emus would attempt to slash at him with its talons, but Lad seemed to sense when this was about to happen and leaped away so deftly that they never came close to touching him.

Everyone breathed a sigh of relief when the two emus trotted back into the pen. Everyone except Lad, of course, who waited with visible impatience until one of the volunteers had shut the gate securely, and then bounded toward Miss Annabel's yard to work his magic on the four emus there.

"Lad saves the day," Michael said.

"And Spike and Tinkie," Jamie added.

"Yes, if they hadn't barked, we would never have noticed that the emus were escaping," I said. "Extra treats for all the dogs tonight."

We watched until Lad and the volunteers had successfully herded the remaining four emus into the pen, then went down to praise and reward the dogs.

We couldn't possibly have gotten near Lad, who was the center of an immense crowd of admirers. He sat at Seth Early's feet, graciously accepting pats and seemingly indifferent to the fact that Seth prevented people from offering him treats. You had to know Lad to read the signs that he wasn't just gazing at the crowd with friendly interest, but studying us, all the better to figure out how and where he'd herd us if his master suddenly noticed how disorganized we humans were and gave him the go-ahead to deal with us.

Spike and Tinkerbell were more than happy to absorb any treats that happened to fall their way. I could tell from Spike's self-important strutting that he considered the return of the emus a personal triumph.

The festivities were slowly breaking up. A lot of people were gathered around the emu pen, watching as Clarence examined the emus, particularly the one who had been trapped in the mess tent, to make sure none had suffered any injuries during their escape attempt. The kitchen crew had hauled the mess tent back to its site and were attempting to untangle it and set it up so it would be ready for breakfast. Here and there small clumps of people, a mixture of volunteers and townspeople, were discussing the joust or the emu chase. But everyone was slowly drifting away, the volunteers to their tents and trailers, the townspeople to their cars.

Michael and Natalie took the boys over to the mess tent area, in the hope of begging a bedtime snack. I fetched food and water for Spike and Tinkerbell, since we'd decided to let them roam the emu pen overnight. They seemed happy there, and the emus seem to like them, particularly Edward Everett Horton. Maybe the dogs would sound an alarm if an intruder approached the emus—or Miss Annabel's backyard. As a team, they actually were pretty good security. A year or so ago, when the human occupants of our house were all over at Mother and Dad's farm for a party, a hapless burglar had tried to break in. He'd heard Spike barking and decided not to worry about a dog that small and yappy, but it was another story when Tinkerbell suddenly loomed out of the darkness, knocked him down, and sat on him for the next six hours.

Maybe instead of the emu pen I should put them in Grandfather's trailer for the night. We'd been so busy catching the emus that no one had had much time to question how they'd escaped. Had someone turned them loose to create a diversion? And if so, had his plans failed, or was he still planning something against Grandfather?

I leaned against the fence and gazed at Miss Annabel's house. I wondered if she'd been watching the joust through her binoculars. There was only one light on at her house, and that in an upstairs room. She was probably almost ready for bed.

I made a mental note to drop by tomorrow morning to check on her. I'd forgotten to ask if the generator and security companies had come as promised. And I could ask if she needed anything. Collect the emu inventory if she'd found it.

I reluctantly turned and headed back to the main part of camp. Halfway there I almost collided with Thor.

He looked like death warmed over.

"How much sleep did you get last night?" I asked.

"Enough," he said.

"And you were out with the crew all day today," I said.

"I managed to grab a nap in the afternoon," he said.

Strange, how motherhood had given me an almost supernatural ability to detect prevarication. Just call me Meg, the human lie detector.

"Yeah, right," I said. "Look—the wranglers will be patrolling the area tonight. To protect the emus, and the horses, and all those expensive bikes."

Actually, the wranglers weren't planning anything of the kind, at least not that I knew about, but as the words came out of my mouth I realized what a good idea it was.

"You're sure?"

"Follow me."

I kept an eye on Thor to make sure he didn't slip away. Although there wasn't as much chance of his doing so as there had been earlier, when he could so easily have lost himself in the crowd.

Clarence had finished his examination and was standing by the emu pen, gazing contentedly at the newly recaptured flock.

"Did Grandfather talk to you about recruiting some volunteers to patrol the camp tonight?" I asked.

"Not yet, but I think it's a sound idea," Clarence said. "I'll take care of it right away."

"Have the guards keep an eye on those two houses in addition to the camp, will you?" I pointed to Annabel's and Weaver's houses.

"Any special reason?" Clarence asked. "Are they emu haters?"

I explained about Cordelia—not my connection to her, but the murder, and her cousin's suspicion about Theo Weaver's involvement.

"And Miss Annabel is not an emu hater," Thor put in. "She and Ms. Delia were the ones who had me feed the emus. I think Mr. Weaver is, though. You don't want him anywhere near them. He tried to get the police to shoot them."

"We'll definitely keep an eye peeled that way, then," Clarence said, and hurried off to recruit his patrols.

"You see?" I turned to Thor and put my hands on my hips. "And we're also leaving our dogs there, for additional security. You can rest easy."

"Okay," he said. "But maybe I should just find a place to bunk down here. I'm not sure there's anyone left who can give me a ride back."

"That's why I'm driving you," I said. "Follow me."

I dropped by the tent to let Michael know where I was going and stayed long enough to help him stuff the boys into pajamas and give them their goodnight kisses. I hadn't decided what to do if Thor keeled over fast asleep while I was with the boys, but fortunately he was still upright— just barely—when I'd finished, so I led the way through the almost-deserted camp to the Twinmobile.

Thor craned his neck toward Miss Annabel's house as we drove down the dirt road, and seemed to relax a little when a pair of men waved to us from the far end of the emu pen.

"Miss Annabel and the emus will be fine," I said.

He nodded and leaned against the window. I stayed silent for a few miles, so he could doze if he liked. But every time I glanced over, I saw his eyes, wide open.

"Thor," I said. "You've lived here all your life, right."

"So far," he said, reminding me of the sign at the edge of town with the painted-out population total.

"And you think Miss Annabel's right about what happened to her cousin? I asked. "That Theo Weaver killed her?"

He didn't say anything for a few long moments. Maybe he, too, thought Miss Annabel was a nice old lady with an unreasonable obsession, and was trying to figure out a polite way to avoid my question.

"I hope it's not true," he said finally. "But you know what I think?" His voice was suddenly shaking with anger. "He did it. He's a total creep. He did his best to make the ladies' lives miserable, and then he killed Ms. Delia, and we shouldn't let him get away with it."

"Is he getting away with it?" I asked.

"He was an old buddy of Chief Heedles's dad," Thor said. "So the chief thinks he's an okay guy. But he's not. She's a nice lady, the chief, but way too trusting for a cop, if you ask me. Mr. Weaver's a mean, nasty old man and I think Miss Annabel's totally right, but they're not going to arrest him on her say-so. Everyone thinks she's kind of . . . well, you know."

"Eccentric?" I suggested. "Or maybe even crazy?"

Thor nodded.

"She seems pretty sensible to me," I said.

"Except for the whole never-going-outside thing, she's totally sensible," he said. "And one of the nicest ladies I know. And if it wasn't for her and Ms. Delia, I wouldn't be going to college. Miss Annabel tutored me in English and Social Studies, and Ms. Delia bossed me around to do my homework, and then they found this association that was offering scholarships for deserving engineering students, and thanks to them I'm going to be the first one in my family to go to college."

"That's really cool," I said. And I meant it. Later on, I would probably feel pangs of jealousy that he'd gotten to know my grandmother so well when I'd never get to meet her. But right now, I only felt happy and proud of her.

"Our house is three blocks west," Thor said, pointing. We'd reached the town square, and I turned onto the western road. At Thor's direction, I pulled up in front of a small bungalow, tidier and in better repair than most. There were a couple of lights on inside, and I heard the unmistakable sound of a generator chugging away in the back yard.

"I'll see you tomorrow," he said.

"Sleep well," I replied.

As he was turning to close the van door, he paused.

"You know," he said. "I just thought of something. Every picture you take with a cell phone has GPS coordinates in it, you know."

I nodded. I hoped he wasn't about to explain some abstruse engineering concept at this late hour.

"I took a lot of pictures of the emus over the last couple of years," he said. "Not just when we were feeding them, but any time I saw them. You think maybe those pictures would help Dr. Blake find them all? You know, seeing where they liked to hang out."

"Couldn't hurt," I said. "Why don't you send them to Caroline? When the power's back."

"My Internet's working fine," he said. "We have a generator, and a satellite connection."

"But I doubt if hers is." I pulled out my notebook, tore out a sheet of paper, and wrote down Caroline's e-mail address. "Wait until the power comes back."

"Okay," he said. "Or I could drop by tomorrow with a flash drive."

"An even better idea," I said. "Thanks."

"See you tomorrow," he said, and ran toward his house.

I waited until I saw the door open and Thor disappear inside before I drove off, just in case he had any notions of sneaking back to camp.

And I would have bet anything he'd stay up for an hour or two, going through his photos to get them ready for Caroline. Nothing I could do about that.

I should probably drop by the caravan and leave her a note to explain why she was about to be inundated with emu photos. And would she know how to access the GPS data in each photo? Should I start looking for someone to help with that?

I suspected Stanley would, although I hadn't seen him all day, and had no idea if he was back in camp or still down in Richmond, snooping around in Theo Weaver's and Cordelia's pasts.

It was getting late. The moon was out, and three quarters full, so it wasn't too dark while I was in town. Then I hit the wooded stretch of road that separated Miss Annabel's neighborhood from the rest of town and the trees closed in on either side and made the way surprisingly dark. But when I emerged from the trees into the more open area, all four white Victorian houses almost glowed in the moonlight.

No lights showed in the two houses across the street. I could still see the same dim but steady light in one of the upstairs rooms in Miss Annabel's house. Presumably her LED lantern, since the power was still out. Why hadn't she gone to bed? Or had she fallen asleep with her light on? No harm, with an LED lantern. Still, maybe I should stop and check.

There was also one light on in Theo Weaver's house. A

flickering light, which seemed to suggest that he was relying on candles or oil lamps. And, oddly, his door was open a crack, so the light inside spilled across his porch.

I parked my car in front of Miss Annabel's house, but the oddity of Mr. Weaver's cracked door still bothered me. Maybe I should check on him as well, even though he'd probably resent rather than appreciate it. I walked back and stood in front of the house.

"Mr. Weaver?" I called.

No answer. I walked slowly up his front walk, calling a couple of times. When I came to the open front door, I knocked, called again, and waited for long moments, listening for any sound inside.

All was quiet. But was it just my imagination, or was I smelling kerosene?

I pulled my phone out of my pocket, turned it on, and used its screen to light my way.

"Mr. Weaver," I called again.

Then I pushed the door open all the way.

Mr. Weaver was lying sprawled in the middle of the hallway and at the foot of the stairs, partly on the hall rug, which had been knocked askew, and partly on the weathered oak floorboards. His eyes were wide open and staring toward the living room, but he obviously wasn't seeing anything. His head was lying in a pool of blood. I couldn't quite see from where I was standing, but while his face was free of blood and wounds there was something odd about the back of his head. I suspected someone had whacked him there. I couldn't see any telltale fireplace pokers or baseball bats lying nearby, but then the light wasn't that strong.

Near his outstretched right hand was a large kerosene lamp. The bottom part, the part that held the kerosene, was broken, and kerosene had spilled all over the bunched up rug around it.

A lot of kerosene to come from one lamp. And if the kerosene was supposed to have spilled when the lamp fell and broke, why were there glistening splotches of kerosene on Mr. Weaver? All the way down to his feet.

I glanced up at the hall table and saw that the flickering light was coming from a candle that had fallen over. No, it hadn't fallen over—it looked as if someone had pulled out the table's drawer and balanced the candle on the edge of the table and the edge of the drawer. The bottom of the candle, still inserted in a heavy, old-fashioned pewter candle holder, hung over the edge, which meant that the longer the candle burned, the smaller and lighter the wick end grew. Eventually the candle would get short enough that the weight of the candle holder would drag the whole thing down on top of the kerosene-soaked rug.

Someone had killed Mr. Weaver and then rigged the candle to start a fire once he or she was gone.

I pulled out my cell phone and snapped a few quick pictures of the rigged candle. Then I pocketed my phone, stepped over to the table, carefully took hold of the candle with one hand, and smothered the flame with my fingers, to keep from blowing sparks around.

Then I stepped back to the door, pulled out my phone again, and called 9-1-1.

Nothing happened.

Chapter 22

I muttered a few words I tried not to use when the boys were around. And kicked myself for not snagging a spare radio when I'd left mine with Michael. Should I drive back to town for help? Go next door to Miss Annabel's to see if her phone was working? Run over to Camp Emu for help?

I decided to start by checking Mr. Weaver's own phone. If his landline wasn't working, odds were Miss Annabel's wouldn't either, so I wouldn't have to disturb her. Of course, to try his phone I'd have to walk through the crime scene. Chief Heedles probably wouldn't like that. Then again, there might not have been much crime scene left for her to see if I hadn't already disturbed it by putting out the candle, so if she wasn't happy, tough.

The foyer was large, with the same generous twelve-foot ceilings as Miss Annabel's house. Starting about twelve feet back, the stairway ran up the right side, and to its left was a hallway that probably led to the kitchen. An open archway on the right led to the living room. I leaned over as far as I could and studied what I could see of the room. No phone in sight. On the left side of the hallway were French doors, and what I saw through the glass panes looked like an office. Definitely a place I'd want a phone extension, so I resolved to start my search there.

I tiptoed around the edge of the hallway, not only to give Mr. Weaver's body a wide berth but also to avoid getting any more kerosene on my feet. Yes, the room behind the French doors was an office. Built-in bookshelves lined two walls, although they held more trophies and decorations than books. He also had a few file cabinets and a large mahogany desk. Either Weaver had been a disciple of the clean desk policy or he hadn't done all that much work in his office. His desk held an old-fashioned green glass banker's lamp, a few manila file folders, a wooden pencil holder with a few pens and pencils in it, and a telephone.

A dead telephone. Evidently the landlines were still down, too.

I hung up the useless phone and stood for a moment trying to decide what to do. Should I run over to the camp or wait until I could flag down a passerby?

I was staring ahead of me as I pondered, and suddenly realized I was looking at something rather interesting. The three middle shelves of the bookcase at my elbow held a collection of mineral specimens. I found myself wishing I'd seen them at some time when I actually had the leisure to examine them. In fact, I did pause for a few moments to appreciate the display.

The specimens were neatly labeled and arranged in alphabetical order, from amazonite through vivianite. A line of smaller type beneath each mineral's name gave the location where it was found—the amethyst in Amherst County, Virginia, the turquoise in Campbell County, Virginia, apophyllite in Fairfax, spessartite garnets in Amelia. All towns and counties in Virginia. I was disappointed to find that kyanite, Rose Noire's new fascination, was not represented.

Or had it been? There wasn't a blank space between hematite (Alleghany County, Virginia) and pectolite (Mitchells, Virginia), but the specimens on that shelf were spaced a little farther apart.

And there were marks in the dust that seemed to indicate that something had been removed, and the hematite, pectolite, and the other specimens on that shelf spaced out a little more to conceal the absence. Not a lot of dust—clearly whoever cleaned Mr. Weaver's house did a good job on the shelves. But enough to see that something had been moved. Recently. Very recently.

It might have nothing to do with Weaver's murder, but you never knew. I took a few pictures of the mineral collection, from a distance and close up, showing the dust marks. And then some pictures of the office itself. I wasn't sure why. Maybe in case the device in the hallway wasn't the only booby trap the killer had left. Then I left the office without disturbing anything else and walked carefully around Mr. Weaver and the kerosene. I took a few pictures of him, just in case. Then I escaped onto the fresh air of the front porch.

I walked down the front steps, taking deep breaths to clear the smell of kerosene from my lungs. I felt slightly dizzy, and perhaps a little nauseated. Should I ask Dad about the possible side effects of inhaling kerosene fumes? Or would that only make me feel worse?

Focus. I wasn't urgently in need of Dad's services. First, I needed to call for help. Preferably without leaving the crime scene unguarded.

I had a sudden inspiration. I fished in my pocket for my car keys, aimed the remote at the Twinmobile, and pressed the button that set off the alarm.

My car began honking furiously. Surely they'd hear it over in Camp Emu. I strolled to the edge of Miss Annabel's fence, where I could keep an eye on Mr. Weaver's front door while watching for anyone who came to check on my car.

Sure enough, a few minutes later several people came loping through Miss Annabel's yard. Rob and two other men from Blake's Brigade.

"See, I told you that was Meg's car," Rob was shouting. "Meg! Where are you? Are you okay?"

"I'm fine," I called out. "But Mr. Weaver isn't. Someone attacked him."

"Want me to fetch Dad?" Rob asked.

"He's past that," I said. "Can someone go to town to get the police?"

"Police?" Rob echoed. "He's dead?"

"We should call 9-1-1!" one of the other men exclaimed.

All three of them pulled out their cell phones. I waited patiently until they'd all three figured out that no, the cell phone towers hadn't miraculously started working again. Then I assigned one of the brigade guys to run back to camp to get his car and drive to town for the police. I assigned the other to watch the back of Mr. Weaver's house from outside the fence. Rob and I stayed in front to keep an eye on his door.

As soon as the two men had raced back through Annabel's yard, I saw her door open a crack.

"You keep an eye on the front door," I told Rob. "I'm going to let Miss Annabel know what's going on."

Chapter 23

"Meg, what's wrong?"

Annabel opened the door as soon as I stepped onto the porch. I had to shade my eyes with my hand against the glare of the little LED headlight she was wearing on her head.

"Sorry," she added. She pivoted the headlight so it shone up rather than into my eyes and stepped back so I could enter.

"No problem," I said. "And sorry about the noise. One of those guys who came running through your yard just now to check on me will be driving into town to get the police. It looks as if your next-door neighbor has been murdered."

"Weaver? Murdered?"

She didn't look happy. I suppose that should have been a relief. But as she absorbed the news, her expression changed from surprise to dismay.

"Damn," she said. "Just damn. Contrary to the conclusion Chief Heedles will probably jump to, I didn't want Weaver dead. I just wanted him punished for what he did. Properly, legally punished. And for your information I'm on record as a staunch opponent of the death penalty."

"If it makes you feel any better, I don't see you as a prime suspect for this," I said.

"Maybe not," she said. "But I bet Chief Heedles will. And why don't you see me as a suspect? You don't think I'm spry enough?"

"I think you'd have done a better job of it," I said. "The

killer rigged up a clumsy device intended to start a fire after he was gone. I'm not sure if it would have worked even
if I hadn't come along. If he'd done a better job, Chief Heedles would be dismissing this as a tragic accident. And
for that matter, however clumsy the device was, it would
have had a lot better chance of working if the killer had
bothered to shut the door behind him."

"That door's always been tricky," Annabel said. "Unless you pull it tightly shut and wiggle the knob a bit to
make sure the latch engages, it will drift open eventually.
Could be five seconds later, or five hours, but eventually.
And in case you're wondering how I know, Cordelia lived
there for the first decade of her life. We used to spend as
much time over there as here. I know that door as well as
my own."

"And Mr. Weaver never had it fixed?"

"He may have tried," she said. "A lot of people have
tried, but the fix never lasts. The old folks used to say there
was a ghost doing it, but I don't hold with that. Sit down.
Would you like some lemonade? Or I could heat some
water for tea—I've got a little propane stove."

"Don't go to all that trouble," I said. "Lemonade will
be fine."

I sat down in one of the white wicker porch chairs
and stared out over the lawn. I could see a pale shape near
the road that was Rob's white shirt, and the occasional
firefly. The faint sounds of a few people singing over in
Camp Emu were almost drowned out by the frogs and
crickets.

"Here." Miss Annabel handed me a glass. "It's lukewarm, but at least it's wet."

We were still sipping in silence when I caught the first
sounds of a siren approaching.

"I'd better get over there," I said.

A police cruiser pulled up in front of Mr. Weaver's

house, closely followed by a blue sedan. A uniformed officer got out of the cruiser and began talking to Rob. I strolled over to where Chief Heedles was getting out of the sedan.

"Meg can tell you," Rob was saying as I reached them.

The chief turned to me.

"What happened here?" she asked.

"I was driving by on my way back to camp," I said. "And I noticed that Mr. Weaver's door was hanging open. And I was a little worried about him. He's elderly."

She stood there, poker-faced, while I told my story. She looked without apparent interest at the photos I'd taken on my phone and nodded absently when I offered to send them to her. Actually, I did see the ghost of a smile when I explained about using my car's emergency button to summon help without leaving Mr. Weaver's door unguarded. But when I'd finished, she sighed.

"So you think someone whacked Mr. Weaver over the head with this missing chunk of kryptonite and rigged up this complicated booby trap for some reason."

"Kyanite, not kryptonite," I said. "I wasn't really thinking of it as a possible murder weapon—I doubt if it's big enough to do much damage. I just noticed it was gone. And as for why they rigged up the candle, obviously they were hoping to make it look like an accident. Poor Mr. Weaver, finding out the hard way just why fire departments keep telling us to use battery-powered flashlights and lanterns instead of open flames in a power outage."

The chief glanced over at Miss Annabel's house. Annabel had gone back inside but there were lights on downstairs. Probably several of her little LED lanterns.

I could hear more sirens approaching.

"Miss Annabel's up?" she said.

"She is now," I said. "I'm afraid I probably woke the whole camp when I sounded the alarm. I think she was upstairs getting ready for bed when I arrived. There was only one small light on in her house, upstairs."

Chief Heedles nodded.

As we watched, Miss Annabel's downstairs light went out. The chief sighed.

"I'll need to talk to her eventually," she said. "But it can wait till tomorrow."

Two fire engines pulled up in front of Theo Weaver's house.

"I'd appreciate it if you stayed around for a bit," Chief Heedles said. She didn't wait to see me nod—just strode over to meet the firemen.

I glanced around. Rob was standing on the sidewalk, near the border between Annabel's house and Mr. Weaver's, with a couple of other people. I decided that I could use the company. As I approached, I realized that one of the others was Stanley Denton.

"Weaver's dead?" he asked.

"Murdered," I said.

I told them what had happened, thinking as I did so that this was efficient, telling them both at once. Stanley needed to know what had happened because it probably affected the case he was pursuing for us. And Rob was dying to know what had happened, and would save me the trouble of telling the rest of the camp.

"Damn," Stanley said when I had finished.

"Yeah," I said.

"I should go back to camp and tell them what's up," Rob said.

He loped off through Miss Annabel's yard. I could see that there were already a few people from Camp Emu peering over the fence to see what was going on. They seemed excited to see Rob heading their way.

Stanley and I watched as Chief Heedles and the fire chief conferred and then went into the house together.

"You think she's getting the fire chief's opinion on whether the evidence matches my story?" I asked.

"Or maybe just checking to see that there's no danger of a fire starting up," Stanley said.

Another car pulled up and a bearded middle-aged man in khakis and a polo shirt strode swiftly into the house.

"Medical examiner, most likely," Stanley said.

We watched for a few minutes as firemen and police officers went into the house and occasionally came out again.

"Interesting turn of events," Stanley said. "And yes, I know your mother always calls something interesting when there's nothing nice she can say about it. I meant it in that sense."

"Damn," I said. "And here I was hoping Weaver's murder would be the last little bit of evidence you needed to solve Cordelia's case."

"Does Chief Heedles know about your relationship to Cordelia?" Stanley said.

"Not that I know of."

"I'd tell her, then," he said. "It might have nothing to do with Weaver's murder or Cordelia's, but you never know. It might be a fact she needs."

"And she'll find us a lot more suspicious if we don't tell her and she finds out later," I said.

"That too," Stanley said. "So—let's look at the possibilities. First, maybe Weaver was murdered out of revenge—because someone thought he killed Cordelia."

"In which case, Annabel is her prime suspect, and I might be second on her list. Along with the rest of my family."

"It's a long list," Stanley said. "Your family, a few other people out at Camp Emu who knew her, at least by reputation, as the instigator of the emu rescue, and at least half the town. Cordelia was well loved. She was cantankerous and bossy and drove people crazy, but they loved her."

He was making her sound a lot like Grandfather.

"Chief Heedles will be working her way down that list," I said aloud.

"And as I said, it's a very long list, and she doesn't have a lot of manpower to help her," Stanley said. "So it could be a while before she looks beyond the revenge theory at any other possibilities."

"Like the possibility that whoever killed Cordelia also killed Weaver," I said. "I hope the similar M.O. will make her consider that early on. But why would anyone kill either of them, much less both?"

"Perhaps Cordelia's killer had reason to suspect that Weaver could finger him," Stanley said.

"Then why wait six months?"

"The killer only recently realized that Weaver knew something?" Stanley suggested. "Weaver said something indiscreet, maybe?"

"Or maybe it's our arrival that set the killer off," I suggested. "The killer saw Weaver talking to a PI and a nosy bystander and started to worry."

Stanley nodded. I could tell he didn't like the possibility that his investigation might have anything to do with Weaver's murder. I wanted to suggest that if anything had triggered this new murder, it was all the fuss and bother caused by Grandfather and his brigade that were to blame, not anything he had done. But he knew that.

"Or maybe the killer's someone in Blake's Brigade," I suggested. "Someone who only realized since coming to Camp Emu that Weaver's house isn't vacant like the ones across the street and there might be a witness to his crime?"

He smiled at that.

"Anything's possible," he said. "So, theory one, Weaver was killed out of revenge. Two, he was killed because the killer was afraid he witnessed Cordelia's murder. Three, they're completely unrelated."

"I'm not buying that."

"Or four, they were both killed for the same reason. Whatever that is. Like they both saw something or knew something."

Chief Heedles had come out of the house, talking with the bearded man we'd pegged as the medical examiner. They shook hands briskly, and the man went back to his car. The chief looked around, spotted us, and headed our way.

"Evening," she said, nodding to Stanley. Then she turned to me. "Is there anyone who has a complete list of who's been at your camp?"

"Do you mean the people who have been camping there?" I asked. "Or everyone who was out there tonight?"

"Half my town's been out here tonight." The chief sounded just a little bitter that so many of her citizens were complicating her life. "But I know who lives here. Need to find out who else is around."

"Right," I said. "The best source would be a woman named Sherry Smith, who makes sure everyone who shows up signs a photo release, so the film crew doesn't have to worry about bystanders wandering into their shots. I can't swear that her list will be one hundred percent accurate, but she's pretty diligent."

"Were they filming tonight?" she asked.

"I have no idea," I said. "If they did, Sherry will probably be lying down with a cold compress over her head, because there's no way even she could have gotten releases from everyone who showed up last night."

"She gets releases from the locals as well?"

"If they hang around camp long enough for her to spot them, yes," I said. "Anyone who appears on camera, even in the background of a shot, they like to have a release, just in case."

She looked at her watch.

"I know it's late," she began. "And people in the camp have probably gone to sleep . . ."

"But you have a murder to investigate," I said. "And you want to talk to Sherry and the film crew and maybe some of the other people on Sherry's list. I'll meet you back at camp, by the mess tent. Or where the mess tent used to be—I'm not sure they managed to get it set up again."

"Can you give me a ride there?" Stanley said. "I hoofed it over the fields to get here, and it's been a long day."

Stanley and I got into my car. The chief was already waiting for us in hers, so we led the way.

We rode in silence for half a minute or so. Then, as we approached the turnoff for camp, Stanley spoke up.

"Is there any chance that the killer went thataway?" He was pointing along the road that continued past the entrance to Camp Emu, and then, a half a mile farther on, led into the neighboring county.

"I don't even know that he or she left by this road," I said. "Whoever did it could be hiding in the woods. Or out in Camp Emu. Or he could have gone back to town."

"Understood," he said. "But did you pass any other cars on your way out here from town?"

I thought for a moment.

"No," I said. "Not a single car. I remember thinking how peaceful it was. And the candle booby trap couldn't have been burning all that long."

"Good," Stanley said. "So if the killer fled by car, he had to have gone thataway. Into the adjacent county."

"Why is that good?" I asked. "Chief Heedles won't have jurisdiction there."

"But the State Police would," he said. "I might be able to use this. To get Heedles to involve the State Police. Or, if they hear about it, they might step in whether she likes it or not."

I nodded. I realized that I no longer distrusted Chief

Heedles. She seemed well-meaning and honest, and not as biased as Miss Annabel seemed to think her. But at the same time I didn't have much confidence in her ability to solve what was, for Riverton, a veritable crime wave. And she didn't seem like the kind of person who found it easy to ask for help. That was one of my failings, and I'd gotten pretty good at spotting others who shared it.

"Maybe it's just as well I hadn't yet spent a lot of time investigating all the brigade members," Stanley said, as I parked my car in a space as close as I could find to Michael's and my tent. "Since Heedles will be doing it."

"Did you find out anything interesting so far?" I asked.

"Not really," he said. "You've got one volunteer who has a criminal record, but I checked him out pretty thoroughly."

"What did he do?" I asked.

"Chained himself to a tree as part of an environmental protest," Stanley said. "A very peaceful protest, as far as I could tell, but he and his fellow protestors happened to come up before a very unsympathetic judge."

"Still, we should keep an eye on him," I said. "Which one was it?"

Stanley pulled out his notebook and read me the name. It didn't ring a bell, but I pulled out my notebook to jot it down anyway.

Chief Heedles was parking near us.

"Nothing else suspicious?" I was forcing back a yawn, and since Stanley seemed to be doing the same, I wasn't expecting anything exciting.

"Nothing else even remotely interesting," he said. "Unless you count it interesting that one of your volunteers is a retired mine company executive."

Suddenly I was very wide awake.

"Mine company executive?" I asked. "Which one."

"Guy named Williams," Stanley said.

"Jim Williams?"

Stanley nodded.

"Weird," I said. "Jim Williams was the one who'd brought me the core drill sample."

"Not so weird," Stanley said. "It would probably take someone in the industry to recognize that. Look, it's been a long day. If Chief Heedles wants me, I'll be in my trailer."

He looked so beat that I merely nodded. And made a note to open the subject again in the morning. Yes, it made sense that anyone in the mining industry would know a core drill sample when he saw one.

Then why had Williams told me he'd learned about core drilling samples on one of Grandfather's previous expeditions? If I'd known his background, I'd have given all the more weight to his identification of the core drill sample. He hadn't just failed to tell the whole truth—he'd lied.

I should have asked Stanley what mining company Williams had worked for. Of course, if it had been Smedlock Mining, he'd have said something.

But what if Williams had worked for Amazonite Unlimited? I was so tired I couldn't remember if I'd told Stanley about Anne Murphy's discovery. If I hadn't, and if he hadn't yet uncovered the relationship between Amazonite Unlimited and Smedlock . . .

I'd talk to him tomorrow.

"Isn't that the police chief?" Clarence Rutledge appeared at my elbow. "Is something wrong? What's with all the commotion over there at the houses?"

"There's been a murder," I said. "She wants a list of everyone here in camp. Do you know where Sherry's camped?"

"Clipboard Sherry? Yeah."

The chief joined us, and Clarence led the way. We passed the film crew's trailers, and I pointed them out to the chief as we passed.

"They're usually still up at this hour," I said. "I guess they decided on an early night for once."

"I'll try to wait till they're up," she said.

"Sherry's in that small RV." Clarence was pointing to the RV in question.

"That's small?"

"For an RV." Clarence shrugged.

I still thought "small RV" was an oxymoron. You could make two Twinmobiles out of the thing.

Chief Heedles had to knock on the RV's door several times before Sherry appeared, uncharacteristically disheveled and blinking sleepily. I'd have expected her to be one of those people who snap awake instantly able to do long division in their heads, and the fact that she wasn't seemed strangely reassuring.

"Sorry to disturb you, ma'am," the chief said. "But I'm told you're the best person to ask for a complete and accurate list of who's here in camp."

That jolted her awake.

"Has one of our volunteers been causing a problem?" she said.

"There's been a problem," the chief said. "I don't yet know if it's one of my townspeople causing it or one of your volunteers. I could use that list."

"Of course." She fidgeted briefly with the thick blond rope of hair that hung down her back, as if hoping it would curl up on its own into its usual French braid. Then she disappeared back into the RV and appeared almost immediately carrying the familiar clipboard.

"This is my only copy," she said. "I'd need it back. Is there someplace in town where you could make a copy?"

"Let's find a place with better light and I can take a picture of it," Chief Heedles said.

"We have some good LED lanterns over at the administration tent," Sherry said. "Would that do?"

The chief nodded. Sherry strode off. Clarence followed Sherry. I didn't, and the chief paused for a moment to look back at me.

"Do you need me any more tonight?" I asked. "Or would it be okay if I went back to my tent and tried to get some sleep."

"That's fine," she said.

She turned to go.

"Just one thing," I said. "I have no idea if this is at all relevant, but—there's a guy here in camp who used to work for a mining company. His name is Jim Williams."

"Is that relevant to the murder?" She frowned as she said it, and glanced in the direction Sherry had gone.

"I have no idea," I said. "It's just bugging me because he—well, he didn't exactly lie about it, but he wasn't forthcoming, either."

"I suspect not everyone in Blake's Brigade is a big fan of mining companies," the chief said. "Maybe he's just afraid people will ostracize him."

"Could be," I said. "But do you know what a core drilling sample is?"

She shook her head.

"Neither did I, until Mr. Williams showed me one and explained what it was. And he told me he had learned about core drilling on another one of Grandfather's previous expeditions."

"Which could be true," the chief said. "You don't know what he did for this mining company. Maybe he never went out in the field."

"Maybe," I said. "And I don't know what company Williams worked for, and maybe the fact that Theo Weaver was also connected with a mining company is just a wild coincidence. Maybe I've just wasted your time with something that has nothing to do with the murder."

She gazed at me for a few moments.

"I'll keep it in mind," she said. "Thank you."

I stumbled back to our tent and crawled carefully onto my air mattress. Michael and the boys were sound asleep. As tired as I was, I should have followed their example immediately. But I kept fretting. Had I just given the chief the clue that would solve the murder? Or distracted her from the real solution? Had I identified the killer—perhaps of my grandmother as well as Theo Weaver? Or fingered an innocent man for a police chief who might be so eager to solve the crime that she'd be all too ready to find him a suspicious character?

I tossed and turned for what seemed like an eternity. When I finally looked at my watch, it was two a.m. The boys would be awake in four hours. Maybe less. I resigned myself to a night without sleep.

And of course, as soon as I gave up trying to catch the sandman, he ambushed me.

Chapter 24

I awoke still tired and already cranky. When I found that Michael had whisked the boys away before they could wake me up, my first reaction was irrational annoyance. Didn't he think I'd want to see them? What better remedy for a bad morning than a little unconditional toddler love?

Clearly, I needed caffeine.

I threw on my clothes and trudged over to the mess tent. Michael, Natalie, and the boys greeted me with enthusiasm.

So did Chief Heedles, which was much more surprising and a lot less reassuring.

"Just the person I needed to see." She was sitting at a table at the far end of the mess tent, a setup that seemed designed to give her a chance to have reasonably private conversations. "May I have a moment of your time?"

"As much as you need," I said. I waved at Michael and the boys and sat down by the chief.

She had a notebook open on the table. She flipped to a new page and picked up her pen.

"You said you stopped to check on Miss Annabel on your way back from town," she said. "Just what were you doing in town?"

"Chauffeuring Thor Larsen home," I said. "And maybe I shouldn't have. He'd spent the previous night lurking in the shrubbery, keeping watch over Miss Annabel and the one emu we caught the first day. And nothing happened that night."

Heedles nodded.

"But last night you organized patrols," she said. "With Dr. Rutledge in charge. Why?"

"I guess I was a little spooked. By Thor. And Miss Annabel. Look, there's something I haven't told you that probably isn't related to the murder, but you never know, so here goes. We didn't just come here for the emus. I didn't anyway. Cordelia—Ms. Delia, as everyone here calls her—she was my grandmother."

Heedles looked up from her book with a puzzled frown.

"I was unaware that she and Mr. Mason had children," she said.

"They didn't," I said. "This happened before she and Mr. Mason ever met."

I gave her the condensed version of the family history.

"Well, I'll be," she said, when I'd finished. "Even from beyond the grave, Ms. Delia continues to astonish me."

"I have no idea if it has anything to do with Mr. Weaver's murder," I said. "And if it turns out it doesn't, I'd appreciate it if you could keep it quiet."

"I don't think people nowadays would find it all that shocking," she said.

"Yes, but Ms. Delia was—and Miss Annabel is—from another generation," I said. "And it's not my secret to share."

"I understand," she said. "And I appreciate your candor. I won't make this public unless it's absolutely necessary, and I can't imagine it would be. Still—you being a cousin and all—any chance you could be there to help out when I go over to interview Miss Annabel?"

"Happy to help," I said. "When?"

"Sometime later today," she said. "I'll be in touch. Give me your cell phone number." She turned her notebook around and offered me a page to write on.

"Is cell service back, then?" I asked, as I printed out my number.

"Not yet," she said. "But they say we'll have power back at least downtown by five p.m. today. Cell towers might come back sooner, and if they don't, I'll come out and pick you up when I'm ready to talk to her. Thanks in advance for your help."

That sounded like a dismissal, so I nodded and joined Michael and the boys.

"Mommy!" Jamie jumped up and hugged me. "Are you helping the police lady catch the bad man?"

"I've explained to the boys that Chief Heedles is trying to find out who let the emus go during last night's joust," Michael said. "And Caroline has suggested that perhaps another expedition in her caravan would be a good plan for today. Steer clear of all the gossip."

"Good idea," I said.

"But Mommy," Josh said. "We need to guard the emus!"

"I have a good idea," I said. "I have to stay here to help the police look for the bad man who tried to let the emus go. So I can guard the emus. And I'll get Auntie Caroline to tell me where you guys are going, so if we finish catching the bad man quickly, I can join you."

"Okay," Jamie said.

"Hey, Meg." Natalie joined us. "I just talked to Caroline. She's going to have Clarence take the emus we've already caught down to the sanctuary a little later today, so we should all go over and say good-bye."

"Only it's not really good-bye, is it?" Michael said quickly, before the boys could react. "Because she's only taking the emus home to live with her at the animal sanctuary, where we can visit them any time we like. So it's more like 'see you later, emus,' right?"

"Go now," Josh said, tugging at Natalie's sleeve.

"Can we give them treats now?" Jamie asked.

"Clarence says it's okay to give them grapes and sliced apples," Michael explained. "And the mess crew kindly prepared a supply for us. Yes, let's go give the emus their treats and let Mommy eat her breakfast."

The boys scurried off, with Michael and Natalie in their wake. I got up and headed for the chow line. There was no one else there, and only one anxious-looking crew member serving.

"Everyone else out hunting the emus?" I asked, as I filled my breakfast plate.

"Most everyone," he said. "Clarence and the other guys who were on patrol are still here, being interrogated. And the police chief told us not to leave town. I thought they only said that in the movies."

"Maybe Chief Heedles watches the same movies we do," I said.

I saw Caroline come into the tent and sit down with her laptop, so I took my plate of bacon, eggs, and fruit and went over to sit with her.

"I hear the boys are going out with you today," I said. "Thank you."

"We don't want them upset by whatever's going on here," she said.

"Does the presence of your laptop mean the power's back?" I asked.

"No, I'm on battery. I just want to make copies of those photos of yours before I send them off."

"Photos of mine?"

"The hundreds of cell phone photos of emus you told Thor Larsen to give me," she said. "Did you say something to give him the idea I wanted them at 5 a.m.?" Oops. She sounded a little frazzled.

"Sorry," I said. "I told him last night to bring them to-day. I didn't think I had to tell him to wait to a decent hour. What's wrong with today's teenagers? I don't recall ever getting up voluntarily before noon when I was his age."

"I don't think he got up, he stayed up," she said.

"Maybe he thought it was urgent," I said. "He seemed to think there was some way you could use them to track where the emus hung out. I don't know how, though."

"Neither do I," she said. "But I'm sure the kid who runs my computer system back at the sanctuary does. So I'm going to send Thor's flash drive down there. As soon as the police are finished with him, Clarence is going to load the emus we've caught and transport them down to the sanctuary. He can take the flash drive with him. I just wanted to make a copy before I send it. Can you keep an eye on my laptop while I run over to the emu pen for a minute? Just make sure no error messages pop up, or if any do, remember what they are."

I nodded, and Caroline bustled off. I studied her laptop screen. She hadn't been kidding about the hundreds of photos. The screen showed that she was copying 1,164 files from the flash drive to her laptop, and was 93 percent finished.

Being careful not to do anything that would interrupt the copying process, I clicked around until I found the folder in which Caroline had stored the photos. Clearly Thor was an avid cell phone photographer. Some of the shots were fuzzy or off center, but a surprising number were reasonably sharp and well composed. I clicked with the thumb of my injured hand while eating with the other hand, and the sight of the emus helped dispel my cranky mood.

Still, one emu looked remarkably like another. After the first few dozen shots, I began to click more rapidly—the computer equivalent of fast forwarding. This was actually kind of fun, because Thor sometimes took fifteen or twenty photos in short succession, so clicking rapidly through them looked like watching a slightly jerky movie.

And then Miss Annabel's face popped up on the screen. I stopped clicking and stared. She was standing face-to-face with one of the emus, And was it my imagination or was there a certain resemblance between them? A certain angular haughtiness.

And if Thor had managed to catch a shot of Miss Annabel, might Cordelia also show up in his photos? After all, I gathered Miss Annabel was only an occasional participant in their emu-feeding expeditions while Miss Cordelia was a regular. I fast-clicked through with new enthusiasm, seeing one or two others with Miss Annabel, but no Cordelia.

Then another familiar face popped up. Jim Williams. He wasn't front and center in the photo—he was off to the side and in profile, but clearly visible behind the emu who occupied the foreground. In the background I saw a faded picket fence—was it the fence around the ranch house up at Biscuit Mountain? I'd taken pictures of that with my own phone. I pulled out my phone and compared the picket fence in the background of the photos of Williams with the one in the shots I'd taken up at the ranch. If it wasn't the same fence it was a dead ringer.

I wondered for a moment if the picture of Williams had been taken over the last couple of days. But no, in it the trees were bare and brown, and yellow leaves had drifted up against the fence. My photo showed nothing but green. I looked at the date of the photo file. Thor's photo had been taken on December 3rd of last year, only a week before Cordelia's death.

I clicked through the rest of the photos. Williams wasn't in any of the other shots. But he was most definitely in this one. Here in Riverton, months before we learned that Cordelia lived here and planned the expedition.

Of course, Miss Annabel and Cordelia had been trying to publicize the plight of the emus for some time. I hadn't heard about it, but maybe someone more actively involved in animal welfare issues would have.

Still . . .

And we'd made him one of Grandfather's bodyguards.

I looked up from the computer screen. Chief Heedles was back at her seat at the table at the far end of the tent, talking to Clarence. I picked up the laptop and went to stand by their table.

"Sorry to interrupt you," I said. "But may I show you something?"

I tilted the laptop so I could show Heedles the picture. And then I let her see the file date.

She frowned.

"Would you excuse us for a moment?" she said to Clarence.

"I'll be at the emu pen." Clarence stood up and strode off.

"Where did you get this?" the chief asked.

"Thor Larsen." I explained the notion of using the GPS data to locate the emus.

"Is there any chance Dr. Blake sent Mr. Williams down as a sort of advance scout?"

"No idea," I said. "You'd have to ask Grandfather."

"How far in advance would his volunteer network have known about his plans for the expedition?"

"He only decided to come here the day before we showed up here, actually," I said. "He probably won't admit that, especially in front of the locals. He'll probably claim he's been intending to come down here for a while. But I'm pretty sure he just decided Tuesday over dinner."

"He pulled this together overnight?" Heedles sounded incredulous.

"His staff did," I said. "He's impulsive, and they're used to it. You should see what they come up with if he gives them a few days' notice. And actually, I think his staff were already planning another expedition, so all they had to do was change destinations. And even though the expedition was last minute, he got the request to rescue the emus months ago. From Miss Annabel. I suppose it's possible that he sent someone down here back in December and just didn't act on the information until this week."

"But not very likely." She was unsnapping the radio from her belt. "I need to talk to Dr. Blake to be sure. Can you get me a copy of that photo?"

I nodded.

"Marvin," she said into the radio. "You're still with Dr. Blake, aren't you? Okay, precisely where are you?"

I left her to it. I took Caroline's laptop back to the table where she'd been sitting and watched as the files finished copying onto the hard drive. Then I sat, clicking through the photos, until Caroline returned.

"Do you have another one of these things?" I pointed to the flash drive. "Chief Heedles would like some of these photos."

Caroline frowned, but didn't ask questions. She darted out of the tent and returned a moment or so later with another flash drive. I copied not just the photo with Williams in it but all the pictures Thor had taken in December.

Chief Heedles appeared at my elbow just as the copy finished.

"Here." I handed her the flash drive.

"Keep this under your hat," she said, and strode off.

I nodded.

"What do Thor's emu shots have to do with the murder?" Caroline asked.

"Nothing, I hope," I said. It wasn't exactly a lie, but it wasn't much of an answer. If it had been just Caroline standing there, I'd have told her, but several other people had arrived to join the chow line and were within earshot. I hated the notion that the killer might be someone using Blake's Brigade as cover for his crimes. I wasn't about to spread rumors to that effect before we were sure.

"I'm going over to see how Miss Annabel is doing," I said.

"Take her some breakfast," Caroline suggested. "She's probably tired of whatever she can fix without her stove."

That sounded like a good idea, so I filled one takeaway box with bacon, sausage, scrambled eggs, ham, breakfast potatoes, and toast, and another with fruit.

I paused long enough to wave at the boys as Caroline's caravan drove off, and take a few cell phone shots of them driving the horse—or at least holding the reins. The horse didn't seem to need much guidance. Then I hiked across the field to Miss Annabel's house.

She opened the back door before I could knock.

"What's going on?" she asked. "Dwight came over to check on me, but he hasn't heard a thing."

"No one's heard much yet," I said. "I'll tell you what I know over breakfast."

"I can't offer you anything but cold cereal."

"Breakfast is on me," I said. "Actually, it's on Grandfather—he likes to eat well on these shindigs, so the quantity and the quality of the food is usually pretty good."

"Monty's paying for all this?" she said. "Good. What's for lunch and dinner? And when is it? You don't need to bring it if you don't have time. I'll send Dwight over."

"You'll hear the bell ring," I said. "No idea what's on the menu, though. Sorry—I should have thought of this as soon as the power went out."

I set the takeout boxes down on her kitchen table and opened them up. Miss Annabel perked up at the sight of the food.

"You're a lifesaver," she said. "Dwight! Chow's on."

As she and Dr. Ffollett dug into the contents of the takeout boxes, I told them everything I knew. Including the suspicion that had suddenly fallen on Jim Williams.

"A mining engineer!" Annabel exclaimed. "Now that's highly suspicious."

"We don't know that he's a mining engineer," I said. "Only that he used to work for a mining company. He could have been a bookkeeper in their accounting department for all we know."

"Still—a mining company."

"You've got something against mining companies?" I asked. "They're not all environmental menaces hell-bent on pillaging the countryside."

"No, but the bad ones do exist," Annabel said. "And it only takes one bad one to ruin things for everyone here. And it worries me that someone from a mining company has been sniffing around up at Biscuit Mountain."

"Sniffing around for what—do you have any idea? Like kyanite, maybe?" I remembered that the blue crystal Rose Noire loved was found on Biscuit Mountain.

"Kyanite and kaolin," she said. "They're related minerals. Not as valuable as gold or diamonds, but they have their industrial uses."

"Kaolin's what you make porcelain with, right?" I asked. "I remember reading that the Biscuit Mountain Art Pottery Works dug its own china clay."

"Yes, so it's valuable for that," she said. "And also there's something called mullite, which is pretty hot these days in the ceramics industry. Only occurs naturally on the island of Mull, in Scotland, but you can refine either kyanite or kaolin to make it. And there were small deposits of both up there. Still are, actually."

"So there is a reason for mining companies to be snooping around on Biscuit Mountain," I said. "Something more than just speculative exploration."

"Maybe," she said. "The vein of kaolin the Biscuit Mountain Works used was pretty much depleted. That's part of what drove it out of business—not just having to buy their clay all of a sudden, but the money they spent trying to find a new vein. And they never did find one. Not one that was worth the cost of digging. Just piddly little deposits."

"That was nearly a hundred years ago," I said. "Technology's come a long way. What if someone thought those piddly little deposits were worth mining? Or at least worth checking out?"

"We did check it out about five years ago," Annabel said. "I looked into buying the land back and trying to do something with it. Maybe start up the pottery works again. Or mine the minerals. The town could use some industry. So I got a mining geologist out here. He seemed to think the kaolin and kyanite were exploitable—his word. But he didn't think the profit margin would be big enough for any reputable company to be interested. To get at them in sufficient quantities, you'd pretty much have to take the top off the mountain. A great big open-pit mine all up and down the side of Biscuit Mountain. The side the town can see, because the other side is in the National Park. Not a legacy I want to leave to the town."

"But if there's no profit in it," I began.

"Not enough profit to be worthwhile for a legitimate operation," Annabel said. "He warned me that it might be pretty tempting to some kind of fly-by-night outfit that would try to weasel out of every environmental and safety regulation on the books."

"So you were worried that a mining company might try to buy it," I said.

"The wrong mining company," she said. "A company that wouldn't have to live with the visual blight or the rest of the environmental impact. Mining kaolin generates a lot of dust, and refining it uses—and dirties—a lot of water. The stuff's even got its own disease—kaolinosis. A lot like asbestosis."

"Other people in town might not care," Dr. Ffollett said. "Not many jobs here. If a mine brought in jobs, people might not care about how the mountain looks or whether it kills them in the long run."

"Okay," I said. "The kaolin and kyanite might be sufficient motive for someone from a mining company to be sniffing around Biscuit Mountain. But are they motive for murder?"

We all looked at each other for a few moments.

"Sounds plausible to me," Annabel said. "Not hard for some scummy company to figure out we'd fight them tooth and nail and maybe cost them so much they couldn't turn a profit."

"Yes, Cordelia would have led the charge against any attempt to start an open-pit mine up at Biscuit Mountain," Dr. Ffollett said. "But she can't now."

"That was another reason we tried to buy the place," Annabel said. "Not just for the emus, although that was important. We were going to work on getting it declared a historical site. Maybe look into deeding it to the National Park Service when we went. Make sure the land—and the town—were protected."

"And frankly, that was one reason Cordelia had Annabel write to Dr. Blake," Dr. Ffollett said. "She thought if we got him up here to take care of the emus, he'd also see how beautiful and unspoiled the area was, and then if necessary we could enlist him to fight against developing the property."

"But when you tried to buy the ranch, the bank turned you down," I said.

"Probably because Theo Weaver was on their board of directors." Annabel's hands were clenched into fists. "What do you want to bet they were in league with some mining company?"

"Possibly the Smedlock Mining Company," I said.

"What's that?" Dr. Ffollett asked.

"Weaver was also on their board," I said. "You didn't know he was connected to a mining company?"

"No," Dr. Ffollett said.

"I didn't until you told me last night," Annabel said.

"Yes," I said. "When I was asking if you could think of any connection between Cordelia and mining. Was there a reason you didn't mention your fears that a mining company might buy Biscuit Mountain last night?"

"You said any connection between Cordelia and Smedlock Mining," Annabel corrected. "And there wasn't. I'd never heard of Smedlock before, and I try to keep tabs on who's sniffing around our mountain."

"I gather the mining engineer you hired wasn't from Smedlock," I said. "Are you sure he wasn't with one of its subsidiaries?"

"He was an independent consulting engineer who's done a lot of work for environmental groups," she said. "Because I wanted a hard, cold look at the real environmental consequences of mining up on Biscuit Mountain. What about this Williams person? Is he retired from Smedlock?"

"No idea," I said. "Chief Heedles will find out, I'm sure."

Or I could hunt down Stanley and ask him. Probably better not to mention that possibility to Miss Annabel, who was definitely fired up by this conversation, pacing up and down the kitchen with her fists clenched, eyes blazing as if about to lead a charge.

"This might give someone a motive for killing off Cordelia," I said. "Assuming they wanted to mine the kyanite on Biscuit Mountain and knew she'd do anything she could to stop them. They might figure even if she couldn't stop them, she could cause them so much trouble that their profit margin would disappear. But what about Mr. Weaver? In this scenario he's one of the bad guys. Why would they kill him?"

"Thieves fall out," Annabel suggested. "Maybe he killed Cordelia, and his accomplices were afraid he was about to get caught and spill the rest of their plan."

"Only I thought our new theory was that the same person killed Cordelia and Weaver," I reminded her.

"Then perhaps the killer was someone Weaver knew," Dr. Ffollett suggested. "Someone who was afraid of being identified."

"What if you did see Mr. Weaver running away the night of Cordelia's death—" I began.

"No 'what if' about it," Annabel snapped.

"—but instead of being the killer," I went on, "he was the inconvenient eyewitness who could identify the killer. And the killer, tired of feeling threatened by him—"

"Or possibly tired of being blackmailed by him," Annabel put in.

"—decided to eliminate the danger of discovery by eliminating Mr. Weaver."

"I like it," Annabel said. "It covers all the facts. And Weaver makes a perfectly plausible blackmailer."

"It doesn't much matter what we like," Dr. Ffollett said. "What matters is what Chief Heedles thinks."

"And what she can prove," Annabel said. "And thanks to Meg, at least she's actually doing something now. Meg got her moving, where I failed."

"No thanks to me," I said. "It was Mr. Weaver's murder that got her moving."

"But is she moving enough?" Annabel said. "Why isn't she doing more next door? I expected to see CSI people swarming all over Weaver's house."

"Oh, so Riverton has CSIs?" I asked. "I thought Chief Heedles only had half a dozen officers."

"Don't the State Police have CSIs?" Annabel asked.

"Yes, but someone has to get them involved," I said. "Preferably the chief. And she might not be all that keen on having them butt in."

We all fell silent. Dr. Ffollett picked at a slice of toast on his plate. Annabel helped herself to seconds—or was it thirds?—of the bacon, eggs, and hash browns.

"Luckily it's Chief Heedles's job to figure all that out," I said finally. "She wants to see you sometime later today."

Miss Annabel stopped in the act of spearing a slice of bacon.

"Oh, dear," she said. "I'm not sure I can bear it."

"I told you so," Dr. Ffollett muttered.

"If it would help, I can plan to be here when she comes," I said. "For moral support."

"That would be nice," Annabel said. "And I suppose I can wear my veil. I'd hardly have to look at her, now, would I? It would be almost like talking to her on the telephone. In fact, why don't you suggest that she just call me once the phones are back," she added. "It would be so much more convenient for her."

"She won't go for that," Dr. Ffollett asked. "Not even if your phone were already working. You'll have to face this."

"Don't you have someplace else you need to be?" Annabel snapped at him. "Seeing a patient or something?"

"With no power in town?" Ffollett said. "I *thought* I was being useful here."

The two glared at each other for a few seconds. Then Annabel sighed.

"Sorry," she said. "You are. I'm just on edge at the thought of having to talk to the chief. But I'll do it if I have to."

"Be as cooperative as you can," I suggested. "I don't

know that she's entirely abandoned the idea that you might have killed Weaver out of revenge."

I was surprised at how agitated Annabel looked. She'd taken to me so easily that I'd temporarily forgotten about her reclusiveness. Or, perhaps, forgotten that I was wearing a face so familiar that it outweighed her naturally reclusive nature.

She looked so anxious that I relented.

"But I'll tell the chief how little you saw," I added. "And you never know. Maybe before she finds the time to interview you she'll catch the culprit and won't even need to talk to you."

Actually, I didn't think it all that likely, but Miss Annabel brightened so much that I was glad I'd said it.

"That would be so nice," she said. "And it's not as if I saw anything. After things calmed down over there in your camp, I went upstairs and read in bed for a while. I guess I fell asleep with the lantern on, and the next thing I knew, your car was honking up a storm in front of the house. That's all I can tell her."

"I'll let the chief know that," I said. "By the way, did you find Cordelia's emu records? It would help to know if the eight Grandfather has caught are the whole herd or just a drop in the bucket."

She chuckled.

"A good start," she said. "But only a start. I seem to recall there were thirty-four of them last fall. More if any of them succeeded in hatching eggs this winter, but the young wouldn't be full grown yet, and would tend to stay with their father and siblings until the next mating season. I've copied out the relevant records—that's why I was up so late last night."

She handed me a list, printed in neat, elegant, almost calligraphic letters that reminded me of Dad's printing.

"Great," I said. "Thanks."

I went out Miss Annabel's back door and headed back to camp, feeling guilty every step of the way. After this second murder, shouldn't someone be guarding Miss Annabel? Someone other than the devoted but hardly robust Dr. Ffollett? And yet I knew if I suggested it, she'd probably bite my head off.

Both murders had taken place in the middle of the night. So given that, plus the level of activity around the camp, she was probably safe until dark. That gave me all day to figure out some way to make her safe.

And all day for Chief Heedles to identify and arrest the killer.

Not that I was counting on that.

I sped up my pace and headed for the mess tent, which was usually information central. I spotted Stanley sitting there.

Chapter 25

"Morning," I said. "Has the chief made any progress?"

"Not that I've heard," he said. "But there's nothing wrong with her methodology."

"What do you have on for today?" I asked, taking a seat beside him.

"Not quite sure," he said. "Most of the lines of inquiry I've been following are now very definitely on Chief Heedles's radar. Not a good idea to get in her way, now that she's moving on the case again."

"Is she moving on Cordelia's murder, or just on Weaver's?" I asked.

"That's the big question," he said. "Don't know yet, and until I do, I think I should lie low and stay out of her way. So I was planning to get out of town. Find someplace with power and a working photocopy machine, make duplicates of all my paperwork on the case, and then come back and hand everything over to Chief Heedles. In a day or so we should know a lot more. Or at least we can see if she has any viable suspects."

"I may just have given her one," I said.

"If you mean Thor, I don't think I'd call him a viable suspect," Stanley said, through a mouthful of toast. "He may have been hanging around keeping an eye on Miss Annabel, and he may have mouthed off a couple of times about Weaver. But I don't see him as a killer."

"I wasn't talking about Thor," I said. "Does Heedles really suspect him?"

"She spent a hell of a lot of time interrogating him this

morning," Stanley said. "And sent him away in a police car. Who were you thinking of?"

"Jim Williams."

"Just because he used to work for a mining company?" Stanley sounded skeptical.

"Because he used to work for a mining company and was photographed snooping around a place with known mineral deposits a week before the main local opponent to any attempt to exploit those deposits was probably murdered," I said. "And Thor's the one who did the photographing, so I'm hoping that's what Heedles is interrogating him about."

"I hope so, too," Stanley said. "Because Thor seems like a nice kid, and I thought Heedles was definitely barking up the wrong tree there. If nothing else, I think a kid with his mechanical and technical skills could have rigged up a much more efficient way of setting a fire to cover his tracks."

"Did Williams happen to work with Smedlock Mining?" I asked. "Or one of its subsidiaries?"

Stanley shook his head.

"That's good."

"I'd have mentioned it if he did," Stanley said. "In fact, that was going to be one of my lines of inquiry. Seeing if there was any connection whatsoever between Smedlock and any of the places he worked."

"Do you remember the names of any of the places where he worked?" I asked.

Stanley pulled out his pocket notebook and read me five company names. None of them rang a bell, but I wrote them down in my notebook, just in case.

"Of course," Stanley went on, as he tucked his notebook away. "If the chief's looking at him as a suspect, I'd better hold off on that. I might just go home to Caerphilly to do my copying—I heard from Muriel that the power's back on and the diner's open again. I could do my laundry and get some home cooking while I'm there."

I had to smile at that. No one in Caerphilly had yet figured out whether Stanley was romantically interested in Muriel, owner of the local diner, or if he just appreciated her cooking. Either way, he would clearly enjoy the trip home.

"Sounds like a good idea then," I said. "Though, could I make a suggestion? Could you come back before nightfall and keep an eye on Miss Annabel's house? Maybe I'm being paranoid—"

"Or maybe you're being sensible," he said. "She could be a target. I'll plan to get back tonight, then."

"And I'll keep you posted on anything that happens while you're gone."

"Thanks," he said.

But as the day wore on, I grew less and less confident that I'd have anything to report. Chief Heedles and her officers spent an hour or so searching one of the tents and a nearby silver van—presumably both belonging to Williams. They hauled off the contents of van and tent in a pickup truck.

Sherry, the Valkyrie, found this highly unsatisfactory.

"Why didn't they take the tent as well?" she asked. "And his van's still here. What are we supposed to do with them?"

"Not our problem," I suggested.

"And why are they interrogating him?"

"He was in town around the time of Cordelia Mason's death," I said. "And he used to work for a mining company."

"A mining company!" She looked ashen. "Which one?"

"He's worked for several," I said. "I don't remember the names offhand." I didn't mention the fact that I had them in my notebook. What if in her fury against the mining companies Sherry did something to complicate Stanley's—or Chief Heedles's—investigation. "Does it matter which ones?"

"Well, yes," she said. "Some of them are reasonably responsible, and some are just horrible. Who would know?"

"Stanley Denton," I said. "The PI. I'll ask him when I see him."

"I'll ask him now," she muttered.

She strode off before I could tell her that he was gone for the day. I wondered if her reaction would be typical. Clearly, she was upset by the possibility that someone with ties to the hated mining industry had managed to infiltrate the brigade.

I wandered through the camp, feeling at loose ends. Should I go out and join the emu hunt? Go over and keep Miss Annabel company? Or maybe see if the library was open so I could resume my research?

I ran into a woman sitting in front of her camper, knitting so rapidly and with such a thunderous expression on her face that I couldn't help thinking of Madame DeFarge in *A Tale of Two Cities*. Was this woman recording everything that happened here in camp? If I could read the pattern of her stitches, would I learn the truth about Weaver's murder?

Actually, I suspected this might be Millicent, creator of the emu turtleneck, which made her no less ominous a figure.

"Morning," I said.

"What do you think?" She held up her knitting, which turned out to be a scarf, already three feet long, in a hideous shade of puce. "Isn't this a lovely purple?"

What did I think? That she needed to know the difference between lavender and puce. That far from being lovely, it was the sort of puce that reminded you that "puce" was French for "flea." That if I were going to spend all that time knitting, I'd at least pick a more attractive color. And should I mention that she appeared to have dropped a few stitches about a foot from the start of the scarf, creating a hole that was already unraveling? Probably better not to. At some of the snootier craft shows, where knitters would be insulted if you called them that instead of "fiber artists," I'd occasionally met avant garde practitioners of the art, who considered dropped stitches and even giant gaping unraveled holes an important, organic part of the creative process. With my luck, she'd turn out to be one of those.

"Very distinctive," I said aloud. "Distinctive" was my new buzzword, since far too many people these days knew my mother had taught me that if I couldn't say anything nice I should fall back on "interesting."

"I decided to switch to scarves because I sensed a certain resistance to the effort involved in helping the emus put on the sweaters," she said. "But they can't complain that this is too much trouble, can they?"

I had a sudden vision of Clarence Rutledge trying to wrap a scarf around an emu's neck and being dragged through the woods with his feet hopelessly entangled in a woolly puce death trap.

"Ingenious thinking," I said. "Ingenious" was another of my new substitutes for "interesting."

As I planned, she mistook this for a compliment. She beamed.

"Do you knit?" She began rummaging in a basket at her side. "I have several pairs of needles and plenty of yarn."

"Alas, no." I held up my bandaged hand. "And with this injury, I'm afraid it's not a good time to learn."

I decided it was time to make my escape, in case she'd been experimenting with one-handed knitting and was in the mood to share. Besides, even thinking of my hand made me realize it was throbbing slightly.

And I was so tired from several days of inadequate

sleep that I decided to go back to our tent and rest. Maybe even nap.

I was about to head for our tent when I saw two motorcycles approaching the camp, escorting a truck with a horse trailer attached. I stayed to watch as Dad and two of the motorcycle wranglers unloaded another pair of emus into the pen.

"Clarence here?" one of the wranglers asked.

"He's making a run down to the sanctuary with the other emus," I said.

"Then I'll give these two a quick once-over," Dad said. "To make sure they weren't injured in transit. Is Thor here? It'd be nice to know their names. So we can put them on their tags."

"I think he's down at the police station," I said. "As a witness," I added, seeing the startled look on Dad's face.

"Oh!" I could see that Dad was torn between his desire to hear about the case and his duty to the emus.

"I'll tell you all about it when you're finished with the birds," I said. "And unless you think the emus are really attached to their human names, I'll think of names that fit in with Cordelia's trinomial system. Are they male or female?"

"One of each," he said. "A mated pair, we think."

"How about Elizabeth Barrett Browning and . . . Martin Van Buren?"

"Perfect!"

I watched as Dad checked the emus out. I figured he'd want to hear all about what had happened here at camp, so I decided to hang around and make him happy.

But when he let himself out of the emu pen—carefully checking the gate latch—and walked over to where I was standing, he didn't immediately pepper me with questions.

Instead, he gazed mournfully at the back of Miss Annabel's house.

"How's she taking all this?" he asked.

"Miss Annabel? I think she's frustrated," I said. "She's not happy with how the chief handled her cousin's murder, and I think that makes her a little pessimistic about the chances of solving this one."

He nodded.

"Why don't you go over and talk to her?" I asked.

"She's a recluse," he said. "What if she doesn't want to talk to me?"

"She talks to me," I said. "Why wouldn't she talk to you? You're family. Even closer family than me."

"I'm still getting used to it all," he said.

I realized that he wasn't quite staring at the back of Miss Annabel's house. He was staring at the remains of the shed.

"Used to what?" I said. "The idea that your mother was living less than an hour away all this time and never once contacted you? The fact that if Grandfather had started this quest a year earlier, we might have gotten to meet her? Or maybe the feeling of guilt that you occasionally find yourself wishing that Miss Annabel had gone out to tend the generator that night instead of your mother?"

He glanced up with a surprised expression.

"All of it," he said. "And especially the last. I feel guilty about it, but I couldn't help thinking that."

"So did I at first," I said. "But not so much since I got to know Miss Annabel. You should meet her. She's pretty cool, actually, in a sharp, suffer-no-fools-gladly way. I imagine I can see something of Cordelia in her."

He nodded. But he still looked glum.

"Hey, maybe it's a good thing we never met Cordelia," I said. "Because I'm having a hard time calling her anything but Cordelia. I look at her photo and I don't think 'Grandmother' or 'Grandma' or 'Granny.' Just Cordelia. I'm not sure a lady of her generation would like that very much. I'd get my knuckles rapped."

He smiled at that.

"It took a while with your grandfather, as I recall," he said. "We managed, eventually."

"And got sucked into all his projects," I said. "Before Grandfather showed up, I don't think I ever aspired to appear on television bottle-feeding baby porcupines."

"And until he showed up, I never managed to get myself arrested." Dad made it sound as if this was a singular accomplishment, instead of a dangerous misadventure while Grandfather was trying to break up a dogfighting ring.

"What do you suppose Cordelia would have us doing if she'd been the one to survive instead of Annabel?"

"Rescue the emus, for sure," he said. "And solve Annabel's murder. I'm starved—let's go see what's for lunch, and you can tell me all about why Thor's suddenly such an important witness."

In the mess tent we spotted Dr. Ffollett filling several carryout boxes. I waved, but he scurried off.

"Strange man," I said.

"Dr. Ffollett?" Dad said. "Seems nice enough."

"You've had a chance to meet him, then," I said. "Talk to him. He probably knows a lot about Cordelia. I get the feeling she was more than a patient. Talk to him, doctor to doctor."

"I already tried," Dad said. "He's not very talkative. And it turns out he's a *dentist*."

That didn't sound like Dad. He'd never shown any particular aversion to dentists. In fact, he and my childhood dentist had been kindred spirits. Mother had finally banned him from accompanying me to checkups after he and my dentist had traumatized me with a particularly graphic discussion of whether trench mouth or scurvy had done more to affect the course of world history.

"What have you got against dentists all of a sudden?" I asked.

"Nothing," Dad said. "But—a dentist. Their dentist. And also a friend. It must have been so difficult for him. Poor man."

I was puzzled for a moment, and then I got it. Cordelia had been identified by her dental records. I hoped that didn't mean that Dr. Ffollett had had to go down to the morgue and—

I shoved the thought out of my mind.

"He could probably use a little sympathy, then," I said. "I offered them meals from the mess tent as long as their power is out. He'll probably be back at suppertime. Why don't you lie in wait and see if you can chat him up then?"

"I will." Dad looked cheerful. "There are some fascinating new developments in dental science that I could ask him about."

Grandfather and the wranglers returned shortly afterward with another eight emus. I wasn't sure which made Grandfather happier—the inventory itself, or the news that they had now rounded up over half of the emus. The whole crew was in high spirits over lunch, and I seriously considered going out with them for the afternoon's hunt. And then decided to stay on at camp. I spent much of the afternoon sitting near the emu pen in a lawn chair, pretending to read a book and actually keeping an eye on the emus and Miss Annabel's house.

And then shortly before dinnertime, a hugely pregnant volunteer who'd been having a cup of tea in the mess tent suddenly shrieked that her water had broken. Most of the other volunteers were men, and evidently none of the few women present had much experience with childbirth—all of them froze in panic when she made her announcement.

"Someone find Dad," I ordered. "And does anyone know where her husband is?"

Everyone else in the mess tent fled, presumably following my orders, leaving me alone with a woman who had either failed to read the "Labor and Delivery" chapter of *What to Expect When You're Expecting* or had forgotten everything it said. Fortunately Dad appeared a few minutes later, and after a brief exam, he and Clarence bustled her off in Clarence's station wagon.

"When you find her husband, bring him along," he said, as he was getting the woman settled in the backseat.

"Bring him along where?" I asked. "I don't remember seeing a hospital in Riverton."

"Richmond," he said. "VCU Medical Center. Her obstetrician will meet us there."

"Richmond?" I exclaimed. "That's at least an hour away. Maybe two with traffic. And it's rush hour, so there will be traffic. Can she last that long?"

"It's her first." He was climbing into the car with his patient. "We should get there in plenty of time. And if we don't—I've delivered plenty of babies, and Clarence can help."

"Clarence is a vet," I protested.

"She's an animal lover," he said. "It'll be okay."

Just then a Riverton police car pulled up, lights flashing.

"Ready!" the officer called out.

"See you in Richmond!" Dad waved at me before turning to his patient.

The police officer started his siren and took off, faster than I'd have thought possible on a dirt road. Clarence fell in behind him, keeping pace with surprising ease.

Dad was loving it, I knew, but I hoped the police escort was overkill.

I didn't manage to locate the husband until over an hour later, near the top of Pudding Mountain. I drove him down to Richmond—fighting our way through heavy traffic— kept him from getting lost in the maze of the medical center, and steered him into the delivery room only half an hour before we all welcomed little Blake Langslow Rutledge Parker into the world.

I grabbed a quick dinner in the hospital cafeteria, enjoying the air conditioning but wondering resentfully what gourmet fare they were serving back at Camp Emu.

Then I set out for the long drive back to Riverton. Dad and Clarence were staying on for an hour or two to check on Fred, the poisoning victim, but I was in no mood to tarry. As it was, Michael and the boys would be asleep by the time I got back to camp. And while I had cell phone service in Richmond, where the power was back in most neighborhoods, evidently the towers near Riverton were still out, so I didn't even get to wish the boys goodnight over the phone.

"What a wasted day," I muttered to myself, more than once, on my long drive back.

Riverton was dark when I finally reached it, at nearly ten o'clock. Was there anything darker than a small town in a power outage? I counted the buildings that had any lights on as I drove through town—seven of them, including the police station.

The narrow, tree-lined road to camp was even darker.

But as I approached the little enclave containing Miss Annabel's house, I realized that some lights were on there.

One in Miss Annabel's house.

And one in Mr. Weaver's.

Chapter 26

In fact, not only was there a light on in Weaver's house, it was moving around. It started out upstairs, then grew dim briefly before reappearing downstairs on the left-hand side of the house, where Weaver's home office was.

I drove past Miss Annabel's house and parked along the road, just out of sight. I made sure my headlight was in my pocket. And my cell phone, although odds were it would still be useless if I needed it for anything other than snapping a picture of whatever was going on.

I walked quickly and quietly until I was in front of Weaver's house. The light was more stable now, staying in the same place, although it still twitched and wavered slightly.

If I were an intruder intent on rummaging Mr. Weaver's office, and had brought along a flashlight to do so, I'd put it down in some convenient place—like on one of the shelves—so I'd have both hands free for my work. But if I were wearing one of the LED headlights that were so popular here in Riverton . . .

I crept up to Weaver's door, trying to be quiet without looking furtive. The moon gave enough light to keep me from stumbling. The crime-scene tape still barred the door. I ducked under it and found the front door unlocked.

Inside, I paused for a few moments to let my eyes adjust, though there was enough light coming through the doorway of the office to let me see after a second.

Miss Annabel was sitting at Mr. Weaver's desk, reading a sheet of paper.

I tiptoed forward with my hand on the switch of my own headlight. When I was in the doorway, I pressed the button.

"Good evening," I said.

Miss Annabel was a cool one, I'll give her that. She barely started when the light hit her—just looked up and raised one hand to shield her eyes from my headlight.

"Either call the cops on me or stop shining that thing in my face and help me."

"Since the cell towers still seem to be down, calling the cops isn't an option," I said. "I could drive back into town and get them, but by the time they arrived, you'd be back in your own house and it would be your word against mine that this ever happened. Why don't you tell me what you're doing?"

"Searching Weaver's papers for clues," she said, looking back to the paper she'd been reading. "Investigating. Since I'm still not sure the police will bother."

"When the police do this, it's investigating," I said. "When you or I do it, it's called burglary. Have you found anything interesting?"

"Not really," she said. "The police took his computer, or I could see what's on that."

"Without power?" I said. "And for that matter, are you sure he even had a computer? I don't recall seeing one when I was here last night."

"You could be right," she said. "Anyway, his papers are pretty boring. He's got every mutual fund statement he ever received and every nasty letter to the editor he ever sent, but not much else. No hobbies, for example."

"Maybe mutual funds and writing letters to the editor were his hobbies," I suggested.

"Evidently."

"What were you hoping for?" I asked. "A tell-all diary? 'June second. Six whole months since I murdered my annoying neighbor, and the police still suspect nothing. Mwahaha!'"

"I don't know," she said. "Someone disliked him enough to kill him. I can certainly understand that. But who? Don't killers ever write threatening letters to their intended victims these days?"

"Not if they have half a brain and ever watch TV cop shows," I said. "I thought you were feeling better about Chief Heedles, now that you know she agrees with you that Cordelia was murdered."

"She hardly spent any time here," she said. "I've been watching. Only an hour or two."

"Maybe she was planning to come back."

"I hope she does."

"And finds traces that you and I have ransacked the house? That should go down well. And what if you do find something incriminating?"

"If I find anything incriminating, I'll tell you, and you can figure out a way to see that she finds it herself," she said. "Are you going to help me or stand there arguing?"

"I give up," I said.

We spent the next hour searching Weaver's papers, and then the rest of his house. About the only even slightly interesting thing we found was the twin to the candlestick that the killer had used to make his unsuccessful arson device.

I did a last pass through the house to make sure we hadn't disturbed anything and came back to the office to find Annabel sitting in Weaver's desk chair, reading a paper.

"Found anything interesting?" I asked.

"Not interesting," she said. "Just annoying. Some kind of memo from a vice president at First Undermountain Bank. That's the greedy bastards who foreclosed on the emu farm and wouldn't sell it to me."

"He probably gets a lot of memos from them," I said. "He's on their board, remember?"

"Was on their board," she corrected. "Our killer just created a vacancy. This is a memo someone wrote complaining about how the repossessed emu farm is costing them too much and asking how soon their plan for unloading it can go forward."

"Maybe that spells good news for your hope of establishing an emu sanctuary."

"We won't need that now that we've finally got your Grandfather to pay attention to the birds," she said. "I still might like to buy it, but I think the emus will be fine with this Caroline person. And anyway, this letter is from eight months ago. They've turned us down again since then. Whatever plan they've got doesn't involve us or the emus, that's all I know. Not sure it's significant. I just wonder why this was sitting out in his inbox."

"No idea." I scanned the memo over her shoulder. Then I took a picture of it, just in case.

"Then again, maybe it's good news," she said. "What if Weaver was somehow working to block the sale of the property to us. Well, to me now. Maybe if I asked again, they'd sing a different tune. Even though we don't need the farm quite as much now, it would be interesting to see."

"Maybe," I said. "But why don't you wait until they catch Weaver's killer before you approach them. Because jumping in with another offer right now might make the chief think you have a serious motive for getting rid of Weaver."

"I thought the chief was set on this Williams person as the culprit," she said.

"She's leaning that way," I said. "Don't distract her. And let's get out of here. I think we've established that if Chief

Heedles spent more than an hour searching Weaver's papers she was wasting her time."

She nodded.

We crept to the front door, turned our headlights off, and waited until our eyes adjusted to the dark and we could be sure the coast was clear. Then we stepped out onto the porch.

"Maybe we should turn our headlights back on," I suggested. "You don't want to fall down in the dark."

"Maybe we should wait till we're safely in my yard," she said, as she lifted up the crime-scene tape. "Unless you're afraid of falling down. I have eyes like a cat since my cataract surgery."

We slunk along Weaver's front walk and then down the sidewalk until we were in front of Annabel's yard. Then we both straightened up, turned on our headlights, and strolled up the walk to her front porch.

Dr Ffollett was waiting just inside Annabel's front door.

"Where have you been?" he hissed to Annabel. "I got here with your groceries and the house was empty and the door open! And what's she doing here?" He glared at me.

"She's been over at Mr. Weaver's house, snooping," I said. "And although I disapprove of the snooping, I'm here to make sure we have our stories straight, in case anyone spotted her over there and called the cops. How about 'we thought we saw something suspicious, so we went over to check it out.' Work for you, Miss Annabel?"

"Works fine," she said. "Thanks."

"You didn't," Dr. Ffollett groaned.

"So now what?" I asked Annabel.

"I have no idea."

"I'm going to send Stanley the picture I took of that memo," I said. "As soon as I get someplace where there's a cell phone signal. Or I'll show it to him tomorrow."

"You think it's significant?" She sounded eager.

"No," I said. "But it's the only even mildly interesting thing we found."

"True," she said. "Why would a bank that's dying to sell a millstone round its neck turn down a legitimate offer?"

"You're sure your offer was competitive?" I asked.

"I—we made several increasingly large offers," she said. "Our last one pretty much asked them to name their price. And they know we can afford it."

"Are they your bankers?"

"I'd sooner trust my money to a pack of hyenas," she said. "But banks have ways of finding out these things. They knew."

"So it's puzzling," I said. "Let's see what Stanley can find out. Can you get us copies of your correspondence with the bank?"

"Of course." She walked over to a small secretary desk, flipped down the hinged desktop, and sat down in front of it. She selected a pen from a small blue-and-aqua pot—more Biscuit Mountain Art Pottery, I was sure—and pulled out a five-by-eight-inch three-ring notebook with an elegant flowered cover.

"Our attorney has all the paperwork," she said. "I'll write a note asking him to make copies for you. Dwight can drop it off with him in the morning."

As she spoke, she was writing down something in the notebook. I suddenly realized I was Miss Annabel's equivalent of my notebook-that-tells-me-when-to-breathe.

It was almost like watching a much older version of myself. Although I doubted I'd ever learn to keep my notebook as clean and tidy as Annabel's. Well organized, yes, but scruffily so. I could never hope to write as neatly and precisely as she did.

She pulled out a sheet of notepaper and began penning her note, while I looked on. She had fine, old-fashioned copperplate handwriting, and when she occasionally printed a word, for emphasis, her printing had the same elegant, calligraphic quality as Dad's, as I'd noticed before on the emu inventory. Was there a genetic component to handwriting style? Would Cordelia's printing have looked even more like Dad's? And why hadn't I gotten a little more of that particular gene?

Annabel finished her note, and was reaching for an envelope when she noticed me looking over her shoulder.

"Sorry," I said. "Didn't mean to hover."

"I don't mind having someone watch me work on my memorandum book." She tucked the note in the envelope as she spoke, and licked and sealed it. "Just don't ever touch the notebook. Drives me insane."

"I feel the same way," I said, patting the tote that currently held my own bulging three-ring notebook. "Ask me to do something, fine; but hands off the notebook."

She nodded with matter-of-fact approval, as if I'd made the only sensible reply—and the one she expected of me.

Something suddenly clicked. Not just the fact that she had a fraternal twin of my notebook. The similar way our minds worked. Her fierce anger at Grandfather. The disconnect between the timid Annabel others described and the strong, forceful woman I'd come to know.

"You're not Cordelia's cousin, are you?" I said aloud.

She looked up and frowned slightly. Dr. Ffollett made a little squeaking noise, but we both ignored him.

"You're Cordelia, aren't you?" I said. "You're my grandmother."

"Took you long enough," Annabel—or, rather, Cordelia—said, with a slight chuckle.

Chapter 27

I just stared, and she sat there, smiling slightly, her head cocked to one side expectantly. But what was she expecting? A hug from her long-lost granddaughter? A rebuke for having kept me in the dark so long? A volley of recriminations? I wasn't sure myself which was most appropriate. All the anger, sadness, and sheer bafflement I'd been dealing with since Stanley had told us his news boiled up and again it was a while before I trusted myself to speak.

I tried to keep my face from showing how I felt, but I suspected Cordelia could tell. Just as I could tell that she was faking her calm, smiling expression.

"Why?" I asked when I finally thought I could manage a calm voice.

"So many possible *whys,*" she said. "Which one do you want me to start with?"

I wanted to start with "Why the hell didn't you ever try to get in touch with us?" but I didn't think it would make for a very good start to our suddenly redefined relationship. "And how could you do this to your own son?" was even worse. I'd decided now how I felt toward Cordelia. Mad as hell. Probably a feeling I should grapple with in silence, rather than lashing out and spoiling things forever.

"Let's start with why you were pretending to be dead." That seemed safe.

I could tell from Cordelia's expression that she was relieved to start with such a relatively neutral question.

"Weaver didn't hate poor Annabel," she said. "He hated me. I didn't realize he hated me enough to kill me, or I'd have taken precautions. But standing over her body, I knew I was in danger. At least I thought I was. And I also thought if he figured out I was still alive, he'd try again, and I wouldn't even have Annabel as a witness."

"I assume you got Dr. Ffollett to switch your dental records," I said. "So they'd think she was you."

"I did nothing of the kind!" Dr. Ffollett snapped. "They didn't identify her body from her dental records. They identified her—*mis*identified her—from her partial plate."

"I'm sorry, but isn't that more or less the same thing?" I asked.

"No! It is very definitely not the same thing!" he exclaimed. And then seeing my puzzlement, he elaborated. "In some states dentists are legally required to mark any removable prosthetic or orthodontic device with the name or social security number of the patient to whom it belongs. And even in states where it isn't required, it's a responsible thing for a dentist to do. I've always done it."

"And Dr. Ffollett has been the family dentist for years," Cordelia added. "He'd made partial plates for both of us."

"With their proper names on them," Dr. Ffollett muttered.

His indignation amused me, and I had to work to keep from smiling or even giggling. I glanced toward Cordelia and realized she was doing the same thing. A little of the anger I'd been feeling toward her fell away.

"So the police found Cordelia's partial plate with Annabel's body and assumed they'd found Cordelia." I turned to Cordelia. "I don't suppose Annabel really went out to the shed wearing your partial plate by mistake, now did she?"

"She didn't," Cordelia said. "I put it there." And then, seeing from my face that I wasn't satisfied with the answer, she went on. "Here's what happened. Just the way I told you before, except it wasn't me who went out to turn off the generator. I was feeling poorly. Bad head cold. I suggested we just leave it on for the night, but Annabel said don't be silly, she could do it. She knew how—she just didn't like doing it much, and most nights I didn't mind. She was already ready for bed—had her plate soaking in the bathroom—so she just put on her bathrobe and ran out to the shed. I wasn't lying about keeping an eye on her. She wasn't as sturdy as me. She went behind the shed, the generator stopped—and then less than a minute later the flames shot up. I knew right away the fire wasn't an accident. I went out there and saw . . . saw . . ."

She closed her eyes and swallowed. Then she set her jaw and opened them again, with a fierce expression. A little more of my anger faded.

"There was no hope for Annabel. I could see that. She was dead, and the fire had already reached her. And I knew who'd done it. I saw a figure sneaking away toward his house, and I was sure it was him. And I figured once he found out he'd killed the wrong cousin, he'd try again. So the first thing I did was run inside to get my partial plate from the medicine cabinet. By the time I got back out, the fire had spread so far I couldn't get near where she was lying, so I just threw the plate in and hoped the police would assume it had fallen out when she fell or something."

"And they did," Dr. FFollett put in. "I knew as soon as I heard about the accident—"

"The non-accident," Cordelia corrected. "The murder."

"The fire, then—I knew it was a mistake. That it couldn't possibly be Cordelia."

"Why not?" I asked.

"I don't wear the plate anymore," she said. "Got an implant—how long has it been, Dwight—thirty years?"

"Thirty-two as of April," he said. "I checked my records. I assumed the police would be requesting them. I came over to warn Cordelia that I wasn't going to lie. That when the police questioned me, I'd tell them it couldn't be her. That it was Annabel."

"But the fools never asked," Cordelia said. "So since Dwight promised to keep my secret until they did, for now I'm safe."

"And my professional ethics are in tatters," Dr. Ffollett said.

"It's your ethics or my life," Cordelia snapped. And then her face softened. "I understand that if you're asked, you have to tell. And I'm as disappointed as you are that they never asked, because that would have meant they were taking the case seriously. Instead of hoping people would forget about it. Or maybe hoping I'd die and stop bothering them."

"I'm surprised the medical examiner didn't compare the plate they found with Annabel's teeth," I said. "Unless of course the two of you were missing precisely the same tooth or teeth—"

"We were," she said. "It's a genetic condition. Runs in the Lee family. It's called—"

"Peg lateral," I said.

They both stared at me.

"How do you know about that?" Dr. Ffollett asked.

"Dad has it, too," I said. "He's missing one of his lateral incisors. And while my brother, Rob, and I weren't affected, my sister Pam is missing the same tooth."

"Upper right side?" Cordelia asked.

I nodded.

"Fascinating!" Dr. Ffollett exclaimed. "Have you ever sent in your DNA to the National Geographic's Genographic Project? You might have Native American ancestry. Peg lateral tends to be more common in certain Native American tribes. Although usually both upper lateral incisors are affected and the tooth is very small rather than completely missing. This could be a different mutation entirely! I've always thought it would be a fascinating subject for a paper, and now with two more subjects—"

"If you had an implant over thirty years ago, why did you still have your partial plate lying around?" I asked Cordelia.

She shook her head.

"Beats me," she said. "Why do we have kerosene lanterns and butter churns lying around? Seemed a waste just to throw it out. Or maybe I had a premonition that someday the old plate would be useful."

"A pity you didn't also have a premonition that the old kerosene lantern in the shed would cause problems," Dr. Ffollett said.

"I'm not even sure that was our kerosene lantern," Cordelia snapped. "I think someone planted it. Weaver. Or whoever killed Annabel."

"Did you really think you'd get away with it?" My voice was perhaps a little sharper than it needed to be. I wasn't completely past the anger. "Didn't you realize that sooner or later someone would find out?"

"I didn't think I needed to get away with it," she said. "Not for long. I thought the police would investigate, get the goods on Weaver, and arrest him. With him locked up, I'd be safe, and I could come out of hiding. If I'd known the whole thing would still be dragging on six months later, maybe I'd have taken my chances."

"Chief Heedles said you'd given her a statement right after the murder," I said. "Didn't she suspect anything?"

"One little old lady looks pretty much like another to most people," Cordelia said.

"Then there's the fact that you pretended to be so overcome with grief that you had taken to your bed with a cold compress over your eyes," Dr. Ffollett said. "One little old lady with a washcloth covering her whole face does look pretty much like another, I'll give you that."

"If you gave a false statement to the police—" I began.

"I never lied," she said. "I never pretended she was me. I always referred to her as 'my cousin' or 'she.'"

"I assume you attended the funeral," I said.

"Heavily veiled, and leaning on poor Dwight for support," she said. "We were much the same height, Annabel and I, and since she was known to be such a recluse, everyone pretty much left me alone."

"And what about your cousin's estate?" I asked. "Does she have beneficiaries who might not be too pleased with you?"

"She never married, and I never had any other children," Cordelia said. "I'm her beneficiary, as she would have been mine if I'd gone first. And Dwight's the executor."

"And since I'm not keen on going into court under false pretenses—" Dr. Ffollett began.

"He's been dragging his heels, on my orders," Cordelia said. She sighed and shook her head. "It was never supposed to last this long. But maybe now's the time to come clean. Whether Weaver did it or this person the chief has locked up, I should be out of danger."

"Or maybe you're in just as much danger as ever," I said. "What if Mr. Williams isn't the killer either? But yes, I agree—you need to come clean. To the chief, if nothing else. If she'd known the truth before, maybe she'd have taken your evidence more seriously."

"Why?" She sounded puzzled. "Am I a more credible witness than Annabel?"

"Where were you when you saw Weaver?" I asked. "Here in the house? Or out by the fire?"

"Out there," she said. "Almost at the fire."

"The way I heard it—and the way the chief heard it— you were here in the house. Much farther away, under conditions that weren't exactly optimal."

"You have a point," she said. "Conditions weren't optimal for observation out there, and from way up here in the house? And I'm beginning to wonder if I only thought it was him because whoever it was ran straight toward his house."

"And even if it was him, what if he wasn't the killer?" I suggested. "What if he saw something going on and ran out to see what it was—he loved to snoop, I've noticed that already. And then when he saw Annabel dead, maybe he thought, 'Holy cow! What if they blame me?' He'd have run away, back to his house, right?"

"Instead of trying to administer first aid or at least save her body from the fire?" she asked. "Yes, probably. And that makes more sense. Because I'm pretty sure it was Weaver."

"Pretty sure," I echoed. "Not positive. Still, even with pretty sure, do you think maybe Chief Heedles might have taken your identification more seriously if she'd known that you were within five or ten feet of the fleeing figure, rather than forty or fifty feet?"

"I realized a few days later," she said. "But by that time it was too late. I couldn't very well go down and give a different statement. I couldn't go down at all."

"And Heedles wasn't going to buy another washcloth-draped interview," Dr. Ffollett put in.

"But if I confessed why I lied, maybe she'd believe me," Cordelia said.

I nodded.

"And if she doesn't believe me and thinks I killed Weaver because he tried to kill me and got Annabel instead, then I could probably get off on self defense," she said. "Might be interesting."

"Good grief," I said. "You sound just like Dad. He always finds it fascinating to be a murder suspect. I'm so glad I don't seem to have inherited that peculiar trait."

"It's too late to talk to Chief Heedles tonight," Cordelia said. "I'll sleep on it."

"In the meantime," I said, "is it okay if I tell one other person about your real identity?"

"You mean your father?" She sounded a little wistful.

"Actually, I was taking it for granted that you'd tell him. I meant one person in addition to Dad. We should definitely tell him right away."

"Are you sure this is the right time?" she asked. "With all this going on?"

"I think it's long past time," I said. "How about I break it to him gently tomorrow?"

"Yes," she said. "And before you tell Chief Heedles, if that's who else you have in mind. James deserves to be the first. Well, after you. But you guessed it. Who else were you thinking of telling?"

"Michael," I said. "My husband. And in fact, make that two other people. Stanley Denton. He's been working very hard to solve your murder. For all I know, this might be just the bit of information he needs to crack the case."

"Somehow I doubt that," she said. "But yes, do tell them. But first, let's tell your father. First thing in the morning."

"Even if he may not be able to keep your secret?" I said. "Not because he won't try, but because he won't be able to hide his exuberance."

"You think he'll be exuberant?" She smiled slightly. "Yes, even then."

"First thing in the morning, then." Dr. Ffollett stood up, evidently feeling this was a good note on which to depart. "You'll probably want to keep that a family affair."

"Come over beforehand and help me keep from going crazy," Cordelia suggested, moving toward the front door.

Dr. Ffollett nodded and went out. I figured she was tired, so I prepared to take my leave. Probably a good thing

I had an excuse to leave. So far I'd managed to avoid expressing the anger I'd been feeling. And it would be a lot easier to get past that by myself.

But more questions were still nagging me. Maybe one more wouldn't hurt. One that didn't go too much farther.

"Before I go," I said. "One more *why*?"

She cocked her head in interrogation.

"You never had any children," I said. "Other than Dad, I mean. Was that a choice?"

"Of sorts," she said. "Robert—my late husband—didn't know about your father. When we were courting, I didn't know how he'd take it. By the time I figured out my past wouldn't have been an issue, there was a bigger reason to keep the secret."

"Bigger reason?"

"When we hit our fifth anniversary with me still not pregnant, Robert suggested we ask our doctor if he could do tests. And I'd already figured he'd get around to that sooner or later. So by the time he brought the subject up, I'd already briefed the family doctor, in confidence, about my history, and got him to agree that if Robert insisted on testing, he'd do the tests—or pretend to. And if there wasn't much hope, then he should say I was the problem."

"You knew he'd take it hard."

"It would have killed him," she said. "Made him feel as if he failed me. I know it sounds silly now, but those were different times. I don't think it would have bothered me nearly as much. Then again, how do I know? By the time Robert and I met, I'd already had your dad. I knew I could have kids. It all became part and parcel of the big secret I was keeping."

"So he never knew about Dad."

"Heavens, no!" She shook her head vigorously. "After a while, I wished I could tell him, but I couldn't do that to him. I don't think your father's existence would have bothered him so much as the fact that we hadn't had any children together. He went to the grave thinking it was my fault, and he never blamed me. Not once."

Her answer to this *why* raised at least as many questions as it settled. Like why not adopt? And why not find some reason for keeping in touch with Dad—like pretending to be his adoptive parents' oldest and dearest friend, a friend who, not having children of her own, became like a second mother to him.

Time enough to talk about all this, instead of trying to do it standing in a doorway with both of us nearly falling asleep on our feet. So I nodded and was turning away when Cordelia gently took my arm and stopped me.

"I never stopped thinking about your father," she said. "About all of you. I realized pretty quickly that having me around really bothered your father's adopted parents. Made them worry that I'd take him back. So I watched from afar, because that was all I thought I could do. Wait—let me show you."

She pushed the front door closed and strode back to the living room. I followed her to the small desk. She opened a drawer and took out a key.

"Annabel never approved of this," she said. "She always said that if you spend too much time craning to see the road not taken, you're sure to trip and break your neck. So she pretended this didn't exist."

She unlocked a nearby armoire—I'd assumed it held a television. But instead, I saw a shrine to my family. The large space where I'd expected to see a television contained a pair of wrought-iron candlesticks I'd made, and pinned to the inside of the cabinet were pictures of Mother and Dad, of my sister Pam and her family, of Rob, and of me with Michael and the boys. Most of the pictures were obviously taken from publications. Rob on the *Business-week* cover the year his first computer game, *Lawyers from*

Hell, was a runaway success. A photo of me at my anvil from a craft magazine. Mother and Dad's wedding picture from the *Yorktown Crier*. Michael in his costume from the cult TV show he'd appeared on for several years.

"I suppose some people might call me a stalker," Cordelia said. "But I think I had reason." She was pulling open one of the armoire's drawers to show that it contained scrapbooks. Copies of some of Rob's games. Several more bits of my blacksmithing work, including one of the simple little hooks I often made as a demonstration and gave out to members of the audience.

"And this is a prized possession." She bent over to open the bottom drawer.

I was leaning over to see the contents when something hit my head, hard, and everything went black.

Chapter 28

"You can't leave her lying that way." Cordelia's voice hit my head like a sledgehammer, pounding away with every syllable. No, wait. My head was doing the pounding. Her voice only made it worse.

"She could suffocate," Cordelia went on.

I flinched, and wondered if there was a polite way to tell your own grandmother to shut up.

"I said—" Cordelia began.

"Shut up, you bossy old cow!" said another voice. Irrationally, the words made me mad. Okay, I wanted peace and quiet, but where did she get off, telling my grandmother to shut up? That was my prerogative. And I wouldn't have been so rude.

And who was she, this rude person? The voice was tantalizingly familiar. I could figure out who it was if my head would just stop pounding.

Or maybe it would work just as well if I took a look at her.

I opened my eyes. Didn't help. I was looking at a small stretch of white wall and white-painted baseboard. And they wobbled slightly in a way I didn't think walls and baseboards were supposed to be capable of.

"You can't—"

"Shut up! I'm trying to think!"

I recognized the voice now. Sherry. Valkyrie Sherry. Clipboard Sherry. What was she doing in Cordelia's house?

"I could make it look like arson," Sherry said, "so Chief Heedles will think it's the same killer as last time."

"What do you mean, 'think it's the same killer?' " Cordelia asked. "Don't pretend you didn't kill both Annabel and Theo Weaver."

I moved my head ever so slightly so I could see them. Cordelia was sitting in a chair a few feet away from me. Her hands were tied behind her back. Sherry was standing nearby. She had a gun in her right hand. I liked the fact that it was pointed at the ceiling rather than at me or Cordelia, but not the fact that Sherry was tapping it rather absentmindedly against her other hand.

"But she's already arrested someone for that," Sherry went on.

"You should have thought of that before you attacked us," Cordelia said. If the tendency to mouth off when it would be smarter to keep silent was a genetic trait, I now knew where I'd gotten it.

"I'll need to find someone else to pin the blame on," Sherry mused. "Preferably someone who can be blamed for the other murders as well. And a better way of starting the fire this time. If Weaver's house had burned down the way it was supposed to—well, it can't be helped. But I'll have to find something that works better this time."

"Are you asking me for advice?" Cordelia said.

"No, I'm telling you to shut up." Sherry pointed the gun at Cordelia. "If you shut up and let me think, I'll knock you out before I start the fire. If you keep yakking, I'll make sure you're awake for it."

I already knew I disliked Sherry. And I liked her even less now, since evidently she was the reason I was lying here with my head pounding and my arms tied behind me, listening to her threaten my grandmother and brainstorm on how to get away with adding us to her death toll.

"I think you're the best candidate." Sherry was studying Cordelia. "She'll have a knot on her head—I'll set it up so it looks as if you knocked her out and were planning to burn down the house with her in it and fell down while running away."

"You really think they'll buy that I tried to burn down my own house?" Cordelia asked.

"Not your house." Sherry sounded exasperated. "Weaver's house next door. That way we'll also be rid of any inconvenient evidence that might be there. And Chief Heedles will assume you were the culprit all along and with nosy Meg out of the way, too, everything will be fine."

Clearly her definition of fine was radically different from mine.

"You don't have to do this, you know," Cordelia said. "There's not a shred of evidence against you in either of the two cases. Why not quit while you're ahead?"

"And let you turn me in? No thanks."

"You could claim you ran in and found me hitting Meg over the head," Cordelia said. "It would be your word against mine, and everyone in town thinks I'm crazy."

"But that won't solve the real problem, will it?" Sherry said. "That horrible Dr. Blake will still be running around trying to ruin my family. He wants to keep us from mining the kyanite, and if we can't get another project going soon, we'll go bankrupt."

"Dr. Blake is here to rescue the emus," Cordelia said. "He isn't here to stop your mine."

"That's because he doesn't know about it," Sherry said. "As soon as he finds out, he'll attack us again. So I have to get him before he finds out. And that means I have to get rid of you so you won't warn him."

Her matter-of-fact tone chilled me as much as the fact that she was talking about killing three people—one of them me, and the other two the grandparents who'd only recently entered my life.

"I don't think Dr. Blake—" Cordelia began.

"It's Blake who's ruined everything," Sherry snapped.

"Him and people like him. First the unions come in and force us to coddle our workers. The way they carry on you'd think we kept slaves instead of paying people to work in our mines. Then it was the tree huggers trying to tell us what we can do on our own land. And then just when we find a natural gas deposit good enough to keep us from going under, along comes Blake and stops us—and for what? A stupid toad! A toad so ugly we'd be doing the world a favor if we did make it extinct. You know what I think I'll do when I've gotten rid of Blake? I'll round up my brothers and we'll go out in the woods and have us a toad hunt. We'll use the slimy little things for target practice, and when we run out of bullets we'll go after them with clubs. You want to talk about extinct? I'll show you extinct."

She was practically shrieking now, and her face was beet red and contorted with fury. I was relieved to see that Cordelia, though obviously tempted to reply, had clenched her jaw tightly shut.

"Yes, once I've gotten rid of Blake, I can finally stop pretending to be a stupid tree hugger." Sherry smiled with satisfaction and hurried out of the room.

Cordelia watched her go. The front door opened and closed again. Then she craned her head again to look down at me.

"Are you okay?" she asked.

"My head hurts," I said. "And when we get out of this, I'm going to have Dad check me out for a possible concussion. But apart from that, I'm okay."

" 'When we get out of this,' " Cordelia repeated. "Does that mean you have a plan to rescue us?"

"No, but I'll work on it," I said. "If you have any bright ideas, now's the time to share them."

She pursed her lips and sighed.

"So she's doing this because she thinks Grandfather

wants to stop her family from mining the kyanite on Biscuit Mountain?" I asked.

"Yes," Cordelia said. "She's a Smedlock. She joined Blake's Brigade under her married name, but she was born a Smedlock—part of the family that owns that dreadful mining company."

"The company whose fracking plans Grandfather foiled."

"Precisely," she said. "And they're still plenty mad about it and out for revenge. They blame him for the fact that they're nearly bankrupt. And none of them would think of doing anything responsible like getting an honest job. So the only thing they've come up with to keep themselves afloat is strip mining the kyanite on Biscuit Mountain. She killed Annabel—thinking she was me—because she knew I'd fight it all the way. Once I'd seen the report from my own mining engineer and knew what a disaster it would be for the town, I was pretty vocal about my opposition to any mining on Biscuit Mountain."

"Was she also behind the attempt to poison Grandfather?"

"Yes, she's been plotting that for a long time," Cordelia said. "Out of revenge for his ruining their fracking plan, even before he showed an interest in Biscuit Mountain. And the lethal candy box was supposed to be punishment for me, for inviting him down here."

"But why did she kill Weaver? Assuming she did, of course."

"He saw her kill Annabel," she said. "And he was blackmailing her. Demanding a bigger share of the proceeds from the mine. Pretty stupid, if you ask me. He knew she was a killer."

"She certainly told you a lot," I said.

"I think she's been dying to get it all out of her system," Cordelia said. "The strain of operating within enemy territory. And, of course, she has no intention of letting me live to report any of it. In fact—"

Just then we heard the sound of the door opening. Cordelia looked away, no doubt to avoid calling Sherry's attention to the fact that I was awake.

I decided that was my cue to pretend to be more out of it than I was. I closed my eyes almost all the way, and slumped on the floor again.

"The coast is clear!" Sherry chirped, in the sort of bright, cheerful tone some people use when they have been put in charge of children and neither like nor understand them.

Cordelia didn't say anything. I decided to continue playing dead.

"You can get up now." Sherry's voice had a bit more of an edge to it.

"I'm still tied to the chair, you know," Cordelia said. "And for all I know you've given her a concussion."

I opened one eye wide enough to watch as Sherry carefully went round to the back of Cordelia's chair and undid something. Then she grabbed Cordelia by the elbow and hauled her up out of the chair, her hands still tied behind her.

"Ow!" Cordelia protested. "Be careful! Old folks like me have brittle bones."

Sherry ignored her words and took something off her wrist—I realized she'd been wearing a roll of silver duct tape like a bracelet. She ripped off a strip of it and stepped behind Cordelia to wrap it over her mouth.

Cordelia kicked her in the shins.

"Ow! You'll pay for that, you old bat."

She grabbed Cordelia's arms roughly and forced her to her knees. Then she taped her mouth and hauled her back to her feet.

Cordelia didn't look cowed. A pity looks really didn't

kill, or our only problem would be getting ourselves untied.

Sherry ignored the glare in Cordelia's eyes and turned to me.

"Don't try anything," she said.

She strode over and planted her foot on my back, making sure I didn't have a chance to try anything. She tore off another strip of duct tape and applied it to my mouth. Then she jumped back as if worried that I'd try something in spite of being bound and gagged.

"Get up," she said, kicking me in the ribs by way of emphasis.

I moaned slightly, trying to suggest that I didn't know if I could get up.

"You can whine on your feet or die on the floor," Sherry said. "Take your pick."

It occurred to me that Sherry probably wanted to avoid shooting me—odds were that a gunshot would bring someone over from camp to investigate. But that didn't mean she'd have any qualms about killing me in some other, quieter way. Hitting me on the head with the gun, for example. Or with whatever blunt instrument she could find. Neither Annabel nor Theo Weaver had been shot.

I struggled to my feet. It wasn't easy, and I made sure it looked even harder than it was. And that it took as long as possible. I figured delay was on our side.

"Get going," she said. "Both of you."

She herded us into the hallway. According to the grandfather clock ticking away there it was nearing 2:00 A.M. Not a time when anyone was likely to be passing by the house, unfortunately. Sherry opened the door and then stood well back as we exited. Then she closed—but did not lock—the front door.

I had a bad feeling about this. My head still throbbed.

My lacerated hand was throbbing in time with it. My shoulders were aching from the awkward way in which Sherry had pulled my hands behind my back. I felt more than slightly queasy. And with every step we took, we drew closer to Weaver's house, where Sherry was planning to do away with us, and I hadn't yet figured out a plan for getting us out.

I should try to make a break for it, I decided. And before we left Cordelia's yard, because her backyard only had the wire fence between it and Camp Emu. Mr. Weaver's yard also had all that overgrown thorny shrubbery that would make it even harder either to get over the fence or attract any attention from this side of it.

We were getting close to the gate. I needed to make my break soon.

I glanced over at Cordelia. She didn't look frightened. She looked calm and focused and mad as the proverbial wet hornet. And suddenly I didn't feel nearly so bad. I wasn't in this alone. I had Cordelia. My grandmother. I might still be a little mad at her, but I already knew how much she thought like me. If I made a move, she'd figure out what I was up to before Sherry did, and she'd do what she could to help.

I think she smiled at me—it was hard to tell underneath the duct tape. Her eyes flicked to the right slightly. There was a large camellia bush there. Maybe a good place to make my move. Our move. If I could lurch into Sherry and shove her into the bush . . .

We were about five feet away from the bush and I was tensing to leap when someone stepped out of the shrubbery.

"Hey! What's going on?" It was Thor. "Why are you— Ms. Delia?"

At the unexpected sight of Cordelia's face, Thor froze. Just for a moment, but that was all it took. Sherry kicked him in the groin and Thor doubled over like an abandoned rag doll.

If Thor had been a vicious thug, I'd have applauded Sherry's quick thinking and capable execution of a highly effective self-defense measure. But since Thor was our would-be rescuer, our now-disabled knight in shining armor, I couldn't help but deplore her underhanded tactics.

"Take that, you creep!" she hissed. She kicked him in the stomach, hard. I could hear a slight *oof!* as the air went out of him. She aimed another kick at Thor's face.

The kick never landed. Cordelia head-butted Sherry, sending her staggering toward me. I deliberately hurled myself toward Sherry's oncoming form. We collided hard and fell in a tangled heap of thrashing limbs.

For a few seconds, I kicked Sherry as hard as I could and tried to roll on top of her to keep her down, while she struggled to heave me away. Out of the corner of my eye I could see Thor curled in a fetal position under the camellia bush and Cordelia staggering toward the backyard. Good; the backyard was our goal. The backyard, and the wire fence, and beyond it Camp Emu, where dozens of potential rescuers lay sleeping.

"Get off of me!" Sherry hissed. She scrambled to her feet, aimed a kick at my still-throbbing head—ow!—and turned to see where Cordelia had gone.

Thump! Thump! Thump! Thud-thud-thud! Thump! Thump! Thump!

Cordelia hadn't reached the wire fence, but she had reached her house's old-fashioned flat metal cellar door and had begun jumping up and down on it, thumping out an SOS in Morse code. The sound was surprisingly loud in the peaceful, generator-free night air, but would it be enough to rouse the camp? And would anyone in camp recognize Morse code when they heard it?

"Stop that!" Sherry hissed. She ran toward Cordelia. I staggered to my feet and took off toward the back fence.

Thump! Thump! Thump! Thud-thud-thud! Thump! Thump!—

I could hear the sounds of a scuffle as I ran past, but I didn't stop to see what was happening. I had my head down and was charging toward the fence. If I could get over it before Sherry stopped me . . .

Behind me, I could hear more hissed orders from Sherry. I didn't waste energy trying to figure out what she was saying or whether she was hissing at me or Cordelia. Always the possibility she'd finally lose patience and shoot me in the back, but I could only hope she was still trying to avoid shattering the silent night with gunfire. And she'd have to be an awfully good shot to hit me with both of us running. And every second I ran was another second for Thor to get his breath back or Cordelia to recover from whatever Sherry had just done to her. Or for someone to spot us. Where was Stanley? He'd agreed to stand guard. He was probably doing it from the across the fence, but surely he'd have noticed something by now.

"Stop right now or I'll shoot!" Sherry hissed, from alarmingly close behind me.

I didn't stop. I was approaching the back fence.

Suddenly I spotted something lying on the ground near the fence. Not something—someone, trussed up and gagged. The silver duct tape gleamed slightly in the moonlight.

It was Stanley. Evidently, he had been on guard, and had become Sherry's first captive. As I approached, I saw him squirm closer to the fence and hunch his back oddly.

He was making himself into a step to help me over the fence. He probably figured helping me escape was his best chance for survival.

I had a few seconds to figure out what to do. I should probably avoid his back. And his neck. I jumped up onto his rear end and from there I managed to vault over the fence.

I landed with a thud. Across the fence, I heard rustling noises, and cursing. Evidently Stanley had managed to wriggle into Sherry's path and trip her.

I staggered back to my feet and looked around, trying to orient myself.

Sherry sailed over the fence, slammed into me, and knocked me back to the ground.

"You're ruining everything!" She was flailing at me— not very effectively, but some of her blows hit home. And I'd landed painfully on my lacerated hand.

Barking erupted from somewhere nearby. The dogs! We were near the emu pen. Lad, Tinkerbell, and Spike were in there with the flock. I silently promised them a pound or two of treats if they barked loud enough to raise the camp.

Sherry was on top of me, still pounding and cursing as I wriggled frantically, trying to get into a position where I could kick her. I realized that she wasn't just pounding with her fists. She still had the gun in one of them, which hurt a hell of a lot more than her fist. And at any moment she could realize she'd lost the battle for silence and use the gun to silence me permanently. I struggled harder.

Suddenly something big landed on us. Sherry was so startled she screamed—yay! And then she kept screaming as the something—more than one something, actually—trampled over us, pounding heavily like a herd of elephants.

No, like a flock of startled emus. Evidently the emus had surged against a section of chain-link, knocking it over on top of us, which allowed the emus to escape by scrambling across the downed portion of the fence. Luckily the fence protected us from their claws. Then they thundered off—away from camp, where sounds showed that at least a few people had been roused and were on their way. The emus were running toward Cordelia's backyard. Good. Yesterday's emus would probably have headed in another direction, but these emus, who had never been cornered by Cordelia's fence, didn't know they were making a tactical mistake. And even better, I could see Lad trotting purposefully after them.

I should stop worrying about the emus. I wasn't out of the woods yet. Sherry heaved herself up, lifting the section of chain-link fence. With both hands, I noted. So where was the gun?

I spotted it at the same moment Sherry did. And I was closer to it. Which might have done me some good if my hands weren't still tied behind my back. I scrambled, crablike, to get my feet in position to kick her when she reached for it.

"Aha!" she exclaimed. I noted with dismay that she didn't make much of an effort to say it quietly. She reached down and—

"Aaiiiii!" Sherry screamed again, and I flinched, expecting to be trampled by another wave of emus. Then I realized that Sherry was waving her hand around with something attached to it.

Spike! His familiar irritable growling was somewhat muffled by the large portion of Sherry's hand in his mouth, but he hung on for dear life and kept growling until Sherry finally did something that caused him to squeal and let go. She kicked him off into the night. I didn't hear a thud or squeal—was that a good thing or a bad thing? He'd probably landed on grass, right?

I'd have to worry about Spike later. If I got to have a later. Sherry, still cursing softly and massaging her Spike bite, was bending down again to pick up the gun. A large flying shape appeared out of the darkness and knocked her down.

"Oof!"

"Grrrrrr." Tinkerbell's soft bass growl made it very clear how she felt about any struggles Sherry might be trying to make. Tink was probably also drooling on the back of Sherry's neck, not because she was particularly bloodthirsty, but because Rob had trained her to expect a liver treat whenever she knocked down potential burglars and prowlers. Halloween visits to our house could be a little overstimulating for children who didn't already know and love Tinkerbell.

"What's going on here?"

"Who let the emus loose?"

"Meg? What happened?"

People were approaching. They'd have to wait for an answer until someone arrived and removed the tape from my mouth. I lay back to wait.

And then a small form appeared out of the darkness. Spike. I was relieved to see that he wasn't limping. He seemed fine.

But definitely in a bad mood. He stopped a few feet from Sherry. He growled at her. And then he darted forward and sank his teeth into her right wrist.

Sherry screamed, and started to shake her hand. Tinkerbell growled and put one paw on Sherry's arm. She froze. The three of them remained in the same pose, motionless, until the first of my human rescuers arrived.

Chapter 29

"I'm fine," I said, as I fed another liver treat to Tinkerbell. I was sitting in one of the Adirondack chairs on Cordelia's front porch, watching the sun come up over Biscuit Mountain. Trying to watch it, anyway.

"You still could have a concussion," Dad said. Not for the first time. "How many fingers?"

"Two," I said. "And don't worry. As soon as Michael gets the boys ready, we'll head down to Caerphilly so Dr. Gridwell and your neurologist friend can check my head out. Let's just enjoy the view for a few minutes."

The view of the mountain really was spectacular, or would be if Dad would stop waving fingers in front of my face to make sure I wasn't developing double vision.

He had been one of the first to arrive on the scene. He had helped truss Sherry up with her own duct tape and then he'd helped untie me, Cordelia, and Stanley—apparently Sherry had ambushed and tied him up on her way over from Camp Emu to Cordelia's house. Had she been planning to drag him inside to die with Cordelia and me? And how was she planning to blame killing not one but two able-bodied adults on a single elderly woman? Clearly Sherry wasn't much of a criminal genius. At any rate, by the time the first Riverton police officer had arrived, Dad had bandaged all our wounds—even Sherry's—and was fussing over my head while Clarence checked out both dogs.

Cordelia didn't seem to have been injured—at least she'd looked spry enough when she fled inside as soon as someone untied her. And she'd given me no clue whether I was allowed to reveal her identity to anyone other than Dad. So I decided not to tell him until there were no other prying ears around.

I'd been waiting for several hours now.

But things were quieting down. The emu rescuers had taken the birds back to their pen and had gone to camp to celebrate over breakfast. Michael was packing up the boys and enough books and toys to ensure that we could turn our anticipated long wait in the Caerphilly Hospital ER into a nice stretch of quality time as a family. Stanley had already taken off for the ER under the care of a brigade member with EMT training. Sherry was headed to jail in the back of a patrol car. Chief Heedles was inside, interviewing Cordelia.

And only Clarence Rutledge stood in the way of my telling Dad Cordelia's secret. It would be nice to get that done before Michael whisked me away. But Clarence was just sitting nearby, holding Spike in his lap, and stuffing the Small Evil One with bacon-flavored treats. Perhaps Dad had enlisted him to help keep watch over me. Clearly he wasn't going to leave on his own.

"Why don't you take the dogs back to camp?" I said to him. "And you can check on what's keeping Michael."

"Good idea." Clarence stood up, still holding Spike. "Come on, Tink."

He waved a bacon treat suggestively as he went down the steps. I held up my hands to show that they were empty of liver treats and Tink went loping after him.

"How many fingers?" Dad asked. He held up his right hand as if taking the Boy Scout oath.

"One hundred and forty-seven," I said. "That's the total number of fingers you've held up since you got here. I've been counting."

"We need to make sure—"

"Never mind the fingers!" I snapped. "There's something I need to tell you."

"What?" He looked worried. "Are you feeling queasy? That could be a sign of—"

"You know, there's another patient you haven't checked out yet." I jerked my thumb toward the house behind us.

"I wasn't sure Miss Annabel would want me to," he said. "Given that she's a hermit. I assumed someone would fetch her regular physician. Of course if you think she would want me to—"

"Yeah, I think she would," I said. "Because she's not Annabel. She's Cordelia."

His mouth fell open and he stared at me for a few moments.

"No," he whispered. "It can't be."

"I only figured it out last night, a few minutes before Sherry attacked me," I said. "And she and I had just agreed that we'd tell you first thing in the morning. And only you, which is why I've been waiting until everyone else finally cleared out. She's Cordelia, not Annabel. Go in and talk to her."

Dad just sat there, staring at me.

"Dad?" I was a little worried. Was he going into shock? "You're sure?"

"Well, we only have her word for it. We can do what Grandfather did when he first discovered us and get a DNA test. But her handwriting's a dead ringer for yours and she has a notebook-that-tells-her-when-to-breathe. I'm betting she's the real thing."

"I hadn't entirely given up hope." He was blinking away tears. "And then we got the news she'd been murdered."

"Annabel was murdered. But Cordelia knew she was the intended victim. And figured the killer would try again if she turned up alive. So she's been pretending to be her cousin all this time."

Dad just blinked and stared at me.

"Why don't you go on in and meet her?"

What was wrong with him? He didn't seem to be show-ing any signs of the anger I'd been feeling. But he also didn't look all that happy to have one of his lifelong dreams coming true.

Of course, he hadn't gotten to know Cordelia as I had. Maybe he was worried that he wouldn't like her. Or more likely, that she wouldn't like him.

"She's with Chief Heedles," he said finally.

"Who's also in the know by now," I said. "And I'm sure would understand the reason for your interruption."

"Oh, my." He scrambled up to his feet, looking first at the front door and then down at himself. He was wearing Crocs, a faded Blake's Brigade T-shirt, and blue-and-white striped pajama bottoms that might have been quite snazzy in their prime but were now faded and stained with Sher-ry's blood and quite a bit of red clay.

"I look a mess," he said.

"You look fine," I said. Actually, he did look a little scruffy, but no more than usual. Was he really worried that his mother would care about his appearance? Or was he using this as an excuse?

"I should go back to camp and clean up," he said. "I don't want her to think I'm a slob."

"Dad, she—"

"I'll be back as soon as I can."

I watched as he scurried around the side of the house.

"Well, that didn't go the way I thought it would," I said, to no one in particular.

After thinking about it for a moment, I pulled out my cell phone. To my delight, I had a signal, so I called Mother.

I got her voice mail, of course. At this hour, Mother would still be fast asleep with her cell phone muted and a sleep mask over her eyes to prevent the light from waking her before she was good and ready.

"I think Dad needs you," I said after the beep. "We just found out that his mother is alive after all, and even though that's good news, it's also a pretty big shock. Call me when you can."

I hung up and began trying to think who I could call to go over and wake her up. Nearly everyone I would normally ask to do it was up here. Maybe I could send Rob down to fetch her.

The door opened, and Chief Heedles stepped out.

"I thought you were going to the hospital," she said.

"I am," I said. "As soon as Michael gets here to take me. How did your interview with Cordelia go?"

"Lord." She rolled her eyes, then closed them and sighed. "Ms. Cordelia and I have agreed that neither of us really has a right to say 'I told you so.' She was right that it was murder, and right that Mr. Weaver was up to no good, but dead wrong about who the killer was."

"Sorry if I complicated things by steering you to Mr. Williams," I said.

"He looked suspicious to me, too." She shrugged. "And you did figure out the mining connection. I confess, that was all news to me. Speak of the devil—here's Mr. Williams now. Although I don't know why my officers are bringing him here instead of taking him back to camp. I'll see you later."

She strode down the walk to the road, where Jim Williams was getting out of the police cruiser. I watched through half-closed eyes as they talked briefly. Then they shook hands. The chief got into her car and drove off. Williams came up the walk and stopped at the bottom of the steps.

"I heard about last night's excitement," he said. "You okay?"

"I'll be fine," I said. "Are you okay? I hear you had to spend the night in jail, and it's all my fault."

"No problem." He shrugged. "It's a comfortable little jail, and they have a generator, so I had a hot shower while I was there. It made an interesting change. No need to apologize."

"Yeah, there is," I said. "I jumped to conclusions. I shouldn't just apologize, I should grovel a bit, but my head's still not back to normal, so will you take a rain check on the groveling?"

"No need to grovel at all." He laughed, and I was relieved that he clearly didn't hold a grudge. "I can't blame you for suspecting me."

"Suspecting you just because you used to work for a mining company." I shook my head. "Thereby demonstrating exactly why you chose not to tell everyone in the brigade about your background. I'm sorry."

"Don't be," he said. "I was flying under false colors in the midst of a murder investigation. And as it happens, you were right. There was a mining company behind the murders. Just not my old company, which even your grandfather acknowledges is one of the good guys in the industry. Unlike Smedlock Mining, which has such a low reputation that my most rapacious, laissez-faire former colleagues would be embarrassed to have anything to do with it. And evidently Oberführer Sherry was working for them."

"Actually, it turns out she is them," I said. "Smedlock is her maiden name."

"I knew I never liked that woman."

"Me neither," I said. "And it's such a relief to be able to say so."

"Instead of nodding cheerfully whenever someone said how efficient she was," Williams said.

"Just out of curiosity, what were you doing up here in December?" I asked.

"Checking out the kyanite and kaolin deposits," he said. "Some company wanted to partner with my old company in developing them. I recommended against it. The mineral veins weren't rich enough to offset the cost. Not if you went about it the right way, with proper environmental controls and a budget for restoration of the site after the veins were exhausted. Of course, you could make a packet if you did it the cheap, sleazy way, which is doubtless what the Smedlocks had in mind."

"Any chance the company who wanted to partner with yours was Smedlock?"

"They didn't tell me who it was," he said. "But I bet it was Smedlock. I plan to find out. And I'm afraid I may have helped trigger Sherry's attack on Miss Annabel. One of the major points in my report was that anyone trying to mine Biscuit Mountain could expect protracted and potentially expensive opposition from the local citizens. Not hard to figure out who'd be organizing that opposition."

"Not your fault," I said. "You didn't recommend killing off the opposition. And I think Mr. Weaver already knew she'd be a problem."

"No doubt," he said. "Anyway, the reason I had them drop me off here is that I wanted to talk for a moment to the lady of the house, if she'll see me."

I wasn't surprised when the door opened a few seconds after he said that.

"Mr. Williams." Cordelia strode out and offered her hand. "I'm Cordelia Mason. I'm pleased to see that you're no longer suspected of killing me."

"My condolences on the death of your cousin," he said. "And may I say that I'm very glad you survived to carry on your work."

"My work?" Cordelia tilted her head slightly as if puzzled.

"Protecting the emus," he said. "And preserving Biscuit Mountain." He nodded slightly toward where we could see the mountain looming up in the distance, still clad in a few wisps of early morning fog, "If Smedlock Mining—or anyone else—tries to start a mine that would ruin that, I'd be grateful if you'd call on me to help you stop them. I've had some experience in that area."

He handed her a business card.

She took it, studied it for a moment, and then tucked it in her pocket.

"Have you got another one of those?" she asked. "I'm slowing down a bit. Sooner or later I'll need to pass the torch along to the new generation. Let's make sure my granddaughter also knows how to reach you."

She put her hand on my shoulder and squeezed it with a surprisingly strong grip.

So she'd decided in favor of full disclosure about her connection to Dad—and me. I couldn't help smiling with delight.

Williams blinked slightly. He'd heard the story of how Grandfather had discovered his long-lost son. I could see him putting the pieces together.

"Of course." He actually only paused for a few seconds before reaching into his pocket, taking out his wallet, and handing me another of his cards.

"And now if you'll excuse me," he said. "I'm told the mess tent is serving a special celebratory brunch this morning. The Riverton jail may be comfortable, but the cooking can't hold a candle to Camp Emu."

He nodded, then strode down the steps and headed for the backyard.

"Of course, I'm hoping we can resolve the question of the mountain pretty amicably." Cordelia let go of my shoulder. I heard the creak of the old-fashioned screen door as she went inside. A few moments later another creak announced her return. I cracked an eye open to see her setting a tray with a white china teapot and several matching cups and saucers on the table beside me.

"There's hot tea if you want it," she said. "I had a little talk this morning with the president of the First Undermountain Bank."

"This morning?" I eyed the teapot and decided to let it steep a bit. "It's not even six."

"I wasn't feeling very patient," she said. "I asked him if he thought maybe his board would reconsider my offer to buy the Biscuit Mountain farm, now that the other potential buyers have been revealed as homicidal maniacs who will probably end up doing hard time and are definitely not people he wants to appear to be in cahoots with."

"You think he'll see the light?" I leaned back in my chair and closed my eyes.

"I think he already has." I heard a creaking noise and suspected she was following my example. "I have a feeling he'll be burning up the phone lines this morning, contacting all the other board members. I'll call my lawyer a little later today and get him to go down and start negotiating with them."

"What will you do with it?" I asked. "Set up the emu sanctuary?"

"No," she said. "I think the emus will be just fine at the Willner Wildlife Sanctuary. Contrary to popular opinion, I'm not some kind of crazy emu fancier. Just didn't think the poor things should be abandoned that way. No, I have other plans."

"Like reopening the Biscuit Mountain Art Pottery Works?" I asked.

"Maybe," she said. "Or maybe an arts and crafts center. Plenty of room up there for a lot of studios and kilns and forges. Invite skilled craftspeople to come and do residencies. Teach their craft. And a shop where the artist gets the lion's share of the sales. I might try my hand at pottery myself. Or maybe blacksmithing, if you've a mind to teach me."

"I'd like that," I said. "By the way, what was in the bottom drawer? Whatever you were about to show me when Sherry whacked me?"

"A picture of me holding your father," she said. "At his christening. I was a godmother, you know. But I don't suppose his adoptive parents would have mentioned it."

We fell silent. I could hear noises drifting over from the camp. Maybe I should call Michael and ask him to bring me a breakfast doggy bag. He was probably making sure the boys were well fed before our drive. That was fine with me. I heard a car stop in front of the house. I opened my eyes to see Thor hopping out of a dark blue sedan. He headed up the walk. The sedan drove off. Toward camp, I noticed, rather than back to town. I'd seen that car somewhere before.

"Ms. Delia?" Thor was standing at the foot of the porch steps.

"Good morning, Thor," Cordelia said. "I trust you're not suffering any ill effects from this morning's adventure?"

"No, ma'am," he said. "I just wanted to say how sorry I was about Miss Annabel. And how glad I am that the killer didn't get you, too."

"Thanks in part to your help," Cordelia said.

"Some help I was," he muttered.

"If you hadn't distracted Sherry, we might not be here," I said. "So I guess I have to thank you for disobeying my orders and lurking out here to guard your friend."

"Just lucky." His pale redhead's complexion turned scarlet. "Oh, and Ms. Delia—I know you won't need to be feeding the emus anymore once Dr. Blake has rounded them up, but if you need me for anything else, just call."

"How about tomorrow morning?" she said. "I've been cooped up here too long. Got a lot of friends I need to catch up with. You can drive me. Eight a.m."

"Great! I'll see you then!"

Thor dashed away, grinning from ear to ear. And headed around the side of the house—no doubt he was also looking forward to the celebratory breakfast.

"Well," Cordelia said. "I can go ahead and replace the generator now. On the old spot. Just as well—it cost a lot of money to install the underground propane tank and lay such a long line to the house."

"Good idea," I murmured.

"Then again, I'm not sure I'll need the generator as much. I'm thinking of taking myself off the grid."

"Off the grid?" Surely she wasn't thinking of living indefinitely with ice chests and LED lanterns.

"Going solar," she said. "Plenty of room on my roof for a solar array. In fact, I could install enough solar panels in the pasture to power the town. Start my own little power company. It's the wave of the future, solar."

"Awesome," I said.

We sat in silence for another minute or two. Cordelia was probably plotting her takeover of the local energy market. I had something else on my mind.

"You know," I said aloud. "I just realized that we've been going about this completely backward."

"Going about what?" Cordelia asked.

"Rounding up the emus. We shouldn't be chasing them all over Pudding Mountain."

"Agreed," she said. "What's your idea?"

"We should take some of that fencing and build a big pen around the emu feeding station," I said. "With a lot of gates. And as soon as you get a bunch of emus in the pen, you shut the gates."

"Should work," she said. "I bet someone could build a remote control device for the gates, so you could shut them without having any humans so near that they'd scare the emus."

"Someone like Thor."

"My thoughts exactly. So are you going to tell them now, before I get a chance to see all of Monty's shenanigans?"

"There's plenty of video you can watch," I said. "I think it would be better for the emus if I told them now."

"Good point."

We both fell silent and I pondered, idly, whether I wanted the hot tea enough to sit up and reach for it.

"Meg, dear?"

I looked up to see Mother standing at the foot of the steps.

"What in the world are you doing here?" I sat up and rubbed my eyes, to make sure I wasn't seeing things. It was too soon for her to have gotten my message and driven here.

"What kind of welcome is that?" Mother asked. I was relieved that she sounded amused and indulgent rather than offended.

"I didn't mean to be unwelcoming," I said. "I'm just surprised to see you here. You do realize that we're all camping over there. And eating in a mess tent. And using port-a-potties."

"Yes, dear." Mother shuddered slightly. "I'm not staying overnight. But your father called at five a.m. to tell me what happened, and I came up to make sure you were all right."

"I'll be fine," I said. "And since you're here, perhaps I should make the introductions." I glanced at Cordelia. I should probably start calling her Grandmother. I'd have to work on that.

"This is my mother, Margaret Hollingsworth Langslow," I said to her. "Mother, this is Cordelia Lee Mason, your mother-in-law."

Mother was obviously taken by surprise, but only hesitated for a moment.

"How delightful!" She swept up the steps and leaned down to take both of Cordelia's hands in hers. "You can't imagine how long I've been wanting to meet you!"

"And I you," Cordelia said.

The two of them stayed there for a moment, hands clasped, quite frankly studying each other. I realized, with relief, that they both seemed to like what they saw.

"Let me pour you some tea," Cordelia said, after a few moments.

"I'd love some," Mother said. "What lovely Haviland!"

"Thank you," Cordelia said. "It was my mother's."

"Where on Earth is your father?" Mother turned to me with a slight frown, as if it were my fault Dad was late to the party.

"I think he went back to camp to clean up," I said. "He wants to make a good first impression."

I heard a car pull up and, sure that it would be the Twin-mobile, I started to stand up. But no—it was the dark blue sedan again. The driver got out and I realized where I'd seen it before: the library parking lot. Anne Murphy was scurrying up the walk.

"Ms. Delia!" she exclaimed. She ran up onto the porch and hugged Cordelia. I suspected from my grandmother's expression that she wasn't much of a hugger, but willing to put up with it under the circumstances.

"I'm so glad you're alive," Anne exclaimed. "So sorry about Miss Annabel, of course. But I'm glad that horrible woman didn't get you as well."

"So am I," Cordelia said. "And I'm looking forward to rejoining the book club again."

Another figure had gotten out of the car and was trotting down the walk. Caroline Willner.

"Lovely!" Anne beamed. "The book group needs you—ever since you left, it's been just one tear-jerker after another. I'm hoping you can talk them into doing mysteries again. And oh! You can be the first to know—we're having a special meeting of the book group tomorrow night, with a live author. Dr. Montgomery Blake is coming to talk about his books!"

Caroline, who had reached the bottom of the porch steps, snorted at that.

"Maybe I won't be rejoining quite that soon," Cordelia said. "I've heard Monty talk before."

"And here I was going to offer to introduce you," Anne said. "And invite you to come to breakfast with him and Caroline Willner and me. But I gather you've met Dr. Blake before?"

"You could say that," Cordelia said. "I'm Meg's long-lost grandmother."

"Oh, my!" Anne's mouth fell open and she seemed at a loss for words.

Caroline marched up the steps and held out her hand to Cordelia.

"Caroline Willner," she said. "I'm the one who's taking the emus."

"And I'm delighted that you are," Cordelia said, taking the hand and shaking it warmly. The two were clearly studying each other, and I was relieved to see that, as with Mother and Cordelia, both seemed pleased with what they saw.

"You can come up to visit them any time you want," Caroline said. "And I can give you the grand tour of the sanctuary."

"I'd like that," Cordelia said. "Although I suspect Monty won't."

"I'll make sure he's not around if you'd rather not run into him," Caroline said. "Do you know what he asked me this morning? If I thought people would expect him to make an honest woman of you."

We all burst into laughter at the notion—even Anne, who seemed to be recovering from her surprise.

"Tell him thanks for the thought," Cordelia said, shaking her head and still chuckling. "But he's about seventy years too late. I've been doing just fine on my own."

I glanced down the driveway and saw that my grandfather had gotten out of the car and was standing outside the gate, peering in.

"Monty, you old goat!" Caroline called out. "Stop lurking! Come here and be polite for once in your life."

I glanced over at Cordelia to see if the idea of coming face-to-face with Grandfather upset her. She didn't seem to mind. In fact, she was clearly having a hard time not laughing at his sheepish expression.

"Not his fault, actually." She was looking at Anne. Was the poor librarian shocked by the revelation? Disappointed to find that her idol had clay feet?

"We lost touch at just the wrong time," Cordelia went on. "Blame the Ecuadorian postal service."

Anne looked puzzled at that. I'd explain later about the Galapagos Island connection. For now, I realized that something was about to happen. Grandfather finally stopped peering in through the gate, straightened his shoulders, and began coming up the walk. I'd seen him face wounded wolves and angry mother bears with a more cheerful air. And yet I had to give him credit—he was marching steadfastly toward us, in spite of the calm, steady, and not entirely approving scrutiny from the five women gathered on the porch. Pretty formidable women—well,

four of them were. I didn't consider myself particularly formidable. Although with such good models, I had hopes of
achieving it.

Grandfather stopped at the foot of the stairs, glanced
quickly around at all of us, and finally spoke.

"Morning," he said.

Everyone murmured "good morning" in reply and then
they all waited to see what else he'd say.

"How lovely to see you again," Cordelia was using her
best Southern hostess voice. I could imagine our ancestors
using much the same tone to a Union officer who'd arrived
intending to bivouac his troops on the front lawn.

"Er . . . likewise," Grandfather muttered.

After an awkward pause, I took pity on him.

"Nice of you to drop by to see that Cordelia is okay," I
said. "I'm sure the two of you will have as much time as
you want to catch up later. But shouldn't you be heading
off to your breakfast now?"

"Um, yes." Grandfather looked pathetically grateful.

"Yes, of course," Anne said. "Ms. Delia, I'll drop by
later, if that's okay."

She turned and hurried down the walk.

"Come on, you old reprobate," Caroline said. She took
Grandfather by the arm and led him back down the walk.

"That was very kind, Meg," Mother said, as we watched
the blue sedan leaving.

"I should probably let him know that I don't really hold
a grudge," Cordelia said. "But not just yet."

Just then the Twinmobile pulled up in front of the house.
We watched as a door slid open and Dad stepped out. He
was dressed in a white shirt, khaki slacks, and a blue sports
jacket, and he was wearing the just-in-case tie that Michael
always kept in the glove compartment of the Twinmobile
in case he had to look presentable on short notice. Dad

dithered for a few minutes outside the gate, then squared his shoulders and marched up the walk.

He reached the foot of the steps and stared up at us. I tried to recall the last time I'd seen Dad speechless and failed utterly. He and Cordelia stared at each other for several long moments.

"Why don't you two go inside and get acquainted?" Mother said. She handed Cordelia a teacup and gave her a gentle shove toward the front door. Cordelia obediently went inside. Mother poured another cup and gestured to Dad, who stumbled up the stairs, took the cup, and followed his mother inside.

"I think they could use a little privacy," Mother said as she pulled the door closed. Then she poured a third cup for herself. After glancing at the Adirondack chairs she sailed over to sit regally in one of the white wicker chairs.

"Michael's waiting," she said, gesturing in the direction of the Twinmobile. "Call us from the hospital. I'm sure you'll be just fine, but you know your father will feel so much better once he knows that nice neurologist friend of his has poked and prodded you and given you a clean bill of health."

"Will do," I said.

As I walked toward the car, I realized my footsteps were dragging. I might know the answer to the question of who killed Annabel and Theo Weaver, but I hadn't even begun to ask most of the million questions I had about Cordelia, and Dad's birth, and the Lee branch of my family tree. And how would Grandfather deal with the arrival of Cordelia in our lives? And how would we explain her sudden arrival to Josh and Jamie? And—

Time enough for all that later. Life with my family, never dull, was about to get even more interesting.

When I neared the car, both Josh and Jamie ran out to throw themselves on me.

"Mommy, are you okay?" Jamie asked.

"Daddy brought you a big doggie bag," Josh said. "Can I have some of your bacon?"

As we drove off, I could still see Mother sitting on the porch, sipping her cup of tea and standing guard over the reunion.

Read on for an excerpt from

Lord of the Wings—

the next Meg Langslow mystery from Donna Andrews,
available soon in hardcover from Minotaur Books!

Chapter 1

"Someone's broken into the Haunted House!"

My cell phone almost vibrated from the excitement in
my brother's voice.

"Calm down, Rob," I said. I wanted to add, "And what
are you doing awake before eight a.m.?" but I suspected
he would take it as a slur on his character. I punched the
speaker button, set my phone on the kitchen table, and
went back to painting a goatee on my son Josh's chin.

"But Meg, the Haunted House—"

"Was anything taken?" I asked. "Or broken?"

"Not that we can tell," Rob said. "But Dr. Smoot is
upset."

"That's his normal state of mind these days," I said.
Then I winced, hoping the proprietor of the Haunted House
wasn't close enough to Rob's phone to hear me.

"If you can call anything about Smoot normal." Okay,
even Rob wouldn't have said that in front of the man.
"But definitely more upset than usual. The closer we get
to Halloween, the more hyper he gets."

Josh lifted up his piratical eye patch, twisted to look at
his reflection in the shiny chrome side of the toaster, and
frowned.

"I want to be more hairier," he said.

"Just hairier," I corrected. "I'm working on it. Did you report it to the police?" I added to Rob.

"Not yet," Rob said. "Dr. Smoot says Chief Burke never takes him seriously."

Dr. Smoot was probably right. Of course, it didn't help that while he was still serving as Caerphilly County's medical examiner, Dr. Smoot had taken to dressing as a vampire, complete with a long black cape and fake fangs, and collecting vampire-related paraphernalia. Chief Burke had been vastly relieved when Dr. Smoot had resigned his post to pursue this strange new hobby full time, complete with travels to such vampire meccas as Transylvania and New Orleans. The chief probably wasn't thrilled to have Dr. Smoot not only back in town but also running the Haunted House that played a central role in the town's ongoing Halloween festival.

"Never mind their past history," I said. "If there's any real evidence of a burglary, Chief Burke will want to investigate. In fact, he'll be pretty ticked off if he finds out you didn't call him right away."

"Dr. Smoot says since nothing was actually taken, he thought it was okay to call the Goblin Patrol instead."

"Rob," I began.

"Sorry," Rob said. "The Visitor Relations and Police Liaison Patrol. I still think Goblin Patrol's catchier. I'll call the chief. But Dr. Smoot's upset—he really wants to talk to you."

"I'm putting the boys into their costumes for school," I said. "And then Michael and I are going along as chaperones for today's school field trip to the zoo. And—"

"Great," Rob said. "The Haunted House is right on your way. You could just drop in for a few minutes—"

"After the field trip," I said. "Or if more than enough parents come to wrangle the kids, I might be able to break away once we've delivered our carload to the zoo. Call the police, and tell Dr. Smoot I'll be there as soon as I can."

"Roger," Rob said.

"Uncle Rob," Josh said. "I'm a pirate today."

"A pirate?" Rob echoed. "I thought you were a cowboy."

"A cowboy? Yuck. That was yesterday."

"Today he's a pirate," I said. "I've been trying to explain to the boys that when their teacher said they could wear costumes every day this week, it didn't mean a different costume every day."

"But it's more fun this way," Josh protested.

"Absolutely!" Rob said. "Goblin Patrol, over and out."

"Rob," I began, but he'd already hung up. "Josh, can you punch the button to turn off my phone? My hands are full."

He obliged, then turned back to me and lifted his chin as if silently demanding that I add another layer of painted beard.

"Mommy—look!" I turned to see Jamie, Josh's twin. "See my new costume! Isn't it cool?"

"Very cool!" I stopped myself before asking, "But what is it?" and studied his outfit for clues. Like most first graders he had only rudimentary costume-making skills, so at first glance, his new outfit looked exactly like Monday's dog costume, Tuesday's raccoon, and Wednesday's penguin. They all used as a base the same set of faded beige footed pajamas. Today he'd stuck tufts of fur rather than feathers to the flannel, so I deduced that he was a mammal rather than a bird. The catlike whiskers stuck on his cheeks with Scotch tape didn't help much, but then I noticed that the rope he'd tied around his waist, leaving one end trailing six or seven feet behind him, now bore a tuft of fur at the tip.

"So you're going as a lion today?" I guessed.

Jamie beamed.

"Look, Josh," he said. "Rowrrrr!"

Josh was studying himself again in the toaster.

"I guess it's okay," he said. "But I want a really cool costume for the real Halloween on Saturday."

"Josh," I said, "that's only two days away. I'm not sure we have time to make another costume. Can't you just go as a pirate or a cowboy or a space alien or a wizard? We can make some improvements to whichever one you choose."

"I want to be a robot," Josh said.

It could be worse, I decided. I could easily make him a robot suit with some cardboard boxes and tin foil.

"But not one of those lame robot costumes like Victor's mother made him out of cardboard boxes and tin foil," Josh said. "A *real* robot costume. It should be metal. And the eyes should light up when I get mad. And you should be able to open up my chest to see my motor."

"I'll think about it," I said. "No promises," I added. "You know I'm pretty busy with the Halloween festival."

"But I really want to be a robot!"

"No whining!" I exclaimed.

Josh recognized the wisdom of shutting up, and shifted tactics. He sighed and donned a look of patient, wistful longing—rather like Oliver Twist holding up the empty gruel bowl.

Maybe Michael could enlist some help in making a robot costume. An extra credit project for a couple of his drama department students with prop and costume shop experience. I could ask him.

And come to think of it, maybe Michael could drive the boys to school, pick up the other two kids we were supposed to transport, and take them to the zoo. Then I could drop by to soothe Dr. Smoot and still meet them there in time for the tour.

"Where's your daddy?" I asked the boys.

"In the backyard, chasing the llamas," Jamie said.

"Why is he chasing the llamas?" I asked. "Are they loose?"

Jamie shook his head.

"Then why—"

"Who's ready for waffles?" my cousin Rose Noire called out, as she sailed in, already dressed in her costume for the day, as Glinda, the Good Witch.

"Yay!" Jamie exclaimed

"Blueberry waffles?" Josh asked.

"*Organic* blueberry waffles," Rose Noire said. "With artisanal maple syrup."

The boys sat down and looked expectant. On mornings like this, I was profoundly grateful that Rose Noire still showed no signs of moving out of the third floor spare bedroom she'd occupied since before the boys were born.

I strolled outside to see why Michael was chasing the llamas.

Actually, he wasn't so much chasing them as being followed by them. He was jogging briskly around the perimeter of their pasture and the llamas, ever curious about human eccentricities, were loping along behind him.

I leaned over the fence and watched until he drew near, then climbed over the top rail and fell into step beside him.

"What's up?" I asked.

"An actor's body is his instrument," he puffed.

"That's nice," I said. "What does that have to do with your taking up jogging?" Then enlightenment struck. "You tried on your wizard costume last night, didn't you?" I asked.

Michael frowned and nodded.

"Too tight?"

"Not *too* tight," he said. "But a little tighter than it used to be. Tighter than it *should* be."

Not surprising, since it had been a few years since

Michael had donned the costume he'd once worn to play the evil wizard Mephisto on *Porfiria, Queen of the Jungle*, a long-canceled cult TV fantasy show. In fact, although die-hard fans kept inviting him to Porfiria fan conventions, he hadn't gone since before the twins were born, and they were six now.

"I could let your costume out a little," I suggested.

"No," he said, and picked up his pace a little. "I need to get down to my proper weight. An actor's body is his instrument."

"Okay," I said. "Carry on tuning your instrument. I'll figure out something healthy and low calorie for dinner."

"Thanks," he said. "And keep all that damned Halloween candy away from me."

"Roger," I said. "By the way, can you take the boys to school and pick up the other two kids we're taking to the field trip? I can meet you at the zoo—I have an errand I should run on my way."

"Goblin Patrol business?"

"Something like that." As I explained about Dr. Smoot, I considered whether I should stop fighting this Goblin Patrol thing. It was certainly catchier than Visitor Relations and Police Liaison Patrol. "If I hurry," I concluded. "I can deal with Smoot and still make the zoo tour."

"I don't envy you," he said. "And yes, I can take the boys."

We'd done nearly a complete circuit of the pasture now, so I decided I'd jogged enough.

"I'm going to peel off now and get ready for my busy day," I said.

"Not as busy as it would have been if Randall Shiffley hadn't hired Lydia," Michael called over his shoulder.

I made a noncommittal noise and headed back to the kitchen.

Yes, if Randall hadn't hired Lydia Van Meter to the

newly created post of Special Assistant to the Mayor, I would probably have been running the whole of Caerphilly's ten-day Halloween festival instead of merely heading up the Goblin Patrol. I definitely preferred my more limited role.

But that didn't mean I had to like Lydia.

Just thinking about her soured my mood. And it wasn't because she was doing a terrible job at organizing the Halloween Festival. Considering that it was her first major project, she was doing okay. Not perfectly—certainly not the way I'd have done it—but things were lurching along, and she was learning. She'd probably have an easier time with the much bigger Christmas in Caerphilly event that would start right after Thanksgiving, because we'd been doing that for several years now, and Randall and I had done a pretty good job of setting up procedures and training the townspeople in them. By summer, when it was time for the Un-Fair, the statewide agricultural exposition Caerphilly hosted every year, she should be in fine shape—again, thanks to all the ground work Randall and I had done on past Un-Fairs.

Since, in the long run, she was going to make my life easier, it was probably ungracious of me to dislike her. Maybe I was the only one who minded her constant griping about how hard she was working and how impossible the job was. I couldn't count the times I'd had to bite my tongue to keep from saying, "You think you've got it bad—I used to do all that and more, as a volunteer." And was it just my imagination, or was she developing an annoying tendency to ask me how I would handle something and then do exactly the opposite?

"Chill," I muttered. After all, Lydia was making it possible for me to spend more time with Michael and the boys, doing things like today's field trip to the Caerphilly Zoo.

And accompanying the boys to the zoo was definitely

important, and not just because I wanted to see their reaction to the brand-new Creatures of the Night exhibit. As the zoo's proud owner, my grandfather was planning on conducting the tour himself, and I knew better than to expect common sense from him. What if he gave in to some first grader's pleas to be allowed to pet the arctic wolves? Or began explaining the curious mating habits of the greater short-nosed fruit bat, as he had a few weeks ago when giving a preview tour to the Baptist Ladies' Altar Guild?

I ran upstairs to throw on the last few bits of my costume—a modified version of the red satin and black leather swordswoman's outfit I wore whenever I exhibited my blacksmithing work at a Renaissance festival. I added the festive black-and-orange armband that marked me as a member of the Goblin Patrol and headed for town.

The first few miles of my journey lay through farmlands—pastures dotted with grazing cows or sheep, fields filled with late crops or post-harvest stubble, and orchards picked clean of all but the latest fruits. Closer to town, I began to see Halloween and harvest decorations on the gates and fences. I particularly admired the farmer who'd used a collection of scarecrows to simulate a zombie attack on his cow pasture. The contrast between the bloodstained shambling figures clawing at the outside of the fence and the Guernsey cows calmly chewing their cuds inside never failed to amuse me.

I was nearing town when my phone rang. Lydia. I considered letting it go to voice mail. Then I sighed, and pulled over to answer it. She was probably calling about something she considered important. Her definition of important rarely coincided with mine, but I'd already figured out that the best way to keep her calm and off my back was to talk to her. She seemed to resent having to leave a voice mail.

"Thank goodness I caught you!" she exclaimed as soon as I answered. "Can you drop by to see me as soon as possible? Something important's come up. Festival business! Thanks!"

"I'm already on my way to take care of festival business," I began. But before I could make the case for discussing whatever had come up over the phone instead of face to face, I realized she'd hung up.

"Damn the woman," I muttered as I punched the button to call her back. But her phone line was already busy.

So I muttered a few words I didn't usually let myself say, for fear the boys would pick them up, and pulled out onto the road again. Dr. Smoot's burglar would have to wait while I tackled whatever crisis Lydia had to offer.

Chapter 2

Even Lydia couldn't spoil my enjoyment of the Halloween scenery. Closer to town the farmlands gave way to houses whose yards almost universally contained some kind of decorations. Strings of orange pumpkin- or skeleton-shaped lights festooned at least half of the fences. Most of the steps bore jack-o-lanterns. Some yards contained miniature graveyards, with or without skeletons or vampires digging their way out of the earth, and I lost count of the number of witches that appeared to have slammed into trees.

In the outskirts of town I passed by the left turn onto the Clay County road that would have taken me to Dr. Smoot's Haunted House and then on to the zoo. Instead I continued on toward the town square.

The official town decorations, though attractive, were somewhat more sedate, reflecting a harvest theme rather than a Halloween one. The streetlights had been enclosed in plastic covers to make them look like pumpkins—just pumpkins, not jack-o-lanterns. Graceful black, brown, and orange garlands hung between the lampposts, and all the trash cans and benches and other public fixtures were festooned with gourds and sheaves of dried grass and flowers. "It's the Caerphilly Garden Club," Randall Shiffley had said in a slightly apologetic tone when he showed me the design. "They always like to err on the side of good taste, and I don't think most of them really like Halloween all that much."

They probably didn't—but they were clearly in the minority. Most of the shops and houses contained enough jack-o-lanterns, faux skeletons, black cat window decals, bat garlands, and rubber rats to make up for any excess of good taste on the part of the Garden Club.

It was early enough that I had no trouble finding a parking spot near the courthouse. As I climbed the long marble steps up to the front portico, I could see that the two small groups of protesters were already on duty. I turned to study them for a moment. To the right were a small group of people who objected to our Halloween festival on the grounds that it was a godless pagan holiday that a respectable town shouldn't be celebrating. To the left was a group of about the same number of devout pagans who were protesting our commercialization of what was for them an important religious holiday and our use of decorations that perpetuated society's negative stereotype of witches.

Neither group had started picketing yet, only milling around as if waiting for something. The arrival of the first tourists, perhaps.

If I'd been in charge, I'd have long ago sent a couple of local ministers out to placate the Halloween haters and tasked Rose Noire with figuring out what we could do to calm down the pagans.

Then I saw them all perk up as two figures approached. It was Muriel, owner of the local diner, and one of her waitresses, both carrying trays laden with doughnuts and carryout cups of coffee. Muriel began serving the pagans while the waitress continued on toward the Halloween haters.

"You were right," said a voice from over my shoulder.

I looked up to see Randall standing at the top of the steps, gazing down at the protesters. His buckskin costume already looked wrinkled, and his Davy Crockett-style coonskin hat was askew.

"I usually am right," I said, as I made my way up the

rest of the steps. "What in particular am I right about today?"

"We never should have tried to chase them off," he said, nodding at the protesters. "Should have killed them with kindness from the start."

I refrained from saying that it was Lydia who tried to order the protesters away, and demanded that the police step in when her efforts failed. Fortunately Chief Burke had a cool head and a strong respect for the First Amendment.

"I see you're taking my idea about the refreshments," I said.

"Yup." Randall smiled with satisfaction. "Coffee and doughnuts every morning from Muriel, and tea and cookies every afternoon from one of the churches. If the forecast calls for rain, we put up those little canvas shelters for them, and they know they're always welcome to use the courthouse bathroom."

"You're spoiling them," I said.

"And we're down to about a third of the number we had last week this time," he said. "Clearly it's no fun protesting people who seem perfectly happy to have you stay around. What brings you downtown? I'd have thought you'd be out at the zoo with the first graders today."

"I will be," I said. "As soon as I talk to Lydia and find out what's so important that she had to drag me all the way downtown."

Randall winced, and I felt slightly guilty for venting at him.

"Sorry," he said. "She means well, and she's learning."

Not learning fast enough to suit me, but I refrained from saying so aloud. I just nodded, went inside the courthouse, and took the elevator up to the third floor where Lydia had her office, a few doors down from Randall's office.

As usual, Lydia was on the phone. Not just on the phone,

but switching back and forth between the two lines on her desk phone while texting something on her cell phone with her right hand and clicking something on her computer keyboard with the left. She nodded and smiled when she saw me, and held up two fingers, like a peace sign. Her intent, of course, was to say that she'd be with me in two minutes. I knew better by now.

I sat down in one of her desk chairs and resigned myself to wait. If I were a snarkier person, I'd have brought along a thick book—*War and Peace*, perhaps—and made a show of settling down to read it while she talked. Instead, I pulled out my notebook-that-tells-me-when-to-breathe, as I call my giant to-do list, and made productive use of my time.

Other people rarely understood how comforting I found it to spend time with my notebook. Knowing that everything on my plate was captured between its covers cleared my brain to concentrate on whatever I was doing. Since the boys' arrival, life had grown even more complicated than before, and I'd traded in my original spiral notebooks for a small three-ring binder, but apart from that my system was the same. My notebook gave me peace of mind, and all it asked in return was that I tend it for a few minutes here and there. I marked a few tasks as done and added a few new ones.

"Yeah, yeah," Lydia was saying. "I'll take care of it."

I glanced up to see that she was scribbling something on a yellow sticky note.

She stuck the sticky on the left side of her computer monitor, where it was largely indistinguishable from the hundred other yellow sticky notes that clung to the monitor, gradually encroaching on the viewing space. Her calendar and the wall it hung on were similarly encrusted. As I watched, one lonely yellow square gave up hope of ever being read and let itself fall to the floor.

By contrast, her desk contained only a few sticky notes, hidden here and there among the books, folders, paper stacks and yellow legal pads that covered every inch of horizontal space and in some places had begun to slide off onto the floor.

Every time I walked into her office, my fingers itched to start organizing it all.

Not for the first time I wondered where Randall had found her, and how in the world she had convinced him that she was good at organizing.

"Chill," I murmured under my breath. Lydia's organizing skills might be overrated, the festival might not be running the way I'd like to have seen it run, but it was limping along adequately without me doing anything other than organizing and running the volunteer security force. I reminded myself to be grateful for that.

"Sorry." She hung up and turned to me with a perky little smile that didn't really reach her eyes. "There's just so much going on."

"Understandable," I said. "What did you need to see me about?"

"Oh!" She began scanning the sticky notes on the left side of her monitor and plucked one off. "Here it is. Dr. Smoot called. He seems to think someone broke into the museum very early this morning. Could you check to see if it's something the police should handle or if he's just being hyper again?"

"You could have told me about it over the phone," I said. "As it happens, one of my volunteers already told me about the break-in, and I was on my way over there when you called. If you'd told me that was why you were calling, I'd be there by now, dealing with it."

"Oh, sorry," she said. "But it's only a little detour, after all."

"Only ten miles." My smile probably didn't reach my

eyes, either. In fact, it was probably more of a grimace. But since Lydia had already half turned away to dial another number on her phone, she probably didn't notice.

I closed my eyes and counted to ten. Then I stood up and left her office, ignoring her cheerful goodbye wave.

Luckily Randall wasn't still at the top of the courthouse steps, so I was spared the temptation to tell him what I thought of his assistant.

The protesters had finished their morning coffee break and were marching up and down their assigned sides of the sidewalk. The anti-Halloween crew carried signs with slogans like "Halloween Is the Devil's Nite." The pagans' signs all had a picture of a spectacularly ugly cartoon witch riding a broomstick. The witch was in a circle with a line through it, reminiscent of a no-smoking sign. During the first few days they hadn't had any slogans on them, giving some of the tourists the erroneous impression that they were against witches, or possibly declaring the town a no-fly zone for broomstick riders. So they'd added slogans like "No Stereotyping" and "Caerphilly Unfair to Witches."

The protesters were all remarkably well-behaved, especially considering the fact that each group probably considered the other its arch-enemy.

Behind them, in the town square, the farmers and craftspeople and other merchants were starting to set up for the farmer's market. I could see merchants and volunteers performing a few last-minute tasks, finishing up the job of switching things over from the Night Side, our evening mode, into the family-friendly Day Side.

In the daytime, we insisted that none of the festival attractions display any excessively graphic or scary decorations, and we discouraged overly gory or provocative costumes. We had no control over what the owners did on private property, of course, but most of them voluntarily complied with the daytime guidelines. Then, an hour after sunset, dozens of volunteers throughout the festival rushed to transform everything. Smiling pumpkin heads turned into evilly grinning ones. Fluffy black cats gave way to snarling wolves. Instead of "Ghostbusters" and "Monster Mash" on the loudspeakers we played "Night on Bald Mountain" and Bach's "Toccata and Fugue in D Minor" and, as the night wore on, truly sinister-sounding mood music. Welcome to the Night Side.

Most of the volunteers found it easier to switch things back before going home, so there was less to do in the morning, but as long as the switch was complete before the tourists streamed in we were okay with it. Members of the Goblin Patrol checked every morning to make sure the switch was complete by eight a.m. That was probably why Rob had been out at Caerphilly Haunted House so early, since the Haunted House and its environs were a hot spot for inappropriate decorations.

My route out of town passed by Caerphilly Elementary and I could see that the children were lined up on the curb in groups of four, being given their marching orders by Mrs. Velma Shiffley, their teacher. I spotted Michael easily. At six-four he towered over all the children—and for that matter, all the adults. He looked very impressive in today's costume—a Union general's uniform that he'd originally acquired for participating in the town's Civil War celebrations. Probably more suitable for a school outing than the over-tight evil wizard costume.

On impulse, I made a U-turn and pulled into the school parking lot. Lydia be damned. Dr. Smoot could wait. I was going to the zoo with my boys.